Love's Scribe

Love's Scribe

Reading Dante
in the Book of Creation

ANDREW FRISARDI

Angelico Press

First published in the USA
by Angelico Press 2020
Copyright © Andrew Frisardi 2020

Translations from Dante's *Vita nova* are reprinted (sometimes
with minor emendations) courtesy of Northwestern University
Press (Evanston, IL), from Dante Alighieri, *Vita Nova*.
English translation, introduction, and notes copyright
© 2012 by Andrew Frisardi. Published 2012 by
Northwestern University Press. All rights reserved.

For information, address:
Angelico Press, Ltd.
169 Monitor St.
Brooklyn, NY 11222
www.angelicopress.com

ppr   978-1-62138-561-5
cloth 978-1-62138-562-2
ebook 978-1-62138-563-9

Book and cover design
by Michael Schrauzer
Cover image: William Blake, *The Youthful Poet's Dream*
Source: Wikimedia Commons

For the Temenos Academy

Nel suo profondo vidi che s'interna,
legato con amore in un volume,
ciò che per l'universo si squaderna.

(I saw there in its depths how what is scattered
like pages through the universe is gathered
and bound by love into a single volume.)

Paradiso XXXIII.85–87

CONTENTS

PREFACE

I N A F E W P A S S A G E S of his writings, Dante identifies himself as "Love's scribe"—the scribe, that is, of *all* love, from natural and human love to the "Love that moves the sun and the other stars." This notion, the source of the present book's title, will arise throughout the chapters that follow, especially the first and last. The subtitle, *Reading Dante in the Book of Creation*, alludes to another fundamental notion in Dante, expressed in the book's epigraph from *Paradiso*, where Dante says that the manifold things of the creation are like pages bound together by love into a unified book. In medieval thought, the book was a rich and frequently utilized symbol, as in St. Augustine's view of the universe as a series of successive analogies of God—a Book written by God, in which images and resemblances of God can be discerned. Dante applies this concept in his first book, the *Vita nova*, which he says draws on material from the "Book of Memory"—the memoried life of the narrator, Dante, which for him would have been written by God rather than created by himself. This way of reading the creation is also a way to read Dante's or any traditional metaphysical-symbolist author's works: as a series of signs that correspond to multiple levels of reality, each resonating with others in the hierarchical chain of being.

This approach to reading is strange for the modern mind, which has been conditioned to presume that empirical matter is the ontologically basic reality, and that nonmaterial realities (love, thought, imagination, God, etc.) are mere epiphenomena of matter. But from the traditional viewpoint that Dante shares, Mind or Spirit ("God") is the essential reality, whose "signature" can be read in all created things. As the twelfth-century theologian Hugh of St. Victor puts it, "Just as some illiterate man who sees an open book, looks at the figures, but does not recognize the letters: just so the foolish and natural man, who does not perceive the things of God, sees outwardly in these visible creatures the appearance but does not inwardly understand the reason."[1] Our challenge in reading Dante, then, is to become literate in this sense, through informed and intuitive reflection.

---

1   Hugh of St. Victor, *De tribus diebus* (On the Three Days) IV.94–104; quoted in Charles S. Singleton, *An Essay on the "Vita Nuova"* (1949; 2nd ed., Baltimore: Johns Hopkins University Press, 1977), 47.

This book's chapters, which originally were written as individ-ual essays or as pairs of lectures, have been arranged and somewhat remolded into a thematic sequence: from chapter 1, which describes Dante's discovery of love and its spiritually transformative effects; to chapter 2, which is about Beatrice, Dante's beloved, his muse and the agent of his transformation; chapter 3: Dante as the Orpheus who, by means of his "realism," integrates love and spiritual knowledge with music and poetry, rather than sacrificing one for the other; chapter 4: Dante's understanding that self-purification is a precondition for the realization of such an art; chapter 5: his view of nobility as the seed of the virtues that enable this purification; chapter 6: Dante's expan-sion into philosophical inquiry, guided by his muse after Beatrice's death, Lady Philosophy, the "friend of Nobility"; chapter 7: his quest for knowledge and for an understanding of how philosophy relates to love, visionary insight, and the pursuit of virtue; chapter 8: Dante's representations of Rome and Jerusalem as figures for the pilgrimages of life and of the spirit; chapter 9: the symbolic, cosmic imprint he weaves into the *Divine Comedy* itself; and lastly, chapter 10, circling back to the book's opening two chapters: Dante as Love's scribe, receptive to inspiration as a "divine gift," as he calls it, the beginning and end of both speech and silence.

Most of this book's content is self-explanatory and accessible to anyone with an interest in Dante. The point of the introduction is to explain the perspective I bring to these readings, some reasons that Dante for me is the most exciting, brilliant, and inexhaustibly reward-ing author. He is by no means an easy or simple author, however, and commentary and scholarship are essential for appreciating and integrating his richness.

Reader: may the readings in this book supplement and enhance your own readings of Dante.

Andrew Frisardi
Castiglione in Teverina
June 2020

NOTE ON EDITIONS
AND TRANSLATIONS

THE FOLLOWING EDITIONS and translations are used in this book, unless otherwise stated. Some of the translations are slightly emended.

Aquinas, St. Thomas. *Commentary on the Metaphysics.* 2 vols. Translated by John P. Rowan. Chicago: Henry Regnery, 1961.

———. *Expositio libri Posteriorum Analyticorum* (Commentary on Aristotle's *Posterior Analytics*). Translated by Fabian R. Larcher, O.P. Albany, NY: Magi Books, 1970.

———. *Summa contra Gentiles.* Translated by Anton C. Pegis et al. Edited and updated by Joseph Kenny. New York: Hanover House, 1955–57.

———. *The Summa Theologica of St. Thomas Aquinas.* 2nd rev. ed., 1920. Translated by Fathers of the English Dominican Province. Online ed. copyright 2008 by Kevin Knight. New Advent website, www.newadvent.org/summa.

———. *Super Boetium de Trinitate* (On Boethius's *On the Trinity*). Questions 1–4, translated by Rose E. Brennan. New York: Herder, 1946. Questions 5–6, translated by Armand Mauer. Toronto, 1953.

Aristotle quotations are taken from *The Works of Aristotle.* Translated into English under the editorship of J. A. Smith and W. D. Ross. 12 vols. Oxford: Oxford University Press, 1908–52.

Bible quotations are from the Revised Standard Version and the Vulgate.

Dante. *Commedia.* Edited and with a commentary by Anna Maria Chiavacci Leonardi. Milan: Arnoldo Mondadori Editore, 1991, 1994.

———. *Convivio: A Dual-Language Critical Edition.* Edited and translated by Andrew Frisardi. Cambridge: Cambridge University Press, 2018.

———. *De vulgari eloquentia.* Translated by Steven Botterill. Cambridge: Cambridge University Press, 1996.

———. *Epistles.* Translated by Paget Toynbee as *The Letters of Dante.* Oxford: Clarendon Press, 1920.

———. *Monarchia.* Translated and edited by Prue Shaw. Cambridge: Cambridge University Press, 1995.

———. *Vita nova.* Translation, notes, and introduction by Andrew Frisardi. Evanston, IL: Northwestern University Press, 2012. Citations from the *Vita nova* have both chapter numbering systems currently in use. The more recent system has chapter numbers in Arabic numerals and the older one in Roman numerals.

Dante's Poetic Gnosis

GNOSIS AND ORTHODOXY

A RECENT INTRODUCTORY BOOK about Dante makes a distinction that, for me, raises questions. The context is a reference to canto XXIV of *Paradiso*, where Dante recites the Nicene Creed, adding his own comment on that bedrock statement of the Christian faith. In this passage, Dante says that the Three-in-One of the Trinity is "so one and so threefold that it takes 'are' and 'is' simultaneously." Dante is saying that in speaking about the Trinity, one must use both the singular and the plural forms of the verb *to be*, since the Trinity is simultaneously a plurality and a unity. Prue Shaw, a distinguished Dantist and the author of this book, parenthetically remarks that Dante's comment "confirms . . . [that] Dante has the temperament of an intellectual and not of a mystic."[1] I was surprised by this statement, since this passage of Dante is hardly exceptional in its intellectual content. Dante's prose and poetry are full of such speculative insights, and he even wrote entire works and passages modeled after formal scholastic inquiries. I assume that Shaw comments on this particular statement in *Paradiso* in this way because it occurs in the middle of Dante's affirmation of his faith, which requires an intellectual leap from the definitions and comfort zone of reason. She is pointing out that, even in matters of faith, Dante is always thinking, always intellectually engaged. This is certainly true, but I think Shaw's statement also suggests a conflation that is common in modern thought.

By "mystic" it would seem she means a person whose religious life is characterized primarily by an affective, devotional engagement with religion — "voluntarist" or "fideist," as this inclination has been called. *Mystical* can mean other things, including its etymological sense related to "knowledge of the mysteries," but the contrast above with *intellectual* suggests the former use of the word, just as it has when some modern scholars of Islam have asserted that the sage Ibn ʿArabī was not a real

---

1 Prue Shaw, *Reading Dante: From Here to Eternity* (New York: Liveright Publishing, 2014), 177; quoting *Paradiso* XXIV.139–41.

1

mystic. By "intellectual," Shaw seems to mean the current general under-standing of that term: someone who has a gift and habit for critical thinking, probably is bookish, and perhaps is engaged in scholarly, ana-lytical research. Dante was all of these things, but his statement about the Creed actually *combines* devotional and intellectual perspectives or atti-tudes; he is *both* ardently devout *and* intellectually rigorous. Of course, this could be said about many medieval authors. Is Meister Eckhart, for example, "mystical" or is he "intellectual"? Similarly, in Dante ardent love coexists with intellectual acumen. In short, I think Shaw's statement presents a false dichotomy. There are many gradations between these two categories, and even more importantly, there are vast intellectual tradi-tions associated with religion, with the arts, and with all areas of learning that encompass much more than analytical thought or book learning can access — more things in heaven and earth, to borrow from Shakespeare, than are dreamed of by modern philosophers and intellectuals.

The modern secularized mind tends to equate intellection with ratio-cination and knowledge with empirical science; intuitive and supra-rational modes of knowing are usually ignored or dismissed. On the other hand, many Christians equate faith with dogmatic belief that has no need of knowledge or understanding, and "gnosis" (Greek for "knowledge") or "gnostics" with a certain Manichean heresy of the early Church, or with disembodied metaphysical Neoplatonists, or with medieval alchemists or Renaissance magicians — with various views, in short, that they consider disagreeable or heretical. And yet, while the word gnosis appears twenty-nine times in the New Testament, only once is it used in a pejorative sense, where St. Paul warns that gnosis may "puff up" the believer. In all other instances in the New Testament, it is highly to be desired, as in the Gospel of Luke, where Zacharias prophesies the Christ, who will "give the *gnosis* of salvation to his people in the forgiveness of their sins."[2]

Scholars of Dante are wary of the word for other reasons. A number of studies have referred to Dante's gnosis with the associated claim that he was clandestinely "transgressive" or "heterodox" or "esoteric"

---

2 1 Corinthians 8:1; Luke 1:77. These references are taken from Wolfgang Smith, *Christian Gnosis from Saint Paul to Meister Eckhart* (2008; new ed., Kettering, Ohio: Angelico Press / Sophia Perennis, 2011), 5. Smith's book is an eloquent defense of the importance of the concept of gnosis to religious contemplation, and of the essentially *Trinitarian* nature of Christian gnosis.

in a somewhat vague and shady way redolent of conspiracy theories. Authors who have used the word in this sense often make the claim, with no historical evidence, that Dante was a member of an esoteric and quasi-heretical initiation-sect in Florence, the so-called *Fedeli d'Amore* (Devotees of Love), a phrase that Dante use in the *Vita nova* to refer to his group of youthful poet-friends. I want to clarify, then, that I am not using *gnosis* in any of these senses (which I have no objection to per se, as long as they are recognized as theories not facts). Explicitly occult or esoteric interpretations of Dante are sometimes interesting—René Guénon's *Esoterism of Dante*, for instance, has its merits, though he too avows Dante's membership in an esoteric society—but are often reductionist and formulaic. Dante himself is much more exhilarating, evocative, profound, poetic, and "gnostic" in the sense I am about to describe than are the "esoteric" interpretations of him.[3]

What I mean by gnosis is the contemplative or visionary knowledge implicit in traditional doctrines based on divine revelation and scriptures. Gnosis is principial comprehension; contemplative, unitive knowledge that arises from and remains consonant with being. As such, it is unconditioned and participatory; it is knowledge that can no more be seen from outside than the eye can see itself. As will be discussed further in chapter 7, "The Quest for Knowledge," this essential thought arises from the substance of the mind, which is knowledge of the

---

3 Such theories tend to reduce all poetic figures in Dante to merely a disguised language or pretext for secret initiatic doctrines, where every word and image is a cipher for "corrupt Church," "heretical," "Cathars/Templars," and so on. Some of these interpreters are more subtle than others—Luigi Valli, for instance, though his judgment too is predetermined by the theory he has superimposed on Dante's imagery. Valli proposed that Dante and his poet-friends wrote in a secret language—that words such as *women* or *death* were codes for meanings that would have been heretical at that time. For example, for Valli, *women* in the *Vita nova* refers to other *Fedeli d'Amore*, the faithful of Love who knew the secret anti-ecclesiastical meanings of the texts; *death* refers to the Church that had betrayed its spiritual mission in favor of political power; and so on. Valli believed that these poets formed a secret (heretical, in the Church's view) society that aimed at renovation of a materialistic and corrupt Church and of all Christian society. Since their activities and writings were heretical and therefore punishable, perhaps by death, argues Valli, they used a secret language in their poetry, with very specific meanings attached to recurrent images and words. Luigi Valli, *Il linguaggio segreto di Dante e dei "fedeli d'amore"* (Milan: Luni Editrice, 1994). For a recent overview of this approach and its main representatives, more sympathetic to it than I am, see Tommaso Priviero, "On the Service of the Soul: C. G. Jung's *Liber Novus* and Dante's *Commedia*," *Phanes* 1 (2018): 28–57. See chapter 2 for a few examples of this approach to interpreting the *Vita nova*.

divine Substance.[4] The latter notion is embedded in orthodox Christian theology itself; scholastics such as Thomas Aquinas were aware that their theoretical writings were the outer shells of an inner kernel of truth (and so Aquinas after visionary experiences near the end of his life would say that his writings looked "like straw" by comparison).[5] In this sense, much high Christian theology is implicitly "esoteric."[6] Without, of course, using the word gnosis per se, Dante himself refers to it as the *divina scienza*, or theology (recalling that *theology* literally means "knowledge of God"):

> The divine science . . . is replete with peace, a peace which admits no dissension of opinions nor of sophistical arguments because of the supreme certainty of its subject, which is God. And with reference to this science, He [Christ] says to his disciples: "My peace I give you, my peace I leave to you," giving and leaving His teaching to them, which is this science I am referring to. About this science, Solomon says: "There are sixty queens and eighty concubines, and young maidens without number: one is my dove and my perfect one." He calls sciences queens and friends and handmaids; but this one he calls "dove" because she is without any blemish of controversy; and he calls her "perfect" because she makes us see the truth perfectly, by which our soul is calmed.[7]

Note that Christ's teaching in this passage is oral, direct, and experiential. Gnosis proper is distinct from theoretical and doctrinal articulations of it, which constitute, as the scholar of Islam Seyyed Hossein Nasr has put it, "the theoretical dimension of salvific knowledge."[8] The

---

4 This is Frithjof Schuon's pithy formulation, repeated in a few of his publications: *La substance de la connaissance est la Connaissance de la Substance.*

5 *Omnia que scripsi videntur michi palee respectu eorum que vidi et revelata sunt michi*: "Everything I have written appears to me as straw compared to what I have seen and has been revealed to me." Dominicus Prümmer, O. P., ed., *Fontes vitae S. Thomae Aquinatis: Notis historicis et criticis illustrati* (Toulouse: Apud ed. Privat, Bibliopolam, 1912), 377.

6 See Smith, *Christian Gnosis*, 150.

7 *Convivio* II.xiv.19–20; quoting John 14:27 and the Song of Songs 6:7–8.

8 Seyyed Hossein Nasr, *The Garden of Truth: The Vision and Promise of Sufism, Islam's Mystical Tradition* (New York: HarperCollins, 2007), 149. Although this book is about Sufi gnosis, it is a useful source for understanding the concept of gnosis in general.

latter is synonymous with the *philosophia perennis*, or perennial philosophy, pure metaphysics as found in sages such as Meister Eckhart or Śaṅkara or Ibn ʿArabī, or theology in the sense Dante uses above. Such sources trace the return to our human archetype *in divinis*, while we are still in our bodies in the present life. While most religious teaching emphasizes cultivating the spiritual life of prayer and charity for the sake of salvation in the afterlife, from the perspective of sacred science the "otherworld" is here and the "afterlife" is now. This is not to deny postmortem states; rather, it is the awareness that all of time is present in the eternity of God. Indeed, in the state of visionary gnosis, which in reality is God knowing himself through us, the distinction between "in this life" and "not in this life" is transcended. In the divine union or "deification" no such dualism is possible.

All of this is pertinent to Dante. To return to the quote from Shaw, this is what makes Dante an "intellectual" — but not in the post-Enlightenment, reductive understanding of that word. Again and again in the *Comedy*, Dante reminds us that he made the journey to his vision in the Empyrean while he was still in his body. Symbolically, this means that his depictions of Hell, Purgatory, and Heaven apply not only to the afterlife but, even more urgently, to spiritual states in the present life.[9]

Importantly, there is no essential conflict between the above and Dante's orthodox, devout Catholicism. While Dante's prophetic invective in the *Comedy*, from damned popes to allegorical apocalyptic visions, confronts and challenges Church corruption, Dante entirely believed in the Church as the Bride of Christ and in scripture as the revealed word of God. In fact, his orthodoxy is indispensable to his poetic gnosis, which requires intellectual austerity and self-denial for the sake of truth. As Zygmunt Barański has put it, for Dante as for Catholic opinion in general, to deliberately or arrogantly misinterpret scripture "was a heinous sin and a hallmark of the heretic.... In the medieval imaginary, heretics were obstinate, intellectually arrogant, deceitful and, of course, invariably wrong. They lacked the capacity — refined by faith and humility — to discern the truth."[10] In his

---

9 I have chosen to capitalize Hell, Purgatory, and Heaven, not as names of archetypes, but as proper place names in Dante's cosmology, which (as I will elaborate) is closely associated with the realism of his poetic gnosis.

10 Zygmunt G. Barański, "(Un)Orthodox Dante," in *Reviewing Dante's Theology*, 2 vols., edited by Claire E. Honess and Matthew Treherne (Oxford: Peter Lang, 2013), 2: 288; and see this essay in general on the subject of Dante's orthodoxy/unorthodoxy. See also

treatise on monarchy, Dante quotes from Augustine's *De doctrina christiana* (On Christian Doctrine), the most important guide throughout the Middle Ages to the orthodox way of reading the Bible: "Faith will waver if the authority of the Holy Scriptures is shaken."[11]

It is important to note Dante's orthodoxy in the context of a discussion of his gnosis, since mention of the latter has often been accompanied by extravagant claims about Dante's *un*orthodoxy or "heterodoxy," or by misleading statements about the relationship between individual spiritual experience and religion. Institutional religion is a human interpretation — sometimes guided by spiritual wisdom, but sometimes not — adapted to time and circumstance, of divine revelation and scripture, the revealed Word of God. While it is right to point out that the spiritual experience ultimately is the cause of religion, in practice the reverse has been true for countless sages, saints, and ordinary believers, for whom the experience of the sacred has arisen *from* their religion. Etymologically, orthodoxy simply means correctness of opinion or belief. If there is truth, there is error, and if nothing is false, there is no truth. But the statement "there is no truth" is a truth-claim, so it contradicts itself. In other words, there is no way that human beings can get around or avoid the question of truth and falsehood. Orthodoxy interprets divine revelation to ensure the correct praxis and principles for realizing the truth. As Nasr writes, "Authentic esoterism [or gnosis], far from being heterodox, lies at the heart of orthodoxy and orthopraxy in their most universal sense."[12]

A common tendency in our own time is to approve of "spirituality" but to be dismissive or distrustful of "organized religion." Given the oppression and idolatry often perpetrated by religious institutions, to say nothing of everyday religious bigotry and narrow-mindedness, this attitude is understandable. And yet it is a destructive oversimplification. Those who too easily dismiss orthodoxy as mere "dogmatism" ignore the essential point that truth realizes itself in the human mind within a matrix of form. Truth does not *deny* forms, but goes beyond them from within, much as an artist who has mastered

---

the essays collected in *Dante and Heterodoxy: The Temptations of 13th-Century Radical Thought,* edited and with an introduction by Maria Luisa Ardizzone and with a conclusion by Teodolinda Barolini (Newcastle upon Tyne: Cambridge Scholars Publishing, 2014).

11   *Monarchia* III.iv.9.

12   Seyyed Hossein Nasr, *The Heart of Islam: Enduring Values for Humanity* (San Francisco: HarperSanFrancisco 2002), 97.

form can discover formal freedom in creative inspiration. Dante was fully aware of this. He honored orthodoxy for protecting values that human beings cannot simply reinvent individual by individual (as is often implied in our individualistic culture). That Dante clearly did think for himself as well is not at all inconsistent with his orthodoxy. Independent thought has always resided within Catholic orthodoxy, even as certain articles of faith are fundamental. Such articles — the Nicene Creed, which I mentioned earlier, is one authoritative summary of them — are like the soil in which one plants the seed of one's thought, as it were, not cemetery ground for burying the cadaver of thought. This is why Dante felt free — obliged actually — to criticize the Church. For example, he spared no harsh word for the so-called decretalists, the keepers of "decretals" or papal decrees, whom he blasted for their greed (they offered dispensations to the credulous faithful and substitutions for vows in exchange for money), and perhaps even more so for their privileging canon law over the inspired authority of the Bible and the Holy Spirit. We know that Dante did not disparage canon law per se, since he celebrates Gratian, the compiler of the *Decretum*, in *Paradiso*, when he encounters the doctors of the Church.[13] Intention and integrity are always at the fulcrum of Dante's ethical distinctions.

The most pertinent scene in the *Comedy*, in terms of Dante's independent thinking about Christian doctrine, is where he asks the just rulers in *Paradiso* xix how it can be that a devout and holy person born in a place that afforded no possibility of ever hearing about Christ or the Gospels could be denied eternity in Paradise. The just rulers answer, in the collective form of an Eagle that speaks in one voice, that on the Day of Judgment many non-Christians will be closer to Christ than some Christians will be. In addition, Dante places the pagans Trajan and Ripheus among the beatified Christian and Hebrew rulers. The salvation of these souls confounds ordinary Christian understanding, the Eagle explains, because God's Intellect and Justice so infinitely transcend our own. So, as always, Dante

---

13   Dante lambasts the decretalists in more than one passage: see, e.g., *Paradiso* XII.82–87, *Monarchia* II.x.1, and *Convivio* IV.xxvii.13–14. On Dante and the decretalists, and his relation to ecclesiology in general, see Paola Nasti, "Dante and Ecclesiology," in *Reviewing Dante's Theology*, ed. Honess and Treherne, 2: 43–88.

defends the spirit over the letter, essential truth over fossilized form.[14] Inevitably, this has led some to question his orthodoxy. For example, his treatise on monarchy—an early argument for the separation of Church and State—was publicly burned in Bologna after his death and remained on the Vatican Index of Prohibited Books for centuries. Another interesting example, which I discuss in chapters 1 and 2, is the Counter-Reformation censorship of certain words in the *Vita nova* that were considered scandalous or heterodox. In short, Dante was a gadfly for Church authorities.

At the same time, he was entirely orthodox in his view of the providential mission of the Church. To confirm this, we need only note that, starting with canto XXIII of *Paradiso*, Dante presents five consecutive cantos dedicated to the Church as the body of the faithful in Christ. In the Empyrean, the vision of the Trinity, the divinity outside of time and space, will be the dominant theme, but these earlier cantos present the triumph of the Church—the archetype, so to speak, of the earthly institution—in her historical reality. In canto XXIV of *Paradiso*, where St. Peter examines Dante on the theological virtue of faith, Dante tells Peter that holy scripture is what awakened faith in him. For Dante, the Bible in relation to human intelligence is like the sun in relation to the eye: it enables the believer to see. This canto repeats in dramatic form what the *Convivio*, which he had written many years earlier, had stated in abstract prose: faith sees perfectly what reason is blind to. The profound insight in this canto of *Paradiso* is that truth itself is grasped in a flash of intuition, inspired by scripture and divine revelation, which enable the intellect to become conscious of its own nature. Commenting on St. Paul's definition of faith in his letter to the Hebrews, Dante says that faith on earth is itself the reality of the things that we hope for—the existence of God and of eternal life—and therefore proves the existence of things we cannot see.[15]

---

14 Kenelm Foster, *The Two Dantes and Other Studies* (London: Darton, Longman & Todd, 1977), 152, says that for medieval theologians considering pious Muslims and "pagans," their approach "was to distinguish between explicit and implicit faith, and to find the concept of implicit Christian faith confirmed by such texts as Hebrews 11:6.... For St. Thomas this included all that a pagan need believe in order to be saved; for to believe in God as rewarder—or more simply, to believe in Providence—is implicitly to believe in Christ. Nor was he by any means the only theologian of his time to suggest this kind of hidden contact between the pagan soul and God's fatherly love."

15 *Paradiso* XXIV.61–66.

METAPHYSICS AND POETRY

Christian Moevs's study *The Metaphysics of Dante's "Comedy"* (2005) is the first sustained treatment of Dante's metaphysical thought and its place in his poetry.[16] As Moevs says, we must learn how to grasp Dante's metaphysical perspective, his understanding of fundamental reality, free of post-Enlightenment prejudices, if we are not to misread him.

Moevs locates Dante's view of reality in the nondualist, nonmaterialist, Western tradition, in its various Aristotelian and Neoplatonic permutations, from Pseudo-Dionysius and Augustine to Bonaventure and Eckhart. He outlines a few principles that pervade this tradition, which informs Dante's work from start to finish but which is most fully realized and expressed in the *Comedy*. The principles are:

- God is Being or actuality or form, pure awareness or Intellect itself, which is not a "thing" but is the active power to be everything and nothing. This principle derives from the Aristotelian insight that to answer the question of where or "in what" the cosmos exists, there must be a reality that is no thing, since all things by definition are part of the cosmos itself and so could not account for where it exists. That "no thing" is consciousness or *nous* (substituted in Dante by the Empyrean, which is further discussed below), the divine Intellect-Being (God), on which the entire visible universe is dependent at every instant.

- Matter is ontologically dependent upon Intellect, but Intellect is self-subsistent. Aristotle, and Aquinas after him, saw that our belief that the world is "made of matter" is an illusion because matter is nothing in itself; it is a principle of continuity in change — which is why all attempts to define it only describe a form that matter has assumed. Matter's being derives from the principle of form, or consciousness. This is the meaning of the Aristotelian maxim, *Forma dat esse materiae*, "Form gives being to matter."

- Each thing that exists does so only as a qualification or participation in Intellect-Being (the One or God). In an absolute sense, only God is; all else merely participates in this reality. The universe is radically contingent, dependent in every instant on what gives it being.

- Human awareness, the rational soul, is a special case within the creation, "a special sharing in or affinity with the ultimate ontological

---

16 Christian Moevs, *The Metaphysics of Dante's "Comedy"* (Oxford: Oxford University Press, 2005). Page numbers for quotes from this will be given in parentheses after the quotes.

principle"—hence its immortality, its freedom from spatiotemporal parameters, and its potential for ecstatic contemplation and deification or union with the divine.

The latter point is important in this context since it underlies the journey of Dante to the Empyrean in *Paradiso*. As Moevs puts it: "Dante's *Comedy* is built on the principle that when the individual subject of experience, having shed the *scoglio* or slough . . . of the exclusive self-identification with the finite, fully awakens to itself, it finds itself in the Empyrean, knowing itself as (one with) the awareness-actuality-being-love that—since it is nothing in itself—is not *in* the world but rather *contains* the world" (169). On the question of how the human soul or intelligence can experience itself as deiform, Moevs writes: "If Intellect is the principle of Being-in-itself, then human intellect comes to know God, and all things, by truly knowing itself, or knowing its true self, the ground it shares with *what is*. This revelation can come only through surrendering or sacrificing everything it thinks it is or needs or wants: that is, every thing" (59).

The idea of Intellect as the ultimate ontological principle upon which all else depends is the cornerstone of the Western spiritual and philosophical tradition up to the Enlightenment, and is present in most Indian and Asian spiritual teachings. Moevs quotes or cites Ibn 'Arabī and Avicenna (Ibn Sīnā), as well as other Muslim sages, in this connection; and he refers briefly to similarities with Vedic nondualistic thought, as in the Advaita Vedānta of Śaṅkara, pointing out that Christian medieval thought, too, "believes that reality is *ultimately* one and *ultimately* spiritual," and that "if the *Comedy* has a philosophical or theological foundation and 'message' that is it" (172).

Moevs's survey of Western metaphysical thought raises other key ideas that are related to the above principles. The world of space and time does not itself exist in space and time; it exists in Intellect, the Empyrean, pure conscious being. Intellect-Being is what is; it is unqualified, self-subsistent, without attributes. "It has no extension in space or time; rather, it projects space-time 'within' itself, as, analogously, a dreaming intelligence projects a dream-world, or a mind gives being to a thought." As Moevs points out, this understanding of "the radical contingency of 'created' things is the wellspring of medieval Christian thought, without which the rest of medieval thought makes little sense" (5).

Dante expresses this symbolically, in the final cantos of the *Comedy*, as the relation between the Empyrean and the Primum Mobile, or First Mover.[17] Much of Moevs's discussion focuses on cantos XXVIII–XXX in *Paradiso*, where Beatrice's instruction to Dante finally enables him to grasp that the creation is a projection of the divine Mind, that the Primum Mobile is "the nexus between pure being and the differentiation of being into identity" (33). In *Paradiso* XXVIII, Dante sees a brilliant point of light reflected in Beatrice's eyes, a point that is as much smaller than the smallest star as that star is smaller than the moon as they appear from earth. This is the *punto*, or point, between spatiotemporal extension and self-subsistent Being, what St. Bonaventure called the *apex mentis* or *apex affectionis*, through which the mind that has entered itself leaves behind every idea and thing, focusing itself in single-pointed attention on its ground, ultimately to pass beyond itself into pure Being. The entire universe depends upon this point, which is the reflexivity of conscious being. It is the ultimate ontological principle, as Aristotle defines it in his *Metaphysics*, "the thought that thinks itself," upon which "depend the heavens and the world of nature." These last words, quoted from Aristotle, are the very words that Beatrice first speaks in her discourse on the point of light and the angelic hierarchies around it.[18]

Many Christian sources refer to the concept of the *punctum*, including Bonaventure, Richard of St. Victor, Augustine, and Meister Eckhart. In Neoplatonist sources, too, there is the notion of the divine point through which existence flows from nonbeing into being. It is the same as the point through which the mind enters and goes beyond itself, until, in Bonaventure's words, it is "totally transferred and transformed into God." This is the sense in which Meister Eckhart said the eye with which we see God is the same as the eye with which God sees our essence. The notion appears in modern spiritual writers as well. William Blake, probably drawing on Plotinus, opposed the concept of

---

17 Briefly, the Primum Mobile is the swiftest, outmost sphere, which imparts motion to the other spheres in Dante's Ptolemaic cosmology. The Empyrean or tenth heaven was a Christian addition to the Aristotelian-Ptolemaic cosmos; its theoretical justification was to provide a sphere outside the rotating spheres, consistent with the Christian emphasis on the transcendence of the Deity. It absorbed the functions of Aristotle's Unmoved Mover (which was based on the idea that change or motion in itself is unintelligible without a principle from which it proceeds, which is not subject to change).

18 Aristotle, *Metaphysics* XII.7, 1072b14.

the *punctum* to the Newtonian concept of empty space and extension. He said that modern science's depiction of human insignificance in the immensity of space—the "soul shudd'ring vacuum" of the Newtonian universe—results in spiritual passivity, since it falsely extracts consciousness from space, treating the latter as a detached entity. The *punctum* can be seen, Blake wrote, in flowers and their perfume, which are opening centers, as it were, through which Eternity manifests.

Moevs applies metaphysical principles to notions of the Empyrean, matter, form, and creation, for interpreting the *Comedy* and for understanding Dante's poetics. Especially important is Moevs's setting aside of the frequent misconception that the *Comedy* is simply a metrical vehicle for doctrinal instruction. Such an approach would be anathema to Dante, since for him truth is not merely a set of beliefs or ideas; rather, truth transcends language, history, and every contingency—the *Comedy* included, as Dante certainly knew and in fact expresses in the very fabric of the poem. "Understanding is practical," says Moevs (and "understanding" here is "gnosis" in the sense I am using it), and must not be confused with doctrine or belief: "it is to have experienced the true nature and foundation of reality, to know it as oneself, and thus to live it" (171). Even the most doctrinal passages in the *Comedy* have one aim: "to reveal being.... Every signifier, every form, and every concept that Dante can use must necessarily also eclipse what it reveals" (9). In other words, Dante is perfectly aware that what he has created, awe-inspiring as it is, is itself provisional and contingent. The *Comedy* is a great and mighty wave of the creative imagination, but it is still ultimately just a wave on the ocean of Being. In the *Comedy*, salvation is a self-awakening of the Real to itself in us, "the surrender or sacrifice of what we take ourselves and the world to be, a changed experience that is one with a moral transformation" (8).

Dante extols saints like Francis and Dominic, not because they taught truths people already knew, but because Dante believed they *saw* and *embodied* the truth, the irreducible reality in which all things and thoughts consist. As Dante repeatedly emphasizes, his lay contemporaries and the leaders of the Church often simply used doctrines to remain comfortable in a delusional sleep—obviously a pitfall of religion in every age. Dante expresses this symbolically in his placement of the blessed in the celestial Rose: divided *equally* between those who lived before Christ and those who lived after. Salvation is not merely predicated on knowing about the historical Jesus; it is the capacity to recognize Christ in the present, "the loving self-sacrifice of the self-subsistent to and as the contingent," as Moevs puts it. Dante's whole point is transformation, since he, in the great line of Western gnosis or pure metaphysics, has the conviction that "the mind's obsessive self-identification with the contingent, finite objects of its own experience" is what obscures the intellect. In *Inferno*, we see an enactment of "the web of desires, attachments, emotions, passions, and fears that are the fabric of human life, and the habit of a mind that does not know itself" — for "the obsessive identification with the body makes human love carnal and spawns insatiable desire, *concupiscentia*: to experience oneself only as a body in space and time is to conceive all things as other than oneself, and to seek to overcome this limit and isolation by *consuming* or possessing the world . . . through the senses" (88). Could there be a more lucid description of what underlies the current global economic, political, and environmental crisis?

In sum, the doctrine of the *Comedy* points beyond itself, the way that Beatrice's deconstruction of space-time in *Paradiso* XXIX leads the intellect of Dante to a knowledge of itself, one with self-subsistent Being. The *Comedy*'s aim, then, is "the self-experience of *what is*" (9), not an inculcation of beliefs in symbolic form or an art-for-art's-sake poetic fiction. In terms of Dante's view of poetry, this distinction is crucial, and helps to resolve the centuries-old, sterile scholarly debate over Dante-*poeta* (the fiction of the *Comedy* as "poetic posturing") versus Dante-*theologus* (the *Comedy* as pretext for imparting theological and philosophical doctrines).

In *De vulgari eloquentia* (On Eloquence in the Vernacular), Dante's unfinished treatise on poetics and language, which he wrote before beginning the *Comedy*, he defines poetry as "nothing but an invention or fiction composed through rhetoric and music."[19] Unusual for his time, Dante's definition does not include the content of poetry as one of its terms. This does not mean, as is clear from Dante's writing, that he considered content unimportant. Moevs believes that Dante's definition of poetry is the foundation of the *Comedy*'s "transcendent enterprise and truth-claims" (180), its prophetic function. The content of poetry is transparent or not, depending on the level of inspiration of the poet. Religious content alone does not necessarily make a work of art more

---

19   *De vulgari eloquentia* II.iv.2.

spiritual than a mundane subject; inspiration does. Moevs compares Dante's view of poetry to that of Augustine, which disparages poetry that is "the emblem of temporality, mortality, ephemerality, change-ability," and praises only poetry of the Holy Spirit, which remains "one with faith, with openness or expectation, a currency stamped with the image of Christ" (180). I view these matters in Dante differently from Moevs; Dante's attitude toward poetry strikes me as less monolithic than that of Augustine or Aquinas. He clearly does favor spiritual poetry, but he does not simply dismiss "secular" poetry either. His admiration for poets such as Ovid and Horace shows that he appreciates them as more than "false coinage" or "liars" (as the theologians sometimes called poets). Classical poets are in Dante's Limbo, it is true, but Dante is proud to be one of their company of masters of the art.[20] He is entirely the poet in this regard.

Also pertinent to a discussion of Dante's theory of poetry is a passage in *Purgatorio* XVII about the epistemological validity of imagination. For Dante as for Aristotle and Thomas Aquinas, most human knowledge derives from the senses. Sense images are presented to the intellect either by the so-called estimative or cogitative faculty (the power that enables us to judge the veracity of the images we receive from the senses), or by the imagination (which for Dante and medieval thought in general is the faculty that produces or stores images from previous sensations). Imagination orders sense experience into cohesive wholes. But in *Purgatorio* XVII, reference is made to a light or intelligence, a *lume che nel ciel s'informa* ("light that is formed in heaven"),[21] which takes form either spontaneously or through divine will and moves the imagination, focusing the mind on images arising within it that make the senses inoperative. This happens when the mind is freed from the outer world and its distractions or attachments. The process corresponds to the *imaginatio vera*, or to what Henry Corbin called the *mundus imaginalis*, the imaginal world, which mediates between the purely intellectual and the sensible worlds.[22] As Moevs writes:

---

20 *Inferno* IV.39.

21 *Purgatorio* XVII.17.

22 On the imaginative faculty as described here, see *Purgatorio* XVII.13–18, IX.13–18; also *Convivio* II.viii.13, where Dante argues for the immortality of the soul on the basis of its capacity for prophetic dreams, the idea being that the silencing of the soul's corporeal sheath allows the soul to communicate again with the divine world that is its origin and destiny.

> When the human intellect is dissociated from spatiotempo-
> ral form, finite forms arise spontaneously within it as they
> arise in angelic intelligences, or in the divine mind itself:
> the human mind "takes dictation," so to speak. Such images
> or intuitions, undistorted by a finite point of view... or by
> sensation, are self-revelations of reality, with the same actu-
> ality, truth, or being as the sensory world. This phenomenon,
> which grounds prophecy and divinely inspired art—and
> thus (according to the *Comedy*) the *Comedy* itself—can
> occur only because of the affinity (*proporzione*) between
> human intellect and angelic intelligence: when the human
> intelligence is freed from body, sensation, and thought, it is
> assimilated to a "separated substance," an angel. (76)

Such ideas are behind Dante's conviction that divinely inspired
poetry, the subject of chapter 10 in this book, can be a vehicle for
truth. In the case of Dante's masterpiece, truth is conveyed by means
of fiction presented as a historical, concrete fact. As Moevs says, the
Comedy asserts itself as *literally* true because it claims to embody or
give finite form to (incarnate) Truth/Being, like scripture or like Christ.
It is a *non falso errore*, or not false illusion, in Dante's phrase,[23] "contingent form disguising the reality it makes manifest by giving it finite
attributes.... It understands itself to be a finite form 'transparent' to
the reality it embodies, a reality that, in those who have eyes to see,
can come to recognize and awaken to itself by reading this text." The
Comedy's "realism" is intrinsic, then, to its purpose: "to understand
how this fictive textual world becomes inescapably real is to awaken to
the sense in which the spatiotemporal world is fictive (contingent or
relatively unreal)." In the *Comedy*, along with the pilgrim-protagonist,
we slowly awaken like a dreamer who has forgotten he or she is dreaming—"so we come to live only 'inside' the physical universe, and not
in the Empyrean which sustains it" (10).

The realism in the *Comedy* is the poetic equivalent of gnosis: it
evokes participation in incomprehensible reality. In canto IV of *Paradiso*,
Dante writes that God revealed scripture in images to adapt divine
knowledge to the human mind, which relies on the senses. Clearly,
Dante does something similar with the marvelous pictures he creates

---

23   *Purgatorio* XV.117.

in his poem. For Moevs, Dante's great breakthrough in his poem was to show that "to journey toward self-knowledge is to assimilate as oneself, through direct poetic experience, the entire breadth of human experience in history, in its concrete and particular reality." Through this identification with the totality of possible experience, the obsessive point of view and attachments of the individual ego begin to dissolve, and "the subject of all experience, reflected as the individual mind, begins to awaken to itself" (10). This is why Dante's masterpiece is "a great wake-up call" (11) — as much so now, if not more so, as when it was first published.

DANTE THE SYMBOLIST

Between pure metaphysics and poetry, there is the poet, Dante, who, even when he composes his philosophical treatise the *Convivio* ("Banquet"), is far from being a rationalizing Neo-Aristotelian. As is clear from any number of passages in his writings — from book III of the *Convivio*, which draws heavily on *De causis* (On Causes), a Neoplatonic treatise, to the opening lines of *Paradiso*, which says that the One that moves all things penetrates the universe, reflected in some parts more and in others less — the presence of Neoplatonist thought in Dante is pervasive and poetically fruitful. Accordingly, much recent scholarship has toned down the old emphasis on the Neo-Aristotelian and Thomist Dante, while granting that these elements indeed run deep in his thought, in order to highlight him as a symbolist poet.[24]

As Zygmunt Barański points out, the scholasticism of Dante has been exaggerated by scholars because it conforms to modern rationalist biases. For example, Dante does not organize his presentation in the *Convivio* according to the eleven sciences or fields of learning he names in book II,[25] as was done by medieval encyclopedists such as Cassiodorus, Martianus Capella, Hugh of St. Victor, and Alan of

24 On Dante's symbolist, "nonrationalist" approach, important recent studies have been Lino Pertile, *La puttana e il gigante: Dal "Cantico dei cantici" al Paradiso terrestre di Dante* (Ravenna: Longo, 1998); Zygmunt G. Barański, *Dante e i segni: Saggi per una storia intellettuale di Dante Alighieri* (Naples: Liguori, 2000); Paola Nasti, *Favole d'amore e "saver profondo": La tradizione salomonica in Dante* (Ravenna: Longo Editore, 2007). For a study in English, see Paul Priest, "Dante and the Song of Songs," *Studi danteschi* 49 (1972): 79–113.

25 Seven of which belong to the trivium and the quadrivium, which were the foundation of medieval education: grammar, logic, rhetoric; arithmetic, music, geometry, astronomy. The other four are physics, metaphysics, ethics, and theology.

Lille. The *Convivio* has a much more fluid organization, interweaving the various sciences, not only within individual books or treatises, but even within single chapters — a method "that clearly departs from the standard form of 'encyclopedic' organization and which anticipates the apparent liberty with which knowledge is organized in the *Comedy*."[26] In this and other ways, Barański demonstrates the prominence of "non-rationalist" (importantly, very different from *anti*rationalist) influences in Dante's writings, and shows that Dante implicitly criticizes Aristotle and the rationalist approach to knowledge even in some of his most Aristotelian and scholastic passages. Instead, Dante favors a hermeneutics of signs that emphasizes knowledge as divine illumination. As the beatified heads of state tell Dante in canto XIX of *Paradiso*, "There is no light if it does not come from heaven, from the serene light of God, which never darkens; the rest is total darkness, the shadow of the flesh or its poison."[27] In other words, only the divine Intellect ultimately can bring light to the human intellect. Poet that he was, Dante preferred "the greater flexibility and creative liberty of exegesis to rationalizing rigor and to the obsessive, divisive anxiety of Neo-Aristotelean philosophy and theology."[28] The signs of the mind of God that Dante saw himself reading were two: the creation itself and sacred texts, the Book of Creation and the Book of Scripture (the Bible). Dante's semiotics are conspicuous, for example, in his use of Bible commentary, whose style and methods Dante imitates in his prose works the *Vita nova* and the *Convivio*. Paola Nasti has shown that the prose in the *Vita nova* recalls commentaries on the Song of Songs, which leave traces also in Dante's erotic-lyrical language and in some explicit echoes of the Song in his works. Even the *Vita nova*'s and *Convivio*'s prosimetrical form, blending poetry and prose, is reminiscent of Bible commentary.[29]

I have already referred to the important place of imagination in Dante's epistemology. And in fact, a dream-vision announces his poetic vocation in the opening poem of the *Vita nova*, a sonnet written when he was eighteen years old. This poem describes the seizure of his being by his love for Beatrice. As Dante describes the vision in his commentary in the *Vita nova*, written about ten years after the poem:

26 Barański, *Dante e i segni*, 86.
27 *Paradiso* XIX.64–66.
28 Barański, *Dante e i segni*, 64.
29 Nasti, *Favole d'amore*, 43–85.

I seemed to see a fiery cloud in my room, inside which I discerned a figure of a lordly man, frightening to behold. And it was marvelous how utterly full of joy he seemed. And among the words that he spoke, I understood only a few, including: "Ego dominus tuus" [I am your lord]. In his arms I thought I saw a sleeping person, naked but for a crimson silken cloth that seemed to be draped about her, who, when I looked closely, I realized was the lady of the saving gesture, she who earlier that day had deigned to salute me. And in one of his hands it seemed he held something consumed by flame, and I thought I heard him say these words: "Vide cor tuum" [Behold your heart]. And when he had been there awhile, it seemed that he awakened the sleeping lady, and he was doing all he could to get her to eat the thing burning in his hands, which she anxiously ate. Then his happiness turned into the bitterest tears, and as he cried he picked up this woman in his arms, and he seemed to go off toward the sky.[30]

It is instructive to note, as Barański does, that after this episode in the *Vita nova* Dante says that the people who interpreted the poem for him were poets, not academicians or philosophers. For Dante and his poet-friends, poetry was a way of knowledge — inner knowledge that engages the whole person. So, love was inseparable from it; love is what makes knowledge personally transformative and imitative of God's knowledge. For Dante, to be a poet was to follow the example of the symbolic art of the Creator, the *Deus artifex*. Poetic knowledge is the living presence of what is realized and known; it is the thought of the heart (understanding "heart" in the nonsentimental sense, as the core of one's being, not the physical organ). This is why, as several chapters in this book will illustrate, Dante used individual poems in the *Vita nova* and *Convivio* as occasions for contemplative and philosophical insight. They were landmarks along his heartfelt philosophical and spiritual pilgrimage.

The high metaphysics that I sketched above is *dramatized* in the context of the *Comedy*, where it becomes *experienced* knowledge. In the crisis of epistemology brought about by Aristotelianism in Dante's

30 *Vita nova* 1.14–18 (III.3–7).

time, forms of knowing were themselves objects of discussion, and for Dante poetic knowledge is privileged knowledge, not dictated by encyclopedist categories and philosophical *summae*.[31] It has often been claimed that Dante left off the unfinished *Convivio* to write the *Comedy*, in 1307 or so, because he had outgrown an erroneous attachment to rational philosophy that still gripped him while he was composing the *Convivio*. When I was translating and annotating the *Convivio*, however, I was never able to conceive of its author as a poet who had gone the way of rationalizing Neo-Aristotelian philosophy. An abundance of Neoplatonist metaphysics, as well as the poetry and often imaginative poetic prose of the *Convivio* persuaded me otherwise. Rather, I think that when Dante left off the *Convivio* he had come to realize that the kind of language he was using in that book could not express what he most needed to say. For Dante the solution was poetry—a poem that includes everything—as the privileged vehicle of knowledge, because, as Barański puts it, "compared to other knowledge systems, it is able to combine effectively the form and the content of the creation, and can therefore provide a better analogy of divinity."[32] The many-faceted symbolic and poetic language that Dante used for the *Comedy* is indicated throughout this book, and is the express focus of chapter 9, "The *Divine Comedy* as Cosmos."

WOMAN AS INITIATOR

"Lady Philosophy," who has much in common with Solomon's Sapientia or Wisdom, is the subject of chapter 6 in this book. This fluid, feminine figure is not associated with abstract, detached knowledge, but with the knowledge that involves loving participation, and so naturally is associated with poetry and inspiration, or poetic gnosis. No discussion of Dante's inspirational sources, and no introduction to the chapters that follow, which often refer to the image of woman in Dante's works, would be adequate without considering the place of women in his creative imagination. After all, we have it from Dante himself that he awoke to his life's calling, his vocation as a poet-prophet, through his overwhelming, first unrequited then bereaved love for Beatrice—whose name in Italian means "She who blesses," or "She who brings bliss." The passage from the *Vita nova* quoted above shows

---

31   Barański, *Dante e i segni*, 34.
32   Ibid., 100–101.

how literally consuming this awakening to love was for Dante. This theme often comes up in this book, but is especially the focus of chapters 1 and 2, "Love and the Soul" and "Beatrice." In addition, as just mentioned, the chapter on Lady Philosophy, while ostensibly about a different inspiring feminine figure for Dante, will show how even in a work supposedly modeled after Aristotelian rationalism, a female muse is his initiator. If knowledge or gnosis for Dante ultimately was *poetic* knowledge, women and feminine wisdom brought that knowledge to fruition in his intellect and imagination. The final cantos of *Purgatorio* and all of *Paradiso*, in which Beatrice is his guide to celestial realities and even his final vision of the Trinity is mediated by the Virgin Mary, are high proof of this.

The word *donna* or *donne* (woman or women) occurs 208 times in the *Vita nova* alone. In Dante's time this word, from Latin *domina*, had connotations of *signora*, lady. *Femmina* had and still has in Italian a more physical-biological connotation; this is why Dante refers to the seductive siren who appears to him in a dream at the start of *Purgatorio* XIX as a *femmina*, not a *donna*. The traditional courteous stance of the courtly lover is extended by the protagonist to all of the women in the *Vita nova*. Courtly love, about which much will be said in chapter 1, signaled a break from the misogyny of the times. One only has to read Augustine and Aquinas on women and compare that to what Dante says about them in any number of poems to see that the denigration of women in Christian theology had been transformed for Dante and his poet-friends into value and dignity. There is no question that for Dante the word *donna* held great importance and quasi-numinous power; the Virgin Mary herself is referred to as a *donna* in the last canto of *Paradiso*.

Women, as Dante says in the *Vita nova*, are the ones who understand the truth of love; they are guardians of the insight into love that the protagonist is blindly and awkwardly seeking. He observes them mourning; informs them about his decision to write poetry in praise of his lady even if she refuses to acknowledge him; sees them coming from Beatrice's house in mourning after the death of her father; and tells them of his terrible delirious waking premonition of Beatrice's death. A woman, the so-called Donna Gentile (noble or gracious woman), comforts Dante in his grief after Beatrice's death. Women are the poet-protagonist's ideal readers on matters of love, as Dante makes clear when he comments in the *Vita nova* that he is writing in vernacular so that women can read his works (since at that time few women had opportunity to learn Latin). Just as Beatrice is the image of other women's perfection, they are more accessible Beatrices. Women for Dante are the great teachers of the heart and the crucial guides for the soul's salvation.

Years later, when Dante composes the *Comedy*, the function of Beatrice as Dante's initiator will be explicit. In the final canto of *Purgatorio*, Beatrice reminds him that her wisdom is far beyond that of the *dottrina* (teaching) of *quella scuola* (that school), the merely human knowledge with which Dante once had been too enamored.[33] Dante's awakening to greater gnosis comes a short while later in this canto, where Beatrice leads Dante to drink of the waters of Eunoë (a name coined by Dante, from the Greek for "well-minded"), which conventionally has been interpreted as an allegory for the restoration of one's memories of the good, but which, at this climactic point in the Earthly Paradise, must have a more substantial and profound sense than this apparently bland phrase would suggest. "The Good" is more than a moral quality, it is fullness of being. So Eunoë signals the restoration of the good of the primordial self, the very substance of the intelligence, in other words gnosis, which enables Dante's climb with Beatrice through the celestial spheres.

Another instance of many in which Dante emphasizes Beatrice as initiator occurs near the start of canto XXVIII of *Paradiso*, which is discussed below in another context. Dante recalls his looking at Beatrice in the ninth sphere or Primum Mobile: "Thus my memory recalls what I did looking into her lovely eyes with which Love made the knot to snare me." Dante has just looked into those eyes by means of which Lord Love had taken hold of him years ago, as he recounts in the *Vita nova*. He compares his seeing of a brilliant light in Beatrice's eyes to a man seeing a candle flame in a mirror he is facing, who turns and sees that the candle really is there behind him. Similarly, when Dante turns to see the light he sees reflected in Beatrice's eyes — the light of God in the Empyrean — he knows it actually *is* there. Allegorically then, Beatrice-Wisdom is the sight which makes inner vision possible. She is gnosis itself, and only gnosis can impart gnosis, as the sages always teach. And because she is his beloved, the knowledge she brings is

---

33 *Purgatorio* XXXIII.85–86.

infused by love. As Beatrice tells Dante in canto v of *Paradiso*, things that seduce us in this world with their beauty or desireableness are *traces* of the light he sees in Beatrice's presence, and they are things that are *mal conosciute*, not properly recognized for what they are.[34] The so-called *intellectus amoris*, intellect or understanding of love, is a theme in Dante's writing from very early on. The concept is repeated in *Paradiso*, where Beatrice states that one whose intellect is not ripened by the *fiamma d'amor*, or flame of love, will not understand why God chose Christ's sacrifice for human beings' redemption.[35] The memory of her presence, her being, effects this ripening in Dante's mind.

POET-PROPHET

The first phase of Beatrice's initiation of Dante culminates in her charging him, by the grace of God, with his prophetic role. Near the end of *Purgatorio*, Beatrice predicts the eventual delivery of the Church from its current abuse by papal and royal powers, and orders Dante to take note of what she is saying, to report her words back to people on earth, by means of his poem.

The other major stage in Dante's taking on the mantle of poet-prophet occurs in the middle cantos of *Paradiso*, where he encounters his ancestor the crusader-knight Cacciaguida, who urges Dante to speak out fearlessly against corrupt religious and civic leaders. For Dante, the principal causes of social disintegration and malice in society are the Church's betrayal, led by corrupt popes, of its mission to be the Bride of Christ, and the absence of a just political leader (an emperor) who can unite contentious factions in Italy and rein in people's tendency to waywardness.

The mid-twentieth-century scholar Bruno Nardi compared Dante to the Old Testament prophets, who spoke in the name of a direct revelation from God, were at odds with sacerdotal institutions, decried corruption, and announced the coming of an Anointed One who would restore the throne of David — something that Dante mirrors in his prophecy of renewed empire.[36] As Nardi notes, Dante's politics are visionary politics, like those of Plato or the Gospels, so the fact that

---

34 *Paradiso* v.10–12.

35 *Paradiso* vii.58–60.

36 Bruno Nardi, "Dante profeta," in *Dante e la cultura medievale,* edited by Paolo Mazzatini, 2nd ed. (Rome-Bari: Editori Laterza, 1990), 265–326.

his prediction of a restored Church and Empire did not come to pass is not a "failed" prophecy:

> Dante's illusion lies in having faced in the course of time . . . an eternal idea which, in itself, is outside of time and does not affect human events other than as an aspiration to "surpass a limit," a limit which can never be actually surpassed in time, like the "Kingdom of God" in the Gospels, which, as long as man is on earth, say the theologians, is no less utopian than Dante's dream. As Jesus said, "Regnum meum non est de hoc mundo [My kingdom is not of this world]."[37]

Like any prophet, Dante is called to remind his society of the eternal verities amid the wreckage of the present, and therefore of the first principles upon which to base a renewed order. His great-great grandfather Cacciaguida gives fathering support to Dante, who is to fulfill his prophetic role even though he is impoverished and in exile, relying on the hospitality of others. At seven hundred years' remove, we may take it for granted, but the circumstances of Dante's poetic-prophetic vocation are remarkable. He was dependent on others' generosity for his very survival, and still he held nothing back in his writing, criticizing whomever he thought was corrupt, even though they might have helped him at some point in his exile. Cacciaguida comforts Dante by assuring him that the blows of fate and the changing fortunes of Florence and of Dante are ultimately only contingencies, like musical notes in the *dolce armonia* or sweet harmony in the mind of God. Immediately after this, Cacciaguida delivers the *Comedy's* ninth and final prophecy of Dante's exile, the number of lines of which exactly total the previous eight prophecies combined. Yet all of Dante's "prophecies" are a fiction, made possible by narrating his journey in the *Comedy* as having taken place in 1300, before his exile and other events had occurred. This fiction is consistent with Dante's method throughout the *Comedy*: it creates verisimilitude — what I am referring to as his realism — making his story convincing in terms of time sequence, character, place, and so on. Since Dante knows perfectly well that most of his readers are going to understand that much of what he is saying is invented for

37 Ibid., 320.

the poem, *he* knows that *they* know that *he* knows it is a fiction. But the point, in effect, is this: when Dante says (following Beatrice's and Cacciaguida's instructions), "I learned these things in the other world and now I am writing about it," he is symbolically saying, "I have seen into the root causes of things, of the corruption and evil in this world, and into the divine order that the world tends to forget, and now I am sharing those insights so that others may benefit from them."

When Dante encounters the poet-prophet King David in the Heaven of the just rulers, his description of David as poet — for Dante, *the poet of the Spirit* — clearly also alludes to his own role as poet-prophet. David has already appeared in canto x of *Purgatorio*, figured in a bas-relief, dancing before the Ark of the Covenant (in which the Jews kept their most sacred objects), to seek forgiveness from God for his sins. There, David's dancing like a commoner is a sign of his profound humility before God, unashamed of letting go of his kingly reserve and dignity. In *Paradiso* he appears in the pupil of the eye of the Eagle, which is composed of all the just rulers united and speaking as one. Dante says, "He who shines in the middle of the pupil [of the eye] was the singer of the Holy Spirit, who moved the Ark from town to town; now he knows the merit of his song, insofar as it is the effect of his judgment [*consiglio*, counsel], by means of the reward [in Heaven] he now enjoys."[38] *Consiglio* is one of the Seven Gifts of the Holy Spirit, which Dante mentions in the *Convivio*.[39] It refers to the faculty of discernment, the ability to make choices consonant with the true nature of things, or God's will, and therefore is associated with the proper use of free will. Chapter 10, "Love's Scribe," which refers to this episode in the *Comedy*, discusses at length the centrality of inspiration in Dante. But what Dante is referring to here is David's conscious and disciplined engagement in the craft of poetry, his mastery of the art as a spiritual discipline, which will be further discussed in chapters 3 and 4. Dante certainly believed that David was taking dictation from the Holy Spirit when he composed the Psalms, but the *consiglio* in the above quote refers to the conscious choices and skills that contributed to David's salvation, since to craft sacred poetry is to participate *freely* in the inspiration of the Spirit. Conscientious artistic labor is an act of humility before God, and this scene shows that Dante viewed his

38 *Paradiso* xx.37–42.
39 *Convivio* iv.xxi.12, drawing on Isaiah 11:2.

own poetic discipline as one means of spiritual purification that would make him worthy to stand before God. This is behind his passionate outcry in the opening of *Paradiso* xxv, where he refers to the long self-sacrifice demanded by his labor at his *poema sacro*, or sacred poem, and imagines being crowned some day with the poet's laurels in the cradle of his faith, the Baptistery in Florence. As with David, and in keeping with Beatrice's words to him at the end of *Purgatorio* about his prophetic role, dedication to poetry in service of his spiritual calling was a key to Dante's salvation. Obviously, this is not a puritanical exaltation of uninspired work, but an acknowledgment that joyful artistic realization can only come to those who labor to realize it.

When Statius and Virgil, at the end of canto xxviii of *Purgatorio*, smile at the mention of Parnassus, the ancient poets' mythical source of inspiration, as a pre-Christian Eden or Earthly Paradise, we are in similar symbolic territory to Dante's encounter with David. In all such episodes there is the implication that poetry at its most essential is a return to primordial knowledge, to gnosis. As Dante says in canto xxv of *Paradiso*, the spiritual energy and hope in his writing rains down on people, and he himself received this hope from King David and St. James. So the *Comedy* is like a cloud that formed in the air when the rain from David and James condensed in the sky, and now, as Dante writes it and the poem spreads through the world, the rain is falling again. His writing finds its moving power from the spiritual energy he imbibed from his holy forebears in the art of poetry.

POETIC TECHNIQUE AND POETIC GNOSIS

The chapters in this book reflect on Dante's use of imagery and symbolism, his poetic strategies, his cultural and religious perspective and background. In them, the goal is to draw closer to Dante's poetic thought, its subtleties and transformative power. Of course, everything that can be said *about* poetry, especially great poetry, cannot do justice to what it *is*. All the Dante scholarship and commentary, including the pages in this book, fade from view when the reader directly encounters the poem with whatever he or she brings to it. A poem is an experience, not a theory. On one level, poetry is not *about* anything, it is an *invocation* of the thing that it is about. This is why poets are often more interested in appreciating how a poem is made than the ideas in it, which lose all their life in paraphrase. When Dante listens in on Virgil and Statius's conversation about the art in their episode late in *Purgatorio* (recounted and analyzed in chapter 4, "The Dream of Leah and Rachel"), we can imagine that he is taking notes on the tricks of his trade. Dante's mastery of his art is unsurpassed, and is a vast subject unto itself. He knows very many poets' tricks indeed, all designed to bring life and grace and force to his subject matter. This is what makes his otherworld so palpable; it is physically and existentially present by means of Dante's astonishing imagination and art.

Realism is not a noun that people generally associate with visionary or spiritual poetry, and it is true that Dante is not a realist the way modern novelists are realists. We have already observed that Dante is fundamentally a symbolic thinker, yet he works with symbols as though they are concrete things. This "realism" is his crucial tool for establishing that the *fiction* he is telling is *real*. One rhetorical device that he uses for this purpose is the figure of simile. The stunning similes in the *Comedy* — and there are over four hundred of them — permanently plant the poem's narrative moments in the reader's memory. So, the fifteenth-century commentator Cristoforo Landino praised Dante's uncanny ability, reminiscent of Ovid, to "make the impossible seem believable."[40]

Dante was not the first Christian author to write about the otherworld — Bede and Peter Lombard, for instance, had depicted Purgatory — but Dante's brilliant stroke is to place his imaginal world in the context of an empirical one. As chapters 8 and 9, "On the Way to Rome and Jerusalem" and "The *Divine Comedy* as Cosmos," describe, Dante gives a *geographical* placement for Heaven, Hell, and the world in between (often through observations about the positions of the stars and sun in relation to different compass points on earth). Very frequently, especially in *Inferno*, Dante mentions geographical and topographical features familiar to his audience, earthly landscapes that are similes for the landscapes of Hell or Mount Purgatory. In addition, phenomena that occur in the supernatural landscapes of the *Comedy* are given naturalistic causes, as when, at the end of canto XIV of *Inferno*, Virgil explains to Dante that the flames falling from above, in the third level of the circle of the violent, are snuffed out by vapors rising from the stream along whose margin they will be walking. Or supernatural phenomena are depicted with naturalistic detail, as when Dante and

40   Quoted in Robert Hollander's commentary to *Paradiso* XX.25–29, in *Paradiso*, translated by Robert and Jean Hollander (New York: Anchor Books, 2008).

Virgil are passing through the wall of fire that is between the terrace of the lustful on Mount Purgatory and the Earthly Paradise, and Dante's shadow (since he is still in his body) darkens the sunlit flames.

His narrative strategy, too, is consummately artful. Dante always varies the pacing of the narrative, and handles transitions between scenes and cantos, with a feel for keeping the story unpredictable and vivid. For example, in canto XXIII of *Inferno*, where he narrates the transition from the *bolgia* or "pouch" or zone of the hypocrites to that of the thieves, Virgil carries the protagonist Dante down the rubble of the broken bridge between *bolgia*s, which Dante focuses on for many lines. In this way, he conveys a sense of the labor involved, physically and morally, to pass to the next, more inhuman and ferocious levels of Hell. At the same time, this interlude gives the reader a chance to adapt to the new and startling scene where the thieves are attacked and metamorphosed by serpents. Often, Dante's realistic portrayal of a character makes him or her as alive as someone you might meet on the street, even if the personage happens to be a mythological figure like Chiron, the most humane and cultured of the centaurs, who uses the butt-end of his arrow to part his beard from his mouth before he speaks.[41] Visionary as Dante surely was, his powers of observation of the world of the senses is what gives his verse such authority, particularly for the modern reader. When he describes the change of color of the thief who is merging with the serpent who has gripped him, he evokes the alteration by calling on the reader's memory of the color of a burning piece of paper.[42] And the realism is often psychological or perceptual as well. For example, when Dante sees the Provençal poet Bertran de Born carrying his own head like a lantern in the *bolgia* of the schismatics, he expresses the weirdness and import of it by making the extraordinary claim that his conscience assures him he is telling the truth as he writes it down.[43] By referring to himself in the moment of writing, as though he is recalling something that really happened—a technique he uses many times in the *Comedy*—he renders the scene more credible and immediate.

Concrete figural *language* is also fundamental to Dante's style, another way of conveying the sense that his fantastic story actually

41 *Inferno* XII.77–78.
42 *Inferno* XXV.64–66.
43 *Inferno* XXVIII.113–15.

happened as told. One example is where he says that he has previously seen the face of one of the sinners he encounters in the first *bolgia* of the eighth circle of Hell: *Già di veder constui non son digiuno*, literally, "I am already not lacking the food of seeing this man"; in other words, "I have already been sated with the sight of this man," or more abstractly, "This is not the first time I have seen him." A good example of how Dante in translation loses his concreteness (and by this I mean no criticism of the translators per se; translating Dante's poetry, I know from experience, is virtually impossible), his figurative manner of expression, can be seen in Mark Musa's translation: "I know this face from somewhere, I am sure."[44] Another example from the same canto of *Inferno* (line 108) describes the disgusting fecal mold of the second *bolgia* as smelling so bad that *con li occhi e col naso facea zuffa*, literally, "it was brawling or battling with my eyes and nose"—a vivid way of saying, "it stank." Musa renders this as "disgusting to behold and worse to smell," and Robert and Jean Hollander as "offending eyes and nose." All the power of the expression is gone in translation, and above all the concreteness of its figure and even of the dense, bodily sound of the word *zuffa*. This is hardly the writing of a disembodied "gnostic," in the Manichean sense of that word, though Dante's insight into the meaning of "Hell" underlies the brilliant technique.

Even in theological passages, which occupy much of *Paradiso*, Dante's poetic art makes the ideas tangible, palpable, sensual, human. For example, in various passages of *Paradiso*, Dante employs tortuous, hard-to-follow syntax to communicate a sense of the inscrutable mind of God.[45] To experience this directly, of course, one must read it in Italian—no translation could capture it. But if you know even a few words of Italian, and especially its pronunciation, and first read a clear translation, and then read commentary so that the ideas and similes are all in mind beforehand, and then *reread* the canto glancing at the Italian, you can experience for yourself how the poem tangibly evokes its subject.

There are many instances of the elaborate and amazing techniques of Dante's art—as the chapters in this book will attest—but I will conclude this introduction with just one more. In the opening of canto XXIX of *Paradiso*, Dante expresses the length of Beatrice's gaze at the

44 *Inferno* XVIII.42.
45 See, e.g., *Paradiso* XI.31–36.

still point of light, or God, at the center of the circling angelic hierarchies by comparing it to how long the perfect balance between the
sun and the moon in Aries and Libra, respectively, maintains that
equilibrium on opposite horizons. At this threshold of the Primum
Mobile, the highest celestial sphere before the Empyrean and therefore a
figure for the first ontological plane of manifestation, Dante evokes, as
Christian Moevs puts it, "the fulcrum balancing the manifest universe
against the ground of its being, multiplicity against unity."[46] But Dante
does not stop with the simile; he makes the language itself *embody*
the equilibrium it expresses:

> *Quando ambedue li figli di Latona,*
> *coperti del Montone e de la Libra,*
> *fanno de l'orizzonte insieme zona,*
>
> > *quant'è dal punto che 'l cenìt i'nlibra*
> *infin che l'uno e l'altro da quel cinto,*
> *cambiando l'emisperio, si dilibra,*
>
> > *tanto, col volto di riso dipinto,*
> *si tacque Bëatrice, riguardando*
> *fiso nel punto che m'avëa vinto.*
>
> > *Poi cominciò: "Io dico, e non dimando,*
> *quel che tu vuoli udir, perch'io l'ho visto*
> *là 've s'appunta ogne ubi e ogne quando."*[47]

(When both the children of Latona, covered by the Ram
and by the Scales [Libra], make the horizon their belt at one
same moment, as long as from the instant when the zenith
holds them balanced till one and the other, changing hemi-
spheres, throw off the balance of that belt, for so long, her
face showing a smile, was Beatrice silent, looking steadily at
the point which had overcome me. Then she began, "I will
say what you wish to hear without asking what it is, for I
have seen it [what you wish to know] there [in the *punto*
of God's light] where every *ubi* [where] and every *quando*
[when] comes to a point.")

46   Moevs, *Metaphysics*, 8ff., 151ff.
47   *Paradiso* XXIX.1–12.

Moevs shows how this passage enacts the moment of equilibrium in the image of the sun and moon on opposite horizons. As we see above, the word *quando* (when) begins and ends the passage; the center of the lines is marked by the words *emisperio* and *dilibra*, "hemisphere" and "throw off the balance"; the word *punto*, discussed earlier in this introduction, is balanced around this midpoint in lines 4 and 9, occupying the same metrical position in both lines; and the tercets bracketing the midpoint are balanced by *quanto* and *tanto* ("as long as," "for so long"), both in initial positions. In other words, the very structure of the passage enacts "an instant of cosmic equilibrium" (152).[48]

Moevs's comment on this mind-bogglingly profound passage elaborates: "In gazing 'where all *where* and *when* come to a point,' Beatrice is seeing nothing, that is, no thing, but the source of all things. More precisely, she is seeing the nexus between God and creation, 'where, when, and how' space and time arise from, or within, Intellect-Being" (153). Dante's realism, in other words, appears even in passages that are remote from ordinary experience. Language, syntax, and sonics *embody* or *enact* the intuitive insight—a feature that could be used toward a definition of poetry itself.

48 Citing Robert M. Durling and Ronald L. Martinez, commentary to these lines in *Paradiso*, in their translation of the *Divine Comedy* (New York: Oxford University Press, 1996).

1

Love and the Soul

T HE *DIVINE COMEDY* begins, as everyone knows, with Dante
remembering a time when he had been lost in a dark wood,
in a state of profound agitation and confusion. Trying to find
a way out, he started to climb a nearby hill above which the sun — a
traditional symbol for God, much loved by Dante — was rising. But
since he was not ready to go to the summit, because his soul was still
in a state of having lost *il ben de l'intelletto*, the good of the intellect,[1] three ferocious beasts blocked his way. Just at that moment he
encountered a specter, Virgil, who would be his guide to the depths of
the universe and up Mount Purgatory to the Earthly Paradise, where
Dante would finally be reunited with his beloved, Beatrice, who had
died when they were young. In all these places, he encounters, as he
puts it at the climax of *Paradiso, tutte le vite spirituali*, all states of the
human spirit, *ad una ad una*, one at a time.[2]

This pattern — attempting to integrate the multiplicity of experience
into a unified vision — is a constant in Dante's work. It seems that there
is no area of experience that Dante ignores or fails to discuss in the
course of his writings, in order to discover, often after long struggle,
how multiplicity relates to unity, the ten thousand things to the One.
Common to all these experiences and levels of being — permeating them,
animating them, and connecting them — are love and desire, which in
medieval thought were also known as *voluntas*, or will. For Dante, the
soul is moved by what it loves the way a body is moved by its weight;
the will gravitates to what it loves. This idea is expressed memorably
by Augustine, who wrote: "The body by its own weight strives towards
its own place. Weight is not downward only, but to its own place. Fire
tends upward, a stone downward. By their own weights are they urged,
they seek their own places.... My weight is my love; by that am I borne,
wherever I am borne. By Thy gift we are inflamed, and are borne upward."[3]

---

1 *Inferno* III.18.
2 *Paradiso* XXXIII.24.
3 *Confessions* XIII.9, as quoted in Edmund G. Gardner, *Dante and the Mystics* (1913;
repr., Chestnut Hill, MA: Adamant Media Corporation, 2006), 58–59.

Dante seems to echo this passage of the *Confessions* in the last poem in the *Vita nova*, where he imagines his love for Beatrice after her death, rising from his heart in the form of a sigh. A common trope in the poetry of that time was that the heart of the lover always resides wherever the beloved is. Beatrice had gone to the other world, so naturally Dante's heart — or the sigh from his heart — had to go there too, beyond the widest sphere of heaven, the Primum Mobile or First Mover, all the way to the Empyrean. The same notion of the soul's ascent by the pull of divine love is the basis of Dante's rising with Beatrice in *Paradiso:* the soul whose will is purified, explains Beatrice, *naturally* ascends, in the same way that fire rises. In the great germinal experience of Dante's youth, his love for Beatrice, he had a vision of love as an incitement toward eternity, a transitory glimpse of "the love that moves the sun and the other stars."

But I have started at the end of Dante's journey. The *Vita nova* mostly has to do with his beginnings as a poet and visionary. He composed this book when he was in his late twenties, selecting a number of poems that he had written in the previous ten years or so and adding a prose narrative and commentary that connect them into a story the poems do not tell on their own.

Dante tells us that he fell in love when he was nine years old with a girl who was several months younger than he and who is named Beatrice. His falling in love with her is so powerful that it leaves an indelible mark on his soul, a perception that is reinforced when she greets him in passing nine years later. Because of her, love — that same "Lord Love" or Amor all the love poets of the time wrote about — comes to dwell in his heart. Following courtly love conventions, according to which the cultivation of pure love required secrecy or privacy, he pretends to others that his love, which his behavior cannot hide, is actually directed toward a woman other than Beatrice. When this woman moves out of the city, leaving Dante without his cover, he invents another "screen-woman," or *donna schermo*. Beatrice catches wind of malicious gossip regarding her admirer's alleged unsavory comportment toward this second screen-woman, and consequently shuns him. She has no awareness of the effect this has on him. Eventually he finds peace for his unrequited love by resolving to praise her in his poetry independently of her responses to him.

A period follows during which Dante vacillates between ruminations on his lady's beauty, spiritual radiance, and self-possession, and dreadful forebodings of death: the death of Beatrice's father, of her, and ultimately of him. When she actually does die, at age twenty-four, he tells us that it was as if the entire city was widowed by her passing, and that he finally came to realize that there was always a mysterious but inexorable connection between Beatrice and the number 9, which shows that she is a miracle since 3 is the root of 9, and the holy Trinity is a 3 and the root of all miracles. As we will see periodically throughout this book, and especially in the penultimate chapter, number is an important symbolic language for Dante, fitting for a poet, since poetry like music is an art of number.

After her death, still in mourning for her, Dante is briefly consoled by an anonymous beautiful woman who shows compassion for his grief. In the *Vita nova* this woman's metaphorical significance is left to the reader's imagination; in the *Convivio*, written about a decade later, Dante will claim she was an allegorical figure for Lady Philosophy (the subject of chapter 6). He becomes infatuated with her, and feels conflicted between this new movement of love and the loving memory of Beatrice—which, unlike the love for the new woman, is not reinforced by the actual physical presence of the beloved. Finally, Dante renounces the new love and resolves to dedicate himself to the beatified Beatrice, practicing his art and studying so that he can write about her as no woman has ever been written about. Meanwhile, his longing, which takes the form of a sigh, rises into the presence of her spirit in heaven.

Dante and his Italian precursors and contemporaries were inheritors of a kind of love poetry that had first taken hold of Europe's imagination in Provence nearly two centuries earlier—so-called courtly love poetry, the ancestor of what we refer to as romantic love. Courtly love emphasized the ennobling potential of human love, the elevation of the beloved to a place superior to the lover—a cult of the beloved, in effect. It conceived of ideal love as an ever-increasing desire that was never satisfied or consummated. Pure love was extramarital—since marriage then was mainly an economic arrangement between families—and it was usually kept secret from others. Andreas Capellanus in his very influential treatise on love (ca. 1184–86) wrote that pure love consisted chiefly "in the contemplation of the mind and the affection of the heart," but that sexual consummation was not permitted to this form of love, because, as Andreas writes, "this love goes on increasing without end . . . and the more of it one has the more one wants."[4] In contrast, so-called mixed love was focused on the delights of the flesh; it was sexual in its aim. Andreas and the courtly lovers did not condemn this earthier form of love, but considered fine or pure love vastly superior to it.

Such love was the force that inspired the lover to increase in worth and virtue — specifically the virtues of courtesy, chivalry, generosity, and humility. It involved a self-effacing surrender to love's power, without demanding anything in return. Among the Italian poets, *servo*, servant, was often used as a synonym for *amante*, lover. As we saw in the introduction, one of Dante's favorite words in the *Vita nova* — *donna*, woman — comes from *domina*, lady, the female version of *lord*. The lover's lady was his female lord, just as Lord Love was his master whom he served as a vassal served his feudal lord.

These notions of love in Provence and Italy had appeared earlier in Islamic poetry and philosophy — for example in Avicenna's (Ibn Sīnā's) treatise on love, which some have suggested was a source for the Provençal code of love.[5] Avicenna's views on love are very similar to Dante's in the *Vita nova* and the *Comedy*. He encourages the love of external beauty, provided it does not eclipse intelligence or reason, and assigns to human love a positive role in the ascent of the soul to divine love. As long as love of beauty doesn't lead to actions that belong to the animal soul alone, says Avicenna, it can draw the lover nearer to the ultimate object of all love, which is God. This is the same distinction that Dante will make in the Paolo and Francesca episode of *Inferno*, where he says that the lustful are those who *la ragion sommettono al talento*, subordinate reason to desire, the intellect to the appetites.[6] And Dante also concurs with Avicenna that great lovers *can* dwell in Paradise. In canto IX of *Paradiso*, for example, he encounters those lovers, including the prostitute Rahab from the Book of Joshua, whose loving nature had for its ultimate object of contemplation the ardent love of the Holy Spirit.

To return to the culture of courtly love in Dante's youth: the notion of eros and of love of physical beauty as potentially ennobling, and

---

4 Andreas Capellanus, *The Art of Courtly Love,* introduction, translation, and notes by John Jay Parry (New York: Columbia University Press, 1990), 122.

5 "A Treatise on Love by Ibn Sina," translated by E. L. Fackenheim, *Medieval Studies* 7 (1945): 208–28.

6 *Inferno* v.39.

especially the extramarital nature of courtly love, were of course at odds with official Christian doctrine. In addition, courtly love's inwardness and sentimentality could all too easily slip into narcissistic self-absorption or self-indulgence. For this reason, such leading figures as Andreas Capellanus himself eventually renounced this form of love. As Andreas wrote in his retraction of the guide to love he had written in his youth, no one devoted to serving Lord Love could serve God as well. Andreas in his later years noted that love can be a kind of slavery, causing obsession and jealousy and leading the lover to neglect his or her dealings with the world and friends.

This combination of fascination for and reservation about courtly love permeates the *Vita nova*, and for that matter much of Dante's lyric poetry that is not included in that book. But Dante, unlike Andreas, did not ever renounce human love as a way to resolve the ambivalence. Like Avicenna, he remained convinced that one divine reality underlies all love, whether erotic or spiritual.

Many love poets of that time sought ways to reconcile Christian teachings with their own experience of erotic love's tremendous transformative power. The extreme ascetic denunciation of eros — typified for instance by an early Christian father's statement, "When we see a beautiful woman, our intellect is at once wounded by sensual desire"[7] — was rejected by these poets and courtiers. The often misogynist association of women with Eve and original sin was shed in favor of an image of woman as an intimation of celestial bliss. As the Sicilian poet Jacopo da Lentini, the reputed inventor of the sonnet, expressed it a few decades before Dante:

> I have resolved in my heart to serve God so that I might go to paradise, to the holy place where, I have heard, there is perpetual pleasure, play, and laughter. Without my lady, the one who has a blonde head and a bright face, I do not wish to go there, since deprived of her I could not feel pleasure, being separated from my lady. I do not say this intending to commit a sin, but rather because I would want to see her beautiful ways and her beautiful face and her sweet glance, for it would console me forever to see my lady in glory.[8]

---

7 *Philokalia: The Complete Text*, translated and edited by G. E. H. Palmer, Philip Sherrard, and Kallistos Ware, vol. 1 (London: Faber & Faber, 1979), 213.

8 This is the sonnet *Io m'aggio posto in core a Dio servire*, *Rime* XXVII.

Even more boldly, a poet who was an important influence on Dante's sacralization of courtly love themes, Guido Guinizzelli, imagines himself standing before God, who accuses him of making claims for mortal, earthly love that should be made only for divine love:

> Lady, God will say to me, "How did you presume?" when my soul is in front of Him. "You passed through the heavens and came to Me, and you likened Me to vain love: for to Me belong the praises and to the queen of the worthy kingdom, through whom all wickedness dies." I will say to God: "She resembled an angel that was of Your kingdom; it was no fault of mine if I placed love in her."

Inspired by Guinizzelli's example, Dante would come to develop a central theme of the *Comedy*, in which a woman-beloved, Beatrice, leads the pilgrim-lover *to* God rather than *away* from God.

The passage I just quoted comes from Guinizzelli's most famous poem, *Al cor gentil rempaira sempre amore* ("Love always comes to dwell in the noble heart"). This highly influential canzone initiated metaphysical love poetry among Dante and his contemporaries. Using the language of Aristotelian philosophy, it opens by stating that love and the noble heart are in a relation of act and potency. The predisposed heart receives love the way matter receives its informing spirit. As Guinizzelli puts it, just as a gemstone's particular properties or virtues are activated by the star associated with it, the radiant woman ignites the love that is latent in a heart noble by nature. These are the kinds of analogies and associations Dante and the other Florentine poets explored, combining scholastic science and philosophy with the images and conventions of courtly love. They were interested in seeking a union of intellect and love, so much of their poetry approaches love of beauty as a form of cognition or a source of interior knowledge.

The poems in the first part of the *Vita nova* are ones that Dante wrote in his late teens or early twenties, when he was still an apprentice to the poets before him. These poems are derivative and the lover-protagonist of the story, Dante, is caught in the self-centered preoccupations of the unrequited courtly lover—the sort of erotic love that Andreas had warned about in his retraction. The courtly lover was often depicted as full of anxiety that his services might not suffice to gain or keep his lady's love. Accordingly, the young Dante broods alone in his room, humiliates himself at a public gathering where his lady unexpectedly is present, and crumbles when Beatrice refuses to acknowledge him as she passes by. The focus is mostly on the lover's subjective state.

This early part of the book dramatizes the failure of courtly love culture, a theme that preoccupies Dante for many years, most famously in the Paolo and Francesca episode of *Inferno*, where Francesca quotes Andreas Capellanus's much-imitated idea that the lover has no choice but to obey the dictates of eros. The *Vita nova* episode culminates in a sequence of four poems that are derived from the kind of love poetry that Dante's close friend, the older poet Guido Cavalcanti, wrote. Dante admired Guido's brilliant mind and his great poetic talent and skill, memorialized in canto x of *Inferno*, where Guido's father, Cavalcante dei Cavalcanti, alludes to his son's *altezza d'ingegno*, lofty genius.[9] Dante dedicates the *Vita nova* to Guido although Dante and he had fundamental philosophical and religious disagreements, which themselves form an undercurrent running through the *Vita nova*. For Cavalcanti, erotic love is essentially tragic because it *cannot* be integrated with the rational soul. There is no way to reconcile it, says Guido, with the highest human aspirations, as Dante — and Avicenna — emphatically insist *is* possible. As Cavalcanti states in his great canzone *Donna me prega* (A woman asks me), Guido believed that love is a faculty that is *non razionale, — ma che sente*, not rational, but that feels — in other words, that it is located in the so-called sensitive soul, the seat of the passions, not in the rational soul, and so can never lead to a Platonizing ascent to absolute beauty. Rather than bringing harmony and bliss, Cavalcanti said love brings conflict and so is born under the influence of Mars. Cavalcanti's viewpoint reminds us that the root of the word *passion* is "to suffer." His poetry, often echoed by Dante in the *Vita nova*, emphasizes such words as *tormento, distrutto, disfatto, angoscia, morte, pauroso*, torment, destroyed, undone, anguish, death, fearful. The internal dramatization of the lover's state is a battle of dismayed spirits — an image that comes up many times in the *Vita nova*.

Dante himself wrote a number of poems in this vein during his youth, including the four poems leading up to the first big breakthrough in

---

9 *Inferno* x.59. The reference there is to Dante's lofty genius, but by extension and implication to Guido's as well.

the *Vita nova*, where Dante resolves to write poetry that praises his lady whether she acknowledges him or not—the great canzone *Donne ch'avete intelletto d'amore* ("Women who understand the truth of love"), which we will look at in more detail below. Dante places this poem immediately after the group of Cavalcanti-influenced sonnets precisely to emphasize his decision to reject Cavalcanti's fatalistic view of love. For Dante the very essence of being human is at stake in this issue: that there *is* a love which is consonant with intellect, with spiritual knowledge. This is one of the meanings that Beatrice embodies for him, as much of the *Vita nova* attests. But first Dante pays tribute to his friend's influence and to his own ambivalence, in sections of the *Vita nova* that focus on the lover's conflicts about love, his turbulence resulting from the power his lady has over him.

For example, one sonnet in this section is about the humiliation of the lover as he is mocked by his lady in the midst of his besotted state—a conventional theme going back to the troubadours. The fact that the theme is conventional does not mean it has no relation to real experience. Helplessness and humiliation in the face of love are themes in today's pop songs as well. Dante, in keeping with the style of the time, expresses these feelings in an exaggerated way. Hyperbole itself is a carryover from the courtly love tradition, in which even valiant knights and robust magistrates were passive victims in their own poems.

Typical in this sonnet are the personifications of mercy and of Love himself. The imagery of the frightened spirits that personify the lover's emotions draws on scholastic philosophers such as Albert the Great, who themselves had learned from Galen and Avicenna. Cavalcanti first used this imagery, and Dante and others followed suit, depicting the lover's anxieties as devastated or dismayed spirits. The *spiriti* are not metaphysical spirits; they mediate between body and mind. They are neither entirely spiritual nor wholly material, but a combination of both. These little migrating spirits or *spiritelli* are the vehicles for love, the means by which the spirit of love reaches and dwells in the lover's heart. The experience of falling in love was imagined as the movement of spirits from one person's soul to another's. Light was the medium of love. The glances issuing from the eyes of the woman consisted of a fiery beam of spirits which pierced the eye of the lover and made its way to his heart, often with devastating effects, as in the sonnet that I have been alluding to:

With other women you mock my distress,
and never guess, my lady, what gives rise
to my appearing alien in your eyes
when I am gazing at your loveliness.
If you knew, surely Mercy would be less
entrenched in what she typically denies,
since Love, when I am near you, fortifies,
taking on such nerve and brazenness,

he blasts my frightened spirits all about,
slaughtering some, while others he expels,
so he alone is left to look at you.
Meanwhile I am changed to something new—
another man—though I still hear the yells
of anguish from those banished by the rout.[10]

Whatever some interpreters have done to try to make poems such as this fit their idea of Dante, the great author of the *Comedy*, turning them into allegories expressing one esoteric idea or another, I do not believe it is justifiable to do so. The poems of the *Vita nova* are the finely crafted, searching poems of a restless, sophisticated young man who is exploring his powerful attraction to women, using the conventions of the love poetry and the religious and philosophical thought of his time. The prose that was added to them later, as well as some of the more metaphysical poems in the collection, are what suggest an *itinerarium mentis in Deum*, or mind's journey to God. Dante uses the prose to shape the love poems, mystical or not, into a story in which an analogy is implied: God is to the mystic as the god of love is to the poet-lover. His metaphysical and theological poetics find their first expression in the *Vita nova*, where Dante re-envisions all the poetry in the book as stages of preparation for sacred love.

Many passages in the *Vita nova* consecrate courtly love by combining its imagery and language with those of Christian scripture, theology, and liturgy. For example, at the beginning of the tale, Dante writes of Beatrice's effect upon him when she greets him exactly nine years after the first time he saw her: "And passing along a street, she turned her eyes in the direction of where I stood gripped by fear, and thanks to

---

10   *Con l'altre donne mia vista gabbate*, *Vita nova* 7.11–12 (XIV.11–12).

her ineffable benevolence and grace, which now is rewarded in eternal life, she greeted me with such power that then and there I seemed to see to the farthest reaches of bliss."[11] The lady's greeting is a stock theme from courtly love poetry. Since the true lover sought a state of perpetual, unconsummated desire, a sign of acknowledgment was required from his lady — this was the function of her salutation or greeting, about which I will have more to say in chapter 3.

As usual, Dante takes such conventional themes and pushes them further than anyone had done before him. The phrase "ineffable benevolence and grace" in the above passage translates *ineffabile cortesia,* literally "ineffable courtesy." I translate *cortesia* as "benevolence and grace" because these are the two dominant characteristics of courtesy, as the courtly love poets conceived it. This was probably the first time in a European vernacular language that the word *ineffable* was used. Its Latin form, *ineffabilis,* was unknown in classical Latin but commonly used in Christian Latin in reference to the effects of the divine presence. Dante here takes the Italian word *ineffabile* and applies to a woman the attribute formerly reserved for divinity. Dante's readers in thirteenth-century Florence would have picked up on the juxtaposition, in which a term from Italian love poetry, *cortesia,* is combined with another term that until then had belonged exclusively to religious writing.

What would Augustine or Thomas Aquinas have made of such "theologizing" of courtly love? Counter-Reformation authorities dealt with it by censoring parts of the *Vita nova,* excising language that treated profane love in the same breath as spiritual love. In the first printed edition of the *Vita nova,* in 1576, instead of saying that Beatrice was "no woman, but one of the angels of Heaven," she is "like an angel of Heaven"; rather than being *gloriosa,* glorious, she is *graziosa,* graceful; *beatitudine,* beatitude, is changed by censors to *felicità,* happiness; *salute,* salvation, to *quiete,* peace. Indeed, Dante's and his poetic peers' claims about eros and the beauty of a flesh-and-blood beloved as a path to spiritual knowledge has had little place in orthodox Christian doctrine up to the present day, especially in its more dogmatic forms. As Maurice Valency has put it: "Nothing could be further from orthodox ecclesiastical doctrine than the idea that a woman, the traditional source of all temptation, should be an angel of God.... But none of

---

11   *Vita nova* 1.12 (III.1).

the doctors of the church had any idea of involving the female form in the ladder which led to heaven.... The line which divided love, even the truest, from charity had always been jealously guarded."[12] A similar conflict has existed in Islamic culture, where there is a tradition that beauty is a proof or reflection of God's splendor, a revelation of divine essence. This idea was central to such visionaries as al-Ghazzālī, Ibn 'Arabī, and others. Not all Muslim theologians approved of such practices, however, and some considered them heretical since they emphasized seeking God through love dedicated to a beautiful being.

The integration of the language and imagery of courtly love with that of sacred love will be essential in *Purgatorio* and *Paradiso*, where, for example, the archangel Gabriel is described with a term from courtly love: he is *leggiadro*, elegant or graceful, like a lover.[13] And God looks on the human soul the way a lover gazes longingly at the beloved, an effect that Dante achieves by using a verb from courtly love poetry, *vagheggiare*, to gaze with intense desire.[14] The great scene of Matelda in the Earthly Paradise, in *Purgatorio* XXVIII—where Matelda, as the tutelary spirit of Eden, is depicted as a woman in love—draws its language from a conventional genre of courtly love poem, the *pastorella*, in particular a *pastorella* by Guido Cavalcanti. This kind of poem told of an erotically charged encounter between the poet and a shepherd girl. Matelda is singing as she gathers flowers, the way a shepherd girl might behave in one of these poems. Dante comes upon Matelda unexpectedly, just as the poet-protagonist does in *pastorella* poems. Through her graceful behavior and blissful expression, he perceives that she is a woman in love, and in fact he finds out that she truly is in love, though not with him, as he at first believes. Rather, she is in love with God, where all loves ultimately are bound. We will return to this episode in chapter 5, which focuses on the Earthly Paradise. For now, I will note that Dante's portrayal of Matelda in this very beautiful canto in *Purgatorio* uses the language and imagery of courtly love poetry that he first explores in the *Vita nova* for its profound metaphorical implications.

As every close reader of the *Comedy* knows, Dante's writing is dense with allusions to biblical and classical texts. In the *Vita nova* the biblical

---

12   Maurice Valency, *In Praise of Love* (New York: Macmillan, 1961), 247.
13   *Paradiso* XXXII.109.
14   *Purgatorio* XVI.85.

41

echoes predominate. For example, near the beginning of the book, where he describes his first response to seeing Beatrice when they were children, he uses the phrase *In quello punto*, "At that time," echoing a frequent opening phrase in the Vulgate Gospels, *In illo tempore*. Dante repeats the phrase three times, possibly as one of the many numerological allusions to the Holy Trinity that he works into the text of the *Vita nova*. In addition, the first occurrence of *In quello punto* is followed by the words *dico veracemente*, "I say truly," or truly, I say—an echo of Jesus's frequent phrase in the Gospel of John, "Verily, I say," which is used to introduce some important and solemn statement.

There are many other biblical allusions in the *Vita nova*, by means of which Dante consecrates the themes of courtly love. For instance, Lord Love says to Dante, *Ego dominus tuus*, "I am your lord," in a dream-vision that Dante has after his second important encounter with Beatrice.[15] *Ego dominus tuus* echoes words that God speaks to Moses on Mount Sinai, in the Latin Bible. Dante's use of the phrase in the *Vita nova* reflects the familiar theme of Love as the lord whom the lover serves as vassal, while the phrase's source in holy scripture converts the courtly theme into a religious one.

The analogies that Dante notes between Beatrice and Christ will be discussed in some detail in the next chapter. For now I will give one more example from the *Vita nova* of how Dante consecrates courtly love by alluding to sacred scripture and symbol. Near the end of the *Vita nova* Dante relates how at some unspecified time after Beatrice's death he saw pilgrims passing through Florence on the way to Rome, where they would view the cloth of Veronica, on which there was an image of Christ's visage. This cloth was a common goal of pilgrimages to Rome in those times, especially during Holy Week. In both the prose and the poem of this section, Dante notes that the pilgrims seem to be passing by like people who have not heard of the major loss—the death of Beatrice—that the city has suffered. You will notice in this poem that Dante refers to Beatrice in a way that brings out her public, civic function: she is the *beatrice*, or "bringer of blessings," to all, not just the poet-lover. The phrase "the suffering city," which translates *la città dolente*, is also used in canto III of *Inferno*, where the sign over the gate to Hell says, *Per me si va per la città dolente*, "Through me you enter the suffering city." The people in the sonnet I am about to

15   *Vita nova* 1.15 (III.4).

42

read do not "understand a thing about the measure of [the city's] loss," because they do not know about Beatrice's death and what that means for the life of the city. I was struck when I translated this poem how the pilgrims' spiritual obliviousness applies to the movement of people through our own, contemporary cities.

> You pilgrims walking by oblivious,
> your minds, it seems, on something not at hand,
> can you have come from such a distant land —
> the way you look suggests as much to us —
> that you're not weeping, even as you pass
> right through the suffering city, like that band
> of people who, it seems, don't understand
> a thing about the measure of its loss?
>
> If you'll just stop, because you want to hear
> about it all — so says my sighing heart —
> your eyes will fill with tears before you leave.
> For she who blessed the city is nowhere
> in sight: what words about her we impart
> have force enough to make a stranger grieve.[16]

In this episode of the *Vita nova*, Dante echoes the episode on the road to Emmaus, narrated in the Gospel of Luke, in which two wayfarers encounter the resurrected Christ without realizing his identity. He asks them why they are sad, and they respond: "Are you the only visitor to Jerusalem who does not know the things that have happened there in these days?" meaning the death of Christ.[17] This is one of several passages in the *Vita nova* in which Dante implies a parallel between Florence on the one hand and Jerusalem in mourning on the

---

16 *Deh peregrini che pensosi andate*, Vita nova 29.9–10 (XL.9–10).

17 Luke 24:18. The image of the whole city mourning Beatrice's death also harkens back to the narrative poem *Cligès* (ca. 1176), by Chrétien de Troyes (who, no doubt, is also alluding to the Emmaus story), in which the death of Fenice brings about the mourning of the city of Constantinople. Dante takes from *Cligès* not only the motif of the city's mourning the death of the most beautiful creature of the place, but also that of the strangers who are passing through the city oblivious to what has happened there. The citizens tell them in turn that the whole world would be in mourning if it knew of the loss their city had suffered.

other, as depicted in the prophet Jeremiah's Lamentations, where the destroyed Jerusalem is compared to a grieving widow.

The theme of Beatrice's death and of death in general is central to Dante's transformation of courtly love in the *Vita nova*. The first four poems in the book immediately create the atmosphere of elegy. Twenty-one of the thirty-one poems in the *Vita nova* include tears or sadness. Three deaths, including that of Beatrice's father, are lamented. Death is literally at the center of the story. The poems of the book are arranged symmetrically, the watershed poem being the canzone that anticipates Beatrice's death. In the lines at the exact center of that poem, women whom Dante sees in a vision remind him that he too will die.

> While I was thinking about my fragile life, seeing how fleeting it is, Love cried in my heart, where he dwells; at which my soul was so dismayed, that, sighing, I thought: "Surely it is inevitable that my lady will die one day." I felt so dismayed that I closed my eyes, heavy with despair, and my spirits were so driven out by Love's grief that each wandered about aimlessly; and then, seized by frenzied images, unconscious and halluci-natory, I saw women appearing to me tormented and outraged, who repeatedly said to me: "You will die, you too will die."[18]

The vision of the death of Beatrice brings total awareness of mortality, and from that the potential for rebirth. It is possible that Dante was inspired to bring the theme of death into the setting of courtly love via Augustine's *Confessions*, in which, after the death of a dear friend, Augustine learns to recognize the error of loving "a man as if he would never die who nevertheless had to die." In the *Vita nova*, Dante is forced to learn that he must direct his desire toward what is constant in human love, its divine origin and aspiration.

As mentioned earlier, however, Dante's faith does not stay resolute for long. He is attracted to another woman — the so-called Donna Gen-tile or gracious woman — and he loses sight of the vision Beatrice has inspired in him. The fact that, after Beatrice's death, Dante vacillates in his dedication to what she embodies for him will be occasion for her to reproach him when they meet in the Earthly Paradise late in *Purgatorio*.

18 *Donna pietosa e di novella etate* ("A woman compassionate and young"), *Vita nova* 14.21–22 (XXIII.21–22).

Beatrice says to Dante there: "If the supreme pleasure failed you after my death, what mortal thing should then have drawn you into desiring it?"[19]

The inconstancy of love is a problem that Dante discusses with his friend the poet Cino da Pistoia in a letter and a sonnet written ten years or so after the *Vita nova* — where he describes how "love for one object may languish and finally die away, and that... love for a second object may take shape in the soul," and adds that reason and virtue are about as effective against the whims of eros as is a voice in a storm.[20] In the *Vita nova* and elsewhere, Dante shares with us his struggle to come to terms with his own vacillations and ambivalence.

Two forms of Beatrice's absence in the *Vita nova* put Dante to the test and bring about a new awareness in him of what is enduring in love: her death, and, somewhat earlier in the book, her denial to him of her greeting or salutation. Beatrice's denial of her salutation provokes Dante to a disinterested love of her, whereby he praises her regardless of how she responds or does not respond. When some women ask him what might be the point of his love for Beatrice, since her effect on him is so intense he cannot bear to be in her presence, he answers, "The point of my love at one time was the greeting of my lady — to whom, I take it, you are referring — since that greeting was home to the blessedness that all my desires were seeking. But because she chooses to deny it to me, my Lord Love, in his mercy, has transferred my bliss to that which cannot fail me." When one asks him what that might be, he replies: "In words that praise my lady."[21] He has realized that, rather than trying to possess her love or to understand her, he should praise the mere fact that she simply is, that she exists at all. His ideal theme now will be disinterested love; he will try not to focus on his self-centered lover's emotions but rather on the beloved herself.

The immediate result of Dante's resolution is the great canzone of praise, *Donne ch'avete intelletto d'amore.* By writing this poem, Dante in effect overcame his lady's denial by making the poem itself the salutation and blessing he had been denied. This canzone was one of Dante's own favorites among his lyric poems. It had the role of breaking with the past and of ushering in the new metaphysical subject matter and the new limpid style known as the *dolce stil novo,* the sweet new style.

19 *Purgatorio* XXXI.52–54.
20 *Epistle* III.4.
21 *Vita nova* 10.6–8 (XVIII.4–6).

In *Purgatorio* XXIV, Dante is identified by Bonagiunta da Lucca, one of the older Tuscan poets whom Dante was conscious of superseding, precisely as the one who wrote the canzone *Donne ch'avete*. Dante responds to Bonagiunta with the justly famous lines, *I' mi son un che, quando / Amor mi spira, noto, e a quel modo / ch'e' ditta dentro vo significando* ("I am one who, when Love inspires me, takes note, and the way that he dictates [to me] within, I write it").[22] The responsiveness to Love's dictation that Dante mentions here involves transcending individuality in order to communicate an objective intelligible reality. This is the meaning of the opening line of the canzone: "Women who understand the *truth* of love," those women who know the very love which Cavalcanti said was impossible, love that is open to the intellect and therefore *can* be transparent to divine love.

The phrase *intelletto d'amore*, understanding of love, in the poem's first line, compresses the notions of intellection and love—or, in terms of medieval thought, knowledge and will. The phrase translates *intellectus amoris*, used by medieval theologians to encapsulate the union of knowledge and love, a concept that is central to Dante's thought.

The praise-energy of Dante's canzone reflects a metaphysical insight into the beauty of Beatrice, who is spoken of as a *cosa nova*, a new and wonderful creature who emanates light. Thomas Aquinas said that lucidity or *claritas* is the intelligible radiance of form that pervades a being, an idea that Dante echoes in the second stanza of this poem when an angel tells God that Beatrice is "a miracle whose quality / arises from a soul that shines on high." In the opening lines of the canzone the words *intelletto* (intellect, or understanding), *vo'* (short for *voglio*, I want, or will), and *mente* (mind, or memory) echo the three aspects, according to Augustine, which represent *vestigia* (vestiges or traces) of the Trinity in the human soul. The poem is full of such theological and metaphysical allusions, even if they are expressed overall with less precision and rigor than Dante will later achieve.

Donne ch'avete intelletto d'amore has five stages or sections: the first stanza acts as a preface and the fifth as an epilogue or envoy. In between are a stanza that imagines a tribunal in heaven; a stanza that enumerates the four miracles associated with Beatrice's powerful influence; and a stanza that describes her physical loveliness and power. Note that this progression of themes has a descending movement—starting

---

22 *Purgatorio* XXIV.52–54.

in heaven and arriving on earth. In fact, it has been noted that the poem is structured to suggest Neoplatonic emanation, the descent of God's creative power into multiplicity, which Dante will express fully in *Paradiso*. Here, the presentation is more schematic and abstract, as demonstrated in this scholarly analysis of the poem's structure:

> Parts are subdivided at levels that are lower and lower on the chain of being and of value (heaven, soul, body, whole, parts), since in both Platonic and Aristotelean terms the generic is by definition at a higher metaphysical level than the particular.... The subdivided parts themselves naturally become smaller and smaller: part II is three stanzas long; part II.B, two stanzas long; part II.B.2 one stanza long; part II.B.2.b, six lines; part II.B.2.b.ii, two lines.[23]

Indeed, like the *Comedy*, although of course on a much smaller scale, *Donne ch'avete* is a marvel for the way it combines dense intellectual content with passionate poetic language (of which, naturally, my translation can catch only glimmers):

> Women who understand the truth of love,
> I want to talk with you a while about
> my lady—not because I could run out
> of words and ways to praise her, but to set
> my mind at ease. Her worth is so above
> the rest, I feel such lightness in my heart,
> that if speech didn't stammer I'd impart
> new love to those who are not lovers yet.
> And I won't speak so far above my head
> that I go giddy and get lost in haze:
> instead I'll talk about her gracious ways—
> nimbly, approaching her with lightest tread—
> to you, the amorous and wise of us,
> since no one else can grasp what we discuss.

23   Robert M. Durling and Ronald L. Martinez, *Time and the Crystal: Studies in Dante's Rime Petrose* (Berkeley: University of California Press, 1990), 58. Further details can be found in this source, as well as in my notes on this poem in my edition of the *Vita nova*.

An angel clamors in the Intellect
of God: "My Lord, on earth, for all to see,
there is a miracle whose quality
arises from a soul that shines on high."
Heaven, whose absolutely sole defect
is lacking her, requests her from its Lord,
and all the blessèd saints are in accord.
For us, the only one to testify
is Mercy, in the guise of God, who states:
"Chosen ones, suffer it for now as best
you can, since, while I will it, hope will rest
down there, where one about to lose her waits,
who'll say in hell: 'O you who are denied,
I've seen the hope of the beatified.'"

My lady is desired in Paradise.
I'll tell you now about her powers too:
to look more noble all you have to do
is be with her, in public by her side,
while Love casts into vulgar hearts an ice
that makes their thoughts drop dead from shocking cold.
As for the one who manages to hold
his gaze: he's either killed or dignified.
And when she meets somebody who is fit
to see and feel her power to generate —
how she restores the paradisal state —
he yields, forgives old hurt, surrenders it.
And God has granted her another grace:
who talks to her can't finish in disgrace.

Love says of her: "How could it happen that
a mortal is so lovely and so pure?"
He looks at her and tells himself he's sure
that God is set on making something new.
Her pallor's pearly, with this caveat:
it's not so white that you forget she's real.
Whatever good that Nature can reveal
is hers — she's beauty's touchstone on review.

Out of her eyes, whichever way she starts
to move them, issue spirits hot with love,
wounding the eyes of those whose gazes move
on her, and passing straightway to their hearts.
You women see Love's portrait in her eyes,
her face impossible to scrutinize.

I know, canzone, you'll go off and speak
with lots of women once I've turned you loose.
Remember how, wishing to introduce
Love's daughter young and mild, I raised you so;
when you arrive somewhere ask those you seek:
"Show me the road: I am an accolade
for her in praise of whom I'm so well made."
And to avoid a waste of time don't go
where everyone you meet is coarse and dumb;
try, if you're able, only being seen
by men and women versed in what you mean,
whose guidance will be swift, not burdensome.
You'll find Love living in her neighborhood —
tell him about my good points as you should.[24]

This poem is Dante's fullest early statement in poetry about the union of knowledge and will, or intellect and love. In the central cantos of *Purgatorio* — the part of the *Comedy* whose theme is the purification of the soul from disordered love — he will give his mature assessment of the possibility of human love that is harmonious with the rational soul rather than at odds with it. We will return a few times to this crucial episode of *Purgatorio*.

Earlier I noted the strong similarity between Avicenna's ideas on human love as a possible source of the soul's ascent to God and Dante's own views on this subject. For both Avicenna and Dante, attraction to external beauty is an impediment only when it involves a turning of the rational soul away from its final good, which is spiritual or intellectual beauty. Both these great visionaries assign to the lower, animal or sensible soul a role of partnership whereby love of beauty and erotic attraction may serve to draw the soul toward divine love.

24 *Vita nova* 10.15–25 (XIX.4–14).

The morality of human love rests on the free exercise of the rational soul—the use of free will, so strongly emphasized by Dante. The key distinction, made by both Avicenna and Dante, is that human love is unworthy and potentially damaging when it springs only from sensual appetite, since this harms the rational soul by subordinating it to the sensible soul. As Dante puts it in the *Convivio*,

> The nearer the desired object draws to the one who desires it, the greater is the desire; and the more the soul is impassioned, the more it unites itself with the appetitive part and the more it abandons reason; so that the person no longer judges as a human being but practically like an animal: by appearance only, not discerning the truth.[25]

Provided that sensual pleasures do not lead to actions that belong to the sensible soul alone, they are legitimate and beneficial, helping to bring the lover closer to the ultimate source of beauty and the first object of all love. In short, the lover must recall that beauty is the property of heaven. The spiritual struggle that this entails will be discussed in detail in chapters 4 and 9.

The question of how the soul ought to behave in the face of each *novo piacere*, or new pleasure, as Dante calls it in one chapter of the *Vita nova*,[26] is a central concern for Dante throughout his writings, first in his lyrics and finally in the *Comedy*. The *Vita nova* is a dramatization of that solution. Its narrator sees through courtly or profane love, realizing its limitations and possibilities, while also acknowledging at the end of the book that he has only begun to grasp how his vision might be lived in his own life and embodied in his poetry. As he writes, referring to the sonnet that pictures his heart's sigh rising to Beatrice in the celestial realm:

> After writing this sonnet a marvelous vision appeared to me, in which I saw things that made me decide not to say anything more about this blessed lady until I was capable of writing about her more worthily. To achieve this I am doing all that I can, as surely she knows. So that, if it be

25 *Convivio* III.x.2.
26 *Vita nova* 4.11 (IX.11).

pleasing to Him who is that for which all things live, and if my life is long enough, I hope to say things about her that have never been said about any woman.[27]

That woman is the subject of the next chapter.

---

27   *Vita nova* 31.1–2 (XLII.1–2).

2

Beatrice

EARLIER I MENTIONED the Counter-Reformation censorship of the first printed edition of the *Vita nova*. Some words and phrases that Dante had used in connection with Beatrice were disallowed by the Roman Curia, which found it objectionable that a mortal woman should have divine attributes symbolically associated with her.

In the *Divine Comedy* Beatrice is linked to Christ, especially in the great allegorical pageant atop Mount Purgatory in which Beatrice approaches like the rising sun, drawn by a Griffin who most commentators say represents the two natures of Christ. This association between Beatrice and Christ is first made in the *Vita nova*, where her life and death are said to echo his in various ways. Dante quotes Homer early on in the *Vita nova*, as an authority who can justify his extravagant claims for Beatrice, adapting Homer's description of Hector in the *Iliad*: "It can truly be said of her as Homer wrote: 'She did not seem the daughter of a mortal man, but rather of a god.'"[1]

Of course, Dante did not believe that Beatrice was Christ's equal, as his use of the word "seem" in the Homer passage implies. The Counter-Reformation censorship would have come about because of the gulf of understanding which separated the sixteenth century (and rigid dogmatists in the present time) from Dante's era, so that the later period could take for sacrilege what was only a correspondence, one which, understood in its proper terms, is no sacrilege at all. On the contrary, the analogy of Beatrice to divinity would have been viewed by Dante as a sign of the divine nature of God's creation. Like the great saints of the Christian tradition, Beatrice is a *speculum Christi*, a mirror of Christ, certainly not identical or equal to Christ, a notion which Dante himself would have considered sacrilegious, to say nothing of absurd. As a *speculum Christi* Beatrice is also an *imago Dei*, an image of God, in the theological tradition of the analogical relationship between the Creator and His creation. The famous passage from St. Paul's first letter to the Corinthians which states that in this life we see God only

1   *Vita nova* 1.9 (II.8).

53

as if in a mirror, was often interpreted in the sense that we *can* know him now through signs or images, a teaching that also permeates the Quran. In the context of the *Vita nova*, Beatrice is just such a sign. We will return to this theme and its related Trinitarian symbolism below.[2]

But in Dante's story, before Beatrice is a symbol of divinity, she is a girl who lives in his neighborhood in Florence. He tells us that he met her and was seized by love for her when he was nine years old. She was dressed in red, the color traditionally associated in Christian iconography with charity or love.

Dante emphasizes his *physiological* reaction to his first glimpse of Beatrice. The experience of being in love was imagined by the poets of Dante's circle as the movement of *spiritelli* or little spirits — who were noted in the last chapter — passing from the soul of one person to that of another. These poets applied such concepts, taken from scholastic philosophy, to the phenomenology of erotic love. The emotion Dante feels when he sees Beatrice is expressed as the reactions of the spirits in his heart, brain, and liver, stirred to a new awareness. Commenting on Lord Love's new power over Dante's heart, the spirit of life or vital spirit which dwells in the heart says, "Here is a god stronger than I, who has come to rule me." A spirit in the brain, site of the transformation of sensory experience into mental representations, tells Dante, "Your beatitude has now appeared." And the spirit in the liver, where the process of digestion is completed and the basic life functions originate, says, "How miserable! From now on I will be blocked [in my digestion]!"[3] Dante is giving highly stylized and perhaps tongue-in-cheek expression here to feelings often voiced in our own popular songs: the lover's famous loss of appetite. Each of these statements made by the *spiritelli* is in Latin, in Dante's otherwise Florentine text, highlighting the significance of what is being said.

The point is that Dante is changed, changed utterly, marked for life, by the sight of Beatrice. As he adds: "From then on, I swear that Love dominated my soul, which was wedded to him so early, and began to rule me with such confidence and power, by means of the force my

---

2 For the *imago Dei* insight, I am indebted to Lorenzo Dell'Oso for sharing his paper "From Peter of Trabibus' Quodlibets to Dante's *Vita nova*," read at the conference Quodlibetal Culture in Dante's Time: Europe, Italy, and Florence, University of Notre Dame, April 26–27, 2019.

3 *Vita nova* 1.5–7 (II.4–6).

imagination lent him, there was no choice but for me to do whatever he wanted. Time after time he ordered me to search for where I might glimpse this youthful angel; so that in my boyhood I went searching for her often."[4]

Next he tells us that exactly nine years had passed when, one day,

> that marvelous lady appeared to me dressed in pure white, between two gracious women, both of whom were older than she. And passing along a street, she turned her eyes in the direction of where I stood gripped by fear, and thanks to her ineffable benevolence and grace, which now are rewarded in eternal life, she greeted me with such power that then and there I seemed to see to the farthest reaches of beatitude.[5]

Her benevolence and grace are "rewarded in eternal life" because Dante is narrating this story after Beatrice's death in young adulthood. The effect of love on him after her greeting is so overwhelming that he has to withdraw from others to recollect himself. He has a dream-vision in which Lord Love appears to him, carrying his lady in his arms and feeding Dante's heart to her.

Dante tells us early on in the *Vita nova*, in the same section as the above passages, what Beatrice's special significance is for him. He writes that "even though her image, which was constantly with me, was the means by which Love ruled me, it was so dignified in its power that it never allowed Love to govern me without the faithful counsel of reason."[6] As we saw in the last chapter, Beatrice inspired in him the kind of love which was harmonious with the ascent of the soul to divine love, not, as in Paolo and Francesca's case in *Inferno*, the love of those who subordinate reason to desire. It is important to note that by "reason" here, *ragione*, Dante and his contemporaries did not mean only what is usually meant by it in our time, ratiocination. *Ragione* designates both the objective intelligible foundation of things and the human capacity for grasping this foundation: the intelligence in things — their essential being — that communicates itself to the intelligence in the mind. It has to do with the *reasons* or essences of things eternally present in the

---

4   *Vita nova* 1.8–9 (II.7–8).
5   *Vita nova* 1.12 (III.1).
6   *Vita nova* 1.10 (II.9).

divine Logos. The above statement means, then, that Dante's love for Beatrice is consonant with the Logos, which at least partly accounts for her symbolic association with Christ.

On the other hand, some of the poems in the *Vita nova* as well as others that Dante wrote in his youth express his struggle with the darker or more turbulent emotions involved in erotic love. And if we consider Dante's early lyrics *not* included in the *Vita nova*, Beatrice too is implicated in this struggle. In one early canzone—for obvious reasons left out of the *Vita nova*—Dante says that Beatrice wields a deathly power over him, one that threatens to engulf his intellect and paralyze his free will.[7] Note that this is the opposite of what he says in the passage I just quoted about Beatrice and reason. Even in the *Vita nova*, some of Dante's responses to his lady, especially early on in the tale, can hardly be said to be reasonable. In addition, it is easy not to notice that many of the poems in the *Vita nova* that Dante states or implies he wrote for Beatrice were not necessarily written for her, but rather perhaps for this or that other woman Dante was infatuated with at various times in his youth. The poems read in isolation do not have the narrative continuity that we find in the book as a whole. As the last chapter explained, Dante in the *Vita nova* re-envisions his love poems as stages of preparation for sacred love. At some point in his twenties, Dante decided to try to write love poetry that was less centered on the self and more aimed at love as such. Beatrice becomes the embodiment and symbol of this kind of love and love poetry—love that is "so dignified in its power it never allowed Love to govern [him] without the faithful counsel of reason." Beatrice is Dante's pole star for finding his way through love's vicissitudes, in his search for what is constant and eternal in love and desire.

The next section in the *Vita nova* tells of Dante's love for a new woman after Beatrice's death, the Donna Gentile, or gracious or noble woman, who is not only beautiful but who visibly sympathizes with Dante in his grief over his beloved's death. There are many facets to the Donna Gentile episode, but the important thing here is that Dante tells us his love for her threatened to make him forget Beatrice and the kind of love she represents. The code of courtly love, as laid out by Andreas Capellanus, had allowed that after a certain period of grieving—two

7 The canzone is *E' m'incresce di me sì duramente* ("I pity myself so intensely"), *Rime* LXVII.

years, says Andreas—it was permissible to love again. Ovid had written that there is no love sentiment that does not give way to a new passion. But Dante feels great conflict over his capacity to forget Beatrice so soon after her death because a new object of desire, alive and embodied, has presented itself. Dante's canzone *Voi che 'ntendendo il terzo ciel movete* ("All you who, knowing, make the third heaven move"), which is the subject of Dante's self-commentary in book II of the *Convivio*, similarly depicts the speaker's vacillations between his memory for a beloved who is dead and in heaven and a woman whose attractions are increasingly winning the affections of the speaker in his present life. Dante wrote this poem at about the time he was finishing the *Vita nova* (ca. 1295), though the *Convivio* commentary was composed about ten years later.

As we have seen, the human heart's inconstancy in love was a problem expressed in many passages in Dante's writing, from various points of view. In this scene of the Donna Gentile in the *Vita nova*, he expresses this conflict as one between his eyes, which are unfaithful because they delight in seeing this new beautiful woman, and his heart, which cherishes the memory of Beatrice: "By seeing this woman I reached the point where my eyes started to relish the sight of her too much, so that I often felt tormented in my heart, seeing myself as totally loathsome. Over and over I cursed the inconstancy of my eyes, and I told them in thought... 'Never, except after [my] death, should your tears have stopped.'"[8]

A few sections later in the *Vita nova*, Dante has had a renewed vision of Beatrice, who appears to him as she was when he first saw her, and he feels repentant for having let himself be distracted from his love for her. Now, he says, "I started to think about her [Beatrice]; and remembering her as she was in the past, my heart painfully started to repent the desire by which it so basely had let itself be seized for a number of days against the constancy of reason. And once this wicked desire had been driven off, all my thoughts turned back to their most gracious Beatrice."[9] In other words he returned to his dedication to her post mortem—very much as Christians did with regard to some martyred saint.

This means that Beatrice for Dante is the embodiment of love that is transparent to the Absolute, inspiring the integration of desire aroused

8   *Vita nova* 26.1–2 (XXXVII.1–2).
9   *Vita nova* 28.2 (XXXIX.2).

by visible beauty with the longing of the soul for beauty as such, which is intellectual or spiritual. Consequently, Beatrice is even more exalted in her death than she was in life, as a group of poems just before the Donna Gentile section attests, in language that anticipates Dante's representation of Beatrice in the *Comedy*. He emphasizes that death has made her invisible and therefore more sublime:

> the pleasure of her loveliness,
> once it had left our sense of sight behind,
> became great spiritual beauty then,
> which through the heavens sends
> the light of love, which blesses angel-kind,
> and their high intellect, unperishing,
> amazes, it is such a gracious thing.[10]

In a vision, Dante sees that Death himself is altered by Beatrice's death, made peaceful and merciful by her beauty, which now, having entered Death's realm, is veiled and interior:

> I saw her there outspread,
> where women laid a veil upon her state.
> She had such humbleness in her decease,
> it seemed that she was saying: "I am at peace."
>
> I felt so humbled by my suffering,
> to see such humbleness was traced in her,
> that I said: "Death, I deem you most humane;
> you must by now be such a gracious thing,
> considering you have been placed in her,
> that you are full of mercy not disdain."[11]

And in a sonnet at the end of the *Vita nova*, which will be quoted in full later in this chapter and which I referred to earlier in connection with Augustine's words on the gravitational pull of the essential nature of all created things, the dead Beatrice is the celestial center of gravity

---

10   *Quantunque volte, lasso!, mi rimembra* ("Whenever I, alas, recall"), *Vita nova* 22.8 (XXXIII.8).

11   *Donna pietosa e di novella etate* ("A woman compassionate and young"), *Vita nova* 14.26–27 (XXIII.26–27).

for the sigh of love that rises heavenward from the lover's heart. Love for her invisible essence draws his mind to contemplation of the Eternal.

The *Vita nova*'s storyline is a gradual revelation of Beatrice's nature. We witness the protagonist's groping understanding as it is slowly revealed that Beatrice's beauty and virtue are signs of a transcendent power. Early on in the book this understanding is still vague; the images of Beatrice's power are like hints of what is to come. Her quasi-divine status is suggested at the opening of the story by an allusion to the meaning of her name, *beatrice*, which comes from the Latin *beatrix*, "she who blesses." Dante refers to her as "she whom many called Beatrice without even knowing that was her name,"[12] apparently meaning that people talked about her presence as a kind of blessing even if they did not know her name was *Beatrice*.

As the next chapter will elaborate, the salutation of the beloved—the bliss of being acknowledged by love—was a favorite theme in courtly love poetry. In the following passage early in the *Vita nova*, Beatrice's greeting has an effect that is more characteristic of Christian *agape* or *caritas* than of *eros*. The language in this passage uses such Christian terms as *humility* and *charity* even as it also describes the body's trance-like possession by eros:

> I tell you that whenever and wherever she appeared, by virtue of my hope in her marvelous greeting, no one could be my enemy; on the contrary, I became possessed by a flame of charity that made me forgive whoever had hurt me, and were someone to ask me any question at that moment, my response would have been, simply, "Love," my expression clothed in humility.... And when this lovely salve offered me her salutation, Love by no means tempered the unbearably powerful bliss that came over me; rather, by an almost excessive delight it became such that my body, which by then was totally dominated by him, moved like a heavy, inanimate object. Clearly then my bliss depended on her salutation; it was a bliss that many times surpassed and overflowed my capacity to contain it.[13]

---

12   *Vita nova* 1.2 (II.1).
13   *Vita nova* 5.4, 6–7 (XI.1, 3–4).

Returning to the Counter-Reformation censorship of the *Vita nova*, it is surprising, actually, that the censors bothered to alter the phrases I quoted in the last chapter, since the association between Beatrice and Christ is so explicit in certain scenes in the *Vita nova* — scenes that were left unaltered in the Counter-Reformation edition. We have seen some examples of this already. In addition, the chapter in which Dante has a delirious vision of Beatrice's imminent death, in the middle of the *Vita nova*, is especially crucial for establishing the Beatrice-Christ parallels. Dante tells us of a time that he was gravely ill:

> It happened that a painful illness came over a certain part of my body, so I was in bitter pain for nine days in a row, which reduced me to such a weak condition that I had to stay put like a paralytic. I tell you that on exactly the ninth day, when I was in so much pain it was almost intolerable, a thought about my lady came over me. And after having thought about her for a while, I went back to thinking about my incapacitated life; and seeing how fleeting it was, even when it was healthy, I started to weep over such misery. Then, letting out a great sigh, I told myself: "There is no escaping the fact that the most gracious Beatrice will have to die some day."[14]

Note that his vision came precisely on the ninth day of his illness — we will take a look later at the significance of that number with regard to Beatrice.

Then he tells us that he had a terrifying premonition of women in mourning, sobbing with grief, at which point he has a vision of cataclysmic natural events. Here is the description as Dante gives it in the poem in this chapter, the canzone represented by Rossetti in his painting of Dante's vision of Beatrice's death. Dante is relating his delirious vision to some women who are visiting his sickbed. The mention in this passage of women with loose hair refers to a funeral custom at that time; women loosened their hair as an expression of grief and mourning.

---

14   *Vita nova* 14.1–3 (XXIII.1–3).

And I saw many things, grim and abstruse,
as I entered in the unreal vision-scene.
I seemed someplace — just where, I couldn't guess —
where women walked along with their hair loose,
and some shed tears and some unleashed a keen
that discharged fiery arrows of distress.
Then bit by bit it seemed I saw progress
the sun's darkening when first a star appears,
both sun and star in tears;
and the birds flying through the air fall down,
and tremors shake the ground.
A man appeared, spectral and colorless,
who said: "Come on. Do you know what befell?
Your lady is dead, who was so beautiful."[15]

The description here echoes scenes in the Gospels involving the crucifixion of Jesus. The reference to the vision occurring on exactly the ninth day is an allusion to the Gospel of Mark: "And at the ninth hour Jesus cried with a loud voice, . . . 'My God, my God, why hast thou forsaken me?'"[16] Similarly, the natural catastrophes echo signs in scripture of the death of Jesus and the end of the world. So an analogy is made between Beatrice's death and the death of Christ. The canzone continues on to describe Beatrice rising to heaven attended by angels who are hovering beside a white cloud and crying out hosanna, as in Christ's ascension.

In the episode after this important and long chapter on Beatrice's death, the analogy between Beatrice and Christ is stated quite explicitly. It is as though the veil over this knowledge has been removed by the vision of her death. Dante tells us that one day he was sitting somewhere, absorbed in reflection, when he unexpectedly felt a trembling in his heart — several times in the *Vita nova* he tells us that his heart is aware of Beatrice's presence before his eyes are. Then, he says, a vision of Lord Love came over him, announcing the approach of a beautiful and gracious woman, one he knew as the beloved of his best friend, the poet Guido Cavalcanti. The woman's name, it so happens, was Giovanna, the female version of Giovanni or John, but her

15   *Donna pietosa e di novella etate, Vita nova* 14.23–24 (XXIII.23–24).
16   Mark 15:34.

poetic nickname was Primavera, Spring. And right after her, Dante says, came along his divine Beatrice. Dante in this scene makes a meaningful wordplay between the word for "spring," *primavera,* and the words for "she will come first," *prima verrà.* Lord Love, whose presence Dante senses because of the arrival of these ladies, says to him as the women pass:

> That first woman is named Primavera only in honor of today's coming. I moved the one who gave her that name [i.e., Cavalcanti] to call her Primavera, that is, *prima verrà,* she will come first, the day that Beatrice appears, after the imaginings of her faithful one. And if you also consider her given name, you will see that it is practically the same as saying *prima verrà,* since her name, Giovanna or Joanna, is derived from that John who preceded the true Light, saying, "I am the voice of one crying in the wilderness. Make straight the way of the Lord."[17]

What Dante has done here is extraordinary. He has stated that Cavalcanti's lady, Giovanna, is to Beatrice as John the Baptist was to Christ. Her name and nickname were signs of that, as was the fact that the women physically approached Dante one after the other, Giovanna coming first as John did before Jesus. The reference to *primavera* in this poem of the *Vita nova* is most likely an homage to a poem by Guido Cavalcanti, in which Cavalcanti refers to his lady as *piacente primavera,* or "lovely spring." The prose of this chapter of the *Vita nova,* which is famously incongruent with its accompanying poem — since the poem itself gives no hint of the theological and visionary meaning I have just described — is probably suggesting that Guido's beloved preceded Dante's just as Guido's poetics represented a mere preparatory phase for Dante's own superior poetics, initiated in the *Vita nova* by various poems that implicitly reject Cavalcanti's dark and fatalistic view of love.

Lord Love in this scene adds one further comment: "Whoever wants to give the matter subtle consideration would call Beatrice 'Love' because of the great resemblance she bears to me." Given the explicit analogy to Christ that Dante has just presented in this section, the identification of Beatrice with Love or Lord Love echoes the notion of

17   *Vita nova* 15.4 (XXIV.4).

Christ as the incarnation of God as charity or love (*Deus caritas est*). Beatrice now has become the very name of love, so much so that the episode following this one is a theoretical excursus on personification in poetry, in particular the personification of love. Now that Beatrice has been revealed as love itself, Lord Love disappears from the prose narrative and is unveiled as a mere poetic figure.

After the excursus into literary theory — the first passage of literary criticism, by the way, in a European vernacular language — Dante launches into the episode of his story that is the height of the praise-poetry he resolves to write about Beatrice whether she acknowledges his desperate love for her or not. He has realized that he can break away from the narcissistic traps of romantic love by praising his beloved, setting aside his subjective states in favor of what transcends them in constancy: the nobility, grace, and beauty of Beatrice. The imagery of this episode is flagrantly biblical, echoing the Gospels' accounts of Jesus's passage through villages and towns and the reactions of people when they saw him:

> This most gracious of women came to be much admired and sought after, so when she passed along the street people ran to see her — a fact that filled me with wonder and happiness. And when she drew near to someone, such purity of heart took hold of that person he did not so much as dare to raise his eyes or respond to her greeting; and for those who do not believe this fact many could bear witness to it, having experienced it directly.

The last part of this description, about bearing witness, obviously echoes biblical accounts of the reactions of people to the miracles Jesus was working. And in fact the narrative continues: "Many said, before she had passed, 'She is no mere mortal woman; rather, she is one of the beautiful angels in heaven.' And others said, 'She is a marvel; may the Lord be blessed who knows how to work such miracles!'"[18]

A famous sonnet in this chapter, *Tanto gentile e tanto onesta pare*, which many Italians to this day know by heart, expresses this same notion of Beatrice's beauty as a divine manifestation. The first line of the poem ends with the word "appears," *pare*, while the second line

18   *Vita nova* 17.1–2 (XXVI.1–2).

opens with "my lady" or *la donna mia*. There is an express purpose for these positions, as in fact every detail of this poem, as in nearly all of Dante's work, is a wonder of conscious design. The word "appears," occurring at the end of the first line, is like a flash before the manifestation of divinity. In addition there is a sharp enjambment, or line break in the middle of a phrase, that occurs between this word and the words "my lady," which begin the second line of the poem like the epiphany of a goddess. This is a poem of radiant manifestation of the invisible—as the repetition in the poem of the words "appears" and "shows" is meant to suggest.

> So noble and so self-possessed appears
> my lady when she's greeting everyone,
> that every tongue, in trembling, falters dumb,
> and eyes don't dare to watch her as she nears.
> She senses all the praising of her worth,
> and passes by, benevolently dressed
> in humbleness, appearing manifest
> from heaven to show a miracle on earth.
>
> She shows herself so pleasing to the one
> who sees her, sweetness passes through the eye
> to the heart—as he who's missed it never knows.
> So from her face it then appears there blows
> a loving spirit, as if spring's begun,
> which breathes upon the soul and tells it: *Sigh.*[19]

The mention of an incarnation on earth that manifests heaven is an obvious reference to Christ. In what I have translated here as "breathes upon the soul," the original simply says that the loving spirit *speaks* to the soul. But the word *sospira*, sigh, forms a wordplay that Dante and other poets were fond of, with *spirito*, spirit—both suggesting "breath" or *spiritus*. These verbal echoes, combined with the Christ-like portrayal of Beatrice in this poem, suggest that Dante at the end of the poem, where he mentions the spirit telling the soul to sigh, has in mind the biblical scene following Christ's resurrection in which Christ breathes the Holy Spirit—the Spirit of Love—upon his disciples.

---

19   *Tanto gentile e tanto onesta pare*, Vita nova 17.5–7 (XXVI.5–7).

In the same section of the *Vita nova*, Beatrice is credited with the power of creating *ex nihilo*, out of nothing, the way that God creates the world in Genesis. Beatrice is not merely like other women, whose inner and outer beauty can awaken love that is dormant in people. Her power is such that she arouses love even where it is not latent. As Dante says: "I was taken with a wish to write something in praise of this most gracious of women, by means of which I would show how love awakens through her, and how it awakens not only where it is dormant but also where it is not even in potential: working miraculously, she brings it forth."[20] This is just one of the ways in which the *Vita nova* is a celebration of Beatrice as a miracle. In Aristotle's thought, in the background for Dante even at this early stage of his work, potential necessarily precedes act or actualization. Here, however, potential is by-passed altogether and the soul of the one who beholds Beatrice is awakened directly into love, which in effect is created *ex nihilo*.

It is not hard to understand, given the symbolic weight such passages place on the figure of Beatrice, that phrases about her in the *Vita nova* such as *la gloriosa donna de la mia mente*, "the glorious lady of my mind,"[21] would come to be interpreted by some as indicating that Beatrice is *only* an allegory for divine wisdom or theology, not a real person whom Dante knew. The debate between those who take this line of thought and those who accept Dante's statement that Beatrice was an actual person harkens back to Boccaccio's biography of Dante, written about thirty years after Dante's death in 1321. In this text, Beatrice in the *Vita nova* and the *Comedy* is identified as a certain Bice Portinari—"Bice" (pronounced "BĒ-chā") is the nickname for *Beatrice*—the daughter of the prominent Florentine Folco Portinari and the wife of Simone de' Bardi, who was from a family of bankers. In addition, certain other old documents associate Dante's Beatrice with Beatrice Portinari or at least with a real woman who lived in Florence in Dante's time. Many scholars have doubted Boccaccio's account, pointing out that he was, after all, an author of fiction. The fact that Beatrice never talks and in general is phantom-like in the *Vita nova*, and goddess-like in the *Comedy*, has suggested to many readers and critics that she is allegorical from the start, an abstraction whom Dante invents for his symbolic ends. The notion that a boy could fall

20 *Vita nova* 12.1 (XXI.1).
21 *Vita nova* 1.2 (II.1).

in love so entirely and enduringly at age nine has also been doubted, and at times cited as another reason to believe that Beatrice is invented purely for allegorical purposes.

To those who have questioned the truth of Boccaccio's claim about Beatrice's real-life identity, it has been pointed out that Boccaccio made these assertions originally in lecture form, addressing a live audience of Florentines who easily could have refuted him since they would have personally known the families he mentions. In addition, if Boccaccio were inventing, why would he have made Beatrice a married woman, which is nowhere hinted at by Dante, and moreover, the wife of a member of one of the most prominent families of Florence? The Portinaris were employed in the Bardi banking business and Boccaccio himself was associated with this business as an agent of the bank—making it unlikely that he would take such liberties with families to whom he would have to answer. And again, at least three independent Trecento witnesses say that Beatrice was Bice Portinari, two of them in the half-century after Dante's death. And no one at that time made a statement to contradict the claims of these three sources.

The issue as to whether Beatrice was an actual historical figure or a completely allegorical one is not merely an academic curiosity, since the discussion involves a question of major importance to understanding Dante's allegorical method and therefore the deeper undercurrents of his poetry. Leaving aside his later elaborations of this method in relation to the *Comedy,* even in the *Vita nova* Dante says that Lord Love is a poetic figure—in short, that Dante is working allegorically. But we know from Dante's *Convivio* that he considered the literal level of meaning—that of concrete facts—an essential component of allegory. In this kind of explication, he writes, "the literal [sense] must always go first, as that within whose meaning the others are enclosed, and without which it would be impossible and irrational to try to grasp the others, above all the allegorical."[22] This is the approach of medieval writers in general (e.g., Thomas Aquinas) to the interpretation of sacred texts: the literal level was considered the necessary starting point. Although we cannot extrapolate from Dante's statement in the *Convivio* as to how Dante conceived his youthful project, we do know that he includes enough concrete details in the *Vita nova* to make it absolutely clear that he *intends* for us to think of the story as happening in a real place with real people.

22   *Convivio* II.i.8.

The suggestion, then, is that allegorical meanings in the *Vita nova* too are founded on literal or historical fact. Beatrice is a symbol even as she is a real-life person — it seems to me that this is one of the main points of Dante's story. It appears far more in keeping with Dante's style, methods, and ways of thinking that even though he clearly does idealize the plain historical facts of the story of Beatrice, all the poetic flights of fancy are based on a core of concrete experience. A number of Sufi poets did something similar — for example Ibn 'Arabī's description of a sheikh's young daughter as "a slender child who captivated all who looked on her, whose presence gave luster to gatherings, who amazed all she was with and ravished the senses of all who beheld her.... She was a sage among the sages of the Holy Places."[23]

The one-sided allegorical view of Dante was first proposed in the mid-fifteenth century by Giovanni Mario Filelfo, in his biography of the poet. Anton Maria Biscioni followed Filelfo's lead in his 1723 edition of the *Vita nova*. Biscioni writes in his preface: "I do not hesitate in the least to say: Dante's Beatrice was not a real woman, and so was not [Beatrice] Portinari: and the *Vita nuova* is a treatise on love, only intellectual, without any profane element."[24] This characterizes the approach of one-sided allegorists ever since. Whether the interpreter says Beatrice is an allegory for the active intellect of Aristotelean metaphysics; or for the ideal Church; or for Dante's own soul; or for the ideal of the emperor and the pope acting in harmony for the good of all; or for Wisdom, this sort of interpretation implies that the great Dante could not possibly have wasted his time on writing about anything so "trivial" as love for an actual woman. There is a Manichean duality to these approaches, not because they insist on finding allegorical or symbolic meanings in the *Vita nova* — which certainly are there — but because they assert that such meanings preclude the literal sense of the text, however sketchy and attenuated that may be. In the process, some of these critics went very far indeed into the realm of the absurd. For example, one critic interpreted the death of Beatrice's father as "really" about the death of Thomas Aquinas, and another asserted that the

---

23 Quoted in Seyyed Hossein Nasr, *Knowledge and the Sacred* (Albany: State University of New York Press, 1989), 331.

24 Anton Maria Biscioni, *Prose di Dante Alighieri e di messer Gio. Boccacci* (Florence: Per Gio. Gaetano Tartini, e Santi Franchi, 1723), ix. Biscioni adds (xxxi) that the protagonist's love in the *Vita nova* is only for *sapienza*, wisdom.

screen-woman represented "some monastic ideal, possibly the Franciscan Rule, and that in adopting her for a defence Dante allowed it to be believed that he contemplated embracing the religious life."[25] More reasonably, Ernest Robert Curtius allows that

> Dante paid homage to a Florentine woman, whom he called Beatrice; later [Curtius continues] he stylized her into the myth of the Lady Nine.... [The mediatrix whom we encounter in *Purgatorio* XXX] is not the recovered love of [Dante's] youth. She is the highest salvation in the form of a woman — an emanation of God. For no other reason can she appear without blasphemy in a triumph in which Christ himself has a place.[26]

And yet the fact remains that Dante chose a woman whom he says he knew and loved in Florence, rather than, say, a canonized saint as his main guide.

A key in understanding that there is no contradiction between Beatrice as allegory and Beatrice as a real woman in Dante's neighborhood in Florence is the teaching, found in Augustine, Bonaventure, and Aquinas, of the divine traces in the creation, an idea which derives in part from St. Paul's letter to the Romans: "The invisible things of God are clearly seen through the things which have been made."[27] Augustine's term for this, *vestigium*, is echoed by Dante in canto I of *Paradiso*, where he uses the word *orma*, imprint, for the signs of the Creator in the outer world — an imprint that is perceptible by creatures (angels and human beings) endowed with intellect.[28] In canto XI of

---

25   Gertrude Leigh, *The Passing of Beatrice: A Study in the Heterodoxy of Dante* (London: Faber & Faber, 1932), 56. She also interprets the two sonnets about the death of a young woman, in chapter 3 (VIII) of the *Vita nova*, as "no mere empty dirge, but an outspoken contemporary denunciation of the Inquisitions Court"; since Death in these poems is "so vehemently reprehended, is there not some reason to suspect a personification of the most hated tribunal of the Carnal Church, that of the Inquisition?" (60). Note the disdain for "mere" dirges. For Leigh, what was good enough for any number of great poets apparently was not good enough for Dante — or for her agenda with the Roman Church.

26   Ernst Robert Curtius, *European Literature and the Latin Middle Ages*, translated by Willard R. Trask (1951; repr., London: Routledge and Kegan Paul, 1979), 376, 378.

27   Romans 1:20.

28   *Paradiso* I.106.

Inferno, Dante refers to the Creator and this imprint as the "divine intellect" and "its art."[29]

The emanationist understanding of creation, which Dante knew from the Neoplatonic treatise *De causis* (On Causes) and other sources, conceives of reality unfolding in multiple levels, or emanations, hierarchically arranged, starting with the First Cause, which is transcendent, and with each successive level transmitting this Principle to the one below it. A concomitant of this understanding is that the creation may be seen as metaphysically transparent, the "signature" of God's creative act or "God's Book," as both the hermetic tradition and Catholic theology have repeatedly affirmed. Thomas Aquinas wrote that before the Fall in Eden, a spiritual light was available to the human mind, by which divine realities could be seen directly. Since the Fall, human beings have needed a mirror in which to see God. The created world is this mirror, and therefore is a proper object for contemplation. We will have much more to say about this mirror in chapter 4, "The Dream of Leah and Rachel."

To Bonaventure the world is a ladder for ascending to God and the mind ascends through three stages, corresponding to the Trinity: seeing God in external forms, seeing God within the mind itself, and seeing God in transcendent vision. Some commentators have claimed that these stages outlined by Bonaventure are embedded in the narrative progress of the *Vita nova*: the search for the good as found outside the self, where Dante's love still relies on the outward sign of Beatrice's greeting; the stage of *caritas* or *agape* as love that does not seek any recompense, where Dante's praise of Beatrice is its own reward, with or without the salutation or greeting; and the final stage of the ascent of the soul beyond itself, where Dante's sigh rises to Beatrice in Paradise.

In terms of this emanationist view, then, the beauty of the beloved, as an aspect of the creation, *can* be a mirror for divinity. This is certainly a notion behind much of the *Vita nova*. I have already referred to the analogies between Beatrice and Christ and given a few examples of the biblical and liturgical echoes in the text of the *Vita nova* that create this sense of the sacred mystery underlying the surface events of the story. I noted the role of the number 9 in this planting of signs in the text. The very first word of the narrative proper, after a brief

29 *Inferno* XI.100.

prelude, is *nove*, the number 9: "Nine times, the heaven of the light had returned to where it was at my birth, almost to the very same point of its orbit, when the glorious lady of my mind first appeared before my eyes — she whom many called Beatrice without even knowing that was her name."[30] The heaven of the light is, of course, the sun. Dante is telling us he was 9 years old when he first saw her — Boccaccio says it was at a May Day celebration.

This number comes up several times later in the story in connection with various revelations about Beatrice. I have already mentioned the vision of her death that came on the 9th day of Dante's illness. In addition, Dante tells us that exactly 9 years elapsed between his first sighting of Beatrice and the first time she greeted him in passing. It just so happens that this event came in precisely the 9th hour of that day, which would be 3 in the afternoon by the reckoning of medieval Europe.

And there are other episodes as well in which the number 9 is associated with Beatrice. Dante recognizes the significance of this association only after Beatrice's death. Once he has calculated the date of her death according to 3 different calendars — Syrian, Roman, and Arabic — always coming up with the number 9, he realizes that she is a miracle precisely because the number 3, associated with the blessed Trinity, is the root of 9:

> The number 3 is the root of 9, since it makes 9 by itself, without any other number, as we see plainly in the fact that 3 times 3 makes 9. Therefore, if 3 by itself is the factor of 9, and the factor of miracles multiplied by itself is 33 — that is, the Father, the Son, and the Holy Spirit, who are 3-and-1, this woman was accompanied by this number 9 to make it understood that she was a 9, a miracle in other words, whose root (the root of the miracle) is none other than the miraculous Trinity.[31]

Nine will be Beatrice's number right on through the *Comedy:* There are 9 poetic invocations in the *Comedy,* just as there are 9 prophecies of Dante's exile. Beatrice's name is used as a rhyme word in the *Comedy* on exactly 9 occasions. Her name is mentioned 63 times in the *Comedy,*

30   *Vita nova* 1.2 (II.1).
31   *Vita nova* 19.6 (XXIX.3).

which in standard numerological practice produces 6 + 3 = 9. The last time we see Beatrice is at line 9 of the 99th canto of the work (canto XXXII of *Paradiso*).

Guglielmo Gorni has noticed that Beatrice's Latin name, *Beatrix*, can also be read as a cipher that states that Beatrice was "accompanied by this number 9" in quite a literal sense. Referring to a line in *Paradiso* XIII, *Non creda donna Berta e ser Martino* ("Do not think that Lady Berta and Sir Martino"),[32] Gorni points out that "Berta" was used by Dante in a passage of *De vulgari eloquentia* as well, and in his time and place in general, as an antonomasia for "woman." Gorni goes on to show that *Berta* can be seen as an anagram for *Beatr*, which only needs *ix*, or the number 9, added to it to make *Beatrix*. Thus, Beatrice literally is *Beatr* (woman) + *ix* (9): the woman accompanied by 9.[33]

The number 9, as Dante explains after the passage quoted above, signifies the Trinity multiplied by itself, which also produces the number of angelic hierarchies. Therefore Beatrice's number, which is her true self, is a reflection of the angelic world. It is the number closest to perfection, according to the Pythagoreans and to later Christian writers, because of its nearness to the number 10, which contains "all numbers and therefore all things.... Not only is the number 10 necessary to realize completeness, but all things are contained within the decad, since after 10 the numbers merely repeat themselves."[34] Multiplicity again becomes unity in 10: "Nicomachus of Gerasa, a commentator of Plato, said of the number Ten that it 'serves as the measure of the universe, as a square and line in the hand of the Director.'"[35] That the divine tetraktys (1 + 2 + 3 + 4) adds up to 10 "makes clear that 'every whole and perfect thing is ten.'"[36] Augustine refers to the Decalogue and to 10 as the number of the Law.[37] Augustine also wrote:

32   *Paradiso* XIII.139.

33   Guglielmo Gorni, *Lettera nome numero: L'ordine delle cose in Dante* (Bologna: Il Mulino, 1990), 39ff.

34   Vincent Foster Hopper, *Medieval Number Symbolism* (1938; repr., New York: Cooper Square Publishers, 1969), 34. To name just two uses of this number in the *Comedy*: the poem itself consists of 100 cantos, a number that is the product of 10; and Dante begins to describe his vision of the Empyrean at exactly line 100 of canto XXX.

35   Jean Hani, *Divine Craftsmanship: Preliminaries to a Spirituality of Work*, translated by Robert Procter (San Rafael, CA: Sophia Perennis, 2007), 49.

36   Ibid., 117, citing Roger Bacon.

37   *City of God* II.xv.20.

> If truly one adds to nine the number one, by this method
> the form and likeness of unity is satisfied, which makes so
> much complete since number cannot proceed beyond this
> except to return again to one; and this is a pattern which
> is preserved by numbers to infinity. Nine therefore lacks
> one since the form of unity is joined to, and is itself, ten.[38]

This allows us to see that Beatrice represents "the all-but-complete or
all-but-perfect."[39] The number 9 was seen as having the mathematical
virtue of incorruptibility, since "like the salamander, it may change its
shape, but, however often multiplied, it always reproduces itself," based
on the notion that "a number divided by 9 will leave the same remain-
der as the sum of its digits divided by 9."[40] It is interesting to recall in
view of all this that until the Empyrean (associated with the number
10), Beatrice's face is the only one that Dante can see in Paradise. All
the other faces are hidden in light.[41] The number 9, then, can be interpreted as the reflection of the Absolute in the relative, which is to say
what Dante says about Beatrice: it symbolizes the face of holy Wisdom.

In my outline of some episodes in the *Vita nova* in which the number
9 is mentioned in connection with Beatrice, I have intentionally passed
over one episode early in the story. I left it out until now because it
involves the all-important role of Beatrice as Dante's muse, the source
of his highest poetic inspiration. The episode occurs shortly after the
one in which Dante has a dream of Lord Love feeding his burning heart
to his lady, whom Love is carrying half-naked in his arms. Dante is in
such a state of lovesickness that he has lost weight and is generally a
nervous wreck because he cannot stop thinking of his beloved. People
start questioning him, "spitefully curious sorts of people,"[42] as Dante
describes them — lacing into his story yet another conventional theme
from the courtly love tradition, that of the backbiting or malicious

---

38 Augustine, *Quaestiones evangeliorum* (Questions on the Gospels) II.40; cited
in Guzzardo, *Dante: Numerological Studies,* 134.

39 Hopper, *Medieval Number Symbolism,* 11.

40 Ibid., 123, and n. 143 on that page (Hopper is quoting a mathematician there).
On 102, Hopper writes: "Nine was considered circular...because, however often multiplied, it continually reproduces itself in the sum of its digits."

41 See *Paradiso* XXV.118–23 for a direct reference to this fact. There are times, for
instance the beginning of canto XXI, when Beatrice's face is too bright to look at *if
she is smiling,* at which point Dante's vision has to adapt to a new level of beatitude.

42 *Vita nova* 2.3 (IV.1).

person, the *losengier* in Provençal troubadour poetry—who cannot possibly understand the ecstasies and torments of the besotted lover. In this context, Dante uses his neighbors' wrong conjecture as to whom the young Dante is actually in love with (they think she is a beautiful woman who had met his eyes one day in church), to create a "screen" or shield for the true object of his love, Beatrice. Dante tells us that this woman was his screen for a long period of time, during which he wrote "certain little rhymes" for her in order to throw busybodies still further off the scent of the true object of his love.

He says that one day he wanted to compose a poem that would have Beatrice's name in it as well as the name of his screen-woman. The array of beautiful women that Dante mentions in this passage was another stock theme in courtly love poetry:

> During the time when this woman was a screen for this great love of mine, I was taken with a wish to record the name of that most gracious of women [Beatrice] and to place it in the company of many women's names, especially this gracious woman's [the screen-woman]. And I gathered together the names of sixty of the most beautiful women of the city where my lady was placed by the supreme Lord, and I composed an epistolary poem ... which I will not write down here. And I wouldn't even have mentioned it if it were not to say what wondrously took place as I was composing it: the name of my lady would not settle for being in any other position, among the names of these women, but that of the number 9.[43]

This last part of Dante's narrative most likely refers to the exigencies of rhyme: Beatrice's name had to occur in the 9th position of the list of names because he needed a rhyme at that point of the poem. Scanning the *Comedy* for rhymes that Dante uses for *Beatrice* (pronounced in Italian as "ʙᴀ̄-ah-ᴛʀᴇ̄-cha̅") one finds that most often *dice*, he or she says, or *felice*, happy, are used.[44] Does the name "not settle" for any other

---

43   *Vita nova* 2.10–11 (ᴠɪ.1–2).

44   Dante and other medieval poets often used rhymes to suggest affinities—between particular things as well as between texts. So in the *Comedy* we find rhyme pairings that echo (intentionally, it is clear) other passages in the poem.

position in this poem, then, because *Beatrice* "means" *felice*? Yet *dice* also could work, since Dante and other Italian poets often used that verb, which means "telling," to mean "writing poetry." *Beatrice* then is a name that means, as we have seen, the bringer of beatitude or bliss. I think it is likely that this passage implies that *Beatrice* also means — since the bliss she brings is inspiration itself — the one who brings *poetry*. This idea is reiterated at the end of *Purgatorio*, where Beatrice charges Dante with his prophetic mission, instructing him to write everything he has seen and heard in the other world as a sign for the living, whether he understands what he has seen or not, thus becoming, as Dante will put it in another work, a *scriba divini eloquii*, or scribe of divine speech.[45] Beatrice is the source of Dante's decision and drive to write the *Comedy*, as in fact he states explicitly at the end of the *Vita nova*, and as we hear from the character of Beatrice near the end of *Purgatorio*, when she charges Dante with his role as poet-prophet.

We cannot know for sure how detailed Dante's ideas about Beatrice's allegorical significance were when he wrote the *Vita nova*. Enough is said about her in this book, however, to tell us that he already was thinking along the lines of what he says in *Paradiso*, where he compares his experience in the celestial realm to that of the mythical figure Glaucus. Glaucus was a fisherman who noticed one day that the fish he had thrown half-dead on the grass after catching them miraculously revived and leaped back into the sea. Realizing that the grass was the source of their rebirth, Glaucus ate the grass himself, whereupon he was infused with divine life and plunged ecstatically into the sea of being, along with the fish. He became immortal. Beatrice is Dante's guide in Paradise, and so has to do with that which aids Dante in his *trasumanare*,[46] the transformation of his humanity into its primordial and ultimate deiform nature. Thus in his encounter with Beatrice in the Earthly Paradise, Dante identifies her explicitly with holy Wisdom from the Song of Songs, a figure mentioned in the *Convivio* as a symbol of divine science.[47]

This elevated sense of Beatrice's significance is represented in the final sonnet of the *Vita nova*, which I have alluded to a few times in connection with Dante's sigh rising to Beatrice in heaven. In this poem,

---

45 *Monarchia* III.iv.11.
46 *Paradiso* I.70.
47 *Purgatorio* XXX.11–12.

you will notice that the word *to speak* or *speech* is repeated three times in its final lines. As he will do so often in *Paradiso*—and as we will see, this is closely associated with the theme of poetic inspiration—Dante highlights the unspeakableness or incomprehensibility of celestial experience. In this poem the ascending sigh is called a pilgrim-spirit. Dante placed the poem in the *Vita nova* immediately after the section about the pilgrims passing through Florence during Holy Week, on the way to see the Veronica—the much-venerated cloth with the image of Christ's face on it. Here, Beatrice is as it were the Veronica to which the spirit-sigh is making a pilgrimage. The "widest gyre" in the opening line of the poem is the last of the Ptolemaic spheres, the Primum Mobile or First Mover, beyond which is Eternity proper, the Empyrean.

> Beyond the sphere that turns the widest gyre
> rises a sigh my heart cannot contain;
> a new awareness, which Lord Love in pain
> inspires the sigh with, draws him ever higher.
> When he has reached the site of his desire
> he sees a woman there, an honored name
> whose splendor is so luminous a flame
> the pilgrim-spirit's rapt, his gaze entire.
>
> He starts to speak, but I cannot infer
> the meaning of the tale, so subtly spun,
> he tells my suffering heart, which gives him speech.
> I know he's speaking of that lovely one,
> Beatrice, since he often mentions her—
> that much, dear women, is within my reach.[48]

The knowledge that Beatrice brings, then, is both ineffable and transcendent, an insight that will be repeated many times in the *Comedy*. At the same time, when Dante in *Purgatorio* finally sees Beatrice again, in the Earthly Paradise, the first time he has seen her since her death, he emphasizes his personal memory of her, his physical response to this encounter in the Earthly Paradise, saying that, *d'antico amor sentì la gran potenza* ("I felt the great force of the old love"), adding,

---

48 *Oltre la spera che più larga gira*, Vita nova 30.10–13 (XLI.10–13).

As soon as that high power, which had already pierced me before I was out of childhood, struck my eyes, I turned to my left with the trust with which a boy runs to his mother when he is afraid or when he is afflicted, to say to Virgil, "Less than a drop of blood remains in me that does not tremble: I recognize the signs of the old flame."[49]

The journey that starts in Hell and climaxes in the celestial journey is always a journey *toward* Beatrice and then *with* her. Dante finds his way again on the path he had lost by recalling the way of the heart that he had depicted in his youthful work the *Vita nova*. The apotheosis of Beatrice's beauty in the Earthly Paradise, which Dante says surpasses her beauty on earth even more than her beauty on earth surpassed that of other women, is the power that opens his heart to full repentance, completing his purification in Purgatory.

Near the end of *Paradiso*, Dante addresses his final farewell to Beatrice just before she goes to rejoin the blessed in her place in the Empyrean. This hymn to Beatrice uses language that, so characteristically in Dante's work, combines the sublimest thought with warm-blooded emotion. Very significantly indeed, for the first time in his writing he addresses Beatrice using the familiar pronoun *tu*, you—until this point he had always used the respectful formal *voi*. He expresses his gratitude to her for humbling herself for his sake, descending to the hell of Dante's own making in order to guide him out of it: *O donna in cui la mia speranza vige / e che soffristi per la mia salute / in inferno lasciar le tue vestige* ("O lady in whom my hope is strengthened, and who suffered [*soffristi* is informal second-person singular] for my well-being and salvation, leaving your [*tue*, again, informal second-person address] footprints in hell").[50] One last time, Dante is likening Beatrice's role in his life to that of Christ, who descended into Hell to save souls. His farewell address to Beatrice continues, using the informal second-person pronoun throughout:

Of all the things that I have seen, I recognize grace and virtue from your power and from your goodness. You have drawn me from servitude to liberty on no matter what the

49 *Purgatorio* XXX.39–47.
50 *Paradiso* XXXI.79–81.

path, using every means that you had in your power. Preserve your magnanimity in me so that my soul, which you restored to health, may release itself from my body at death in a condition that is pleasing to you.[51]

Why would Dante switch in this climactic scene to addressing Beatrice with the familiar *tu?* Obviously it is not because his deferential respect for her is diminished. Rather, perhaps the shift signals that, as Beatrice leaves off being his guide, as she has taken her seat among the beatified saints, she is now recalled one last time in Dante's writing as the historical woman or the immortal individual spirit whom Dante originally knew in his youth. That is, the informal *tu* may be a final human gesture of Dante toward the beloved of his youth. Alternatively, the informal pronoun *tu* may not signal a *closing* of the distance between Dante and Beatrice, but rather a widening of it, since *tu* is used in Italian for addresses to a saint, or in prayers offered to Christ or the Virgin Mary. Once again, then, even in Dante's most mature and exalted writing, Beatrice is both the young woman he knew in Florence and an exalted beatified spirit — the glorious lady of his mind.

---

51 *Paradiso* XXXI.82–90.

3

Dante, Orpheus, and the
Poem as Salutation

A S DANTE WRITES in his letter to Cangrande della Scala, his host in Verona to whom he dedicates *Paradiso:* "It must be understood that the meaning of this work [the *Divine Comedy*] is not of one kind only; rather the work may be described as *polysemous*."[1] We have seen in the introduction and the first two chapters how subtly and pervasively Dante weaves veiled or multiple meanings into his text. A further, interesting example of this is what Dante does with the myth of Orpheus and Eurydice — which in fact he never refers to anywhere in his writing. It is a conspicuous omission, given the theme in that myth, which Dante knew from Virgil, Ovid, and Boethius, of a visit to the *oltretomba*, or Otherworld.[2]

In this story from ancient Greece, Eurydice, the beloved of the musician-poet Orpheus, is bitten by a viper and dies and goes to the Underworld, or Hades. Orpheus journeys to the Underworld to retrieve her, where he sings and plays his music so beautifully that Hades and Persephone, the king and queen of the Underworld, allow him to take Eurydice back to the world of the living. But the condition for this release is that Orpheus must walk always in front of Eurydice and not look back until they both emerge into daylight. As Orpheus walks ahead, however, he turns around to make sure Eurydice is still there, so she vanishes back into the Underworld forever.

Dante never mentions the name Eurydice in his work, and only twice does he mention Orpheus. In the *Convivio*, he refers to Orpheus in the context of a discussion about the traditional four levels of interpretation: literal, allegorical, moral, and anagogical or mystical. Poetic allegory, says Dante, communicates truth by fiction that pleases the listener — *sotto bella menzogna*, beneath a beautiful lie — a craft at which Orpheus was especially skillful, charming even stones and plants with his song. The other mention of Orpheus in Dante's writings is in *Inferno*,

---

1   *Epistle* XIII.20 (ca. 1316).

2   In *Inferno*, Dante explicitly or implicitly compares himself to Theseus (IX.54) and Hercules (IX.98–99), who also made the descent to the underworld, but never to Orpheus.

where Orpheus is among the noble pagans in Limbo.[3] However, Dante never mentions Orpheus's love for Eurydice or his visit to Hades to bring her back to the land of the living. It is well known that Dante designed his poems down to their minute details. Why might he have left out at least a passing mention of this story that was so close to his own?

The scholar Guglielmo Gorni has suggested that Dante fails to mention the Orpheus-Eurydice myth because he sees himself as a new Orpheus rewriting and Christianizing the tale. An obvious sense in which Dante and Beatrice's story is different from Orpheus and Eurydice's is that the male-female roles are reversed: Dante is the poet-Orpheus for whose sake Eurydice-Beatrice descends to Hell, to save Dante, who is trapped in the dark wood of his own spiritual death. Beatrice, as Dante tells us in canto II of *Inferno*, was sent by St. Lucy, who in turn had been sent by the Virgin Mary, to tell Virgil to go to the Dark Wood to lead Dante on his journey. Also, the two stories have opposite outcomes. While Orpheus in the ancient story disobeys the one condition for his being reunited with Eurydice — he looks back at her as they are leaving the Underworld, so that he loses his soul completely — Dante is reunited with his beloved through his Christian faith and therefore is saved. This pattern suggests another way in which Dante reverses the Orpheus myth. Whereas the latter is a tragedy, Dante's narrative is a "comedy" in the medieval sense: it is written in the vernacular, and, contrary to tragedy, begins with misfortune and ends with redemption. At the same time, there are also parallels between the characters of Dante/Orpheus and Beatrice/Eurydice. As Gorni notes, the names *Eurydice* and *Beatrice* rhyme in Italian and have the same number of letters, just as *Dante* and *Orfeo* have five letters each; and Dante acts as Orpheus does in that he saves his Eurydice from eternal darkness by resurrecting Beatrice through his poetry.[4]

Such indirect associations between Orpheus's and Dante's stories might be taken as mere coincidences fancifully interpreted, if there were not blatant textual evidence in the *Comedy* itself that Dante is thinking about the Orpheus-Eurydice myth even as he does not explicitly mention it. The scene is in canto XXX of *Purgatorio*, where Dante is finally reunited with Beatrice in the Earthly Paradise after his

---

3 *Convivio* II.i.3–4; *Inferno* IV.140.

4 Guglielmo Gorni, introduction to the *Vita nova*, edited by Luca Carlo Rossi (Milan: Mondadori, 1999), v–xxxix.

descent into Hell and the ascent of Mount Purgatory. Virgil has just disappeared forever from the story, because Dante, purified through his ordeals in Hell and Purgatory, has outgrown his need for the Roman poet's guidance. As the embodiment of natural virtue and artistry that does not have access to the Logos, to Christian revelation, Virgil's task has been to lead Dante into the presence of Beatrice, who embodies the divine wisdom that will lead Dante through the heavenly spheres.

In the *Purgatorio* scene, Dante has just beheld Beatrice for the first time since their youth, so that *d'antico amor sentì la gran potenza*, he felt "the great force of the old love." He turns to tell Virgil that *men che dramma / di sangue m'è rimaso che non tremi: / conosco i segni de l'antica fiamma*, "not even a drop of my blood is left unshaken: I recognize the signs of the old flame" — lines which mimic the description of Dido's love for Aeneas in Virgil's *Aeneid*.[5] Dante continues, now echoing lines from Virgil's *Georgics*:

> *Virgilio n'avea lasciati scemi*
> *di sé, Virgilio dolcissimo patre,*
> *Virgilio a cui per mia salute die'mi.*[6]

(Virgil had left us deprived of him, Virgil the tenderest father, Virgil to whom I gave myself for the sake of my salvation.)

In the *Georgics* passage, Orpheus's voice, calling his lost Eurydice, resounds along the River Hebrus on which his severed head is floating. The name Eurydice is repeated three times there, just as Dante repeats Virgil's name three times.[7] In echoing the tragic separation of Orpheus and Eurydice, Dante's verses suggest a parallel between that bereavement and his own wrenching away from Virgil. As Gorni puts it, "In order not to lose Beatrice, Dante loses — he has no choice but to lose — Virgil,"[8] his master and highest poetic authority. He must let go

---

5 *Purgatorio* XXX.39, 46–48; *Aeneid* IV.22–23.

6 *Purgatorio* XXX.49–51.

7 *Eurydicen vox ipsa et frigida lingua / A miseram Eurydicen! anima fugiente vocabat, / Eurydicen toto referebant flumine ripae* ("[Orpheus's] voice of itself and his cold tongue called, 'Eurydice, O poor Eurydice!' with his fleeting breath, 'Eurydice,' the banks echoed all along the river") (*Georgics* IV.525–27).

8 Gorni, introduction to *Vita nova*, xxviii.

of his mortal Eurydice to gain another, immortal one. It is the price that Dante has to pay in order to become an Orpheus who is saved by Eurydice, reunited with her forever.

A few verses later in *Purgatorio*, Beatrice speaks to Dante for the first time since her death — beginning with his name, which, very significantly, is not mentioned anywhere else in the *Comedy:* "Dante, although Virgil is leaving now, do not cry yet, do not cry yet; because you will need your crying for another, greater affliction."[9] In this second triple invocation (repeating *piangere* or "cry" three times), Dante is echoing another passage from the Latin poets, this one in *Metamorphoses*, where Ovid's description of the dead Orpheus repeats the word *flebile* (mournful or sad) three times.[10] In contrast with the earlier invocation that echoes the *Georgics*, which put Dante in the position of the Orpheus who mourns Eurydice-Virgil, this one identifies Virgil with Orpheus, mourning his (spiritual?) death and departure. Dante intertwines his story with the Orpheus passages in Virgil and Ovid, not to create fixed correspondences between their respective characters, but to lead his readers into reflecting on symbolic parallels. So, in this pivotal scene of the *Comedy*, the myth of Orpheus-Eurydice leaves its traces even though it is never mentioned overtly. And of course, throughout *Inferno* and *Purgatorio*, Dante is clearly Orpheus-like in that he is a great poet who confronts supernatural ordeals in order to be reunited with his beloved.

Beatrice's vital role in Dante's imagination begins, as we have seen, in the *Vita nova*, whose central themes, as in the Orpheus-Eurydice story, are love, death, and bereavement. The *Vita nova* relates two major crises in Dante's life — two losses of Beatrice's blessing — just as Orpheus loses Eurydice twice to death's kingdom. Dante compensates for his loss by interiorizing his love for Beatrice, while Orpheus loses his love by nostalgically looking back. The first crisis for Dante is the absence of Beatrice's salutation, or greeting. In the conventions of courtly love the greeting of the beloved was the equivalent of being granted life. What is more, the Italian *saluto*, greeting, has the same etymological basis as

---

9 *Purgatorio* XXX.55–57.

10 ... *caput, Hebre, lyramque / Excipis et (mirum!) dum labitur amne, / Flebile nescio quid queritur lyra, flebile lingua / Murmurat exanimis, respondent flebile ripae* (*Metamorphoses* XI.50–53) ("Yet by a miracle the River Hebrus / Caught head and lyre as they dropped and carried them / Midcurrent down the stream. The lyre twanged sad strains, / The sad tongue sang; sad, the river banks and reeds / Echoed their music") (*The Metamorphoses*, translated by Horace Gregory [New York: Viking Press, 1958], trans. modified).

salvezza, salvation, and *salute*, health. So the Vulgate of Psalm 51 says, *Redde mihi laetitiam salutaris tui*. "Restore to me the joy of thy salvation"; and Christ is referred to in the Bible and in Christian tradition as *salus nostra*, "our health" or "our salvation." In Dante's prodigious symbolic imagination, then, the "greeting" of courtly love poetry had become yet another indication of the Christ-like nature of Beatrice.

In the *Vita nova*, Dante decides to praise Beatrice even though she is aloof and unattainable. The immediate poetic result of this decision is his first great canzone, *Donne ch'avete intelletto d'amore* ("Women who understand the truth of love"), which we looked at in chapter 1. In effect, then, the poem itself becomes the salutation that Dante has been denied. We have also seen a second crisis in Dante's devotion to Beatrice, her death at age twenty-four, and Dante's subsequent vacillation and confusion. As Patrick Boyde puts it, commenting on the *Vita nova*: "Paradise is twice lost from external causes, and twice regained through a deeper understanding of love coming from within."[11] Dante's love will survive Beatrice's physical death because she awakens interior knowledge in Dante, as her death and ascension to Heaven prefigure the movement of Dante's own individual soul in the *Comedy*.

So, we might say that Dante Christianizes the Orpheus-Eurydice story by overcoming absence and duality with love and faith. Most medieval commentators interpreted Orpheus's backward glance and subsequent loss of Eurydice as an emblem for temptation and the state of sin. Dante's treasured author Boethius was one of the early sources for this interpretation. For Boethius, Orpheus's lapse represents the worldly mind's inability to focus on essential reality.[12] In Dante's case, rather than resisting the backward glance at Beatrice-Eurydice he relocates the beloved: Beatrice is above, in Heaven, instead of behind him, below. Throughout *Inferno* and *Purgatorio* Dante is drawn toward purification by the promise of seeing Beatrice again. Separation is seen through by faith that praises the invisible source of love.

In fact, as will be discussed in more detail later in this chapter, the gnosis that Dante develops as a devotee of Amor *depends* on separation from Beatrice-Eurydice. This is a symbolic variation on the courtly love tradition of passion that had to remain unrequited or unconsummated.

---

11   Quoted in Stephen Bemrose, *A New Life of Dante* (Exeter: University of Exeter Press, 2000), 20.

12   *Consolation of Philosophy* III, m. 12.

Impossible, unrequited love, not marriage, was the ideal. It is desire, not its satisfaction, that is an analog of the soul's longing for God. With this in mind, Henry Corbin writes that the "prayer of the heliotrope" described by the Neoplatonist Proclus is an image of the lover's or pious person's devotion: the sunflower "prays" by inclining toward its "celestial prince," the sun, and this is "the *act* ... through which the invisible angel draws the flower toward him." In this way, "the Lord becomes known through his vassal," which, for a poet, surely means that the poem itself, and the technique that goes into its making, is the heliotrope's blossom: the poem is a form of prayer.[13] This is why, for Dante, the art of poetry is inextricably joined to his devotion to Beatrice, which in turn is inseparable from his religious faith. As we saw in the introduction, artistic technique in Dante is something sacred, an essential aspect of his spiritual praxis.

Dante's passion for verse forms and the art of poetry appears time and again in his works. It is clear that, unlike much theology of his time, he had high regard for poets and poetry, and would have rejected as missing the point any critique that reduces poetic craft to a utilitarian "vehicle" of doctrine or theology. As a matter of fact, Dante was never shy about vaunting his mastery of his medium per se, and often praised poets who did not have much to do with his vocation for philosophical and spiritual poetry but a lot to do with his art: Ovid, Lucan, Sordello, Arnaut Daniel, and others. The point is this: while Dante clearly *did* view his poetry as a vehicle for philosophical and theological as well as prophetic truth, he also viewed language itself and his crafting of it as an *embodiment* of that truth, not merely a superfluous container. To write imperishable verses in the ever-metamorphosing language of a particular time and place is to marry the contingent with the essential, the temporal with the eternal. His test as a poet was that there would be a unity between concept or doctrine and the verse form it took.

Dante's esteem for poetry anticipates Renaissance humanism. In choosing the greatest Roman poet as his guide through Hell and up Mount Purgatory — and Statius as his companion when Virgil is left behind — he was already at work on the fusion of classical and Christian cultures that would occupy the artists and scholars after him. His

13 Henry Corbin, *Alone with the Alone: Creative Imagination in the Sūfism of Ibn ʿArabī,* translated by Ralph Manheim (1969; repr., Princeton, NJ: Princeton University Press, 1997), 107.

admiration of naturalism or realism in art is another important anticipation of this cultural revolution. In the description of the Annunciation scene in *Purgatorio*, for example, where Dante and Virgil view
the bas-reliefs that illustrate examples of humility, Dante says that
the archangel Gabriel appeared so real that it seemed as if he had just
pronounced *Ave*, "Hail," and how the Virgin's face reflected the words
Ecce ancilla Dei, "Behold the handmaid of God."[14] Dante says that
the marble on which the bas-reliefs were carved was "decorated with
engravings such that not only Polycletus but Nature herself would pale
by comparison."[15] Such beauty came into being because the sculptor
of the work is God. There is no intermediary of Nature between God
and his art; his artworks emanate directly from the perfection of the
divine archetypes, the sign of which, for Dante, is their life-like realism.
Indeed, as we have seen, Dante's realism is a signature feature of his
work—even as his poetry is packed with symbolic significance. For
Dante, literal, everyday realities convey multiple layers of meaning.

So, despite his incomparable imaginative power, he chose to make
250 of the approximately 600 characters in the *Comedy* historical figures
from his own time; and many of these people were friends or acquain-
tances. The *Comedy* immediately places us in historical time—*nel mezzo
del cammin di nostra vita*, in the middle of our life. Dante here is
drawing on the biblical tradition that the typical human life span is
seventy years long; we know, then, that Dante-Everyman is thirty-five
years old at the beginning of the story. Later in *Inferno* the date is even
more precisely specified: Good Friday, April 8 (or, say some commentators, March 25), 1300, is when Dante and Virgil's descent begins. Hell
itself is a cone-shaped abyss directly beneath Jerusalem, along an axis
the other side of which is Mount Purgatory, an island in the watery
Southern Hemisphere. As chapters 8 and 9 of this book will elaborate,
no visionary narrative before or after places its protagonist—here, the
author himself—in such a specific time and place and in such concrete
circumstances. Dante's incarnational theology justifies this approach;
the Bible and the classical poets, especially Virgil, show him the way.

The historical emphasis in Dante anticipates our own era's historicist
tendencies, as does his choice of writing the *Comedy* in the vernacular.
For these reasons, the American poet Robert Duncan called Dante "the

---

14 *Purgatorio* x.40–45.
15 *Purgatorio* x.31–33.

first of modern poets," purifying the language of his tribe to such an extent that Florentine dialect (which became the model for modern Italian) was "the first language in modern poetry."[16] Dante's writing in Florentine dialect offended the sensibilities of some of Dante's immediate successors, early humanists such as Petrarch, who believed that great themes should be written about in Latin, not in the common tongue. But the decision to write in the vernacular was pivotal in Dante's life as a poet. He wanted — as he says at the start of the *Convivio* — to write so that everyone could understand and benefit from his work. Dante was by no means a "populist" in the trite sense, but he loved the common tongue of his *patria* with a passion, so much so that he said that the *volgare* in general, not just that of Florence, was nobler than any language acquired through conscious study — for the vernacular is rooted in our birth and destiny.[17]

Dante is not a realist in the contemporary understanding of realism, since he views art as a copy of God's offspring, Nature, and Nature as the archetypal pattern existing in the mind of God, not the externalized object of empirical investigation. Nevertheless, his manner of maintaining this distinction differed considerably from that of his medieval predecessors. As mentioned, many characters in the *Comedy* were historical figures from Dante's own time, some of whom would have been personally known by his audience — a tactic no postclassical writer had attempted. The attraction to precision and detail in individual portraiture had appeared for the first time about a century before Dante's birth, in the figures of the western portal at Chartres. Gothic sculpture, the art of Duccio, Giovanni Pisano, Cimabue, and Dante's contemporary Giotto: these are instances of a new vision of the human being, no longer as a type but as a concrete individual.

So, although Dante was indeed a prophetic voice of the Christian tradition, he was so in terms that were suited to a new age. Another sense in which Dante was a forerunner of the Renaissance was his attitude toward ancient myth, different from that of most medieval Christian writers. The theologians had often been dismissive or hostile toward Greco-Roman myths, notes William Anderson, while Dante's

---

16   Robert Duncan, "The Sweetness and Greatness of Dante's *Divine Comedy*," in *The Poets' Dante: Twentieth-Century Responses,* edited by Peter S. Hawkins and Rachel Jacoff (New York: Farrar, Straus & Giroux, 2001), 195.

17   See the opening of *De vulgari eloquentia.*

"rediscovery of the inner psychological and mystical meanings of pagan mythology, anticipated and prepared the ground for the makers of the Renaissance."[18] Whereas Augustine says in *City of God* that the old gods of Rome were demons, Dante in the *Convivio* equates the pagan gods with the angels or celestial Intelligences, and says about the great historical pagans of ancient Rome: "Certain and evident it must be, recalling the lives of these ... divine citizens, that not without some light of the divine goodness, over and above the goodness of their own nature, were there so many miraculous actions."[19] It is true that the demon-guardians of Dante's Hell (Charon, Minos, Plutus, etc.) are mythological figures from pagan mythology, but Dante presents them, by and large, like the goddess Fortuna, as agents of God's justice, not rebels against it.

An essential aspect of Dante's passion for the art of poetry, and another way that he anticipates Renaissance thought, is his exaltation of poetry as a means to truth. The *Comedy* is an implicit challenge to Augustine's and later theologians' negative view of poetry's epistemological validity. This tradition had denied that imaginative literature may be a valid means to truth, since the former is overly reliant on the senses and tends to fire the emotions rather than, as with philosophy or theology, foster mental tranquility and detachment. Thomas Aquinas accordingly argued that there is a shortage of truth (*defectus veritatis*) in poetry. Through his Augustinian appreciation of scriptural poetics, he acknowledges that sacred scripture communicates through metaphor, and that it employs poetic language to communicate fundamental truths, but he compares poetic fiction unfavorably to theology since by its nature poetry resists abstraction and speculative thought.[20] Dante's attitude on this subject, however, is closer to that of the early Renaissance humanists: Albertino Mussato, for instance, who says that poets were the theologians of ancient times; Boccaccio, who in his life of Dante praises poetry as theology; or Cristoforo Landino, who places poetry as the highest of liberal arts.

---

18   William Anderson, *Dante the Maker* (London: Hutchinson, 1983), 322.

19   *Convivio* IV.v.17.

20   See, e.g., Paul Murray, "Aquinas on Poetry and Theology," *Logos: A Journal of Catholic Thought and Culture* 16, no. 2 (Spring 2013): 63–72; Jacques Maritain, "Concerning Poetic Knowledge," in *The Situation of Poetry* (New York: Philosophical Library, 1968); and chapters 11 and 12 of Ernst Robert Curtius, *European Literature and the Latin Middle Ages*, translated by Willard R. Trask (1951; repr., London: Routledge and Kegan Paul, 1979).

Importantly, Dante's affirmation of poetry as a way to truth is related to his application of traditional methods of Bible interpretation to the *Comedy*. Dante insists on the distinction between allegory as it is practiced by the poets—the "beautiful lie" he mentions in the *Convivio* passage cited earlier—and allegory as it is used by theologians. Theological allegory is what Dante says he had in mind for the *Comedy*. He makes this claim in his letter to Cangrande, where, writes Robert Hollander, Dante "puts forward the disturbing (to use a mild word) idea that [his] poem was written with the same keys to meaning as was the Bible."[21] This is important for the present discussion because "the principal tenet of theological allegory is that it holds certain (but not all) historical events in the Bible as a privileged and limited class of texts.... Dante has adapted the techniques of theological allegory to the making of his poem. Characters and events in it are portrayed in a historical mode and as part of a historical continuum."[22] The reason Dante did this, again, was to affirm "the 'right' of ['lay'] poetry to truth." Dante could either

> admit that poets are literally liars who nonetheless tell moral and philosophical truths through (poets') allegory, or he had to find a new answer to the attacks on poetry by friars like Thomas. Typically, he went his own way. If religious detractors of poetry say it lacks truth, he will give them truth. The *Comedy* is presented, from end to end (no reader can possibly miss this fact), as a record of an actual experience.... Since the pretext of the poem is that he indeed saw all that he recounts as having seen, his own experience, in completely Thomistic spirit, comes first.[23]

For this reason, two-dimensional allegorical interpretations of Dante (e.g., "Beatrice" = "Theology") miss the point.[24] As Hollander says, "What is allegory? Simply put, it is the interpretive strategy of

---

21 Robert Hollander, introduction to *Inferno*, translated by Robert and Jean Hollander (New York: Anchor Books, 2000), xxxi.

22 Ibid., xxxi–xxxii.

23 Ibid., xxxii–xxxiii.

24 Approximately a quarter of commentators in the first couple of centuries of Dante commentary interpreted Virgil as reason; and in English too, the Temple Classics edition of the *Comedy* interprets him as "Worldly Wisdom."

understanding one thing as meaning not itself but something other."[25] This was the method of reading Dante that the earliest commentators established, in keeping with that age's predilections, and it has often been followed by subsequent commentators. Hollander admits that

> since something like this [medieval allegorical method] does seem to occur in the course of the poem, we can sense why the formulation has its appeal. The problem is that it short-changes the entire historical referentiality of the poem.... The reader is not asked by the poem to see Virgil as Reason, Beatrice as Faith (or Theology or Revelation), Francesca as Lust, Farinata as Heresy, etc. We may banish such abstractions from mind, unless Dante himself insists on them.[26]

And in fact, if we read without preconceptions, Virgil at times appears more allegorical than at other times, and Beatrice likewise.[27] Allegorical method never does away with their presence as historical figures—Virgil the poet-prophet mentor of Dante's adulthood, Beatrice the beloved of Dante's youth. In this way, Dante restores poetry to its Homeric, classical directness. He writes on the highest theological and metaphysical themes, but does so with the physical immediacy and realism of the ancient Greeks and Romans. Hollander adds: "It is important to grasp that, by breaking out of the lockstep of other poets, who give us narratives that are utterly and only fabulous, i.e., patently untrue in their literal sense, Dante wanted to take poetry somewhere new."[28] No wonder, then, that he chose Virgil as guide, given the high theme and vivid physical immediacy of the *Aeneid*.

---

25 Hollander, introduction to *Inferno*, xxix.

26 Ibid., xxx, xxxiii.

27 See, for example, Virgil's bungled negotiations with the demon-guardians, such as the rebel angels at the Gates of Dis (*Inferno*, canto IX) or the demons in the *bolgia* of the barraters (canto XXI). Virgil as reason is shown in these scenes to be deficient without divine grace, and to that extent he is allegorical. But Dante and Virgil in these passages become comic-realistic characters as well, as, for instance, when Virgil speaks in an uncharacteristically popular ("comic") register when he realizes he was fooled by the demon Malacoda: *Mal contava la bisogna / colui che i peccator di qua uncina* ("The one who gives sinners the hook over here didn't tell it straight"); *Inferno* XXIII.140–41. There is no doubt that, in Hell at least, Dante can have a wicked sense of humor.

28 Hollander, introduction to *Inferno*, xxxiii.

Another justification for Dante's emphasis on literal, historical detail is his emanationist theology. As mentioned earlier, the emanationist view depicts a hierarchy of being that connects all levels of creation, from the lowest life forms to the highest angels. For Bonaventure, the world is a ladder for ascending to God and the mind ascends through three modes, corresponding to the Trinity: it sees God through the outer body, its sees God within itself, and it sees God above itself. The first of these modes, in which the sensible world is perceived as a mirror-reflection of God, would validate for Dante the attention paid to the literal and the historical.

In addition, the realism of Dante may be viewed in terms of the Aristotelian notion of the *habitus*. The *habitus* refers to an acquired yet entrenched state of moral character that orients our feelings and desires in a situation, and therefore influences our conduct. As Erich Auerbach writes, the *habitus*

> is an acquired attribute, not the substance of man himself, but an enduring disposition which enriches and modifies the substance; it is the residuum in man's soul of his soul's history.... Dante was the first thinker-poet since antiquity to believe in the unity of the personality, in the concordance of body and soul; and so it was that reason reinforced his power to portray a man in the attitude and gesture which most fully sum up and most clearly manifest the totality of his *habitus*.... What radically distinguishes the *Comedy* from all other visions of the other world is that in it the unity of man's earthly personality is preserved and fixed; the scene of action thus becomes the source of its poetic value, of its infinite truth, of the quality of direct empirical evidence which makes us feel that everything that happens in the work is real and credible.

Thus, even in her transfigured state, "Beatrice retains her distinctly earthly form."[29] I cannot read these words of Auerbach without recalling Yeats's lines from "Broken Dreams," where the poet imagines Maud Gonne in old age and then in the afterlife, hoping that, even there, she

29 Erich Auerbach, *Dante: Poet of the Secular World*, translated by Ralph Manheim, foreword by Michael Dirda (New York: New York Review of Books, 2001), 85–86, 90.

will "Leave unchanged / The hands that I have kissed, / For old sake's sake." As Auerbach memorably puts it: in Dante, "earthly particularity [is] held fast in the mirror of a timeless eye."[30] Dante's belief in the "concordance of body and soul," and therefore his movement away from the generalities of medieval allegory, prefigure the even greater development of this movement in later authors such as Shakespeare, as the Bard abandoned the allegorical trappings of his early plays.

> ✶ ✶

But we have digressed. What does all of this have to do with Dante's veiled allusion to the Orpheus-Eurydice story, with which this chapter began? We can only speculate, but it is clear that while other figures of antiquity — Aeneas and St. Paul — were explicit predecessors to Dante's visionary journey, the Orpheus story is a submerged current in Dante's narrative. Orpheus in ancient and medieval commentary was often seen as representing the civilizing effect of poetry and eloquence. Aquinas, for example, called him a philosopher-theologian who brought the light of intellect to darkened minds. Dante writes within this tradition when he states that Orpheus has the power to make "cruel hearts mild and humble, and move . . . at will those who have no life of knowledge and art."[31] He makes this statement in a work, the *Convivio*, which he says he is composing for those who have not had the opportunity to seek knowledge, so even here his mention of Orpheus is also an oblique allusion to himself. A variant on the reading of the Orpheus-Eurydice story as an allegory for the relation between knowledge and art was given by Fulgentius in the fifth century and by John Scotus Eriugena in the ninth. These philosophers interpreted Eurydice as representing profound insight into the music which Orpheus himself, like the inspired rhapsode in Plato's *Ion*, could not comprehend. Orpheus, according to them, retained "musical sound without its cause" — his music did not give him knowledge (gnosis) or wisdom.[32] Fulgentius states that "Orpheus is [so] called from *orea fone*, that is, 'best voice,' while Eurydice is 'profound judgment.'"[33] As

30 Ibid., 68.

31 *Convivio* II.i.4.

32 Susan Boynton, "The Sources and Significance of the Orpheus Myth," *Early Music History* 18 (1999): 60.

33 R. Helm, ed., *Fabii Planciadis Fulgentii v. c. opera* (Leipzig: Teubner, 1898), 77.

one scholar comments: "These two... represented two aspects of the art of music—the power of words to move the listener, and the more mystical harmony of tones."[34] Dante and Beatrice, too, can be seen as representing voice (or song) and judgment (or wisdom). Perhaps, if we join the parts of Fulgentius's interpretation, we might say that Dante views himself as the Orpheus who *does* combine gnosis with his music.[35]

From the *Vita nova* on, Dante's challenge is to remember *il ben de l'intelletto*, the good of the intellect, which ultimately is God, the very thing the damned have lost. What does this recollection involve for Dante? Recalling the source of his love, rejecting all idols for the one icon of the face of the Beloved. Not until Dante is reunited with Beatrice in the Earthly Paradise and has cleansed his most indelible sins in Lethe, and has drunk the waters of Eunoë, restoring memory of his primordial nature, will he be free of the danger of forgetting Beatrice by mistaking the object of his love. What Corbin says of Ibn 'Arabī applies to Dante's experience as well:

> Beauty is the theophany par excellence... not a purely aesthetic pleasure accompanied by a joyful tonality but with the contemplation of human beauty as a *numinous*, sacral phenomenon which inspires fear and anguish by arousing a movement toward something which at once precedes and transcends the object in which it is manifested, something of which the mystic gains awareness only if he achieves the conjunction, the conspiration... of the spiritual and the sensory, constitutive of mystic love.[36]

So, Dante is the Orpheus who never really loses his Eurydice precisely because he knows she is always here, in life itself, which is to say she is also in the poetry through which she gives her salutation.

---

34 John Block Friedman, *Orpheus in the Middle Ages* (Syracuse, NY: Syracuse University Press, 2000), 89.

35 Although Dante's direct knowledge of Fulgentius and Eriugena is unknown, it is probable that he would be familiar with their ideas from the numerous commentaries in circulation. See Robert M. Durling and Ronald L. Martinez, *Time and the Crystal: Studies in Dante's Rime Petrose* (Berkeley: University of California Press, 1990), 54.

36 Corbin, *Alone with the Alone*, 274.

4

The Dream of Leah and Rachel

JUST BEFORE DANTE and his guides the poets Virgil and Statius enter the Earthly Paradise at the summit of Mount Purgatory, Dante has a dream. It is his third and final dream in *Purgatorio*, all of them occurring just before dawn. This is the hour, Dante reminds us, for visionary dreams: ones that alert us to essential reality in symbolic form.[1]

In this dream-vision, he sees a beautiful young woman who is gathering spring flowers in a meadow. As she walks along and picks the flowers, Dante hears the words of a song she is singing. The lyrics of the song say that her name is Leah. Still singing, Leah adds that she uses her supple hands to weave a garland of flowers, with which she adorns herself so that she will be pleased at what she sees when she looks in her mirror. Her sister, Rachel, she continues, never tires of gazing into her *own* mirror, which she does all day long, day after day. Leah's song and Dante's dream conclude with these words: "She [Rachel] desires to see her own lovely eyes as I [Leah] do to adorn myself with my hands; seeing [or vision] is her delight, doing [or working] is mine."

Given the timing of this dream, just before Dante enters the Earthly Paradise, it almost certainly is meant to encapsulate something about that place or state of being. Many commentators have interpreted Leah and Rachel, respectively, as representing Matelda (the mysterious figure whom Dante will encounter in the Earthly Paradise) and Beatrice. But others have pointed out that Beatrice's dwelling place is the Celestial Paradise, while Matelda certainly does exhibit characteristics of the women of Dante's dream.

Leah and Rachel in the Bible are the wives of the prophet Jacob. In Christian tradition, Leah is a figure for the active life, the life of doing, while Rachel is a figure for the contemplative or interior life.[2] Clearly, Dante's dream imagery refers to this tradition. We also note that Leah is practicing an art — she is weaving a garland. According

---

1 *Purgatorio* XXVII.94–108.

2 Importantly, Dante places Rachel next to Beatrice in the Empyrean (*Paradiso* XXXII.8).

to the scholastic thought that informs Dante, art is a virtue or power of the practical intellect, a *knowledge* about how to order materials, in this case flowers, to *make* something, here a garland. That Rachel represents contemplation or vision, we can confirm in a passage of the *Convivio*. Dante uses mirror imagery there to convey the nature of true philosophical speculation or contemplation. He writes that the philosophizing soul "not only contemplates the truth, but, moreover, contemplates its own contemplation and the beauty of that contemplation as well, turning back upon itself and falling in love with itself through the beauty of its first gaze."[3] It is interesting to apply this passage to the image Dante gives several times of the beatified spirits in *Paradiso*, who spin around their own axes like tops or millstones, a rotary motion suggestive of the inward gaze of contemplation.[4]

The word *speculation* is related to Latin for mirror, *speculum*. Commentators have often noted Dante's use of mirror symbolism, especially in passages where Beatrice's eyes are mirrors for visionary states. When he and Beatrice reach the Primum Mobile, in a passage referred to in the introduction to this book, he sees the angelic hierarchies as concentric circles reflected in her eyes, first appearing as a brilliant light. Following a Christian tradition that goes back at least to Pseudo-Dionysius, Dante pictures the angelic hierarchies as mirrors of the divine light, and they in turn are reflected in Beatrice's eyes. In the introduction, I described the simile in this *Paradiso* passage of a man who is looking at a candle flame in a mirror, and turns to see that the candle actually *is* there, behind him. Significantly, the candle flame is what enables the man in the simile to see himself in the mirror; he is illuminated by it from behind and thus made visible. His image is made manifest by the reflected light. It is possible that Dante, who often works on several symbolic levels at once, intended this complex figure as a metaphor for the relationship between divine-archetypal forms and created things.

Some close readers of Dante have seen mirrors as an organizing principle in *Paradiso*; as Simon Gilson has put it, there is "a hierarchy of *specula* from the mirror of nature to the mirror of God."[5] Here, the

---

3   *Convivio* IV.ii.18.

4   See, e.g., *Paradiso* XVIII.40–42 and XXI.79–81.

5   Simon Gilson, "Light Reflection, Mirror Metaphors, and Optical Framing in Dante's *Comedy*: Precedents and Transformations," *Neophilologus* 83 (1999): 242, referring to studies on this topic.

mirror is the human soul itself—which is the place, say the theologians, human beings can come to see God. Late in *Paradiso*, Beatrice tells Dante that God is a unity who breaks into countless mirrors yet who always remains one.[6] The contemplative gaze is in love with these mirrors, and for Dante, contemplation is the basis of all art and making. Art requires discernment into the true nature of the thing to be made or represented. As Dante says in the *Convivio*, the artist who wants to represent something "must first perfectly be within that thing's being."[7] Therefore some kind of direct seeing relatively undisturbed by the artist's ego is inherent to it. As Virgil reminds Dante in *Purgatorio*, the person who is distracted by one thought springing from another, in an endless concatenation of associations, loses sight of the *segno* or goal of the spiritually integrated life.[8] The artist needs a steadier gaze.

Also fundamental to the idea of art in Dante's culture is the notion that *all* work and making—not just what we call art today—is the practice of art, by which human beings, made in the image of God, further reflect that image. Dante states this parallel between divine art and human art quite explicitly at the beginning of canto x of *Paradiso*, where the reader is urged to gaze on the cosmic order. The annual path of the sun in relation to the earth, Dante notes with wonder, is so perfectly angled that it enables the succession of the seasons and makes life itself possible on earth. And the cause of this wondrous order is "the art which that master [God] loves within himself" so much that he never takes his eye off what comes into being in this manner.[9] In other words, the creation itself is the result of the art that arises from the loving, contemplative gaze of God. Human art is a faint reflection of this ontological and metaphysical reality.

In Dante's dream, Leah and Rachel combined can be seen as figures for artistic mastery. Note that Leah too, after she has made the garland, looks into a mirror. The two feminine figures constitute a continual cycle between contemplation and doing, knowing and making. Dante commentators recognize that this dream, which occurs shortly before the dramatic scenes in the Earthly Paradise, represents the perfecting

6 *Paradiso* XXIX.144–45.
7 *Convivio* IV.x.8.
8 *Purgatorio* V.16–18.
9 *Paradiso* X.10–12.

of the active and contemplative lives necessary for regaining that Paradise. I have not seen any mention, however, of an implied association between this active and contemplative perfection and artistic mastery, understood in the broad sense I have sketched. Yet this association is striking when we note that the dream of Leah and Rachel occurs, not only just *before* Dante's arrival in the Earthly Paradise, but just *after* a series of cantos that feature Dante's meetings with a number of poets who represent his own development in the art of poetry.

We will look at the poet-and-poetry episodes a bit later on in this chapter. For now, I would like to note that one key scene takes place between Dante's dream and his entry into the Earthly Paradise. In this scene, Virgil tells Dante that, because his will has been purified, it would be wrong now *not* to follow it. Since Virgil's declaration of Dante's newly purified state comes directly after the dream of Leah and Rachel, a connection is implied between the two: art and contemplation on one hand and self-purification on the other. As we have seen, in Dante's understanding, all art and making requires that the mirror of the artist's soul be polished; the artist cannot represent an object if his or her mind does not grasp the essential reality of the thing to be represented.[10] This idea is common among visionary artists and poets. Wordsworth points out that the poet does not write from emotion per se, but from emotion recollected in tranquility. William Blake argues that a condition for inspiration is the removal of the delusory state of the ego he calls "the Spectre." He describes this process in his poem *Milton*:

> . . . a false Body, an Incrustation over my Immortal
> Spirit, a Selfhood which must be putt off & annihilated alway.
> To cleanse the Face of my Spirit by Self-examination,
> To bathe in the Waters of Life, to wash off the Not Human.[11]

10   See *Convivio* IV.x.8, 10. In scholastic thought the *intentio*, the idea or representation of a subject, is prefigured in the artist's imagination. The idea is that an artist cannot represent an object if his or her mind is not first assimilated or conformed to the species of that object. See Aristotle, *Metaphysics* VII.8, 1033b.22–24. Prominent medieval thinkers such as Roger Bacon likened the rational soul disfigured by sin to a rusty mirror in which the truth of things cannot be seen; the practice of virtue, then, was the polishing of this mirror.

11   *Milton* I, plate 40, lines 35–37, to plate 41, line 1; in *Blake: Complete Writings*, edited by Geoffrey Keynes (Oxford: Oxford University Press, 1966), 533.

The "Not Human" is the spectral self or ego. Both Blake and Dante teach that when the doors of perception are cleansed of ego projections we naturally see God everywhere and see all things in God. This liberated vision is what Dante describes in the Earthly Paradise. As he puts it early on in the narrative there, the Earthly Paradise is given by God as the pledge or bond of Heaven.[12] If we think of art (in the broad sense) itself as the Earthly Paradise, this statement recalls the words of Blake, that poetry, painting, and music are means for "conversing with Paradise" in the present age.

In some passages in his writings, Dante refers to the state of inward receptivity as the good disposition of the material on which the spirit may do its work. In the *Convivio*, for example, he says that the

> divine goodness descends into all things, or else they could not exist; but although this goodness springs from the simplest principle, it is variously received, either more or less, by the things that receive it.... "The Primal Goodness bestows his benefits and gifts on things in a single stream." Indeed, each thing receives from that stream in accordance with the mode of its power and being.[13]

The great opening of *Paradiso* says the same thing: that the glory of the One who sets everything into motion penetrates the universe, shining in some parts more and in others less. In human work or art, the material that is penetrated more or less by this light is the mind or soul of the artist or worker. Self-mastery and self-purification prepare the soul so that *Deus artifex*, God the Artist—who in Christian thought is ultimately the only artist there is—may work upon and through the human artist.[14] At the same time, immersion in our work is vital to our self-transformation and self-realization. This idea is common to many traditions. The *Bhagavad Gita*, for example, says that self-realization comes about by devotion to the work that harmonizes with one's true nature.[15] Plato in *The Republic* even argues that this is the basis of a

---

12 *Purgatorio* XXVIII.93.

13 *Convivio* III.vii.2, quoting *De causis* (On Causes).

14 On *Deus artifex*, see Ernst Robert Curtius, *European Literature and the Latin Middle Ages*, translated by Willard R. Trask (1951; repr., London: Routledge and Kegan Paul, 1979), 543–46.

15 *Bhagavad Gita* III.15–35, XVIII.13–48.

just society. For a Christian like Dante, however, being in the state of original sin means that, from early on in life, the material of our human nature is poorly disposed to the influx of grace.

In the Western hermetic tradition, some have spoken of two phases of the purification or transformation of the soul, the so-called lesser mysteries and greater mysteries. Initiation into the lesser mysteries leads to self-*integration*, where the soul is restored to its essential or primordial state, while the greater mysteries lead to self-*transcendence*. The lesser mysteries enable contemplation of the inner essences or principles of created things—hence their relevance to the work of the artist. The greater mysteries lead to contemplation of God and the spiritual Intelligences. In Dante, the Earthly Paradise on top of Mount Purgatory can be seen as an image of initiation into the lesser mysteries; his vision in the Empyrean or highest Heaven, the climax of *Paradiso*, depicts the greater mysteries. In his treatise on monarchy, Dante describes these two stages of initiation in Christian-Aristotelian terms:

> Ineffable providence has set before us two goals to aim at: happiness in this life, which consists in the exercise of our own powers and is figured in the Earthly Paradise; and happiness in the eternal life, which consists in the enjoyment of the vision of God (to which our own powers cannot raise us except with the help of God's light) and which is signified by the Celestial Paradise.[16]

The climactic scene in cantos XXIX and XXX of *Purgatorio*, in the Earthly Paradise, includes a sacred allegorical procession, which recapitulates Christian history and culminates with the appearance of Beatrice in a carriage drawn by a Griffin. The pageantry of the sacred procession is a revelation of sacred art. It includes many products of artistry: chanting, metal work, dance, solemn choreography, drama, symbolic clothing, and so on. Dante greatly slows down the pace of his narration to describe the procession, in effect at time-lapse speed, in order to get us to share in the sense of revelation and wonder. To use a phrase from the visionary painter Cecil Collins's definition of sacred ritual, the procession in the Earthly Paradise enacts "kinetic participation in

---

16 *Monarchia* III.xvi.7.

incomprehensible reality."[17] This is a striking way to put it, and it nicely describes all truly soulful activity or work, approached with imagination.

The revelation of Beatrice in the Earthly Paradise first appears as a bright flash of light that permeates the forest.[18] Still unaware of what is about to take place, Dante hears a melody drifting in the bright air, exquisite music which he refers to as *ineffabili delizie*, ineffable delights, as well as *primizie / de l'etterno piacer*, the first anticipations of the Celestial Paradise. Right after this, Dante sees that the flashing light has drawn closer. The air under and around the branches of the trees becomes bright like fire, and the sweet sound of the melody has clarified into distinct human voices singing in a chorus. Dante sees what he thinks are golden trees in motion. Next, he realizes that the dazzling trees are actually seven golden candelabras and that the singing voices are uttering a specific word: a joyous *hosanna*.[19] This is the word in the Gospels that the adoring crowds exclaim when Jesus enters Jerusalem on his donkey, with olive and palm branches scattered in his path.[20] Dante immediately follows these lines with an invocation of the Muses, asking for inspiration so that he may put into verse things that are difficult to comprehend. He reminds the Muses of his long and arduous labor at the art of poetry, for which he often went hungry and was cold and awake at all hours of the night. After the invocation, Dante sees the first figures in the procession: twenty-four elders dressed in white who represent the twenty-four books of the Old Testament. As the seven candelabras pass by they leave behind seven long, wide strips of color, their brilliance painting the air high above like a rainbow.[21] And the great allegorical pageant continues to

17 "Why Does Today's Art Lack Inspiration?" in *Meditations, Poems, Pages from a Sketchbook*, edited by Brian Keeble (Ipswich: Golgonooza Press, 1997), 83.

18 For the following, see *Purgatorio* XXIX.16ff.

19 The mistaken perception (referred to as *l'obietto comun*, or "common object," in *Purgatorio* XXIX.47) alludes to a concept from scholastic philosophy, the so-called common sensibles — movement, rest, number, shape, dimension — which are more likely to cause errors of perception than one of these alone. So, for example, a newspaper blowing in the distance may appear to be a cat until we are up close. The movement, shape, and so on, had been interpreted wrongly. On an allegorical level, says the fifteenth-century commentator Cristoforo Landino, this indicates that the mind often is deceived in its conclusions when it is far away from the principles which make accurate judgment possible.

20 Matthew 21:9.

21 These seven colors are usually interpreted allegorically as the seven Gifts of the Holy Spirit: Wisdom, Intellect, Counsel, Strength, Knowledge, Piety, and Fear of God (named by Dante in *Convivio* IV.xxi.12). It has been suggested that the vivid visual

unfold from there. All of this is a prelude to the arrival of Beatrice, who is announced with words from the Song of Songs in praise of divine Wisdom or Sophia, the bride of God.[22] Her appearance reminds Dante of Christ's second coming, when the dead will leap from their graves, singing *Alleluia!* She is compared to the rising of the sun, a familiar figure for the advent of Christ in the mind through sanctifying grace.

Icons are images that lead our intellect to the sacred reality behind those images. A saint or holy person, therefore, is a living icon, and in this scene in *Purgatorio* and elsewhere in Dante's writings, Beatrice herself clearly is an icon of sorts. At the same time it is also accurate to say that unlike the icon, Beatrice herself *is*, at times at least, that sacred reality itself.[23] As mentioned earlier, ever since his early work the *Vita nova*, Dante has depicted her as the *speculum Christi*, the mirror of Christ, and the apotheosis of his art.

In the cantos leading up to Dante's dream of Leah and Rachel and the scene in Earthly Paradise, Dante encounters a number of poets who were significant to him in the development of his art. Each of the poets is undergoing purification for a sin of the flesh — avarice or prodigality, gluttony, or lust. Dante and Virgil encounter five poets in these cantos: the first-century Roman poet Statius; a close poet-friend of Dante in his youth, Forese Donati; the Tuscan poet Bonagiunta da Lucca; the Bolognese poet and immediate predecessor of Dante, Guido Guinizzelli; and the Provençal poet Arnaut Daniel. All of these poets represent different facets of Dante's long apprenticeship to his craft. To better appreciate the connection between self-purification and artistic mastery that is implied in these scenes, I will outline what happens in them.

The first poet who appears is Statius, reinvented by Dante as a late convert to Christianity. Dante pictures Statius as one of the souls saved by Virgil's prophecy of the birth of a child who will usher in a new golden age of peace and harmony. Many in Dante's time interpreted

---

imagery in this scene was influenced by particular works of art that Dante certainly had seen — the mosaics of Sant'Apollinare Nuovo in Ravenna, for example. See Anna Maria Chiavacci Leonardi, introduction to *Purgatorio* xxix, p. 851.

22 *Purgatorio* xxx.11ff. for this scene. On these closing cantos of *Purgatorio*, see Charles S. Singleton, *Journey to Beatrice* (Baltimore: Johns Hopkins University Press, 1977); and Lino Pertile, *La puttana e il gigante: Dal "Cantico dei cantici" al Paradiso terrestre di Dante* (Ravenna: Longo, 1998).

23 See, to give just one example, *Paradiso* xviii.21, where Beatrice's eyes are an aspect of Paradise, not merely a sign of it.

this passage in Virgil's *Eclogues* as his unconscious anticipation of the coming of Christ. In *Purgatorio*, Statius also explains that a passage in the *Aeneid* about the devastating effects of the excessive love of luxury and possessions saved him from his formerly extravagant lifestyle.[24]

Just before Statius appears in the narrative, early in canto XXI, Dante is gripped by curiosity over why, at the end of the previous canto, an earthquake had rocked the mountain. Suddenly, Dante says, he notices a shade walking with him and Virgil. The shade is Statius, who has appeared seemingly out of nowhere, the way the resurrected Christ appeared to the apostles on the road to Emmaus. The shaking of the mountain was caused, Dante learns, by the passing of Statius's soul to a higher level, signifying spiritual advancement. The pious spirits on the mount rejoiced over Statius's newfound freedom, and their loud celebration shook the mountain. Statius had been prostrate on the terrace of the avaricious and prodigal for five hundred years, but his release was sudden. As he says, the will immediately and spontaneously rises once it is purified, since the soul is simply returning to its heart's desire, its inherent state of freedom and joy.

It is clear from details in this episode that Dante identifies with Statius in various ways. He was not made a Christian by Virgil, as Statius was, but Virgil's example made Statius a poet capable of writing about gods and men — an epic poet, in short.[25] Both Dante and Statius learned from Virgil how to use poetry to evoke noble human emotions, such as piety and compassion. Statius tells his two poet-companions that the main model for his sweet verses was none other than Virgil's *Aeneid*, without which he would not have amounted to much. At first, Statius in this scene doesn't realize that Virgil is standing right in front of him. The passage where Statius reacts to finding out that Virgil himself is present is one of the most humanly touching scenes in the *Divine Comedy*. As Statius attempts to embrace Virgil's feet, Virgil admonishes him with the beautiful words, *Frate, / non far, ché tu se' ombra e ombra vedi*, "Brother, do not do that, for you are a shade and a shade is what you are seeing." To which Statius responds with the equally lovely,

---

24 *Purgatorio* XXII.40–41.

25 As Dante has Statius say in *Purgatorio* XXI.126. On line 90 of the same canto, Statius explains that early on he had merited (through his love poems) to be crowned with myrtle, which was for love poets, while laurel would have been for poets of greater weight.

Or puoi la quantitate
comprender de l'amor ch'a te mi scalda,
quand' io dismento nostra vanitate,
trattando l'ombre come cosa salda.[26]

(Now you can understand the extent to which my love for
you warms me, when I forget our emptiness, treating shades
as a solid thing.)

The affectionate exchange between the poets is rather surprising
and even nonsensical if we limit ourselves to the old interpretation of
Virgil as an allegory for human reason or the natural intelligence. It
is true that Dante explicitly associates Virgil with reason and Beatrice
with faith, in *Purgatorio* and elsewhere,[27] but he never explicitly *limits*
Virgil's narrative function to that. If reason and natural intelligence
were all of Virgil's allegorical role, it would have been more appropriate
for Dante to have chosen, for example, Aristotle as his guide through
Hell and up Mount Purgatory. When Dante encounters Virgil at the
beginning of *Inferno*, he does not describe him as the master who
taught him how to reason; rather, he refers to Virgil as the poet-mentor
from whom he learned the style that made Dante a great poet—again,
something that Statius also says.[28]

Virgil in Dante's time was viewed as a poet-prophet, a sage, even a
magician, as well as the supreme master of poetic style. If we consider
the Earthly Paradise as the culmination of the lesser mysteries, Virgil
would be Dante's initiator into those mysteries, with which the development and discipline of Dante's art are closely bound. For both Dante
and Statius, then, Virgil the pagan was an evangelist of sorts—not
only of Christianity but of the good news of the art of poetry. As if
to emphasize the extent to which this is true, Statius says: *Tu prima*
m'invïasti / verso Parnaso a ber ne le sue grotte, / e prima appresso
Dio m'alluminasti ("You were the first to send me toward Parnassus

---

26 *Purgatorio* XXI.133–36.

27 *Purgatorio* XVIII.46–48. See also *Purgatorio* XXV.28–30, where Virgil delegates
to Statius the task of explaining how the rational soul is infused directly by God. Statius is Christian, and so is in a position of explaining transcendent mysteries, whereas
Virgil is not.

28 *Inferno* I.85–87.

to drink in its grottoes and the first to light my way toward God").²⁹ Parnassus was the ancients' sacred mountain of poetic inspiration. As Statius concludes, *Per te poeta fui, per te cristiano* ("I was a poet because of you, because of you a Christian"). And this is where Statius makes the famous comment about Virgil's being a light for others though he himself could not benefit from that light—surely one of the high-tragic moments of Dante's poetry.

> *Facesti come quei che va di notte,*
> *che porta il lume dietro e sé non giova,*
> *ma dopo sé fa le persone dotte.*³⁰

(You were like one who goes along at night, carrying the light behind him and himself not benefiting from it, but teaching the people who follow him.)

I mentioned earlier the names of the other poets Dante encounters before reaching the Earthly Paradise: Forese Donati, Bonagiunta da Lucca, Guido Guinizzelli, and Arnaut Daniel. In contrast to the Latin and classical Statius-Virgil episode, these cantos involve vernacular poets of Dante's own epoch. The only poet in all of these cantos who is not Italian is Arnaut Daniel—who speaks to Dante in Arnaut's native Provençal.

Forese was a very minor poet but a dear early friend of Dante in Florence. He died when Dante was about thirty. He is notable in this context for his youthful exchange of scurrilous sonnets with Dante. For example, to Forese's teasing in a sonnet that the young Dante was a parasite who lives off the work of others, Dante had responded that Forese was a glutton and a thief. In Dante's three extant sonnets addressed to his friend, he accuses Forese of being a good-for-nothing husband, a son who isn't sure who his father really was, a cuckold, and so on. Forese answers in kind, with insults such as the accusation that Dante's father was a usurer and that Dante is a common thief. The mock ridicule of these poems and the slapstick humor in them became a model for Dante's style in certain coarse scenes in *Inferno*.³¹ But for the mature

---

29   *Purgatorio* XXII.64–66.
30   *Purgatorio* XXII.73, 67–69.
31   For a lucid discussion in English and translations of the Dante-Forese exchange of poems, see Teodolinda Barolini, *Dante's Lyric Poetry: Poems of Youth and of the "Vita*

Dante, low or hellish surroundings are the only appropriate place for this sort of poetry. As he puts it in *Inferno*, one sort of language is appropriate for saints in church, another for drunkards in a tavern.[32]

When Dante meets Forese on Mount Purgatory, his old friend is unrecognizable except for his voice. His face, like that of the other gluttonous souls, is distorted by sunken cheeks and darkened eye sockets. He is in an emaciated state, which is an image of the starvation that gluttonous souls undergo to purge themselves of their attachments. Dante comments that it is a wonder Forese is already so high up the mountain, given his friend's rather relaxed attitude toward the spiritual life. He jibes that he would have expected Forese to start out lower on the mountain, therefore needing much more time to reach the penultimate terrace. His interaction with Forese in *Purgatorio* has an affectionate teasing tone reminiscent of the scene lower down the mountain where he encounters the slothful Florentine maker of musical instruments, Belacqua, who enjoys poking fun at Dante's obsessive earnestness. It seems that Dante had a soft spot for unambitious but big-hearted and down-to-earth Florentines. Forese explains that his ascent was expedited by the prayers of his widowed wife, Nella — whose virtuous devotion becomes the foil for Forese's diatribe against shameless and immodest Florentine women. One gets the sense that perhaps Dante and he had enjoyed the company of those very women when they were young. Some critics have speculated that Dante viewed the poem genre he shared with Forese, the scurrilous sonnets I described earlier, as a form of literary gluttony. But those poems are only an outward sign for an interior, moral state. Dante viewed them as an aspect of the dissipation and lack of *gravitas* which he associates with that time in his life. As he tells Forese directly, *quella vita*, that life of being confused, self-indulgent, and dissipated, is what Virgil saved him from when he guided him out of the dark wood at the start of *Inferno*.[33] Dante and his friend share in their common eagerness for contrition and divine pardon, both having recognized the limits of their past.

The dialogue that Dante has with the Tuscan poet Bonagiunta Orbicciani da Lucca takes place in the middle of the Forese episode. Dante has

---

Nuova," with new verse translations by Richard H. Lansing, commentary translated into English by Andrew Frisardi (Toronto: University of Toronto Press, 2014).

32 *Inferno* XXII.15.
33 *Purgatorio* XXIII.115–18.

asked Forese to identify some gluttonous souls who are nearby. One of these, Bonagiunta, was from the generation of Tuscan poets just before Dante. Bonagiunta asks Dante if he is the man who initiated the *dolce stil novo* or sweet new style of poetry with the canzone *Donne ch'avete intelletto d'amore* ("Women who understand the truth of love"), which we looked at earlier. Dante responds to Bonagiunta with the famous lines (also quoted in that earlier discussion) that refer to Dante's taking direct dictation from Love when he writes his poems. Dante's responsiveness to Love's dictation has to do with being open to imaginative and intellectual vision — the very opposite of the self-involved love poetry that Dante has renounced. The new style is possible only for a poet whose powers of contemplation or inward concentration are equal to his technical skill. As Bonagiunta correctly observes after Dante's response, he and the other earlier Tuscan love poets were tied up in knots in comparison with Dante and his poet-friends, the so-called stilnovists (those who wrote in the *stil novo*). Some have speculated that Dante chose Bonagiunta for this scene because he was the author of a sonnet that criticizes Guinizzelli for the new style, and because his own style marked a transition between the Sicilian poets (the historical link between the Provençal poets and the early Tuscans like Bonagiunta) and the stilnovists.[34] In *De vulgari eloquentia*, composed several years before this scene, Dante had dismissed Bonagiunta's style as suitable "not for a court but at best for a city council."[35]

After the interaction with Bonagiunta, Forese, who has been standing nearby, reenters the narrative. The overlapping of Dante's encounters with Forese and Bonagiunta suggests that the two figures are closely if inversely related in Dante's development. While Forese is associated with a period of youthful debauchery and the associated poetry which had to be left behind, Bonagiunta reminds us of the birth of Dante's limpid and sublime poetry through his love for Beatrice.

After Forese's departure from the scene, Dante follows along behind Virgil and Statius while they talk about the ancient Roman and Greek poets and discuss the art of poetry.[36] As they walk, Dante sees a tree on the path in front of them. At the base of the tree, purgatorial souls

---

34 Anna Maria Chiavacci Leonardi, introduction to *Purgatorio* XXIV, p. 695, citing Gianfranco Contini for the second point.

35 *De vulgari eloquentia* I.xiii.1.

36 *Purgatorio* XXII.129.

are raising their hands like children begging an adult for a treat. A voice calls from the branches, reciting well-known examples of gluttony that led to suffering and dissipation. This scene is reminiscent of a passage in the *Convivio*, which describes the illusory nature of desire, by which we *think* we finally will be satisfied when we get the next thing we want, only to find out that we follow that up with a desire for something bigger and better, or simply other:

> And as a pilgrim who goes along a road he has never been on thinks that every house he sees from afar is his inn, and finding that this is not so, puts his hope in the next one, and so on, house after house, until he reaches the inn; just so does our soul, no sooner than it has entered upon the new and untraveled road of this life, direct its eyes to the aim of its supreme good, and thus, whatever thing it sees which appears to have some good in it, believes it to be *that* good.... So we see small children desiring more than anything else a piece of fruit; and further along, desiring a little bird; and then, still further, desiring fine clothes; and then a horse; then a woman; then modest wealth, then great wealth; and then more besides. And all of this happens because in none of these things does it find what it is searching for, while it believes to be finding it just ahead.[37]

This charming passage is a figural expression of Virgil's lesson on love and free will that had taken place several cantos earlier, in the middle of *Purgatorio* and therefore at the center of the entire *Comedy*.[38] In that literally pivotal scene, which will be discussed in detail in chapter 9, Virgil acknowledges that the human soul is created to love instantaneously, spontaneously, and that it is highly susceptible to pleasing things that awaken desire in it. The soul is mobilized by everything that promises pleasure. The next stage of desire occurs when consciousness extracts an image or concept of the external attractive thing and opens out that image in the soul. The soul's inclination or leaning toward that fantasized or internalized object is love in its most general sense. With this inclination or love, desire seizes the soul,

---

37 *Convivio* IV.xii.15–17.
38 *Purgatorio* XVIII.19ff.

compelling it to move toward the loved object until it finds satisfaction and pleasure. So, Virgil teaches Dante in the earlier *Purgatorio* cantos, desire is a spiritual motion, impelling us along from thing to thing throughout our lives — as the *Convivio* passage shows. However, clearly we cannot live in the fully human sense merely by blind desire, since the distinguishing feature of human beings is the intellectual soul, the life of the spirit, which is associated with free will. Dante reasonably asks: if love is simply a response to something that presents itself outside of us, where does free will come in? How is it that some desires lead to bad choices and some to good? Virgil in *Purgatorio* answers that reason and discernment guard the threshold of assent to our conceptual images of desirable things. Thus the proper relation of free will to desire is intimately bound up with the fullest realization of human potential.[39] Dante's definitive expression of this understanding comes in *Paradiso*, in the canto (XXVI) where he is questioned by St. John on the nature of love. As Dante will say there, the promise of some good always rouses love in human beings, and this love is proportionate to the degree of goodness that awakens it. Since God is the good as such, whoever recognizes this truth will love God above all other things.[40] Crucially as well, shortly after Dante has articulated the metaphysical truth of love, his vision is restored by Beatrice; he had been blinded by John's light but now he sees more clearly than ever before. Immediately after this he sees *un quarto lume . . . tra noi,* "a fourth light [in addition to the three Apostles] among us"[41] — none other than Adam, the first human being. Symbolically, this sequence means that to see the nature of love in its metaphysical essence is to see the essentially, primordially human. The pilgrim-Dante in this scene addresses Adam as the *pomo maturo* or ripe apple, an epithet suggesting that Adam himself was the fruit he was seeking outside of himself when he fell from grace by eating the forbidden fruit.[42] As the passage quoted above indicates, to seek ultimate fulfillment by chasing chimeric externals is to lose sight of our own essential nature, rooted in the ground of being, which is God.

---

39   In the opening lines of *Paradiso* IV, the question arises as to whether Dante ascribes free choice to reason or to the will. Since this distinction is beyond the scope of this chapter, the interested reader is referred to those lines and related commentaries.

40   *Paradiso* XXVI.28–39.

41   *Paradiso* XXVI.81.

42   *Paradiso* XXVI.91.

In sum, free will does not consist merely of conscious choices between alternatives in daily life, though it appears that way to us in immediate experience. Rather, it ultimately has to do with a state in which the individual assents to being what he or she already and always is, in the mind of God. Only insofar as human beings master egotistical desires and submit the will of their selves to that which is ontologically prior to them do they realize freedom in God. But those who live in such freedom will only what God wills, because they exist in a state of perfect submission to the good and thus also display the attributes of something that is totally determined. As Piccarda Donati (the sister of Forese) beautifully states in *Paradiso*, *'n la sua volontade è nostra pace*, in His will is our peace.[43]

Of course, asceticism of whatever degree is itself an acknowledgment of the ambiguous revelatory power of love and desire. Dissipation is "sin" because it squanders the chance of spiritual union. Dante's reflection on this crucial subject resembles that of Greek Orthodox saints such as Maximus the Confessor, who articulate in great detail the incremental relations between desire and free choice. As Maximus puts it, "The wrong use of our conceptual images of things . . . followed by the wrong use of things themselves," results in sin. And Maximus adds that "an intelligent use of conceptual images and their corresponding physical objects produces self-restraint, love and spiritual knowledge; an *un*intelligent use produces licentiousness, hatred and ignorance."[44] This is why in all spiritual traditions, watchfulness or vigilance is essential to praxis: habitual thoughts bring habitual patterns of behavior and ways of treating the world and its creatures. As Dante puts it in the *Convivio*, when the most noble part of the human soul, the intellect, is afflicted with various maladies, it is impeded in its function, which "is knowing what things are."[45]

Dante's reflections on this subject play a central role in his work at least as far back as the *Vita nova*. It is a theme that is closely related to his growing understanding of his vocation as poet-prophet. Through Virgil's influence and philosophical-theological reflection, Dante went beyond his predecessors in his understanding of love and desire—and

43 *Paradiso* III.85.

44 *Philokalia: The Complete Text*, translated and edited by G. E. H. Palmer, Philip Sherrard, and Kallistos Ware, vol. 2 (London: Faber & Faber, 1983), 79 and 83.

45 *Convivio* IV.XV.11.

this is intimately bound up with his achievement as an artist. The final encounters with poets in *Purgatorio*, on the terrace of the lustful, reinforce this impression.

Here, Dante meets poets who are burning in the fire of lust: love poets, in particular the father-figure of the stilnovists, Guido Guinizzelli, and Arnaut Daniel, a Provençal poet associated with a highly wrought, difficult style that Dante assumed for certain passages of his own poetry. As was *not* the case with Forese and Bonagiunta, Dante admired and imitated both these poets for their artistry—most specifically for their artful use of the modern vernacular.[46] The *Comedy* itself is in the Florentine vernacular, and poets like Guido and Arnaut were important role models for what the spoken word can do in poetry. When Guinizzelli identifies himself, Dante says he feels an overpowering urge to leap into the flames where Guido is standing, for the pure joy of seeing him. To communicate to us how excited he is, Dante uses a simile from Statius. His urge to embrace Guido is like the zeal of the two sons of the Greek queen Hypsipyle, who saw their mother among armed soldiers who were leading her to her death. The sons threw themselves into the midst of the soldiers and embraced their mother, drawing her away to safety.[47] Dante uses this simile to convey a sense of his filial affection for Guido. Indeed, he refers to Guido as his poetry father, acknowledging him as the founder of the sweet new style. Dante clearly has surpassed his early mentor, however, having adopted the high tragic style he learned from Virgil. Guinizzelli was never more than a fine lyric poet. To be a poet who has the strength, skill, and contemplative focus to write high epic requires extraordinary self-mastery and self-purification, which take years to achieve. John Milton somewhere described an apt image for the difference between composing lyric and epic—something he knew a little about. The lyric poet, he said, drinks wine from an exquisite goblet, while the epic poet drinks water from a wooden bowl.

Guido in the *Purgatorio* scene interrupts Dante's praise by indicating a nearby shade, the love poet Arnaut Daniel, referred to by Guido as the *miglior fabbro* or better craftsman in the mother tongue. The extent to which Dante values mastery of craft can be seen in this canto, where Guinizzelli states that it is foolish to rate another Provençal poet,

46 *Purgatorio* XXVI.112–24.
47 Statius, *Thebaid* v.718.

Giraut de Bornelh, higher than Arnaut merely because Giraut was a poet who wrote on moral themes, a genre Dante views as above love poetry. Arnaut is the better maker, and that surpasses poets who write with lesser art on higher themes.[48] Once Guido has asked Dante to recite the Lord's Prayer for him, he disappears into the flames again. Dante says that Guido in the flames looks like a fish in water darting to the bottom and out of sight. Arnaut is then given the final word in this sequence of cantos about poets and poetry. Dante has him speak in his native Provençal, another honor Dante pays to an important mentor. The gist of what Arnaut says is: "I weep tears of penitence; but if I am saddened by the memory of my faults, I am heartened by the thought of the eternal joy that awaits me." Interestingly, Dante does *not* use Arnaut's poetic *style* for the words he has him speak in Provençal. Rather, Arnaut in this scene uses a simple, plain style, in contrast to his highly wrought and difficult poetry. It is as if Arnaut's lines indicate a kind of poetic asceticism, since his style on earth was sensual and ostentatiously skillful. For Dante, perhaps the presence of Arnaut in this passage alludes to his own spiritual and artistic discipline, which resulted in the down-to-earth and always economical and forceful directness of the *Comedy.*

Now that Dante's encounters with the poets in Purgatory are complete, he passes through the wall of the fire of lust. This wall is the only thing left, Virgil reminds Dante, between him and Beatrice in the Earthly Paradise. The dream about Leah and Rachel that I described at the start of this chapter occurs not long after Dante's passage beyond the terrace of the lustful.

We are back on the cusp of the Earthly Paradise. What are some of the things we have seen in Dante's juxtaposing of self-purification and artistic mastery? Most simply put, we can say that mastery of art *is* interior mastery, since art in Dante's understanding is an intellectual virtue that remains in the artist. For Dante, to master an art means finding a way of working that is in harmony with human nature as such. His journey down through Hell and up Mount Purgatory made him confront within himself what happens to human nature when it is distorted by turning away from the good of the intellect, which is

---

48 *Purgatorio* XXVI.119–20. Dante refers to Giraut as a moral poet, like himself, in *De vulgari eloquentia* II.ii.9, while Arnaut and Cino da Pistoia are mentioned as love poets.

God. On Mount Purgatory he learned how contrition, acceptance, and reverence can restore human nature to its rightful place in the creation.

There is a progression in the late cantos of *Purgatorio:* first the encounters with the poets, through which Dante reflects on his own art and its relationship to sensual attachments; then the dream of Leah and Rachel, the principles of art and vision, the active life and the contemplative life; then Virgil's confirmation that Dante's will is finally purified; then Dante's vision of the sacred procession, art as sacrament; and finally, the arrival of divinity in the form of Beatrice. *Purgatorio* culminates when Beatrice assigns Dante his poet-prophet's role of denouncing the corruption of the Church and renewing Christianity at its roots.[49]

Here are some of the details of the Earthly Paradise as Dante finds it. It is a place of virgin nature, so lovely that the most exquisite spring day on earth is but a faint suggestion of what the Earthly Paradise is like. We know that the beauty of the place is actually spiritual beauty because the phenomena Dante witnesses there do not have natural causes. The gentle breeze does not arise from vapors as it does on earth, according to the science of Dante's time; rather, it is made by the motion of the First Mover, the celestial sphere closest to the Empyrean or highest Heaven. This is why the trees are bending delicately toward the west: the breeze emanates from the east, from God. Dante compares the trees to those in the pine forest on the shore of the Adriatic near Ravenna. The seedless plants in the Earthly Paradise impregnate the air with their innate capacity or virtue, which passes down and generates plant life on earth. In other words, these are the archetypes of what Jacob Boehme and Blake after him called "the vegetable glass [or mirror] of nature." The water flowing in Eden, which is clearer than any water on earth, doesn't come from a spring that is replenished by rain, like earthly rivers, but derives its source directly from God. All of these details are in agreement with the notion that the beauty of God is the source of the beauty of every created thing. In the Platonic formulation, beauty is the splendor of being's intelligibility.

This is why Dante depicts the Earthly Paradise as a state of being in love with the Creator. The spirit or guardian of the place is Matelda, depicted by Dante as a woman in love with the Creator. Dante sees her beside a stream gathering flowers, as Leah was doing in his dream. She

---

49 *Purgatorio* XXXII.105.

is singing a love song to God, the psalm that says, "For thou, Lord, hast made me glad through thy work; I will triumph in the works of thy hands. O Lord, how great are thy works!"[50] In addition, the language that Dante uses to describe Matelda, as well as some of the imagery in this scene, evokes a genre of pastoral love poetry that Dante knew well, the so-called *pastorella*, described in chapter 1. When Dante addresses Matelda, he asks her to come closer to the edge of the water (she is on the other side of the narrow stream), so he can hear what she is singing. He addresses her with the courteous speech of a noble lover, but the only lover his words ultimately refer to now is God. Matelda embodies the state in which human love, freed of illusion, naturally reaches for divine love. The sweet new style used in this scene may seem to contradict Dante's leaving behind his stilnovist past when he spoke to the poets on the upper terraces of Purgatory. The opposite is true, however: the Matelda scene actually embodies the fulfillment or full realization or (in Aristotle's sense) the final cause of Dante's sweet new style.

The sensually vivid poet Ovid, too, is in Dante's memory as he composes this scene. Aspects of Matelda recall Ovid's depiction of Persephone, who was ravished by Hades when he saw her alone, gathering flowers. Ovid's depiction of the Golden Age resembles Eden — as Matelda in the *Purgatorio* scene reminds Dante. She says that the ancient poets who wrote about the Golden Age may have been dreaming of this very place from atop Mount Parnassus. As she concludes: "Here the human root was innocent, here is perpetual spring and every fruit; this is the nectar each of them [that is, those ancient poets] tells us about."[51] In other words, the great poets have always found their inspiration from the primordial state of Eden that the purified Dante has now realized within himself. The connection between purification and inspiration-poetry is now firmly in place. The scene of Matelda and the revelation of the Earthly Paradise indicate that Dante's purification — mental, moral, spiritual, and artistic — is complete. And in fact, several lines later, Dante witnesses the sacred procession that will culminate in the appearance — the apotheosis, in the literal sense — of his art in the form of Beatrice herself.

---

50   Psalm 92:4–5 (King James version). See *Purgatorio* XXVIII.76–81.
51   *Purgatorio* XXVIII.142–44.

5

The Seed of Nobility

Wel kan the wise poete of Florence,
That highte Dant, spoken in this sentence.
Lo, in swich maner rym is Dantes tale:
"Ful selde upriseth by his branches smale
Prowesse of man, for God of his goodnesse,
Wole, that of hym we clayme oure gentillesse."
For of oure eldres may we no thyng clayme
But temporel thyng.

(Well can the wise poet of Florence, Dante, speak in this
manner. Here, in the form of poetry, is Dante's speech:
"Very seldom arises from the small branches [of the family
tree] the noble character of a man, for God in his goodness
wants us to claim our nobility from Him." For we can claim
nothing from our ancestors but temporal things.)

—Chaucer, *Wife of Bath's Tale*, 1125–32
(quoting *Purgatorio* VII.121–22)

WHAT CONNECTION MIGHT there be between art and
purification on the one hand, and nobility on the other?
As we have seen, Dante's purification in Purgatory led to
his reaching the Earthly Paradise, and the latter in turn is associated
with Dante's achievement of artistic mastery. A number of medieval
theologians equated the attainment of the Earthly Paradise with the
realization of the nobility that is inherent to the human soul. In the
last chapter I quoted from Dante's treatise on monarchy, where he discusses the two ends of human life, one associated with the corruptible
or mortal self and the other with the incorruptible or immortal self.
Fulfillment of the former means the fulfillment of full human potential
through the application of the moral and intellectual virtues. As we
will see, for Dante nobility is the source of the virtues, so the human
soul's inherent nobility, when it is realized in life, in fact is closely

connected with the Earthly Paradise and therefore with artistic mastery in its full sense.

We will return to these ideas later in this chapter, but first I would like to consider the significance of Dante's thinking about nobility for our own times. How are the words *nobility* or *noble* taken in current everyday speech? In my experience, there is something like mild embarrassment or irony around them. It is as if there is a prevailing unease that it might be pretentious or hypocritically lofty to talk about nobility or about something or someone being noble. Darwin, Freud, and materialist reductionism in general have left a cynical suspicion that spiritual virtues are merely repressed impulses or instincts. It is true that we might read in the newspapers that a person with integrity, generosity, and courage is "noble-minded." We value incorruptibility, self-possession, honesty, self-denial for the sake of the common good. These are virtues associated with what Dante would call nobility. Yet for Dante they are not nobility itself, which he saw as the spiritual *seed* or source of the virtues.

In Dante's time, the word nobility was a legal and social classification applied to aristocratic families whether they were noble-minded or not. In the *Convivio* Dante refutes the notion of nobility as a sort of aura that emanates from enduring family wealth and fame, a mystique such as we feel even now when we watch a royal wedding. In the United States, where royalty was ousted by the Declaration of Independence, Hollywood and celebrity culture nevertheless have become a flashy substitute. As an American poet has put it, America is where people are famous for being famous. The onslaught of images in the ever-multiplying media ensures that we're constantly reminded of celebrity and popularity. There is a widespread obsession with being "seen" in one way or another—even if only through having one's posts on the internet "liked" by other anonymous people. And in this climate, some lonely or disturbed individuals apparently perceive themselves as so painfully invisible and therefore insignificant that they feel compelled to strike out in attention-getting violence.

It is interesting to reflect, in light of this, that the word *noble* comes from the Latin *noscere*, "to know."[1] *Nobilis* originally meant notable or famous. Over time Roman moral philosophers, and later the Christian

---

1 An etymology which Dante rejects as false, preferring the etymology, from Isidore of Seville, which says that *nobilis* is from *non vilis*, not base.

theologians, developed the idea of *nobilitas animi*, nobility of mind or soul, a concept dear to Dante. This concept enables him to explore such questions as: Is what society praises as *notable* an accurate measure of worth? What is the true, *intrinsic* value of a person or of any thing? From what does this value arise? This is, in essence, what Dante's examination of nobility is about.

As far back as the *Vita nova*, nobility was already central to his thought. He tells us there that the first time he saw Beatrice, at age nine, she was dressed "in the noblest [*nobilissimo*] color, a subdued and dignified crimson."[2] An epithet for Beatrice, often used in the *Vita nova*, is the *gentilissima*, the *most* noble or gracious woman. Other women may be simply *gentile*, or noble, but only Beatrice is *gentilissima*. As Dante says, Lord Love himself "rules over me by the power of that most noble of women."[3] Dante's exalted love of Beatrice is the main theme of the *Vita nova*, and for Dante, love and nobility are inseparable: *Amore e 'l cor gentil sono una cosa*, as a famous sonnet in that book begins, "Love and the noble heart are always one." And we know how central love is to Dante's prophetic and poetic vision.

In his philosophical work the *Convivio*, Philosophy is the Donna Gentile or Noble Lady that Dante fell in love with after the death of Beatrice. As he writes in the *Convivio*, Lady Philosophy is a natural *friend* of Nobility, "for they" — nobility and love of wisdom, which for Dante is what philosophy really is— "for they so love each other that Nobility is always in search of her, and Philosophy casts not her sweet glance anywhere else." This statement comes at the end of the last book of the *Convivio*, whose subject is the nature of nobility. We will return to this later, but in the meantime Dante's pairing of nobility and philosophy is important. As he continues: "Oh, how lovely and great an adornment this is . . . calling her [Nobility] the friend of the lady [Philosophy] whose proper reason has its being in the most hidden depths of the divine mind!"[4] Philosophy here is *theo*-sophical, and Nobility is her intimate companion in the mind of God.

In the *Divine Comedy*, Dante shows that, while he admires certain qualities or attributes *associated* with human nobility, such as magnanimity and courage, nobility in the full sense is something more subtle

2   *Vita nova* 1.4 (II.3).
3   *Vita nova* 4.3 (IX.3).
4   *Convivio* IV.xxx.6.

and far-reaching. In canto x of *Inferno*, Dante meets Farinata degli Uberti, an important political leader of the Florentines, the pride of whose bearing and speech was legendary. Dante and Virgil are walking among the open tombs of the heretics in the sixth circle of Hell, just inside the iron walls of Dis, the city of Hell. While they are talking, Farinata's voice suddenly interrupts, in words that are among the most famous in Italian poetry:

> *O Tosco che per la città del foco*
> *vivo ten vai così parlando onesto,*
> *piacciati di restare in questo loco.*[5]

(O Tuscan, going along, still alive, through the city of fire, talking in such a dignified way, may it please you to pause here briefly.)

Farinata is employing courteous speech in response to the gracious words he overheard Dante using in his dialogue with Virgil near Farinata's tomb. Dante in his portrayal of Farinata clearly wants us to see him as regal and proud: *el s'ergea col petto e con la fronte / com' avesse l'inferno a gran dispitto* ("he was rising [from the tomb] with his chest and forehead as if he viewed Hell with utter contempt"). Some authors in the nineteenth century sentimentalized these lines, thinking that Dante meant to portray a spirit who defies rigid Church dogma and hellfire morality. But Dante is far more probing and subtle than this interpretation, and he is always dead serious about Hell. The arrogance and egotism that underlie Farinata's outwardly noble comportment are revealed a few lines later. While he and Dante are talking, another figure rises suddenly from a nearby tomb—the soul of Cavalcante dei Cavalcanti, the father of Dante's best friend of his youth, the poet Guido Cavalcanti. Although Guido's father after his exchange with Dante will fall back in his tomb with grief over the unknown fate of his son, Farinata goes on talking as though nothing has happened to his neighbor:

> *Ma quell' altro magnanimo, a cui posta*
> *restato m'era, non mutò aspetto,*
> *né mosse collo, né piegò sua costa.*

5 This and the following quotes come from *Inferno* x.22ff.

(But that other magnanimous spirit, near where I had
stopped, didn't change his expression, nor move his neck,
nor bend his side.)

In this passage, as usual, the sounds of Dante's poetry are part and parcel
of its meaning. Dante expresses Farinata's unbending self-sufficiency
with a series of truncated words ending with accented vowels — *mutò, né,
né, piegò* — and a string of other hard sounds: *aspetto, mosse, collo, costa*.

For Dante, the magnanimous great souls in Hell show only the
accoutrements of nobility, not its soul, which is empathic and compassionate. The damned are those whose will has closed itself off to grace,
since Luciferian pride has alienated them from their spiritual roots.
Early in *Paradiso*, Beatrice gives Dante an extended theology lesson
about the incarnation of Christ and the redemption of fallen human
nature. As she says there, because of God's creative love, the human
soul came into being in a state of nobility — a gift, however, that was
squandered by Adam and Eve's fall.[6] The proud souls whom Dante
encounters in Hell dramatize this fallen condition, which is a state of
exile from the nobility that is inherent to the human soul.

Like Farinata, the great pagans in Limbo — poets, philosophers, and
heroes who are residents of the *castello nobile* or noble castle — have
a stately bearing. They move slowly and with poise, and when they
speak, which is rarely, they do so with measured voices.[7] They possess
humanistic virtues such as heroism, patriotism, and intellectual acumen,
but they are neither sad nor happy, and remain forever in a state of
empty longing because of their separation from the Eternal.

Perhaps the most memorable of the proud, great souls in *Inferno*
is Ulysses — another of Dante's damned who was romanticized in the
nineteenth century, most famously by Tennyson. Ulysses, who is among
the so-called false counselors in the next-to-lowest circle of Hell, is
noble only in the non-Christian sense. In the legend that Dante follows,
Ulysses had piloted himself and his crew past the Straits of Gibraltar
and beyond all boundaries of the known world.[8] Dante uses this story

6 *Paradiso* VII.67ff.
7 *Inferno* IV.112–14.
8 The historical background of this story is interesting. The first-century geographer
Strabo said that near the Straits of Gibraltar was a city called Odussea, the "city of
Odysseus." Again according to Strabo, there was a temple to Athena nearby, who was
Odysseus'/Ulysses' protectress, inside which were supposedly pieces of Ulysses' broken

as an allegory for human self-will and reason that exceed and violate their basis in divine knowledge and grace. In *Paradiso* he calls this willfulness *il trapassar del segno*, going past the sign or marker or target set by God. This setting of limits by God has nothing to do with the oppressive Demiurge of the Gnostics or with Blake's joy-killing demiurge Urizen. As Christian Moevs has observed, the boundary is not "an arbitrary limit set by a jealous god: indeed, for Dante the goal of all human life is deification or union with God. To overstep the [boundary, as Ulysses does] is . . . to seek more from the ego and from finite being than what they can provide."[9] And the ultimate effects of this ontological inversion are far-reaching and concrete. The giants who guard the threshold to the lowest level of Hell, in canto xxxi of *Inferno*, are outsized and obtuse representatives of this pride in human beings. Dante notes in that canto that if their massive power and ill will were combined with human reason, the results would be disastrous — as we see vividly in humankind's current devastation of the earth through technological gigantism driven by acquisitiveness.[10] For Dante, Lucifer is the prototype of this inversion, since he was created as the most noble of creatures but claimed that nobility as his own rather than as God's gift.[11]

The lofty speech of Ulysses can easily fool us into thinking that he is advocating for the Good and the True. Dante wants us to be seduced by Ulysses' high rhetoric, just as his crew was. Ulysses in this canto recounts what he told his men, trying to convince them to leave everything behind:

> *Considerate la vostra semenza:*
> *fatti non foste a viver come brutti,*
> *ma per seguir virtute e canoscenza.*[12]

---

ship, which had sunk. A historical work by King Alfonso x ("the Wise"), of Castile, thirteenth century, recounts the voyage of Ulysses and says he was the founder of Lisbon (supposedly from "Ulissipona," the territory of Ulysses), and that Ulysses sank on the way home. Brunetto Latini, Dante's early mentor who will appear later in this chapter, knew Alfonso personally. Maria Corti, "Dante and Islamic Culture," translated by Kyle M. Hall, *Dante Studies* 125 (2007): 57–75.

9 Christian Moevs, *The Metaphysics of Dante's "Comedy"* (Oxford: Oxford University Press, 2005), 101.

10 *Inferno* xxxi.55–56.

11 *Purgatorio* xii.25–27.

12 *Inferno* xxvi.118–20.

(Consider your birthright: you were not made to live like brute animals, but to follow virtue and knowledge.)

Few of us would dispute this beautifully stated noble sentiment. However, as Tennyson put it, a motto for Ulysses could be, "To strive, to seek, to find, and not to yield." Tennyson meant this as praise for what he saw as Ulysses' heroic boldness. As a product of his time, Tennyson failed to see that Faustian overreach was what Dante was trying to get us to see in Ulysses' rationalized unyieldingness. Words that John Milton puts into the mouth of Lucifer in *Paradise Lost* express the rising secular humanism that Dante rejects through the figure of Ulysses. As Lucifer says in Milton's poem, "The mind is its own place, and in itself / Can make a Heav'n of Hell, a Hell of Heav'n."[13] It is hard to imagine a more succinct expression of the post-Renaissance secular mindset, for which man is the measure of all things. For Dante, the result of such solipsism and pride is the shipwreck of Ulysses and his crew within sight of the island of Purgatory. Attempting to reach it by their own power rather than by faith in something beyond their egos, they are doomed to sink.

A starkly contrasting figure to Ulysses in the *Comedy* is St. Francis of Assisi, whose story is narrated in canto XI of *Paradiso*. Dante has Thomas Aquinas tell Francis's story in a humble style, using concrete "Franciscan" language rather than Aquinas's characteristically high cerebral style.[14] Dante portrays Francis as an aristocrat of holiness, whose noble comportment is, ironically, a function of his poverty. For example, he says that Francis is *pusillo*, small. The implication is that Francis paradoxically is *great* because of his self-imposed smallness and humility, and is spiritually *rich* because of his voluntary poverty. He embodies the first Beatitude, "Blessed are the poor in spirit," which Dante had heard sung when he and Virgil were leaving the first terrace on Mount Purgatory, where prideful souls are purified until they achieve this spiritual poverty.[15] Importantly, Francis did not come from a noble family. His father was a wool merchant and therefore of the

13   See *Paradise Lost* 1.242–70. The Tennyson quote comes from the last line of his 1842 poem *Ulysses*.

14   Zygmunt G. Barański, *Dante e i segni: Saggi per una storia intellettuale di Dante Alighieri* (Naples: Liguori, 2000), 66.

15   *Purgatorio* XII.110.

middle class. St. Bonaventure, in his life of Francis, says that when the saint used to hear himself praised as a holy man, he would ask one of his friars to remind him of his low birth. His saintliness and nobility were not to be confused with outer trappings. Dante says that when Francis, barefoot and dressed in shepherd's rags, appeared before the pope in all his pomp and majesty, he did not feel ashamed in the least. He was secure in his true, *God-based* nobility. His supernatural self-confidence even emboldened him to *regalmente*, regally, announce to the pope his intention to form his religious order.[16] Through the figure of Francis, Dante portrays real, spiritual nobility as something that overturns more external social values, including the superficial view of the word *nobilitade* as merely indicating old family wealth and gentrified comportment.

St. Bernard of Clairvaux's speech in the final canto of *Paradiso* brings Dante's treatment of nobility to its fullest figural expression. In his prayer to the Virgin Mary to grant the grace whereby Dante may have his ultimate vision in Paradise, Bernard refers to Mary as she whose holiness so en*nobled* human nature that its maker, God, did not hesitate to become the creature of his *own* creature, by incarnating as Christ. Mary's nobility is such that her presence in the flesh prepared the human receptacle to receive the divine Logos. The Virgin Mary is the human soul closest to God. This, as Thomas Aquinas argues, is the only *true* measure of nobility. In Aquinas's words, "The gradation of nobility and lowliness . . . is measured according to . . . nearness to and distance from God."[17] Any being is noble, therefore, to the extent that it participates in the nobility of God, who alone is completely noble, since, to quote Aquinas again, "that which has being through itself is nobler than that which has being in another."[18] With the Virgin's nobility, then, Dante is dramatizing a theological principle.

The historical antecedents to Aquinas's and Dante's spiritual view of nobility go back to the Greek and Roman authors, through Boethius and Augustine, and on to later theologians. I will not burden this chapter with a historical account.[19] It is enough to note that Christian

16 *Paradiso* XI.88–93.
17 *Contra Gentiles* I.lxx.
18 *Contra Gentiles* I.xxvii.
19 The interested reader can find an account in the fourth section of the introduction to my *Convivio* edition, cited with the other primary sources listed in the front matter of this book.

thinkers emphasized nobility as a spiritual attribute — or a metaphysical essence. For medieval theologians, individual nobility is a recovery of the *original* nobility of man, who is made in God's image, through the imitation of Christ, which enables this recovery. They understood nobility as free conformity to the *imago Dei*, or image of God, in the rational soul. Such authors argued that the common origin of *all* human beings excluded a nobility based merely on exclusive family inheritance. In this distinction, there is the characteristic Christian reversal of conventional values. What the world considers *ig*noble is *noble* in the view of God; and worldly "nobility" is actually base or superficial from the spiritual point of view. For Christians, the human tendency to be dazzled by external appearances had led to a view of nobility that encouraged *superbia*, arrogant pride, which is harmful to the soul. The same is true in other religious traditions. The Quran, for instance, says that the most noble human beings in God's eyes are those who are the most reverent and humble; that is, most aware of their dependence on the all-encompassing divine reality.[20] This combination of nobility with reverence was a sharp departure from the norm in pre-Islamic Arabia, where the two had been considered polar opposites. So the moral order of Arabia, like that of the late Roman Empire, shifted from the emphasis on lineage and grandiose display to the ideals of faith, piety, and submission to the Transcendent.

Readers of the *Comedy* will recall how central the idea of *superbia* is in Dante's understanding of sin and of the soul's alienation from God. In *Purgatorio*, Dante represents this Luciferian puffed-up attitude on the terrace of the prideful. The Tuscan nobleman Umberto Aldobrandeschi is bent under a boulder, facing the earth as compensation for his haughty pride. Dante indicates that a source of Umberto's arrogance had been his attachment to having been born into a wealthy family renowned for its *opere leggiadre*, or chivalrous deeds, and among the oldest noble families of Tuscany. The name of Umberto's father fills out nearly an entire verse, as Umberto tries to impress Dante with his inherited status: *Io fui latino e nato d'un gran Tosco: / Guiglielmo Aldobrandeschi fu mio padre* ("I was Italian and born of a great Tuscan: Guiglielmo Aldobrandeschi was my father"). And Umberto adds that pride about his illustrious ancestry had made him forget that all human beings share a *comune madre*, a common mother

---

20 Quran 49:13.

or origin, in the sight of God, so much so that he had contempt for his social inferiors.[21] Just before this scene, canto XI had opened with a recitation and commentary upon the Lord's Prayer. That prayer and Dante's paraphrase-commentary of it show that what is at stake with atoning for the sin of pride is the proper relation between heaven and earth, and human beings' relations with each other and with the creation. Pride, or vainglory (*inanis gloria*), as it was called in medieval moral treatises, was considered the root of all other vices, which is why Dante places those atoning for it at the base of Mount Purgatory. And like Gregory the Great in his *Moralia*,[22] who names pride as the ultimate source of the deadly sins but places it apart from the seven deadly sins, Dante in the *Inferno* does not include pride among the sins that are punished there, precisely because it is implicitly present in all of them.

In a universe parallel to that of the Christian Church, many medieval poets and authors expressed the notion of true nobility in terms of chivalry and love. The self-sacrificing knight who served his king and queen became a model for the ideal of courtly love, which, as discussed in detail earlier, had a decisive influence on Dante's poetry and view of love. Courtly love emphasized the ennobling potential of human love, the elevation of the beloved to a place superior to the lover.

Of the many poets who wrote about nobility, none was more important to Dante than the father of the so-called *dolce stil novo*, Guido Guinizzelli, whom we have encountered a few times in this book already. Using philosophical concepts which were current at the time, Guinizzelli wrote a very influential poem, mentioned earlier as well, which argues that love and the noble heart are in a relation of act and potential: one is created for the other.[23] Guido asserts that nobility is not a *given* of noble ancestry; it is an individual attribute. A person from a family that is renowned as noble may very well be base or worthless. One with a noble heart, on the other hand, will be a lover.

Guinizzelli uses the metaphor of a gemstone to illustrate the workings of love in the noble heart. The science of Dante's time had a hermetic understanding of the relations between things in the great

---

21 *Purgatorio* XI.58–64.

22 *Moralia* XXXI.xlv.87.

23 The canzone *Al cor gentil rempaira sempre amore* ("Love always comes to dwell in the noble heart").

chain of being. The idea was that there are *meaningful* analogies or correspondences between the various levels of being (which is, by the way, the basis of any symbolism that is not arbitrary or idiosyncratic). So, the scholastic philosopher and Thomas Aquinas's teacher Albert the Great wrote that celestial and planetary powers are operative in precious stones and metals, which makes them more or less noble. Albert's thoughts on this theme may have been a direct or indirect source for Guinizzelli's poem. As Albert puts it:

> Powers descend into natural things in a manner that is either noble or ignoble: noble when the materials receiving these powers are more like things above in their brightness and transparency; ignoble, when the materials are confused and foul, so that the heavenly power is, as it were, oppressed. Therefore ... precious stones, more than anything else, have wonderful powers — because, that is, they are in substance more like things above in their brightness and transparency. On this account, some ... say that precious stones are stars composed of elements.[24]

Guinizzelli applies this line of analogical thought to his poem. He says that certain stones, after being refined alchemically by rays of the sun, derive their virtue or power from the radiation of stars or planets associated with them. Likewise, he adds, a radiant beloved actualizes the love that is *potential* in a heart that is noble by nature. Dante echoes this imagery in the *Convivio* when he states that nobility "descends into us from a supreme and spiritual power, like virtue into a stone from a supremely noble celestial body."[25]

By the time Dante wrote the *Convivio*, then, a few years before starting the *Comedy*, there were many precedents for saying that true nobility is of the soul or spirit. His precursors saw birth into a noble family as an *opportunity* for noble, principled action — an opportunity which it was especially blameworthy to squander. Dante's mentor Brunetto Latini expresses this idea as well. Brunetto is famous to readers of *Inferno* as a sympathetic father-figure whom Dante meets among

24 Albert the Great, *Mineralium liber* II.i (translated by Dorothy Wykoff [Oxford: Clarendon Press, 1967], 61).
25 *Convivio* IV.xx.11.

the damned. In one of his works, he says that the noble soul is created the moment it enters the body, and this is the source of its worthiness since it comes directly from God. Virtue is merely an outer sign of nobility, according to Brunetto, which Dante believed as well.

In addition, Brunetto argues that a proper understanding of true, *inward* nobility could be a good remedy for the turbulent political life of Florence. This idea appealed to Dante. For several years in his early adulthood, Dante held important political offices in his city, and was at the very center of the rapid social changes going on at that time. Before Dante entered politics, legislation had been passed which excluded the old nobility in Florence from political office and gave the guilds — or unions of craftsmen — unprecedented power. Dante at first was excluded from political office because his family was of the minor nobility. Then a change was made to the earlier law that allowed noblemen to participate in political decision making — which Dante promptly did. Considering all this, as well as Dante's politically motivated exile in 1302, it is not hard to see why he would devote so much space in the *Convivio* to explaining what nobility is and debunking false notions of it. He wrote the *Convivio* early in his exile, while he was still embroiled in Florentine politics from afar. As he says, he is forming his argument about nobility "in the face of many adversaries" — no doubt a comment about its political implications. [26]

This background also helps account for the change in direction that Dante announces at the start of his poem on nobility in the *Convivio*, *Le dolci rime d'amor ch'i' solia / cercar ne' miei pensieri* ("Those sweet love lyrics I have long been wont / to search for in my thought"). For the time being, he writes, he is leaving behind the poetry of love, in favor of poetry with an ethical and social scope. Dante begins his commentary on the poem with a renewed declaration of his love for philosophy, personified as a woman. As he puts it, using the first of the many vegetation metaphors in this treatise, philosophy's "rays make blossom, leaf, and bear fruit the true nobility of man."[27] His aim in the first half of his treatise is to shed light on a collective delusion about the nature of nobility in order to dispel it. It is essential that someone do so, since to be in error about the "human goodness which is sown in us by nature," as Dante puts it, is to lose the point of what it means

---

26 *Convivio* IV.viii.10.
27 *Convivio* IV.i.11. For similar passages, see, e.g., IV.xxi.12–14, xxii.11–14.

to be human. It "brings suffering and harm," because "good [people are] held in harsh contempt and the wicked honored and exalted." And this in turn throws the world "into hopeless confusion."[28] Clearly, Dante is alluding to contemporary events, and we can easily think of similar difficulties in our own time. For Dante, the examination of the nature of nobility is part of the project which will engage him in the *Comedy*: social and political renewal by a return to first principles.

He says that the main purpose of his canzone and commentary is to clear up the weed-infested garden of popular, false opinion about the nature of nobility. His task is to uproot the unruly overgrowth to let the real, healthy shoots of truth and understanding come forth. Many have gone astray in their false values, but the worst of all is the person who has the good example of noble ancestors and still goes astray. Far more valuable — or noble — is the one who has no such predecessors but who nevertheless manages to find his or her own way.

The widespread and erroneous view of nobility, Dante says, is that it consists merely of old wealth and refined manners or bearing. He refutes the notion that nobility is old wealth on two grounds: first in terms of wealth, then in terms of time (implied by the word "old"). Because wealth is imperfect by nature, Dante says, it would be a contradiction to claim that it could generate nobility. It is clear that material wealth is imperfect, since however much it is accumulated it cannot bring total peace of mind, and imperfection by definition is that which leaves something to be desired. Rather, wealth stimulates ever-renewed hunger to acquire more. That is because nothing in this life completely fulfills our acquisitive nature, since "the supreme desire of each thing, the primal one given by its nature, is to return to its principle. And since God is the principle of our souls and made them like himself... this soul desires more than anything else to return to him."[29] In addition, possession of riches can be harmful because the rich person lives in constant dread of losing them. And it is a privation of good because one person's possession of wealth means someone else's lack of it. So, since wealth is distant from nobility, like a river flowing along far from a tower, it isn't possible that the fluctuation of wealth — the rising and falling of fortune — could have any effect whatsoever on nobility as such.

28 *Convivio* IV.i.6–7.
29 *Convivio* IV.xii.14.

In addition, Dante argues, the passage of time over generations has nothing to do with whether an individual soul is noble or not. Dante's argument here resembles one that has been made against psychoanalytic theories in our own time: If the cause of neurosis or psychosis is always a father or mother or both, and that parent's disturbance was from theirs, and so on, the illness must go back through many generations. But what caused the disturbance in the first person in this line? Likewise, Dante says that if nobility were the result of inheritance only, a low-born person could never be noble; and a noble son or daughter could never come from low-born or ignoble parents. And if nobility cannot appear in new and unexpected places, then Adam, the first human, must have been base and so we all are base; or Adam was noble and so we all are noble. Or, if no transformation or change to nobility can occur within a family, then the human race must descend from two different origins, a base one and a noble one. Yet clearly these hypothetical situations are not true.

Once false views of nobility have been debunked, the second half of Dante's treatise opens with an enthusiastic turn to the truth. Nobility, Dante says, is actually "the perfection in each thing of its proper nature."[30] Dante's discussion now focuses on the essential, interior dimension of nobility rather than external appearances of it. It is noteworthy that his concept of nobility is not exclusively human-centered. As we saw earlier in Guinizzelli's metaphor of the gemstone, nobility is a property, as Dante writes, "not only of human beings, but of all things as well: for human beings call a stone noble, a plant noble, a horse noble, a falcon noble, and similarly with regard to each thing which is viewed as perfected in its nature."[31] In metaphysical language, we might put it this way: a thing's nearness to the intelligible essence of its kind determines its degree of nobility. So material substances such as gemstones and precious metals are known for their noble qualities, as is the bodily beauty of certain varieties of plants and animals. In human beings, nobility shows in the virtues. Following Aristotle, Dante says that each virtue is a mean between two extremes — one an excess of the quality, the other a deficiency of it. He concludes with the famous Aristotelian saying that virtue is "a chosen habit existing

30 *Convivio* IV.xvi.5.
31 *Convivio* IV.xvi.5.

in the mean," or in the middle between extremes.[32] And he adds that the tendency for this habit arises from nobility, which is virtue's seed. As Dante concludes, the virtues "derive from nobility the way an effect does from its cause."[33]

Nobility is greater and more extensive or comprehensive than virtue. It is like a sky in which the virtues shine like stars.[34] It comprises all the virtues, whose visibility presupposes nobility the way the stars' brightness can't be seen without a sky for them to appear in. So, we recognize nobility, which itself is invisible, by its outer signs, the virtues. For example, says Dante, those with a noble nature, after having committed a wrong, display shame on their faces, which is the noble response to wrongdoing.[35]

People whose nobility is actualized to a high degree are chosen by God. Indeed, says Dante, "those who possess this 'grace,' this divine thing [to a high degree], are 'almost' like 'gods,' unblemished by vice; and God alone can give such a thing."[36] This divine seed is not sown in a family lineage, however, but rather falls on receptive individual souls. God grants this grace especially to the soul that inhabits the individual's body perfectly. A soul that is not so endowed is unable to receive the seed of nobility. This is "similar to how," writes Dante using the gemstone metaphor mentioned earlier, "if a precious stone is ill disposed or imperfect, it cannot receive celestial power."[37] Later in his argument, Dante modifies this apparently elitist view with the observation that "if a person does not possess this seed [of nobility] from his natural root, he can certainly obtain it by means of grafting." In other words, it is possible to cultivate nobility as well, since it is intrinsic to the human being as such.[38] Dante's theory, I think, is meant to account for the obvious exceptional quality of certain individuals, who seem naturally to transcend, as it were, average complacency and egotism.

Dante has now laid the groundwork for a complete definition of nobility: "Human nobility is none other than the 'seed of happiness,' placed by God in the ready soul, that is, the soul whose body is

32 *Convivio* IV.xvii.7; and Aristotle, *Nicomachean Ethics* II.8, 1108b.11–19.
33 *Convivio* IV.xviii.2.
34 *Convivio* IV.xix.5.
35 *Convivio* IV.xix.10.
36 *Convivio* IV.xx.3.
37 *Convivio* IV.xx.7.
38 *Convivio* IV.xxii.12.

perfectly disposed throughout."[39] Dante calls the inclination of the will that springs from the seed of nobility sown in the receptive soul, the *appetito dell'animo*.[40] If this appetite or inclination of the soul is not carefully cultivated through good habit, the seed has fallen on barren ground and will not sprout into anything of value. But through self-discipline and by harnessing the passions, this shoot in the noble soul bears fruit. These fruits are the virtues, the greatest of which is the capacity for and love of contemplation. Nobility finds its fullest expression in the contemplative, spiritual life.

Next in the *Convivio* comes an allegorical passage that exalts the contemplative life as superior to, or more fundamental than, the active life. This allegory shows that nobility is the spirit in us that indicates the way to contemplation. Dante draws on the Gospel scene in which three women arrive at Jesus's tomb, only to find that he has been raised from the dead. Here is the scene from the Gospel of Mark:

> And when the sabbath was past, Mary Magdalene, and Mary the mother of James, and [Mary] Salome, bought spices, so that they might go and anoint [Jesus's body]. And very early on the first day of the week they went to the tomb when the sun had risen. And they were saying to one another, "Who will roll away the stone for us from the door of the tomb?" And looking up, they saw that the stone was rolled back—it was very large. And entering the tomb, they saw a young man sitting on the right side, dressed in a white robe; and they were amazed. And he said to them, "Do not be amazed; you seek Jesus of Nazareth, who was crucified. He has risen, he is not here; see the place where they laid him. But go, tell his disciples and Peter that he is going before you to Galilee; there you will see him, as he told you."[41]

Dante's interpretation of this scene is remarkable. With great imagination and originality, Dante interprets the three Marys as figures representing the three philosophical schools of the active life—Epicurean, Stoic, and Aristotelian. The angel in white vestments who is

39 *Convivio* IV.xx.9.
40 *Convivio* IV.xxi.13.
41 Mark 16:1–7.

seated by Christ's empty tomb represents, Dante writes, "our nobility, which comes from God . . . which speaks within our reason, and says to each of these [philosophical] schools, that is, to everyone who looks for joy in the active life, that it is *not there.*" True joy, which is realized in contemplation, is no longer in the tomb. And the angel of nobility continues on to say, in Dante's commentary: "But go, and tell the disciples and Peter, that is, those who are looking for him and those who have gone astray, as did Peter who had denied him, that he will go before them to Galilee: that is, joy will go before us to Galilee, in other words to contemplation."

Dante's interpretation of Galilee as a figure for contemplation is based on medieval etymology. It was thought that the word Galilee was derived from the Greek *gala*, or "milk." Like milk, Dante says, Galilee is purest white:

> To say Galilee is to say "whiteness." Whiteness is a color more abundant with corporeal light than any other; and likewise contemplation is more abundant with spiritual light than anything else that exists here below. And he [the angel of nobility] says, "Christ will go before you," and not, "He will be with you," to clarify that in our contemplation God always precedes us, nor can we ever reach him down here [in the present life], who is our supreme bliss.[42]

In short, Dante has used the Gospel story to illustrate the limitations of the active life, emphasizing nobility as the awakener and messenger of the contemplative life. This recalls the earlier mention of Dante's portrayal of Nobility as the friend of Philosophy in the mind of God.

Next in the *Convivio*, Dante describes the outward signs or virtues by which the noble person may be recognized. He lays out a developmental theory of nobility, or — to adapt Plato's phrase about time as a moving image of eternity — a moving image of nobility set against its background in eternity. Since in this life we are in a state of becoming rather than in pure being, nobility manifests within us in phases. There are "ages of man," like seasons of life. Since all life on earth is a microcosm of the heavens, and the sky we see is an arc or hemisphere bounded by the horizon line, not a full sphere, our life span has an

---

42 *Convivio* IV.xxii.14–18.

ascending phase, a peak, and a decline: the arc of life. The peak of the arc is at age thirty-five. A key here is that for the visionary imagination the way things appear from our perspective on earth is meaningful; it is *significant* that we see only an arc or hemisphere delineated by the horizon line. It is interesting to note, too, that when Dante's journey in the otherworld takes him to the Southern Hemisphere and the island of Purgatory, he is finally in a position to know the entire sphere, not just the side circumscribed by terrestrial life.

Near the opening of the section on the ages of life Dante gives one of the most striking organic metaphors of the treatise:

> This divine seed . . . spontaneously sprouts in our soul, developing and differentiating into each of the soul's faculties, in conformity with their needs. It sprouts, then, in the vegetative faculty, and in the sensitive and the rational; and branches out into the powers of them all, directing them to their perfection, and always persevering within them until that moment when, with the part of our soul that never dies, it returns to heaven, to the highest and most glorious Sower of seeds.[43]

Since nobility is instilled in us by God, Dante focuses on how the eternal and the temporal intertwine in the span of the arc of life. He portrays the virtues of the noble soul associated with each age. First, early in life, when growth and development of the self are the focus, the virtues shown by a noble soul are obedience, gentleness, a sense of shame, and physical beauty. The virtues associated with young adulthood are temperance, courage, love, courtesy, and respect for the law. All of these are needed for curbing and harnessing the great energy that comes with youth — they are virtues that enable a young person to move toward self-mastery. In middle and late middle age, the characteristic virtues of nobility all have to do with the sharing of this mastery: prudence, justice, generosity, and openness to others. Dante gives a striking metaphor for this: "After one's own perfection," he writes, "which is attained in early adulthood, should come that perfection which illuminates not only oneself but others; a person should open like a rose, as it were, which can no longer stay shut,

---

43 *Convivio* IV.xxiii.3.

spreading the perfume that is produced within."[44] Lastly, in the final stage of life, or old age, the soul turns inward, withdrawing from the active life. As Dante puts it, the aged noble soul "returns to God, as to the port it left when it entered upon the sea of this life; ... it blesses the voyage it has made, since it has been virtuous and good and free of tempest-tossed bitterness."[45]

Dante illustrates each of the four ages of the human lifespan with a story from an ancient Roman poet — a different poet for each age of life. The story representing the virtues of youth comes from Statius; the story for early adulthood from Virgil; and the one for middle age, from Ovid. The allegory he chooses for old age, the most striking of the four, is from Lucan's account of the story of the ancient Roman couple Marcia and Cato.

Cato is an important figure at the beginning of *Purgatorio;* he greets Dante and Virgil at the base of Mount Purgatory, right after they emerge from Hell. Marcia is named in *Inferno* as one of the souls who resides in Limbo, and is recalled in the Purgatory scene with Cato. The historical Marcia, in the first century BC, married the austere and patriotic Cato. In a consensual arrangement with her husband (since divorce was very common and easy to arrange in Roman law), Marcia left him and went with Cato's friend Quintus Hortensius, only to return to her first husband after Hortensius's death. Lucan's account personalizes the story, portraying Marcia as a woman who regretted her decision and returned to Cato after the death of her second husband. Cato, the embodiment of selfless devotion to the common good, welcomes her back. His acceptance of Marcia in the story in the *Convivio* foreshadows his role in the *Comedy* as the old man who greets souls as they arrive in Purgatory.

Ever inventive, Dante turns Lucan's story too into an allegory. Marcia represents the noble soul at all four ages of the lifespan. She is a maiden at the beginning of the story, and so signifies youth. In her marriage with Cato she represents the noble soul in early adulthood. Her leaving Cato is the end of early adulthood and the beginning of middle age. And when Hortensius dies and Marcia returns to Cato, the noble soul is setting out upon old age, returning to God, who is represented by Cato himself.

44 *Convivio* IV.xxvii.4.
45 *Convivio* IV.xxviii.2.

Dante expresses this last stage in words that he imagines Marcia or the noble soul speaking to God in the figure of Cato. Here is Marcia's speech, interspersed with Dante's reflections and narrative asides:

> "Now," says Marcia, "that my womb is weary and I am exhausted for childbirth, I return to you, having nothing to give to another husband." In other words [notes Dante] the noble soul, realizing it no longer has a womb capable of bearing fruit — that is, its limbs and organs, sensing that they have grown weak — returns to God, he who has no need of bodily limbs and organs. And Marcia says, "Grant me the rights of our old bed, grant me so much as the *name* of marriage"; which is to affirm [Dante comments] that the noble soul says to God: "Grant me, my Lord, peace in you; grant, at least, that I may, in this small portion of life, be called yours." And Marcia says, "Two reasons prompt me to say this: the first is that, after me, it be said that I died the wife of Cato; the second is that, after me, it be said that you did not drive me off but that you willingly gave me in marriage." [As Dante concludes:] The noble soul is moved for these two reasons: wishing to leave this life as the wife of God and wishing to show that its actions were pleasing to God.[46]

Having described the virtues that are characteristic in each age of life, near the end of the *Convivio* Dante refutes those who think of themselves as noble merely because they have come from an illustrious family. The individual brings nobility to the lineage, he reminds us, not the other way around.

On the other hand, we do not have to look far in Dante's writings to find passages where he *does* praise noble family lineage. He does not simply oppose a "false" nobility of blood to a "true" nobility of spirit. For example, in *Inferno* Dante expresses pride in his noble Florentine-Roman ancestry when he encounters his father-figure Brunetto Latini. In the great cantos of *Paradiso* where Dante meets his noble ancestor the knight Cacciaguida, he positively basks in his noble ancestry. And in his treatise on monarchy, Dante argues that the nobility of the Romans was essential to the providential role of their empire.

---

46 *Convivio* IV.xxviii.17–19.

Without their noble nature, Dante argues, conditions would not have been auspicious for the coming of Christ, who was born at the height of the Roman Empire. While the *Convivio* argues against superficial or corrupt hereditary nobility, the emphasis in Dante is on "corrupt," not inherited nobility as such. As the *Purgatory* quote in the Chaucer passage at the start of this chapter says, individual nobility is like sap in the noble family tree, which withers without it; God wills it to be this way, as a reminder that the seed of nobility is a gift of grace, not a human possession. Nevertheless, noble lineages have an important function that the individual noble person cannot fulfill alone. Dante values noble family ancestry as a kind of "transpersonal objectification of virtue," as one early commentator put it. It is a *social* expression of the Self with a capital S, and so enhances human life as it is actually lived.[47] Dante encapsulates this insight in a single verse, when he tells Cacciaguida that his ancestor's spiritual nobility "raised me up so that I am more than I."[48] Cacciaguida's presence and speech, Dante is saying, give him a strength that is much larger than any individual could have given, since it comes from the source, the *potenza*, of the father. In short, Dante would have agreed with the conclusion to Yeats's poem "A Prayer for My Daughter":

> How but in custom and in ceremony
> Are innocence and beauty born?
> Ceremony's a name for the rich horn,
> And custom for the spreading laurel tree.

47 A paraphrase and quotation from the commentary on *Paradiso* XVI, by Giovanni da Serravalle (fifteenth century).
48 *Paradiso* XVI.18.

6

Lady Philosophy

ARLY ON IN the *Convivio*, Dante seems eager to distance himself from his youthful writings in the *Vita nova*. A decade or so
of intensely active life has passed since he composed his first
book. He is now middle-aged and famous, as a lyric poet and as a
leading politician of his city, Florence, from which he had been exiled a
couple of years before he started composing the *Convivio*. Since writing
the *Vita nova*, in which he was a poet of love, he has become, as he
says of himself in *De vulgari eloquentia*, written near the time of the
Convivio, a poet of ethical and social vision. As Dante puts it early on
in the *Convivio*, while the *Vita nova* was "fervid and passionate," the
newer work is "temperate and virile."[1]

Close connections between the two works are clear as well, however.
Near the start of the *Convivio*, the final episodes of the *Vita nova* are
given as background material. Like the *Vita nova*, the *Convivio* is a
combination of prose and poetry. In fact, although the *Convivio* is not
a narrative with a beginning, middle, and end, but a multifaceted series
of essays, it is in some ways a sequel to the drama of the *Vita nova*. As
mentioned earlier, a crucial episode in the latter is the death of Beatrice.
Dante's shock of recognition of what her impending death means occurs
at exactly the center of the middle poem of that book—like a hinge
between life before Beatrice's death and life after her death. Dante refers
to Beatrice's death also in the *Convivio*, where he says it is the crisis in
his life that led him to the study of philosophy, which he personifies
as a woman he fell in love with. His love of her is his consolation for
the loss of Beatrice. When Beatrice died, he writes, "I was pierced by
so much grief that nothing could comfort me. However, after a while,
my mind, which was trying to heal, considered, since neither my own
nor others' consolation made a difference, turning to what a certain
disconsolate person had used for being consoled."[2]

The disconsolate person here is Boethius, whose *Consolation of
Philosophy* tells us about Boethius's rising above the most adverse

1 *Convivio* I.i.16.
2 *Convivio* II.xii.1–2.

circumstances through philosophical contemplation, personified as Lady Philosophy. Dante tells us that at this time he also read Cicero's *De amicitia* (On Friendship), in which a man named Laelius, whose friend Scipio has died, claims that the soul does not perish at death. Rather, following the great philosophers and oracles of antiquity, he thinks that our soul has a divine origin and destination, and that after death the soul returns to heaven. So, he says, death did not actually destroy his bond of affection with his friend. Dante writes in the *Convivio* that these works of Boethius and Cicero not only comforted him in his grief, but led him to a newfound passion for philosophy:

> And as it can happen sometimes that a man goes in search of silver and serendipitously finds gold, which a hidden cause presents, I, perhaps not without divine authority, in trying to console myself, found not only the remedy for my tears but words of authors, fields of knowledge, and books. Considering these, I determined then and there that philosophy... was a supreme thing. And I imagined her as a gracious lady, and I could not imagine her in any comportment that was not merciful; so that my truth-sense gazed on her so willingly that I could barely turn it away from her.[3]

The merciful quality that Dante says was intrinsic to philosophy, personified as a woman, is characteristic also of the beautiful woman who appears near the end of the *Vita nova*, after Beatrice's death: the so-called Donna Gentile, or gracious or noble lady, whose compassionate expression comforts Dante. Here is the scene in the *Vita nova*. The phrase "some time later" at the beginning of the passage means that this episode takes place a little after the one-year anniversary of Beatrice's death:

> Some time later, in a place where I was reminiscing on the past, I was so beset by anguish and painful thoughts that I was unable to hide this horrible turmoil. Becoming self-conscious about my tormented state, I raised my eyes to see if anyone was watching me. Then I saw a gracious

---

3 *Convivio* II.xii.5–6.

woman, young and very beautiful, who was watching me from her window so compassionately, to judge by her look, that all compassion seemed gathered in her.[4]

The bereaved poet becomes infatuated with this compassionate woman, only to find that the new love conflicts with his loyalty to his love for Beatrice, who is now in Heaven. In the *Vita nova*, the struggle between the new love and the old is depicted as one between the heart, which is in favor of the new love, and reason, which defends the old love. "Heart" in this case, Dante tells us, means "appetite," or will. Finally, a powerful vision of Beatrice as she was when they first met in childhood moves Dante to renounce the new love. Near the end of the *Vita nova* he repudiates his love for the Donna Gentile and entrusts himself completely to Beatrice in glory among the blessed souls in Paradise. He tells us he plans to commit himself to studying and to developing his skills to the point at which he will be capable of writing about Beatrice as no woman has ever before been written about. And the *Divine Comedy* is proof that he was good for his word.

Yet apparently things were not so simple, since, to the consternation of Dante scholars ever since, Dante says in the *Convivio* that the gracious woman who had temporarily eclipsed Beatrice in the *Vita nova* was none other than Lady Philosophy herself. Dante explains, using the cycles of Venus as his measure of time, that he met the Donna Gentile, or Lady Philosophy, exactly three years and seventy-two days after Beatrice's death on June 8, 1290, adding: "She was so moved by mercy over my widowed life that the spirits of my eyes became great friends of hers. And once they had done this, they so shaped her within me that my will was content to wed itself to that image."[5]

Much has been written about the discrepancies between Dante's account of the Donna Gentile in the *Vita nova* and his account of her in the *Convivio*. For example, in the *Vita nova* passage just quoted he sees the Donna Gentile only a little while after the first anniversary of Beatrice's death, while in the *Convivio* passage I referred to he says that more than three years had elapsed since her death. Also, commentators have asked why the Donna Gentile is supplanted by Beatrice at the end of the *Vita nova*, and is said there to be the *avversario de la ragione*,

4 *Vita nova* 24.1–2 (XXXV.1–2).
5 *Convivio* II.ii.1–2.

adversary of reason,[6] while in the *Convivio* the Donna Gentile replaces the memory of Beatrice. And, of course, since she is Philosophy herself, in the philosophical *Convivio* she can hardly be viewed in any obvious sense as an adversary of reason. None of the theories or explanations for these discrepancies is definitive, and it seems likely that we will never know with certainty what accounts for them.

Since Dante did not always speak in allegory, we do know that he studied philosophy after Beatrice's death and that this study was not merely bookish and cerebral. Rather, precisely because Dante saw love as *intrinsic* to true philosophy—actually, he says outright that love is the *soul* of philosophy, while wisdom or knowledge is its *body*—its effect on him was transformative and all-encompassing. Whatever else she might signify, the Donna Gentile or Lady Philosophy embodies and bears this love, as Beatrice in the *Vita nova* is the vessel for Dante's initiation into love as self-transcendence and intimation of beatitude.

After Beatrice's death, then, Dante read Boethius and Cicero. Boethius was especially dear to him. The *Consolation of Philosophy* is an extended dialogue between Boethius, who is in prison on an unjust charge of high treason, for which he would be tortured and executed, and the allegorical figure of Lady Philosophy. Boethius depicts Philosophy as a great comforter and guide of human existence. By the time Dante wrote the *Convivio* he too had been unjustly persecuted by his political enemies, which led to his exile from Florence. He identified not only with Boethius's misfortune, but also with his transcending of adversity by turning to the truth, to the Real with a capital *R*. Boethius in the *Consolation of Philosophy* addresses questions of fortune and happiness, of evil, free will, and divine providence. As Boethius says in the final lines of a poem in the *Consolation of Philosophy*, human beings would be blessed if our minds were governed by the love that rules the heavens: *O felix hominum genus / si vestros animos amor, / quo celum regitur, regat* ("O happy race of men, if only Love who rules heaven also ruled your minds")[7]—words that are echoed in the famous conclusion to Dante's *Paradiso*: *l'amor che move il sole e l'altre stelle* ("the love that moves the sun and the other stars"). Moreover, Dante learned from Boethius, as well as from other philosophers, the nourishment to be gained by applying thought to an inquiry into the nature and causes of things;

---

6 *Vita nova* 28.1 (xxxix.1).
7 *Consolation of Philosophy* ii, m. 8, lines 28–30.

the truth behind appearances; the relation between eternity, divine providence, and human freedom. Dante became an *amatore di sapienza*, as he puts it in the *Convivio*, a lover of wisdom, whose goal, he adds, was "that supreme delight which suffers no interruption or defect, that is, true happiness, which is obtained through contemplation of truth."[8]

Dante's Donna Gentile in the *Convivio* is reminiscent of Boethius's Lady Philosophy, but Boethius does not represent her, as Dante does his personification of philosophy, as the *lover* of all true philosophers. Also, the Donna Gentile is, like the biblical Sapientia or Wisdom in the writings attributed to Solomon, the companion of God from eternity, but Boethius's Lady Philosophy seems more separate from the eternal and God. Medieval commentators of Boethius — recalling Augustine's conviction that true philosophy and true religion are the same thing — had often identified his Lady Philosophy with Sapientia in the Solomonic books of the Bible. They referred to her as the mother of both wisdom and mercy. This association with Sapientia was influential on Dante's conception of Lady Philosophy, as it was on other writers in Dante's time. Dante however, as usual, profoundly transforms his models. He adds to his depiction of Philosophy the praise of the lady-beloved that was standard in the love poetry of his time, and he introduces her as a way to share with others his own personal experience with philosophy. While the scholars of Paris or Bologna praised Philosophy without them ever appearing in their own writings, Dante turns his treatise, parts of it anyway, into an autobiography. He is a convert to philosophy and his story of conversion is a personal one.

As mentioned in the introduction, the symbolist Dante whose gnosis is poetic naturally would have been strongly drawn to the Solomonic writings in the Bible as a model for his writing and as inspiration for his poetic vision. In the Bible, Solomon is the son of David and Bathsheba and the disciple of the prophet Nathan, who becomes the just and powerful king who secures for Israel a golden age (tenth century BC). In ancient and medieval times, for both the learned and the unlearned, Solomon was one of the most beloved and cited figures of the Bible. In popular medieval lore, Solomon was associated with initiatic mysteries and the secret Egyptian sciences, and some even believed he was the master of Pythagoras. Not rational insight but Sapientia, or Wisdom, is the province of Solomon.

8 *Convivio* III.xi.5, 14.

Readers of the *Comedy* may recall the character of Solomon in the sphere of the Sun in *Paradiso*, and the direct citations from the Song of Songs, referred to earlier, when Beatrice appears in the Earthly Paradise. Lino Pertile and Paola Nasti have shown that the Song of Songs and Proverbs and the rich lore around them and Solomon form the dense symbolism of the Earthly Paradise episode of *Purgatorio*, and demonstrated their pervasive influence on the *Convivio*, Dante's treatise the *Monarchia*, and his political letters as well.[9]

Pertile argues that the tradition around the Song of Songs was Dante's main exegetical and iconographic source for the fantastic scene in the Earthly Paradise, which is considered several times in this book. In the Middle Ages, the love story in the Song was interpreted in terms of both mystical love and eschatological-apocalyptic ideas about the historical destiny of humanity—a blending of love and politics that suited Dante's interests well, intertwined as it was with both Beatrice and the historical mission of the Church. In canto xiv of *Paradiso*, Solomon refers to the resurrection body of the blessed at the end of time. Dante may have chosen Solomon as a mouthpiece for this teaching because the Song of Songs depicts the nuptial union of man and woman, which, according to traditional exegesis, is a figure for the union of the divine nature with human nature in the incarnation of the Word, which enables the resurrection of the flesh.

Nasti clarifies that Dante admires Solomon's writings, not only for their deep wisdom, symbolism, and feeling, but for their stylistic variety and ethical courage. The Proverbs of Solomon were considered a model for a gnomic style, Ecclesiastes for a dry and stoic tone, and the Song of Songs for erotic lyricism.[10] Dante's project in the *Convivio* was unique, in that he composed a "scientific" commentary around an erotic metaphor passed down by the tradition of commentaries on the Song of Songs. Dante mixed the model of Song commentaries

---

9 Lino Pertile, *La puttana e il gigante: Dal "Cantico dei cantici" al Paradiso terrestre di Dante* (Ravenna: Longo, 1998); Paola Nasti, *Favole d'amore e "saver profondo": La tradizione salomonica in Dante* (Ravenna: Longo Editore, 2007). A recent translation of the Dante letters, with commentary, is Claire E. Honess, *Dante Alighieri: Four Political Letters*, MHRA Critical Texts 6 (London: Modern Humanities Research Association, 2007).

10 On the Song as an important influence on the early European love lyric, see Peter Dronke, "The Song of Songs and Medieval Love-Lyric," in *The Bible and Medieval Culture*, edited by W. Lourdaux and D. Verhelst (Leuven: Leuven University Press, 1979), 236–62.

with methods and themes of the more philosophical commentaries on Proverbs and the Book of Wisdom. Aspects of this influence were alluded to in the last chapter, since the frequent vegetation metaphors that Dante employs in his discussion of nobility are a prominent feature in Bernard's commentary on the Song.

In addition to reading Cicero and Boethius, at about the time he was writing or finishing the *Vita nova* and entering the political life of his city, in the mid-1290s, Dante took advantage of the instruction for lay people offered by the religious orders at Santa Maria Novella (Dominicans), Santa Croce (Franciscans), and Santo Spirito (Augustinians) in Florence. Two kinds of instruction were offered by these institutions: the *disputatio ordinaria*, or regular disputation, was reserved for religious students, while the *disputatio quodlibetalis*, or quodlibetal disputation, was open to all citizens, including lay people such as Dante.[11] During this time, Dante read essential theological and philosophical texts, often in the form of compendia or commentaries, and mastered the concepts, technical terms, and modes of argument of scholastic philosophy. He studied logic, mathematics, metaphysics, astronomy, optics, physiology, embryology, ethics, history, and political science.

It is important to keep in mind, however, that Dante's formal education was limited.[12] In addition to the above settings, he probably had some contact with a university environment, such as that in Bologna. But Florence itself was somewhat of an intellectual backwater, being more a commercial capital than a cultural one, so Dante had restricted access to books and to the more advanced intellectual discussions of the time. In addition, since Dante was largely an autodidact, learning from oral sources as well as written ones (e.g., recent scholarship has shown the important influence of sermons on Dante's thought), it is that much more difficult to trace his intellectual formation. The sources of medieval authors, in any case, are difficult to track down. Important sources were often accessed via anthologies or *florilegi*; texts were copied and so appeared in relatively fluid form; and it was impossible to read them without preconceptions since they were always surrounded

---

11   My thanks to Lorenzo Dell'Oso for sharing his paper, "From Peter of Trabibus' Quodlibets to Dante's *Vita nova*," paper read at the conference Quodlibetal Culture in Dante's Time: Europe, Italy, and Florence, University of Notre Dame, April 26–27, 2019.

12   Zygmunt G. Barański, *Dante e i segni: Saggi per una storia intellettuale di Dante Alighieri* (Naples: Liguori, 2000), 9–40, and *passim*, is the source for much of the information in this paragraph.

by commentaries and glosses that were canonical and conditioned their reception. In short, Dante's studies were a varied mix. He is a hybrid thinker who takes ideas from various sources as the occasion arises, and then interprets and blends them. His citations are often imprecise and apparently from memory. He is a poetic thinker, in short, not the systematic versifier of Aquinas's theology many scholars in the nineteenth and early twentieth centuries presented him to be. By the time he was thirty years old, Dante's variegated learning was substantial enough to be source material for his mature writings—as the *Comedy* abundantly attests.

A work that was formative for Dante, and one whose spirit pervades the *Convivio*, is Aristotle's *Nicomachean Ethics*, a copy of which he most likely owned. Questions that Aristotle addresses in the *Nicomachean Ethics* are: What do human beings need to do to be truly happy? How do we become virtuous? What is the good and how do we attain it? Aristotle teaches that right choices are based on knowledge, not opinion, and well-being or happiness is not a matter of luck or fortune. As we will see in the next chapter, Dante in the *Convivio* places ethics above metaphysics in his hierarchy of knowledge—lower only than theology. So highly did Dante consider the love of truth and its ethical application, that he poured scorn on those who studied jurisprudence, medicine, and theology simply for the sake of a livelihood and a prominent social position.

In 1302, a few years after Dante had completed his apprenticeship to philosophy, his political enemies sent him into exile from Florence, never to return. This bereavement was a death on a social level that surely rivaled or surpassed the grief he felt after losing Beatrice. For a period, early on in his exile, Dante tried to stay active in the politics of the political party of which he was a leading figure. The futility of political bickering eventually led him to abandon politics, to turn to *meta*-politics in his writing—a party all to himself, as he says in *Paradiso*. By 1304 he was probably at work on the *Convivio*, and it is reasonable to think of this as the work he wrote to come to terms with the loss of his homeland, as the *Vita nova* had been written to come to terms with the death of Beatrice.

Dante says that his original plan for the *Convivio*, which he never finished, was to compose fifteen treatises or books, including an initial prefatory book. Each of the fourteen principal books would begin with a canzone or long lyrical poem, which would then be interpreted allegorically and used as a basis for philosophical and ethical reflection. He wrote the *Convivio* in his mother-tongue Florentine, rather than Latin, the standard language at that time for scholarly writing, in part to make this work accessible to people — in particular civic leaders — who were too busy with social responsibilities to pursue higher learning. It seems, then, that one of the motives for composing this work was to set things right on the political and civic level by turning to and explaining philosophical first principles and their application in governance and social life. Having abandoned direct political involvement, as well as his introspective *Vita nova* stage, Dante was setting out on his vocation as poet-prophet-reformer — a role that he fully realizes in the *Comedy*.

Dante wanted to pass on to his audience of those engaged in practical life, not only his philosophical insights, but his abiding *love* for philosophy. Since the acquisition of wisdom requires everything we are, body and soul, the philosopher must love wisdom like a beloved who occupies his thoughts day and night. As Dante puts it in the *Convivio*:

> My second love began with the merciful face of a woman. This love, then, finding the life within me open to its burning, lit up like a fire from a small flame to a large one; so that not only when I was awake but also when I was sleeping, her light was conducted into my head. And how great the desire was which Love instilled in me to see her can be neither expressed in words nor understood.... Oh, how many nights there were when the eyes of other people were at rest, sleeping, while mine gazed steadily into the abode of my love! And just as a fire that has spread also wishes to be seen without, since it is impossible to stay hidden, a wish to talk about love came over me which was completely uncontainable.[13]

Dante is quite specific about what he means when he says that the light of Lady Philosophy's love filled his head. He writes that the mind or intellect is not only the highest part of the soul, but it is *deitade*, deity, and this, as he puts it, "is the place ... where Love speaks to me about my lady."[14] In other words, Lady Philosophy is associated with the essential core of

13 *Convivio* III.i.1–3.
14 *Convivio* III.ii.19.

the human being, the intellectual soul, which is made in the image of God. As we have seen in chapter 4 and the mirror imagery associated with Leah and Rachel, philosophy is the reflexive love of intellect.

At the beginning of chapter 1, I quoted Augustine's words about the gravitational pull of things toward their ontological homes. Similarly, in one passage in book III of the *Convivio*, Dante describes the characteristic loves of the various levels of creation. Plants love the places where they flourish. Animals love not only their natural habitats, but each other. In the case of human beings, explains Dante, the intellectual soul gives us the possibility of comprehending the loves of all degrees of being, including those of plants and animals. As Dante writes, voicing a commonplace of medieval theology: "Human beings have their proper love for perfect and dignified things. And since man . . . has divine nature within himself, he can and does have [within himself] all . . . loves" of the various levels of creation.[15] It is possible that Dante's view of this partly draws on the hermetic treatise *Asclepius*, which he could have known either directly or through its frequent mention by Albert the Great. In the *Asclepius* human beings are referred to as a *magnum miraculum*, a great miracle, who, although formed of the substance of mind, are given a "worldly sheath" or physical body by God so that we may love the created universe.[16] So, our proper love, which also enables us to comprehend all the levels of creation, is found in that highest part of the soul, where Philosophy or Wisdom dwells: the intellectual soul.

The great canzone that opens book III of the *Convivio* starts with the line *Amor che nella mente mi ragiona* ("Love, who talks to me in my mind"). Commenting on this line, Dante explains what he means by "love": "Love, taken in its true sense and considered subtly, is simply the spiritual union of the soul with the beloved thing: toward which union the soul goes by its very nature, swiftly or slowly according to whether it is free or impeded."[17] This definition echoes a passage in Aquinas: "Love . . . is a kind of union of the lover and what is loved, since the lover regards the beloved object as himself."[18] In his theory of love, Dante also draws on the Neoplatonic notions of *De causis* (On Causes), which says that forms proceed from the First Cause, or God, by way of the

---

15 *Convivio* III.iii.5.
16 *Asclepius* I.6a, 7c.
17 *Convivio* III.ii.3.
18 Commentary on Aristotle, *Metaphysics* I, lect. v.102.

celestial Intelligences, so that all love in this world is ultimately a desire for union with the good as such, which is God. The soul longs for its essential being, and its being depends on God, so it longs to be united with God. In the great chain of being that is the order of the cosmos, the Intelligences, or first emanations of the divinity, transmit the divine goodness by which the unknowable Deity reveals itself—to the extent that created beings are able to receive this revelation.[19] For Dante in the *Convivio*, love-union with the divinity takes the form of the union of his soul with the Donna Gentile, or Philosophy.[20]

In addition to using metaphors from the sort of courtly love poetry that he published in the *Vita nova*, Dante conveys a sense of this union and love through the ideal of friendship as portrayed by Aristotle and Cicero. The very word *philosophy*, Dante notes, comes from Pythagoras, who, when he was asked whether he considered himself wise, said that he was not a wise man but a lover or friend of wisdom—a *philosophus*. As Dante writes:

> From this stems the term for the philosopher's proper activity, *philosophy*, just as from *friend* stems the term for the friend's proper activity, *friendship*.... Philosophy is simply friendship with wisdom, or with knowing; and thus in a certain sense we can call everyone a philosopher, in accordance with the natural love that generates in everyone the desire to know.... Without love or without devotion one cannot be called a philosopher.[21]

Dante adds that by love for philosophy he also means the study required to win the love of Lady Philosophy—the difficult study of philosophical texts. Here as elsewhere, Dante makes use of the double meaning of the Latin word *studium*, study, which also means zeal, enthusiasm. This is why, as he writes, true scholarship or study is the *applicazione dell'animo innamorato della cosa a quella cosa*, the application of the mind to the thing it is in love with. In short, philosophy is "a loving use of wisdom."[22]

---

19 See *Convivio* III.vi.5 and vii.2–3.

20 See Peter Dronke, *Dante's Second Love: The Originality and the Contexts of the "Convivio"* (Exeter: Society for Italian Studies, 1997), 30.

21 *Convivio* III.xi.6.

22 *Convivio* II.xv.10, III.xii.12.

What is more, like any lady-beloved in courtly love poetry, Lady Philosophy's face has such charm as to awaken love in the one who beholds it. Allegorical treatment of the beloved's physical features was common in medieval love poetry in both the West and the East. For example, the fourteenth-century Sufi poet Mahmūd Shabistarī praises the metaphysical ramifications of his beloved's hair and beauty marks. In the *Convivio*, Dante says that the eyes and smile of the beloved are like two balconies, onto which her soul — her essential form — at times comes out so that the lover can gaze upon it. The goodness of the soul of Philosophy is revealed to the lover as the sensible beauty of Lady Philosophy, for Dante embodied by the Donna Gentile.[23] The soul of Lady Philosophy is of such a high degree of goodness that its beauty appears visibly in her body. This is reminiscent of Plato's famous formulation that beauty is the splendor of the true, or that it is akin to the good.

The poem I mentioned earlier, *Amor che nella mente mi ragiona*, says that *cose appariscon nello suo aspetto, / che mostran de' piacer del Paradiso* ("in her face appear things that reflect / the beauties and delights of Paradise"). Dante specifies that by "face" he especially means her smile and her eyes, which he interprets allegorically: "And here it should be understood that the eyes of Wisdom are her demonstrations, with which the truth is seen with utmost certainty, and her smile is her persuasions, in which the inner light of Wisdom shows beneath a veil. And in these two things that sublime pleasure of blessedness is felt, which is the greatest good in Paradise."[24] And he adds: "The eyes of this lady are her proofs, which, directed into the eyes of the intellect, make the soul that is liberated from its contradictions fall in love. O utterly sweet and ineffable appearances, sudden ravishers of the human mind, which appear in the proofs, that is, in the eyes of Philosophy, when she speaks with her lovers!"[25] The reason for this fatal attraction to Philosophy, says Dante, is that since each thing by nature desires its own perfection, and since the intellect is the foundational principle of man's being, its realization is man's ultimate happiness.

Since Lady Philosophy is the image of human perfection, she is also the source and inspiration for virtue, which is the beauty of the

---

23 See *Convivio* III.viii.
24 *Convivio* III.xv.2.
25 *Convivio* II.xv.4.

soul. Where the canzone I have been quoting states that *Sua bieltà piove fiammelle di foco* ("Her beauty rains small flames of fire"), Dante comments:

> Here it should be understood that morality is the beauty of Philosophy; for just as bodily beauty results from its members insofar as they are harmoniously ordered, so the beauty of wisdom ... results from the order of the moral virtues, which make her pleasing in a manner that is perceptible to the senses. And so I say that her beauty, or morality, rains small flames of fire, or upright desire, which is engendered by the pleasure of moral doctrine: this appetite distances us from innate vices as well as acquired ones.[26]

Lady Philosophy's presence, that is, "gently redirects" us, as Dante writes, when we are "turned away from the proper order."[27] Her beauty is such that she can awaken love, which is the soul's impetus to leave base attachments for its own higher calling.

The visible presence of the divine in Lady Philosophy has a further practical effect: she can awaken religious faith in the one who beholds her. This is another theme that harkens back to the love poetry of Dante's early years. For example, a sonnet by Guinizzelli states that his lady's beauty and grace have the power to convert a nonbeliever to the Christian faith. In the *Convivio*'s use of this theme on a higher level, the idea is that, since Philosophy can help us to see things, by means of reason, which without her help seem fantastic or impossible, the lover of wisdom can come to understand that miracles have higher, hidden reasons. And through this rational basis for a faith in miracles, faith, in a more comprehensive sense, can be born. The canzone says:

> *E puossi dir che 'l suo aspetto giova*
> *a consentir ciò che par maraviglia;*
> *onde la nostra fede è aiutata:*
> *però fu tal da etterno ordinata.*[28]

---

26 *Convivio* III.xv.11–12.
27 *Convivio* III.xv.14.
28 *Amor che nella mente*, lines 51–54.

(And we can say her face helps us aver
that wonder has become our certitude;
so that our faith is all but guaranteed:
thus from eternity she was decreed.)

Dante comments that Philosophy's appearance aids our faith because a principal basis for faith is the miracles performed by Jesus reported in the Gospels, as well as miracles carried out by Christian saints. However, many people are skeptical of miracles and cannot believe in them without visible proof. The Donna Gentile or Lady Philosophy is a *visibly* miraculous thing, which people can experience for themselves — since philosophy has to do with truth accessible to reason. So she can be an aid to faith. Dante concludes that "she was decreed in the mind of God as witness to the faith for those who live in this time."[29] More prosaically, in other words, Philosophy bears witness to faith by the light with which she illumines the intellect and by the moral beauty which she instills in the soul.

Not only is Lady Philosophy or Donna Gentile the beloved of all true philosophers, but she is the daughter, wife, and sister of God. Here Dante draws on the writings of Solomon in which Sapientia or Wisdom is represented as bride, *sponsa*. (As mentioned earlier, Dante says that wisdom is the body of philosophy, while love is its soul — in Aristotelian terms, wisdom is philosophy's material cause and love its formal cause.) Dante suggests that the intimacy of Wisdom with the Deity is obvious because God's own contemplation of Wisdom is simultaneously that of His own essence. In addition, Philosophy perfectly realizes the idea of man that is in the mind of God. One line in the canzone reads: *Ogni Intelletto di là su la mira* ("Every [celestial] Intellect gazes upon her from up in heaven"). Dante comments on this line, "I simply mean that she is made thus as the intentional exemplar of the human essence in the divine mind, and, therefore, in all the other... [minds], most of all in those angelic minds which create with heaven the things here below."[30] What is more, the same poem states that *In lei discende la vertù divina / sì come face in angelo che 'l vede* ("In her, celestial potency descends / as in an angel who beholds it"). Dante explains this image in terms of the hierarchy or chain of being,

29   *Convivio* III.vii.15–17.
30   *Convivio* III.vi.6.

to which he often refers. He says that gradations in the hierarchy of being are continuous, not discrete. For example, there is a gray, mixed area between human nature and the highest animal forms, just as between the most enlightened human beings and the angelic realm there is a connection rather than an unbridgeable gap. This is why, says Dante, Aristotle can refer to the most enlightened individuals as divine. The Donna Gentile herself is such a being, so that, writes Dante, "the divine power, in the manner in which it descends into angels, descends into her."[31]

What is more, there are passages in the *Convivio* that merge Philosophy-Wisdom with the divine Logos or Word. The Logos in Christian and hermetic tradition is the eternal, intelligible pattern of divine Ideas after whose model God creates the cosmos. It is the light of the world, the source of its intelligibility, order, and beauty; through the Logos-Christ, the transcendent God is linked to this world. At the same time, it is the light of the human mind, since in the world of appearances, true knowledge is impossible unless the intellect relates things to their source, which is their being in the mind of God. Likewise, wisdom is seen by Dante as having a harmonizing influence since it is associated with the very cosmic harmony that balances the movement of the sun, the cycle of the seasons, and the natural law that manifests as social order. In *Paradiso*, canto x, he expresses this as a hymn to the celestial order as a reflection of the divine wisdom.[32]

In *Amor che nella mente*, Dante describes the patterns of the sun's apparent motion, and his commentary on this passage evokes the providential cosmic order in which Philosophy participates and which she bestows on the lover of wisdom.

> *Non vede il sol, che tutto 'l mondo gira,*
> *cosa tanto gentil, quanto in quell'ora*
> *che luce nella parte ove dimora*
> *la donna di cui dire Amor mi face.*[33]

> (The sun sees nothing, as he circles all
> the world, nobler than at the hour he gives

---

31   *Convivio* III.vii.7.
32   *Paradiso* x.7ff.
33   *Amor che nella mente*, lines 19–22.

> his light to that part where the woman lives
> about whom Love has made me write and speak.)

Dante tells us that the sun in this passage is intended as a symbol for God, and therefore what is in question is the relation between the celestial powers and life on earth, including natural cycles. He adds: "Now we can see that by divine providence the world is ordered such that, once the sphere of the Sun has revolved and returned to one point, this globe on which we live everywhere receives as much time of light as of darkness. O ineffable Wisdom who ordained things thus, how impoverished our mind is in understanding you!"[34]

Dante goes on to say that Philosophy, like Sapientia in Solomon's writings, is co-eternal with the Creator. Since the divine love is eternal, reasons Dante, its object of love must be eternal—as indeed Wisdom is. He quotes from the Book of Ecclesiasticus or Sirach, where Wisdom says of herself: "From the beginning and before all time I was created, and in the age to come I shall be unfailing." Dante continues, still quoting from the Bible:

> In the Proverbs of Solomon this Wisdom says, "I am ordained from eternity"; and at the beginning of the Gospel of John, her eternity can be clearly ascertained. And from this it arises that wherever this love shines [meaning, God's love of Wisdom], all other loves go dark and are nearly extinguished, since its eternal object immeasurably overwhelms and surpasses other objects.[35]

The beginning of the Gospel of John, which Dante refers to here, of course, states that "In the beginning was the Word," the Logos which is Christ. Dante has identified, as if in passing, Sapientia-Wisdom with the Logos. We should not conclude, however, that Dante is equating the two. After all, earlier in the *Convivio* Dante refers to the Donna Gentile as a *creatura*, a created being,[36] but the Logos in Christian tradition is decidedly *uncreated*. It seems likely, then, that the Logos passage comes out of Dante's familiarity with a Christian tradition

---

34 *Convivio* iii.v.21–22. Cf. Romans 11:33.
35 *Convivio* iii.xiv.6–7, quoting Ecclesiasticus (Sirach) 24:14; Proverbs 8:23; John 1:1.
36 *Convivio* iii.viii.3.

from antiquity that associated the feminine Sophia-Sapientia in Solomon with the masculine Logos, the second Person of the Holy Trinity. The penultimate stanza of Dante's canzone ends with the forceful line: *costei pensò chi mosse l'universo* ("He who moved the universe thought of her"). Dante writes in his commentary on this line that Wisdom herself made the universe — a quite explicit association with the Logos, "through Whom," as the Nicene Creed of Christianity states, "all things were made." As Dante writes:

> In supreme praise of wisdom, I say that she is the mother of all things and the origin of every motion, stating that God commenced the universe with her, particularly the movement of the heaven which generates all things and from which every motion has its origin and on which every motion depends.... That is to say, she was in divine thought ... when he made the universe; therefore it follows that she made it.

Dante supports his point with a famous passage from Solomon's Proverbs, again in the voice of Wisdom herself:

> When God prepared the heavens, I was there; when he set a circle on the face of the deep with a fixed law and a fixed circuit, when he made firm the skies above and set on high the fountains of the waters, when he enclosed the sea within its boundary and decreed that the waters should not transgress their bounds, when he laid the foundations of the earth, I was with him, ordering all things, and I took pleasure every day.[37]

With such passionate and comprehensive statements in the *Convivio* about Lady Philosophy or the Donna Gentile, we may be surprised that she does not appear anywhere in the *Comedy*. Or at least she does not appear directly. Near the end of *Purgatorio*, Beatrice reprimands Dante for going astray in some way after her death; her words have often been interpreted as referring to the Donna Gentile: "As soon as I was at the threshold of my second stage and I changed lives [in

---

37 *Convivio* III.xv.15–16, quoting Proverbs 8:27–30.

other words, when she died], he separated himself from me and gave himself to others."[38] And Beatrice also challenges: "If the supreme pleasure failed you after my death, what mortal thing should then have drawn you into desiring it?"[39] We have already encountered these lines in the discussion in chapter 1 about Dante's transformation of courtly love into sacred love. Beatrice is telling Dante that the world of phenomena no longer should have dazzled Dante after her death, since while she was alive he experienced, through her, the substantial reality — the "supreme beauty" — of heaven. That was all he or anyone ultimately needs.

Beatrice in these lines and others in the scene in the Earthly Paradise — including her mention of a *pargoletta*, or young girl, who was a *vanità* or empty distraction[40] — alludes to some sort of infidelity or inconstancy on Dante's part. We notice that she does not mention the Donna Gentile or indeed any specific woman. As a result countless pages of scholarship have been spent on theories about what behavior or attitude of Dante, precisely, Beatrice is chastising him for. Dante himself, in this Earthly Paradise scene, tells Beatrice that *Le presenti cose / col falso lor piacer volser miei passi, / tosto che 'l vostro viso si nascose* ("Things right in front of me with their false pleasure turned my steps, as soon as your face was hidden").[41] He confesses, in other words, to a bodily or spiritual betrayal of what Beatrice represents, after she was no longer physically present to sustain it in him. Many critics believe that Dante's going astray was an intellectual error, a lapse into worldly thinking. Others say that Dante's inconstancy took the form of a period of licentiousness after Beatrice's death. No one is really sure, though it is clear that Dante suggests some infidelity on his part to what Beatrice embodied or what she inspired in him. In a later passage in *Purgatorio*, Beatrice reprimands Dante for having followed a *scuola*, or school, whose *dottrina*, doctrine, was as distant from the divine as earth is from the highest heaven. This passage does apparently refer to a specifically intellectual or spiritual lapse. Many have thought that it alludes to a period when Dante fell into the error of holding natural reason to be adequate for arriving at the truth of

38 *Purgatorio* XXX.124–27.
39 *Purgatorio* XXXI.52–54.
40 *Purgatorio* XXXI.59.
41 *Purgatorio* XXXI.34–36.

things. Some believe that the *Convivio* arises from and expresses this false direction, which Dante later regrets. A number of current Dante scholars, however, think that this interpretation is unwarranted. We will look at this in more detail in the next chapter, but for now I will note that I find it impossible to think of the writer of some of the *Convivio* passages that I have quoted here as a radical Aristotelian who has jettisoned theology in favor of philosophy.

As discussed earlier, traces of the biblical books of Solomon pervade Dante's writings. When Beatrice first appears to Dante in the Earthly Paradise, the words announcing her arrival are from the Song of Songs: *Veni, sponsa, / de Libano* ("Come, bride, from Lebanon").[42] Beatrice in this scene is called the bride of God, just as Lady Philosophy was in the *Convivio*, so it is clear that aspects of Philosophy-Wisdom have been assumed by Beatrice. And in other ways, too, Beatrice in the *Comedy* has some of the attributes of the Donna Gentile or Lady Philosophy. For example, both women are endowed with supernatural power in their eyes and smiles. In canto VII of *Paradiso* Dante describes Beatrice *raggiandomi d'un riso / tal, che nel foco faria l'uom felice* ("shining me a smile such as would make a man happy even if he were burning in fire").[43] Then Beatrice launches into a long theological discourse on the fall of man and his redemption through Christ's crucifixion. There are two conspicuous features in this passage: Beatrice is speaking; and the courtly love trope of the beloved's mouth, applied also to Philosophy in the *Convivio*, is now used for Beatrice. The same is true of her eyes. In the *Vita nova*, Beatrice's eyes were said to be a source of *spirti d'amore inflammati* ("spirits hot with love"),[44] while in *Paradiso*, as described earlier, Dante sees reflected in Beatrice's eyes a prefiguration of his final vision in the Empyrean: the nine angelic hierarchies as circles around a central point, which is God. In the *Vita nova* Beatrice never says a word; her presence may speak volumes but no *speech* issues from her mouth. The same is true of Philosophy in the *Convivio*: Dante chooses not to represent her as speaking, even though he had the model of Boethius, whose *Consolation of Philosophy* is a dialogue with Lady Philosophy herself. But in the *Comedy*, as the spokeswoman for holy

---

42 *Purgatorio* XXX.11–12.

43 *Paradiso* VII.17–18.

44 *Donne ch'avete intelletto d'amore* ("Women who understand the truth of love"), line 52, in *Vita nova* 10.23 (XIX.12).

Wisdom, Beatrice never hesitates to speak her mind. When Beatrice acts as a supreme authority on theological matters, we note that this position was unusual to say the least for a lay woman in the Church of Dante's time. At one point she opens her discourse with the statement, *Secondo mio infallibile avviso* ("According to my infallible opinion"),[45] so that Dante has implicitly placed Beatrice on a par with or beyond the doctors of the Church.[46] She has become a hybrid of Solomon's Sapientia, Boethius's Lady Philosophy, the *Convivio*'s Donna Gentile, and the young Florentine woman Dante loves in the *Vita nova*.

As for the figure of Philosophy in the *Convivio*, some have suggested that she combines what would become Virgil's and Beatrice's roles in the *Comedy*. Virgil is traditionally interpreted as representing natural reason and virtue; while Beatrice is the figure for theology or holy wisdom, the intellect inspired by divine grace. In this view of Lady Philosophy-Wisdom, Dante in the *Comedy* decided to make two personifications out of one: the Sapientia-Wisdom side of Philosophy is now represented by Beatrice, while the Aristotelian-rational side of her is assumed by Virgil. Such an interpretation works to a point, but it falls short when we observe that neither Beatrice nor Virgil in the *Comedy* can be so neatly pigeon-holed. Certainly Philosophy in the *Convivio* is far more baldly allegorical than Beatrice and Virgil are, and the love story of the *Convivio* is, as Richard Lansing writes, "more an artificial frame than a narrative comprising scenes and episodes." Indeed, the *Convivio* may have been abandoned when Dante realized that "Beatrice and Lady Philosophy could be one and the same woman."[47]

---

45 *Paradiso* VII.19.

46 Teodolinda Barolini has written about "speaking Beatrice," or *Beatrix loquax*, from a gendered perspective, in "Notes toward a Gendered History of Italian Literature, with a Discussion of Dante's *Beatrix Loquax*," in *Dante and the Origins of Italian Literary Culture* (New York: Fordham University Press, 2006), 360–78.

47 Richard H. Lansing, introduction to *Dante's "Il Convivio"* (New York: Garland Publishing, 1990), xvii, xxi.

7

The Quest for Knowledge

A S WE SAW IN THE LAST CHAPTER, one of Dante's main inspirations early on in his philosophical search was Boethius's *Consolation of Philosophy*. Boethius, alone in his prison cell, facing torture and a death sentence for a crime he did not commit, had realized that it is pointless to pursue only the things that belong to the realm of time and becoming. The more wealth or prestige or other advantages we acquire the more we can lose through the various and seemingly random turns of fortune. Real happiness consists in the virtuous life and in the pursuit of wisdom. In fact, philosophy in this holistic sense is the quintessentially human vocation. Citing Aristotle's *Metaphysics* as his source, Dante writes at the opening of the *Convivio*: "All human beings by nature desire to know. The reason for this is that each thing, impelled by Nature's providence, tends toward its own perfection; so that, since knowledge [*scienza*] is the ultimate perfection of our soul, in which our ultimate happiness resides, we are all naturally subject to a desire for it."[1] In the *Nicomachean Ethics*, Aristotle praises real philosophy as a divine activity and wisdom as the highest perfection that man can reach. Happiness is that which is desirable in and of itself, rather than something sought for the sake of something else. The contemplation of wisdom is the only activity that truly can be said to be for its own sake alone. Philosophy is awakened by truth. Truth itself calls on the truth within us, and this in turn awakens the desire to contemplate truth—the contemplation of which is true felicity. Dante puts this allegorically in the *Convivio*, in a passage cited earlier for its mirror imagery: "Philosophy, which is ... a loving use of wisdom, gazes upon herself when the beauty of her eyes appears to her; which is but to say that the philosophizing soul does not only contemplate the truth, but, moreover, contemplates

---

1 *Convivio* I.i.1–2. Dante defines *scienza* in book IV of the *Convivio*, again drawing on Aristotle: "*scienza* is perfect apprehension of things which are certain." *Convivio* IV.xii.12, referring to *Nicomachean Ethics* VI.3, 1139b.18–36. Also pertinent is Aquinas's commentary on Aristotle's *Posterior Analytics* I, lect. iv.32: "To know something scientifically is to know it completely, which means to apprehend its truth perfectly."

its own contemplation and the beauty of that contemplation as well, turning back upon itself and falling in love with itself through the beauty of its first gaze."[2]

For Dante, human intelligence is ultimately of one substance with deity, and true philosophy "has its being in the most hidden depths of the divine mind."[3] Thomas Aquinas also argues that the clearest sign of our capacity to unite with God is in our desire for truth, or, as Kenelm Foster paraphrases Aquinas, the "basic orientation of conscious being as such to union with being in general, and so with Being unqualified and absolute: which is God."[4] This is Dante's experience, too, in symbolic form, when he bathes in the river of light of illuminative knowledge, which is God's own light, in the Empyrean at the end of *Paradiso*. As Virgil instructs him in *Purgatorio*, the divine light (in Aristotelian terms, the active intellect) is that which makes the truth as such discernible to the human intellect, the way that light makes objects visible to the eye. And for Dante in the *Divine Comedy*, Beatrice is the visible reflection of this light.[5]

In any case, from the opening sentences of the *Convivio*, it is clear that to understand Dante's approach to knowledge we must consider Aristotle's influence on it. Aristotle and Aristotelianism pervaded the thought of Dante's time. Until the twelfth century, the works by Aristotle that were in circulation in the West were mainly those on logic, some of them translated into Latin by Boethius in the sixth century. But between 1120 and 1220 — in Toledo, especially, but also in other important centers such as Palermo — translation from Greek and Arabic into Latin made almost all of Aristotle's works accessible in the West. Aristotle became established as the most authoritative guide to philosophy, and a crucial influence on Christian thinkers: so much so that, in the *Convivio* and the *Comedy*, Dante calls Aristotle the "glorious philosopher to whom nature most disclosed her secrets," the "master and guide of human reason," and the "master of those who know."[6] Importantly, medieval Europe inherited an Aristotle strongly flavored with Arab and Neoplatonic thought, since the renaissance of

2   *Convivio* IV.ii.18.

3   *Convivio* IV.xxx.6.

4   Kenelm Foster, *The Two Dantes and Other Studies* (London: Darton, Longman & Todd, 1977), 76.

5   See, e.g., *Purgatorio* VI.45–46.

6   *Convivio* III.v.7 and IV.vi.8; *Inferno* IV.131.

Aristotelian learning also came in the form of Islamic commentaries and of certain Neoplatonic works that were mistakenly attributed to Aristotle. For medieval philosophers, historical authorship was not as important as it is to moderns; whether the text was "Platonist" or "Aristotelian," they tended to view the source as wisdom itself.

For Augustine, and continuing with the Franciscans and others who followed Augustine and distrusted the avant-garde Aristotelian learning, philosophy had always been the *ancilla theologiae*, or handmaid of theology, with little independent life of its own.[7] In the terminology of our own time, we can gain insight into the conflict between philosophy and theology in Dante's era by recalling that modern philosophers going back to Descartes and Kant have argued that philosophy's role is to tell us *what* the world's nature is, but it cannot tell us *why* it is or what lies beyond it. The saint or mystic speaks from direct intuitive experience, but since this experience lacks the usual subject-object relation of rational philosophical inquiry, it cannot be conceptualized or communicated and so, for the modern philosopher (who equates knowledge with the representation of concepts), cannot be called real knowledge. But earlier mystics and theologians in the West, such as Augustine or Richard of St. Victor, and the sages of the East, viewed the matter differently. For them, the profoundest interior experience is the *basis* of philosophical thought, while the role of reason is to clarify the meaning of this and to elaborate upon it.

With Aristotelianism came a much higher estimation of human reason (*ratio*) and therefore of philosophy with respect to theology, and of rational thought in relation to faith. The high regard for reason is present in Dante himself even as early as the *Vita nova*. In the *Vita nova*, Dante praises Beatrice because "even though her image, which was constantly with me, was the means by which Love ruled me, it was so dignified in its power it never allowed Love to govern me without the faithful counsel of reason."[8] And the prose of the *Vita nova*, a love story, is sometimes structured in the form of syllogistic argument. The *Vita nova* tells of dream-visions and feverish hallucinations, but Dante

---

7   On the question of what the words *theology* and *philosophy* actually meant in Dante's time, see Zygmunt G. Barański, "Dante and Doctrine (and Theology)," in *Reviewing Dante's Theology*, 2 vols., edited by Claire E. Honess and Matthew Treherne (Oxford: Peter Lang, 2013), 1: 9–64; 61–62.

8   *Vita nova* 1.10 (II.9).

was quite explicit from early on that he stood on the side of intelligibility.[9] The motive for this, far from being a precursor to modern rationalism, was that Dante, in common with scholastic culture in general, saw reason as a trace of the spiritual intellect in the human soul. Dante never viewed reason, in the Renaissance and Enlightenment manner, as independent of its source in the intellect. Rather, for Dante reason complements faith and is the instrument of man as made in the image of God, which is why man is, as Dante puts it in the *Convivio*, "the divine animal."[10] Reason is not only or primarily a confidence in ratiocination, dialectic, and syllogism, although it is this as well. *Ratio* is the mind's discursive procedure from point to point; *intellectus* its resting, or its capacity to rest, in a truth that is totally apprehended because it is totally interior, in the substance of the mind itself.

It is useful to make these distinctions, since some have portrayed Dante in the *Convivio* as a kind of proto-Renaissance humanist undergoing a major crisis about the relation of philosophy to theology and revelation. In this view, there was an "Averroist" or "radical Aristotelian" phase in Dante's development, during which he wrote much of the *Convivio*, when he supposedly favored philosophy and reason over theology and faith, just as some Latin thinkers influenced by the great Spanish-Arab philosopher Averroes (Ibn Rushd) had done.[11] Others have challenged this characterization, however, arguing that all of Dante's works, the *Convivio* included, ultimately are oriented toward religious and metaphysical truth.

Whatever position we might take on this issue, it does appear that Dante was infatuated with philosophy at some point, as his outpourings about Lady Philosophy-Wisdom in the *Convivio* attest, but there is really no clear evidence in his written works of his pitting philosophy per se against Christian teachings. Dante lived in an age of intense philosophical speculation, when there was much more liberty in Christian thought than there would be during and after the Counter-Reformation. Such figures as Albert the Great, Thomas Aquinas, and Dante himself

9   See *Vita nova* 16.10 (xxv.10).

10   *Convivio* III.ii.14. The background for this idea in Aristotelian thought is *De generatione animalium* (On the Generation of Animals) II.3, 736b.27–28, which refers to the divine nature of the intellectual soul.

11   The label "Averroist" itself is a modern invention, so recent scholars have pointed out that its use in connection with Dante is probably an anachronistic projection. See the introduction in my *Convivio* edition for details.

believed that the truths of religion and philosophy were ultimately compatible. They trusted that revelation, if it is indeed true, must somehow encompass *all* truth, including that of ancient "pagan" philosophers such as Aristotle. Philosophy for Dante supplements religion, it does not cut it off at the roots.

Nevertheless, during the thirteenth century, the idea caught on that philosophy has a distinct purpose as a complement to theology, and that the ethics of Aristotle could be a valuable counterpart to Christian ethics. Theologians referred to the twin benefits of philosophy and theology as a *duplex beatitudo*, or twofold state of blessedness. They viewed the contemplative heights of philosophy as an anticipation of eternal bliss—a view that we find in the *Convivio* as well. As Aquinas expresses it: "Man's happiness is twofold. One is the imperfect happiness found in this life, of which the philosophers speak.... The other is the perfect happiness of heaven, where we shall see God himself through his essence and the other separate substances."[12] (By "separate substances," Aristotle's terminology, Aquinas means the celestial or angelic Intelligences, or pure Forms; they are "separate substances" because they are separate from matter.) Central in Aquinas's thought—and as we read in the *Convivio*, Dante follows him in this—is the idea that our natural desire for knowledge cannot be *fully* satisfied by natural means, since human beings ultimately seek to know the divine essence. If philosophy is love of wisdom and God is Wisdom, humans are destined in this life to remain in a state of longing because we can never be totally united with God. The separate substances or celestial Intelligences *can* know God directly. So, Aquinas and Dante say, if we could know the celestial Intelligences, we would have at least some knowledge of God as well. But in this life it is not possible for us truly to know them either, and so we cannot know God even in this indirect way. Aquinas and Dante conclude that human knowledge on earth is limited by the senses on which it is based. *Nihil sit in intellectu quod prius non fuerit in sensu*, "Nothing is in the mind which was not first in the senses," was a maxim in scholastic philosophy, which Dante echoes in the *Convivio*. Clearly, this is not to say that we cannot know anything beyond the senses. Rather, this maxim affirms that human knowing originates in sense perception, a fact we can see for example by how a child's mental development

---

12 *Super Boetium de Trinitate* (On Boethius's *On the Trinity*), q. 6, a. 4, ad 3.

begins with the simplest sense perceptions and gradually builds upon them through language and increasing ability to reason; and adults cannot think without the use of sensible images. For Aquinas and Dante, external sensible forms, which are the divine Idea impressed on matter, penetrate our senses, moving them from potency to the act of sensing. The essential being of forms outside the soul is the cause of the *intentio* or *species cognoscibilis*, which determines and activates the senses, making them conform to the semblance of the real thing in itself. Through the *intentio*, therefore, the act of perceiving a stone involves the "real" form of the stone acquiring an immaterial being in the subject who perceives or knows the stone.[13]

In addition to his Aristotelian epistemology, Dante at this stage obviously does not deny that the divine vision is possible for human beings in this life. The examples of the apostles at the Transfiguration and of St. Paul when he had his ecstatic vision of the third heaven, as well as the testimony of various other saints and mystics — to say nothing of Dante's early visionary experiences, alluded to in the *Vita nova* — are undeniable precedents.[14] But the beatific vision in heaven is habitual and permanent, while the mystical vision or gnosis of men and women in this life is transient and sporadic. Dante makes a point of repeating many times in the *Comedy* that he is still in his body while he is visiting the *oltretomba* or otherworld. In the *Convivio*, on the other hand, Dante often emphasizes the aspect of human knowledge that is limited by its mortal condition. He writes: "I say that our intellect, through a defect in the power from which it extracts what it perceives — a power associated with the organs, namely the imagination — cannot rise to certain things..., such as substances separated from matter — which, even if we are able to have some idea of them, we can neither grasp nor comprehend fully."[15] As he states elsewhere in the *Convivio*, more poetically this time but echoing Aristotle:

> Not having any perception of [the separate substances] with our senses (from which our knowledge originates), there

---

13   A classic study on this subject in Dante, used in this section, is Bruno Nardi, "La conoscenza umana," in *Dante e la cultura medievale,* edited by Paolo Mazzatini, 2nd ed. (Rome-Bari: Editori Laterza, 1990), 135–72.

14   For Paul's vision see 2 Corinthians 12:2.

15   *Convivio* III.iv.9. And see also III.xiii.5.

still shines in our intellect some light of their essence that
is . . . radiantly alive . . .: just as one who has his eyes closed
affirms that the air is bright by means of a little splendor—as by a direct ray that passes through the pupils of a
bat—because not otherwise are our intellectual eyes closed,
while the soul is bound and imprisoned by the organs of
our body.[16]

Note that while Dante says we cannot know the celestial Intelligences fully, our intellect does receive an intuition of their existence,
what he calls the "light of their essence." Eyes as yet too closed to
perceive the radiance of the divine vision may discern something
of its reflected glory, in a form tempered to our earthly intellect's
limits. We are aware of God and the spiritual beings to the extent
that we make ourselves receptive to them. We can know *that* they
are, but not *what* they are. Our knowledge of them is through their
effects, and we may grasp a part, but only a part, of the causes of
these effects. Metaphysics, then, as Dante uses the term in the *Convivio*, has to do with this kind of indirect, intermittent knowledge.
It is reason's piecemeal view of the spiritual intellect's holistic vision.
Dante expresses this metaphorically in the *Convivio* when he writes
that metaphysics is like the Milky Way. Just as we cannot see the stars
whose clustering creates the effect of the Milky Way, and just as we
are forced to infer in the Milky Way the existence of numerous stars
that we cannot see individually, so metaphysics deals with primary
substances, which we cannot grasp other than through their effects.[17]
Also in the *Convivio*, Dante asserts that only in the next life will it be
possible to see the divine reality completely, which is the fulfillment
of our desire for knowledge.[18]

However, says Dante, the devoutly religious *can* know higher realities
by means of faith. Unlike purely rational philosophers, those with faith
in Christ are infused directly with the knowledge of divine things, even
if this knowledge is elusive and fleeting in our present state. For Dante
as for the Catholic tradition in general, such faith does not do violence
to reason. Rather, faith in the incomprehensible is the consummation or

16 *Convivio* ii.iv.17.
17 *Convivio* iii.viii.15.
18 See *Convivio* iv.xxii.13.

crown of rational knowledge. As St. Paul puts it, in words that Dante will quote in *Paradiso*, faith is the substance of things hoped for and the evidence of things not seen.[19] Much more than blind belief in dogma, faith is the adherence of the will to divine revelation and the intuitions of the spiritual intellect. The sanctified are those whose desire for knowing or seeing God is proportionate to their natural goodness; they have surrendered to that wisdom which the nature of each can comprehend. As Dante says in the *Convivio*, in language that echoes the Neoplatonic *De causis* (On Causes), each thing in creation receives the divine emanation according to its predisposition. The universe of Dante and his contemporaries is composed of a harmonious hierarchy of beings, at the height of which is the pure intellectual light of God, while all (ontologically) beneath God — which is to say all created things — are shadowed to one degree or another by this distance and to the extent that they are obscured by matter or open to the spirit. The measure of perfection of each created thing consists of its greater or lesser capacity to raise itself above matter and to draw near to the infinity of the First Cause that comprehends all. As Dante writes in the *Convivio*:

> The goodness of God is received in one way by the separate substances, that is the angels, who have no coarse bulk of matter, as if they are transparent through the purity of their form; and in another way by the human soul, which on one hand is free from matter, while on the other hand it is impeded (like a man is who is entirely immersed in water except for his head, so that no one can say he is entirely in the water or entirely out of it); and in still another way by animals, whose soul is entirely enclosed in matter (though I will add that it is somewhat ennobled as well); and in yet another way by plants, and in another by minerals, and in another way by earth than by the others, since it is the most material, and thus the most remote and most disproportionate with respect to the primal, utterly simple, and most noble generative power that is purely intellectual: that is God.[20]

19 Hebrews 11:1; *Paradiso* XXIV.64–65.
20 *Convivio* III.vii.5.

The human soul is immersed in matter but is free in its use of the intellect, which, as Aristotle noted, has the capacity to become all things. Dante continues: "Between the angelic nature, which is an intellectual thing, and the human soul there is no gradation, but one to the other is as it were continuous along the sequence of gradations," so that, "some individuals are so noble and of so high a state that they are practically angels."[21] And Dante adds that Philosophy herself is such a being. This closeness of Philosophy to the angelic realm is why she has the power in her speech and comportment to awaken higher love and a faith in miracles. Divinity descends into the human mind through the mediation of Philosophy; thus she is an *anticipation* of paradise on earth.

These various details show that Dante in the *Convivio* is working out the relationship between reason and faith: between applied or rational knowledge and spiritual wisdom. He is convinced that a particular, circumscribed kind of knowledge is realizable through the devoted practice of philosophy; and he allows a certain degree of validity to rational approaches to understanding the mysteries of the divine, as a way to harmonize the contrasting views that were current in his age. Dante denies that the limited nature of our knowledge in this life is a deficiency, since a natural desire can only be satisfied on the basis of the capacity that nature has given. He suggests that if nature has not given us the possibility of knowing God and the celestial Intelligences fully in this life, this means that there is no natural desire in us for this knowledge. Trying to force such impossible knowledge in the present life, then, is an error in the etymological sense, a wandering from the way of nature, the cultivation of an impossible desire like wishing to fly or to be made of crystal. In the final chapter of book III, Dante wonders how it can be that philosophical contemplation can bring a certain kind of fulfilment, if our desire to know cannot be completely realized during our life on earth. He concludes that "human desire is proportioned in this life to the knowledge which we can have here, and does not go past that point except by an error which is outside the intention of nature." So, "inasmuch as it is not possible for our nature to know what God and certain other [divine] things are, we do not, by nature, desire to know this."[22] It has been noted that Dante's thought in this chapter

21 *Convivio* III.vii.6.
22 *Convivio* III.xv.9–10.

contrasts with Aquinas's view of knowledge, which emphasizes it as a single direct motion toward a fixed end, God, whereas Dante accepts the intermediate stages as complete and perfect realizations in themselves. Aquinas's solution to the sort of uncertainty that Dante explores in this passage is totally oriented to sustain the supernatural finality of human desire; while Dante's approach to these matters is closer to that of other philosopher-theologians, especially Albert the Great.

By the time Dante wrote the *Convivio*, he had absorbed several philosophical streams that he was aiming to blend or harmonize. One such influence is the *De causis*, which medieval scholars mistakenly attributed to Aristotle, with its emanationist cosmology in which the divine outpouring descends from the First Cause or Supreme Good, via the celestial Intelligences or angelic spheres, to the lower spheres.[23] From this perspective, Philosophy is a natural mediator, since the angelic Intelligences know her in the divine mind, although human beings receive her mediations at best indirectly and sporadically. Philosophy, contemplative intuition, instills the mind of the philosopher with the first principles, even if these cannot be fully known in themselves. As Dante writes in the canzone discussed in the last chapter, *Amor che nella mente mi ragiona* ("Love, who talks to me in my mind"): *Cose appariscon nello suo aspetto, / che mostran de' piacer del Paradiso* ("And in her face appear things that reflect / the beauties and delights of Paradise").[24] In Dante's commentary on these lines he writes:

> I state that things appear in her face which reveal some of
> the pleasures of Paradise; and among those the most noble,

---

23   The origin and authorship of the *Liber de causis* or *Book of Causes* are uncertain, although it has been attributed to the twelfth-century Spanish-Jewish author Abraham ibn Daud (also known as Avendauth); or, alternatively, to a Syrian source sometime before the ninth century. Brought into Christian culture from an Arabic text, it was translated into Latin by Gerard of Cremona, in twelfth-century Toledo, and circulated as a work attributed to Aristotle, although by the time of Albert the Great its authorship was already being questioned. It was Thomas Aquinas himself who recognized that it was drawn from Proclus's *Elementatio theologica* (Elements of Theology) — hence its obvious Neoplatonist and emanationist outlook. By the 1230s the *Book of Causes* was, along with Aristotle's *Metaphysics*, among the required texts of the First Philosophy at the University of Paris. It was one of the principal sources of Neoplatonic thought — along with the so-called *Theologia Aristotelis* (Theology of Aristotle; an epitome of Plotinus's *Enneads*), Avicenna, Augustine, Pseudo-Dionysius, Boethius, and others.

24   *Amor che nella mente*, lines 55–56.

the one that is the fruit and end of all the others, is to be contented, which is to be blessed; and this pleasure truly, though in another manner, is to be found in her face. For, in gazing upon her, people are contented, so sweetly does her beauty feed their eyes; but in another manner than the contentment in Paradise, for contentment in Paradise is everlasting, which this cannot be for any person.[25]

Again, Dante portrays true philosophy as ultimately transcendent and ungraspable in this life, but the aspect that *can* be fully known—the face of Philosophy, her visible aspect—fulfills a basic human need, here and now.

Dante's pragmatic approach to philosophy, along with his love of the Latin poets and ancient Rome which appears in all his written works, shows that it really *is* accurate to think of him as a humanist—even if, unlike the version of humanism that became common during the Renaissance a century or two later, Dante's is a humanism centered on God rather than on Promethean man. In the *Convivio* the humanist insistence on the integrity of earthly life, without denigrating it in deference to the afterlife or the supernatural, manifests in close attention to applied ethics or moral philosophy, and in a long discussion, as we have seen in chapter 5, on the true nature of nobility. The circumscribed knowledge and realization of earthly life informed by philosophy became for Dante the basis for his ideal of civic order and justice. This ideal permeates the *Convivio* in its very conception and execution. The *Convivio* was written in the vernacular instead of in Latin partly to make it accessible to those—especially civic leaders—whose social functions or lack of educational opportunity prevented them from learning philosophy. Dante believed that political thinking based on first principles and philosophical understanding could create the conditions for a just society. This is the basis for his pro-imperial argument in *Monarchia*, and already in the *Convivio* he refers to the politically beneficial effects of philosophy, where he chides rulers whose advisors care and know little about the purpose of human life: "Consider who is by your side to provide counsel, and count how many times a day the final end of human life has been indicated by your counselors!"[26]

25 *Convivio* III.viii.5.
26 *Convivio* IV.vi.20.

The treatise is called a *convivio*, or banquet, because Dante pictures it as a communal meal of knowledge; each book is a separate course in this banquet, where the poems are the meat and the self-commentary the bread. The banquet is not for professional philosophers or theologians, but for human beings who simply wish to realize human nature, which desires to know. The innate desire for knowledge in man, cited in this chapter's opening, "is a particular case of that instinct given by God to all things, through which all natures are inclined to the universal order."[27] Dante himself is not one of the learned elite, but a man who gathers what falls from the table of the learned, to share it with those still mired in "the wretched life...I left behind."[28] In modern terms, Dante intends this work to be for a "non-academic" audience. The *Convivio* aims for an *integration* of knowledge that is difficult to imagine from the post-Enlightenment perspective, for which knowledge generally is partitioned into areas of specialization with little epistemological common ground.

In the *Convivio* Dante proposes three kinds of human fulfilment: the active life and the contemplative life (discussed in chapter 4) that can be realized during our time on earth are two of them; the beatific vision in heaven is the third. Dante views these kinds of fulfillment hierarchically. The contemplative life is superior to the active, and the beatific vision superior to the contemplative life. But Dante also suggests that the active life is the only one that may be completely and socially realized in *this* life, since contemplation is ultimately fulfilled only in the beatific vision. Dante comes to this conclusion because he views the human intellect in this life as too feeble to realize itself, so it must rely on the divine light of revelation. Consequently, the contemplative life is less human than divine. In this limited, practical sense, then, for Dante philosophical understanding can help us to realize our specifically human task during life on earth. Dante knows that it is not the ultimate fulfilment, but it is within our grasp, and its social usefulness encourages him to argue its virtues. So, he focuses for many pages in the *Convivio* on the positive results that can be attained through the exercise of moral and political virtues, as defined in Aristotle's *Nicomachean Ethics*. As Dante puts it in his letter to Cangrande della Scala, written a decade or so after the *Convivio*: "The

27 Nardi, "La conoscenza umana," 137.
28 *Convivio* I.i.10.

branch of philosophy to which the work is subject, in the whole as in the part, is that of morals or ethics; inasmuch as the whole as well as the part was conceived, not for speculation, but with a practical object."[29] He aims to endow our life here and now with a practical end of its own, although he agrees with the theologians that earthly life is subordinate to the heavenly life, which is the telos and pole star of all human activity.

In a section of the *Convivio* that likens eleven sciences or fields of knowledge to the heavenly spheres, Dante surprisingly places ethics or moral philosophy above metaphysics in the hierarchy of knowledge.[30] Book II of the *Convivio* is a commentary on the canzone that begins: *Voi che 'ntendendo il terzo ciel movete* ("All you who, knowing, make the third heaven move"). To explain what this third heaven is, Dante says first that we have to know that the word *heaven* in this context signifies a science or field of knowledge. The seven planetary spheres of the Moon, Mercury, Venus, and so on are associated with the traditional liberal arts, the trivium and the quadrivium, which were the foundation of medieval education: grammar, logic, rhetoric; arithmetic, music, geometry, astronomy. In this way, learning and knowledge were connected to their transcendent sources or archetypes. Dante associates the sphere of the Fixed Stars with physics and metaphysics; the Primum Mobile or First Mover with ethics or moral philosophy; and the Empyrean or highest sphere with theology or sacred science. Each heavenly sphere, Dante says, revolves around its center, which is motionless, just as each science revolves around its subject, which is also motionless, "since no field of knowledge demonstrates its own subject, but presupposes it."[31] And each science illuminates intelligible things the way each heaven illuminates things. Dante modifies the conception of metaphysics in order to assign it second place in the hierarchy, after ethics. He acknowledges that metaphysics remains *in*

---

29 *Epistle* XIII.40. It is worth noting too that Dante later emphasizes the *practical* wisdom of Solomon himself: see *Paradiso* XIII.94–102.

30 Bruno Nardi, in *Nel mondo di Dante* (Rome: Edizioni di Storia e Letteratura, 1944), 213–14, names some precedents to Dante in this schema: e.g., al-Fārābi (ca. 870–950) in his *Liber de scientiis*, which had been translated into Latin by Gerard of Cremona, where ethics (*scientia civilis*) is placed above metaphysics; and various commentaries on Aristotle's *Nicomachean Ethics* before 1250. The idea is present as well in civic thinkers like Brunetto Latini, who had a decisive influence on Dante's thought.

31 *Convivio* II.xiii.3.

itself the loftiest and most perfect of the sciences, apart from theology. But metaphysics is not the highest science *in practical terms*, since our mastery of metaphysics necessarily remains incomplete in this life. Meanwhile, ethics or moral philosophy is associated with a higher sphere, the Primum Mobile, since moral philosophy moves and guides us toward the other sciences—just as the First Mover orders all the other heavens. As in Plato and Aristotle, in Dante the question of justice involves bringing human life into harmony with the universal order.

The analogical procedure here is an application of the hermetic principle, "As above, so below"; or in other terms, of the operation of natural law in cultural activity. Parallels between the planets and the liberal arts had been proposed before Dante, for instance in Alan of Lille's *Anticlaudianus* (twelfth century); and, in a form identical to that of the *Convivio*, in Michael Scot's *Liber introductorius* (thirteenth century). As Titus Burckhardt shows, the system that Dante outlines is anything but arbitrary; the trivium and the corresponding planetary and other symbolism was "a schooling both in language and in thought," since "it is language which makes man man," and the *quadrivium* was "a means to open the spiritual eye to the beauty of mathematical proportions, and the spiritual ear to the music of the spheres." Burckhardt quotes Thierry of Chartres on this: "Philosophy has two main instruments, namely intellect (*intellectus*) and its expression. Intellect is illumined by the *quadrivium* (arithmetic, music, geometry and astronomy). Its expression is the concern of the *trivium* (grammar, logic and rhetoric)."[32]

Dante says in the *Convivio* that, ultimately, our intellect can approach divine things and therefore the subject of theology only by *un*knowing them. Like Pseudo-Dionysius in his apophatic theology, Dante realizes that eternal "things somehow dazzle our intellect" so that "we cannot grasp what they are; the only way we can approach knowing them is by negating things."[33] Since knowledge has as its object that which is, and God is beyond all that exists, only total ignorance or unknowing can know God. Dante's statement is a hint of the journey he will undertake in the *Comedy*. He recognizes that one's own efforts cannot

---

32 Quoted in Titus Burckhardt, "The Seven Liberal Arts and the West Door of Chartres Cathedral," *Studies in Comparative Religion* 16, nos. 1–2 (Winter–Spring 1984): 57–61; 58.

33 *Convivio* III.xv.6.

penetrate the profoundest mysteries, which, as we saw in the introduction, requires the *self*-revelation of the Real. The *Convivio* is partly a personal account in which Dante tells us of a period in his life when he was full of enthusiasm for the possibilities of philosophy. It is not possible to identify clearly, as critics have tried to do, Dante's alleged *traviamento*, or going astray, in the *Convivio*, followed by a return to Beatrice and theology in the *Comedy*. If nothing else, the placement of the "Averroist" Siger of Brabant next to Aquinas in canto x of *Paradiso* confounds any such reductionist account of Dante's development.[34] Rather, Dante's metaphysical and mystical concerns persist throughout his intellectual life. And what the reader who follows the progress of Dante's work witnesses is his integration of theology and philosophy; his evolving poetic vision; his blending of contrasting elements; and, above all, his strong tendency to harmonize rather than compartmentalize seemingly conflicting views.[35]

However we interpret the movement from the *Convivio* to the *Comedy*, there is no basis for believing that Dante when he wrote his masterpiece had left philosophy behind in favor of theology. Even late in *Paradiso*, in the sphere of the Fixed Stars, Dante claims that his love for God is inspired not only by revelation but by the proofs of philosophy.[36] In cantos xxiv–xxvi of *Paradiso*, the apostles Peter, James, and John question Dante on the theological virtues, using the rational-logical techniques and terminology of scholastic philosophy. Earlier in *Paradiso*, Dante makes it clear that both philosophy and theology are divinely ordained, within their respective spheres. In an ecstatic hymn to sacred science in canto iv of *Paradiso*, Dante affirms

34 *Paradiso* x.136–38. This placement has been interpreted by some commentators as Dante's figural expression of the harmony between philosophy and theology. Siger taught the Averroist doctrine that the intellectual soul or possible intellect is a unique principle separate from the individual soul, one intellectual principle common to all human beings, a unity that does not multiply with the multiplication of human bodies. This "monopsychism" was condemned in 1270 by the bishop of Paris, who said this teaching virtually denied free will and the action of God's providence. So, for some, Siger stands for compartmentalized philosophy, the mind's activity as it speculates by the light of reason alone, with the possibility even that reason will reach conclusions that are *not* those of theology.

35 Simon Gilson, "Dante and Christian Aristotelianism," in *Reviewing Dante's Theology*, edited by Claire E. Honess and Matthew Treherne, 2 vols. (Oxford: Peter Lang, 2013), 1: 65–110; 105.

36 *Paradiso* xxvi.25–27, 37–39, 76–78. In lines 28–30, Dante explains how philosophical argument can awaken love of God.

that the human intellect can be fully realized only by divine illumination. And yet Dante concludes this passage with praise of Socratic openness to the yet unknown: "Questioning arises from the desire to know, like the shoot of a plant at the base of divinely illuminated truth."[37] In *Monarchia*, Dante accepts the Aristotelian notion of the nature of happiness; refers to the *Nicomachean Ethics* regarding the argument that greed is a basic obstacle to justice; and writes a long section that is completely based on Aristotle.[38] And two very late works, the letter to Cangrande and *Questio de aqua et terra*, use the technical, scholastic language that Dante uses in much of the *Convivio*. Nevertheless, as is clear from the *Comedy* itself, in these works and others Dante is far from being a "rationalist." As Zygmunt Barański shows, Dante includes an implicit criticism of Aristotle's limitations even in his most apparently pro-Aristotelian moments. For example, *Questio de aqua et terra* (An Inquiry into Water and Earth), a scientific lecture that Dante gave in Verona in 1320, the year before his death, accounts for the relation between earth and water in the scientific, Neo-Aristotelian terms of the day. Barański notes that Dante probably interrupted his work on *Paradiso* to give the lecture in order to counter rationalistic attacks on the symbolic and mythological language he uses in *Inferno*, establishing his credibility as a rational thinker in addition to his reputation as a poet; and to prove that he used the symbolic language of *Inferno* not out of ignorance but out of poetic and hermeneutic exigencies.[39] So, Barański distinguishes between the microcosmic level of the text, where we see Dante's frequent use of Aristotelian doctrine, and its macroscopic counterpart, where Dante's preferences for Platonism and for symbolist exegesis over Aristotelianism are clear.

Dante states in book III of the *Convivio* that "those who live by the senses cannot fall in love with" Philosophy, "since they are unable to conceive of her."[40] Similarly, in canto XXVIII of *Paradiso*, Beatrice tells Dante that knowledge precedes love: "From this one can see how being blessed is founded in vision, not in that which loves, which then follows."[41] Here, Beatrice is saying that the soul can love only when

37 *Paradiso* IV.130–31.

38 *Monarchia* I.i.4 (cf. *Convivio* IV.xvii.8); I.xi.11; I.v–xv.

39 Zygmunt G. Barański, *Dante e i segni: Saggi per una storia intellettuale di Dante Alighieri* (Naples: Liguori, 2000), 127–46, 199–219.

40 *Convivio* III.xiii.4.

41 *Paradiso* XXVIII.109–11; see also V.7–9, XIV.40–42, and XXIX.139–41.

it has first known or seen the beloved—when it has experienced the Other as itself. Both Augustine and Aquinas likewise taught that nothing can be loved that is not first known.[42] The soul loves only what it has seen; and seeing and knowing are etymologically related, as in Sanskrit *veda*, "knowledge," and Latin *videre*, "to see," and Greek *oida*, "to know."[43] There can be no knowledge of anything to which the will refuses to give its assent. This is why the Christian definition of faith is "assent to a credible proposition": *Credo ut intelligam* ("I believe in order to understand") and *Intelligo ut credam* ("I understand in order to believe"), these two being simultaneous rather than successive.

When Beatrice's role as Dante's guide in Paradise has reached its limit, her replacement in the Empyrean is Bernard of Clairvaux. Commentators have said that Bernard represents the sort of knowledge or illumination which enables the vision of God, the *lumen gloriae* or light of glory, which is God's own light by which the beatified may behold the eternal. Dante describes it as the light *che si deriva perché vi s'immegli* ("that gushes forth [from God, its source] so that we may improve [become better]")—*s'immegli* being a term coined by Dante.[44] Ultimately, knowledge of God is God's knowing Himself through us. Beatrice describes this light to Dante in the Empyrean, in the devastatingly elegant verse: *luce intellettüal, piena d'amore* ("intellectual light, full of love").[45] I have not seen this mentioned by the commentators, but it may be significant that the eleven syllables of this line (the standard line length, or hendecasyllable, in classical Italian poetry) are divided into two halves, the first half dedicated to knowledge or the intellect, the second to love: *luce intellettüal, piena d'amore*. The half of this line allotted to knowledge or vision has one more syllable, six, than the half assigned to love, which has five. The balance between the two is close, swayed by a vowel's breath.

---

42 Augustine, *De Trinitate* (On the Trinity) x.i.3; *Summa theologiae* I-II, q. 3, a. 4.

43 Seyyed Hossein Nasr, *Knowledge and the Sacred* (Albany: State University of New York Press, 1989), 6.

44 *Paradiso* xxx.87. See also *Paradiso* xxi.83–84 and xxx.100–102.

45 *Paradiso* xxx.40.

8

On the Way to Rome and Jerusalem

"WHAT HAS ATHENS to do with Jerusalem?" the Church father Tertullian famously asked. Tertullian is usually quoted out of context, so his question has been interpreted as fanatically antirational, but he probably intended it as an aphoristic way of saying that the revelations of scripture are of a different order from the insights of philosophy. As we have seen, it is likely that Dante himself would have agreed with this distinction, even while he was composing the philosophical *Convivio*. At the same time, for Dante, philosophy's essence is divine and therefore implicit in theological and scriptural truth. Dante expresses this dual authority, civic and holy, not in terms of Athens and Jerusalem, but as the marriage of pre-Christian Rome and the imperial ideal on the one hand and Jerusalem and Christianized Rome on the other—each of them being a fundamental locus for his Christian faith as well as a poetic and political symbol.

In the Ptolemaic map of the universe that Dante follows, Jerusalem is the central point on earth, the *colmo* (highest point) of the *gran secca* (dry land),[1] a land mass situated only in the Northern Hemisphere. The Southern Hemisphere, *il mondo sanza gente* (the uninhabited world),[2] is composed entirely of water—with the exception of the island of Purgatory and its mountain, which rise from the water exactly opposite to Jerusalem. This hemispheric polarity is opposite to how things were at the start of the creation, since dry land was originally in the South. Lucifer's fall from Heaven restructured the earth, when dry land, dreading his approach, fled the South and pushed into the North, which became the hemisphere of sin and exile, where Christ would be born, crucified, and rise from the dead to atone for humankind's fallen state.[3]

Since Jerusalem and Purgatory are antipodes, they share a horizon, which has its terminus at the Ganges River in the East and at the city

1   *Inferno* XXXIV.113–14.
2   *Inferno* XXVI.117.
3   *Inferno* XXXIV.112–26.

of Cadiz in the West. Lucifer is located equidistant between Jerusalem and Purgatory. In an astronomical passage in *Purgatorio*, the two places' symmetrical opposition is emphasized, where Virgil explains to Dante that the sun's trajectory in Purgatory, when one is looking east, appears to the left, while in Jerusalem it appears to one's right; the same can be said about the equator in relation to the two poles.[4] This emphasis on how the sun (which in Dante is always a symbol for God) comes from the left in Purgatory has allegorical significance as well. While the direction of Dante and Virgil's descent in Hell was nearly always toward the left, in Purgatory it is toward the right. The "sinister" connotations of left-wardness in Hell, then, have been replaced in Purgatory by right-mindedness; the sun coming from the left symbolizes the rectifying grace of the divine order. As Virgil and Dante learn, no ascent of Mount Purgatory is possible at night, precisely because the sun is absent.[5] The summit of Mount Purgatory, directly in line with the Jerusalem-Lucifer-Purgatory axis, is Eden or the Earthly Paradise, the site of the primordial human state and its fall from grace.

Further symbolic meaning can be gleaned from this cosmic map, since Purgatory is where souls atone for their sins and Jerusalem for Christians is where the Savior was crucified and rose from the dead to redeem souls from original sin. The Cross itself is the axis that extends through the earth to Purgatory and on through the celestial spheres. The sense of Jerusalem as a spiritual center of gravity is expressed by Dante in one of his letters, where he says that the Florentine exiles, including Dante himself, were longing for their city the way the Hebrews had longed for Jerusalem during the Babylonian exile; and in *Paradiso*, where Dante describes earthly life as *lo essilio / di Babillòn*, the "Babylonian exile" from Jerusalem-Paradise.[6]

There are precedents in the Bible for Jerusalem's central geographical position. Jerusalem is King David's city, the place of the Holy Temple, chosen by God for his people;[7] and it is inevitably associated by Dante and by all Christians with the Heavenly Jerusalem or the City of God — from the account in Revelation 21, to the eighth-century hymn

---

4 *Purgatorio* IV.61–84.
5 *Purgatorio* VII.56–57.
6 *Epistle* VII.30; *Paradiso* XXIII.134–35.
7 Ezekiel 5:5. See also Ezekiel 38:12 and Psalm 73:12.

Urbs beata Ierusalem, always imagined as a city.[8] Emperor Constantine built the Church of the Holy Sepulchre in Jerusalem, which became a cherished destination for Christian pilgrims; this and other sacred buildings on earth were to be modeled after the Heavenly Jerusalem.[9] In this chapter and the next, we will see how both these symbolic expressions—pilgrimage and the sacred architecture associated with Jerusalem—are structural elements of the *Divine Comedy* itself.

The image of Jerusalem appears in various ways throughout the *Comedy.* It is less surprising, perhaps, to find this symbolism in *Purgatorio* and *Paradiso* than in *Inferno*, but it is there as well. Dante's round, concentric depiction of Hell resembles medieval maps in which Jerusalem is circular in shape with a cross in the middle. The abyss of Hell and the cone of Mount Purgatory caused by the fall of Lucifer, which Virgil relates to Dante at the end of *Inferno*, accounts for the symbolic map sketched above, where the Earthly Paradise and Jerusalem have complementary roles in salvation history. When Lucifer fell from the Southern Hemisphere, which is where dry land originally was, his impact was directly opposite to where Jerusalem would be built. The dry land fled before him as he fell, pushing through to the other side and forming the new land mass in the Northern Hemisphere. The land that was displaced in forming Hell pushed up to the side to form Mount Purgatory. So, Lucifer is head-down with respect to Heaven—with obvious symbolic implications. At the end of *Inferno*, when Dante and Virgil climb into the Southern Hemisphere, they have returned to the upright position of human beings in their primordial state and can begin their pilgrims' ascent of the mountain.

And *Inferno* contains further traces of the image of Jerusalem. For example, canto xxxiv opens with a parody from the sixth-century hymn *Vexilla regis prodeunt* ("The banners of the king are advancing"), sung during Holy Week liturgy to commemorate the True Cross. Dante adds a word to the verse to make it, "The banners of the king *of Hell* [*inferni*] are advancing." *Vexilla* in this context refers to Lucifer's six bat-like wings. A frigid wind blows toward Dante and Virgil from Lucifer's three

---

8 See Claire Honess, "The City of Jerusalem in the *Commedia*," in *From Florence to the Heavenly City: The Poetry of Citizenship in Dante* (Abingdon, Oxon, and New York: Routledge, 2006), 107–50; 108ff., for specifics about the New Jerusalem in Old Testament Apocrypha and Christian theology. Honess is a main source for the current chapter.

9 Ibid., 112.

pairs of wings, which, as Claire Honess notes, "may also be seen as an infernal reflection of the two arms and the upper section of Christ's Cross.... Lucifer appears from afar to be almost cruciform."[10] All of this suggests an inverted or demonically parodic relation between Lucifer frozen in the earth and Christ crucified in Jerusalem.

In addition, traditional thinking about the earthly Jerusalem would have influenced Dante's ideas about an infernal city. The Old Testament prophets do not exclusively praise Jerusalem's holiness; they also condemn its worldly and sinful aspects. The Jews' exile and the destruction of the city in 587 BC were seen by the prophets as divine punishments.[11] Isaiah and Jeremiah compare the citizens of Jerusalem to those of the prototypically wicked cities Sodom and Gomorrah.[12] Even Jesus condemns Jerusalem, in the Gospel of Luke: "And when he drew near and saw the city he wept over it, saying, 'Would that even today you knew the things that make for peace! But now they are hid from your eyes.'"[13] Dante commentators have linked a passage in canto I of *Inferno*, where the protagonist Dante is mortally threatened by the three beasts blocking his ascent of the hill, to a section in Jeremiah which warns that three wild animals — a lion, a wolf, and a leopard or panther — will ravage the inhabitants of Jerusalem as a result of their transgressions.[14] And although the sources for Dante's depiction of Hell are complex and numerous, the biblical image of Gehenna is one precedent. Gehenna was a valley outside the gates of Jerusalem where, in ancient times, an idolatrous cult had sacrificially burned children, and where, later, the inhabitants of Jerusalem incinerated their refuse. Isaiah says that God, in vindication of the punishments of Gehenna, will restore Jerusalem and have all the nations come there to glorify him. The people who come will see the bodies of those who have rebelled against God.[15]

A passage in canto XIX of *Paradiso*, discussed in the introduction, combines the images of the corrupt Jerusalem and the Heavenly Jerusalem. In this canto, which takes place in the sphere of Jupiter, the beatified spirits of rulers who exemplified justice glorify God collectively in

10 Ibid., 129.

11 See, e.g., Jeremiah 31:38–40 and Ezekiel 22:3–4.

12 Isaiah 1:10, Jeremiah 23:14.

13 Luke 19:41–42.

14 Niccolò Tommaseo's nineteenth-century commentary to *Inferno* I.49–51; and Jeremiah 5:6.

15 Isaiah 46:24.

the shape of an Eagle. The Eagle, which talks as one creature though composed of many beatified souls, explains to Dante that it (the Eagle) is the archetype of divine justice. As with other spirits in *Paradiso*, the Eagle anticipates Dante's question — which concerns the salvation of non-Christians and what this implies about God's justice. While explaining the latter, the Eagle launches into an excoriation of the rulers of Christendom whose names in the Book of God will be associated with corruption and misdeeds which led people astray, while many non-Christians will sit in judgment on them.

Among the corrupt rulers mentioned in this passage is one of Dante's *bêtes noires*, Charles II of Anjou, who had the title "King of Jerusalem," which he inherited from his father, Charles of Anjou, King of Naples and Sicily, who claimed to have acquired the right to it by purchase. Dante considers the younger Charles vastly inferior to his father, since Charles was a powerful enemy against the restoration of the monarchy upon which Dante had set his hopes for political stability in Italy.[16] This passage of *Paradiso* states that the Book of God will mark an *I* (= 1) for the good that Charles has done, but an *M* (= 1,000) for his evil acts, which therefore far outweigh the good ones. The letters that quantify Charles's malice in Dante's view are derived from a wordplay on the first and the last four letters of *Ierusalemme*, since *emme* is the letter *M* spelled out in Italian. In typically compact and gnomic style, Dante here alludes to Jerusalem's transcendent symbolism as a contrast to the squalor of his nemesis Charles. The play is on the numbers 1 and 1,000, since Dante was aware of the symbolic value of 1,000 as perfection, as he states explicitly in the *Convivio*.[17] Jerusalem, then, contains in its very name both the 1 of the transcendental Unity and the 1,000 of the perfection of the return to the One. It is no coincidence that an earlier passage in the *Comedy* states that the letter *m*, *emme* in Italian, is the very sign of man, between the two *o*'s of *omo*, "man," which Dante sees inscribed on the withered faces of the gluttonous souls he encounters there: their sunken eyes are like

16   *Paradiso* XIX.127–29. See also *Purgatorio* VII.127–29 and XX.77–84 for polemical passages against Charles II.

17   *Convivio* II.xiv.4: "a 'thousand' is the largest number, beyond which further growth is not possible without multiplying it." See also Thomas Aquinas, *Contra Gentiles* IV.83: "'The thousand' means perfection, since it is the cube whose root is ten, which also usually signifies perfection"; in Christian number symbolism, then, the number 1,000 combines the perfection of the number 10 with the Trinitarian number 3.

two *o*'s embedded in the curves of the *m*, the middle line of which is formed by the nose.[18] Dante's symbolic point is that the sign of the *emme* (the human-divine to use a Blakean phrase) is distorted beyond recognition in the intractably dissipated and impenitent sinner — of which Charles II is a prime example.

Despite the well-known Christian notion of the *city* of God, Dante's representation of Heaven is not very urban. The dominant image for the setting of the final cantos of *Paradiso* is the celestial Rose, the petals of which are the resurrected or glorified bodies of the beatified them-selves — who are not *seated* on petals, they *are* the petals, an important and highly suggestive detail. Still however, references to Heaven as a city do occur in the *Comedy*. Sapìa, on the terrace of the envious in *Purgatorio*, refers to Heaven as the place where all are citizens of *una vera città*, a true city or city of truth.[19] And elsewhere, the Heavenly City is referred to explicitly as the Jerusalem that is the destination of Dante's otherworld journey, as if in exodus out of Egypt.[20]

In addition, for Dante and his contemporaries, the image of Jeru-salem was closely linked to popular lore about the Crusades. In the central cantos of *Paradiso*, Dante meets his ancestor Cacciaguida, a knight and crusader who had followed the Emperor Conrad III on the Second Crusade, dying in battle in Jerusalem in about 1147. Clearly, Jerusalem is implicitly evoked when Cacciaguida appears with the other holy warriors in the sphere of Mars, who collectively form the shape of the Cross.

In canto XXIII of *Paradiso*, in the sphere of the Fixed Stars, imme-diately after the descent and re-ascent of the Virgin, Christ, and the archangel Gabriel, Heaven is alluded to as that Jerusalem for which the exiles in Babylon or the souls alive on earth are longing.[21] A little later in the narrative, Beatrice states that, because the theological virtue of hope is so alive in Dante, it has been granted that he come to see Jerusalem, or Heaven, while he is still alive in his body.[22]

Dante refers to the assembly of souls in the celestial Rose as the *beata corte*, blessed court, with the Virgin at their center. He uses

---

18   *Purgatorio* XXIII.31–33.
19   *Purgatorio* XIII.95.
20   *Paradiso* XXV.55–57.
21   *Paradiso* XXIII.133–35.
22   *Paradiso* XXV.56.

ancient Roman and medieval metaphors to evoke the courtly atmosphere. The Virgin is called *Agusta*, a female Augustus; and in an earlier canto, Dante refers to the apostles Peter, James, and John as *baroni* (barons) and *segnor* (Lord), as in feudal lord.[23] In the Empyrean, Beatrice calls Heaven "our city," *nostra città*, which many commentators have interpreted as a reference to the Heavenly Jerusalem.[24] However, the courtly imagery mentioned above, as well as the fact that one of the empty places in the Rose is explicitly reserved for Emperor Henry VII, shows that Dante also has imperial Rome in mind as an image of his Heavenly City. In *Purgatorio* he refers to *quella Roma onde Cristo è romano* ("that Rome where Christ is Roman").[25] It is interesting to note that medieval art sometimes portrays the saints in Heaven as Roman dignitaries. For example, in the great mosaic in the nave of SS. Cosmas and Damian in Rome, Peter and Paul are dressed as and have the gestures of Roman senators. Likewise, the urban image of Heaven in Dante is a *hybrid* of Jerusalem and Rome, as well as of the Rose imagery itself. The Rose recalls several well-known symbols: rose windows in cathedrals, the popular narrative poem the *Roman de la rose* (Romance of the Rose), and patristic and liturgical writings that figure the blessed as flowers and Mary as a rose. This layering of symbolism is consistent with Dante's methods elsewhere in his work: Heaven in the *Comedy* combines biblical imagery with allusions to the *Aeneid* and Dante's monarchical or imperial ideal; and the rose that was an erotic symbol in the French romance is now an emblem of spiritual love. The Eagle in *Paradiso* XVIII–XX, mentioned above, alludes not only to the eagle that was a symbol for the Roman Empire, but also to the Evangelist-eagle St. John, and the eagle associated with Moses in Deuteronomy 32:11. So we can read Dante's statement early on in *Inferno*, that he is *non Enëa, ... non Paulo,* "not Aeneas ... not Paul" (both of whom journeyed to the otherworld and back),[26] as an instance of litotes, stating the negative for rhetorical effect to mean the positive. In fact, Dante follows in the tracks of these two great predecessors, one Roman, the other Christian. In the *Convivio* and the *Monarchia*, Dante stresses that Jerusalem was part of the Roman

---

23 *Paradiso* XXXII.98, 119; XXIV.115, 148.
24 E.g., Anna Maria Chiavacci Leonardi, comment to *Inferno* XXX.130–32.
25 *Purgatorio* XXXII.102.
26 *Inferno* II.32.

Empire at the time of Christ — which providentially created the cultural conditions for the Incarnation. In the *Convivio*, Dante's argument for the providential role of Rome in the salvation of humanity concludes:

> We need look no further to perceive that a singular birth and a singular progression, conceived and ordained by God, belonged to the sacred city [Rome]. Surely I am of the firm opinion that the stones which are in its walls are worthy of reverence, and the soil where it is built is worthy beyond what is proclaimed and affirmed by human beings.[27]

Claire Honess shows that Jerusalem is also alluded to in *Paradiso* through abstracted iconographic details. For example, in the penultimate canto of *Paradiso*, the Rose is said to be divided into two semicircles. The mothers of the people of Israel, seated below the Virgin in the Rose, are collectively referred to as a wall between those who believed in Christ to come, *Cristo venturo*, and those who believed in Christ after his advent, *Cristo venuto*. This image, says Honess, draws on the vocabulary of the long tradition of "civic" heavens and their city walls.[28] The women — Mary, Eve, Rachel, Sarah, Rebecca, Judith, and Ruth — were common allegorical figures for the Church. Since Jerusalem was often viewed allegorically as a figure of *Ecclesia*, the Church, each of these women is also implicitly associated with Jerusalem. Also, the figures in the amphitheater-shaped Rose, beatified spirits whom Bernard indicates to Dante, form the shape of a cross within a circle — a shape which, as stated earlier, was a common indication of Jerusalem on maps.

In addition, Dante's very frequent use in *Paradiso* of the imagery of gemstones and precious metals recalls the representation of the New Jerusalem in the Book of Revelation. Like the *aurum mundum simile vitro mundo* ("pure gold, like clear glass") of the Heavenly City,[29] Dante's sphere of Saturn, the setting of contemplatives such as Benedict, features a ladder the color of gold within a crystal heaven; the just rulers in the sphere of Jupiter form golden letters against a silver background when they spell out the first verse of the Book of Wisdom, which refers to justice; Cacciaguida appears to Dante as a topaz set in the Cross

---

27 *Convivio* IV.v.20.
28 Honess, "City of Jerusalem," 119.
29 Revelation 21:18.

shape formed by the beatified warriors. And there are many other, similar passages that evoke the imagery of gemstones, such as pearls and rubies, and resplendent metal, especially gold, consistent with Dante's emphasis in *Paradiso* on the brilliant play of light in Heaven.

Crucial to Jerusalem imagery in Christian iconography is the association between the Heavenly Jerusalem and the resurrection of the flesh—a connection that Dante highlights. The glorified bodies in white that Dante describes in the Empyrean are the citizens of the Heavenly City, whether Jerusalem or Rome or a hybrid of the two. We may note, for example, the scene in canto xxv of *Paradiso* where St. James examines Dante on the theological virtue of hope. Hope is said to reside in the promise of resurrection, which includes references to the Book of Revelation and the New Jerusalem. As Dante tells James: "Isaiah says that each soul in its homeland will wear a double raiment: and its homeland is this sweet life [in Heaven]; and your brother [John, author of Revelation], where he writes about the white robes [or resurrection bodies], manifests this revelation more clearly to us."[30]

As mentioned, pilgrimage as a symbol for the spiritual journey is an important element in the *Comedy*, another way in which the image of the Heavenly City is present. Dante was heir to the extensive voyage and vision literature that was popular in the Middle Ages. This tradition commonly included landscapes that resembled the known, external world in many of their features but which also were embellished by the imagination of whoever wrote them down. Such narratives—for example, the popular twelfth-century Irish *Visio Tnugdali*, or Vision of Tundale—included a mix of spiritual and moral components, as well as visionary landscapes, similar to those that enable the *Comedy* to portray Dante-Everyman's journey toward initiation, intellectual awakening, and salvation.[31]

In the opening of *Paradiso*, Dante sets out on his journey through the *gran mar de l'essere*, the great sea of being,[32] like a pilgrim sailing to the shore near Rome from the Holy Land. Having arrived in Rome,

---

30 *Paradiso* xxv.91–96. A key passage for Dante's thinking about the resurrection of the flesh is *Paradiso* xiv.37–60, where Solomon instructs him on the subject. On the connection between the resurrection and the New Jerusalem, see Augustine's comment on Revelation 21:2, in *City of God* xx.17.

31 See Eileen Gardiner, *Visions of Heaven and Hell Before Dante* (New York: Italica Press, 1989).

32 *Paradiso* I.113.

the pilgrim would traverse the stations of the city up to the gate of St. Peter's and the Veil of Veronica, where he would behold the visage of the Savior. Similarly, Dante, when he first sees the celestial Rose, is likened to the "barbarous" visitors from northern Europe arriving at St. John Lateran; a few lines later, the narrative states that he resembles a pilgrim reaching the temple-church that was the goal of his journey.[33] While Dante does not name a specific shrine for the latter simile, he is probably thinking of one or more of the most important pilgrim destinations: the Church of the Holy Sepulchre in Jerusalem, St. Peter's in Rome, or St. James of Compostela in Spain. In a third pilgrimage simile in this scene, Dante says that his sighting of Bernard is like that of a pilgrim from Croatia first glimpsing the Veil of Veronica and recognizing the face of the Savior. Symbolically, this means that an image of Christ's face is visible in Bernard's, which is an *impronta* or imprint of the face that Dante has been seeking, that of the *vivace carità*, or living love, of Christ.[34]

The pilgrimage to Rome was especially popular for Christians during the Jubilee Year proclaimed by Boniface VIII in 1300. In his bull *Antiquorum fida relatio* (A Trustworthy Report of the Ancients), Boniface promised "not only full and copious, but the most full, pardon of all their sins," to pilgrims who confessed their sins during the Jubilee and visited St. Peter's and St. Paul's at least (in the case of residents of Rome) once a day for a month or (in the case of nonresidents) for fifteen days. Over two hundred thousand people made the pilgrimage to Rome that year, Dante probably among them: "the Jubilee, therefore, was a triumph for the pope…, for the coffers of the city, and, perhaps especially, for the doctrine of Purgatory," since a pilgrimage was touted as lessening the duration of one's own afterlife penance as well as that of loved ones.[35] The Jubilee is one reason, then, that Dante's otherworld pilgrimage in the *Comedy* takes place in the same year, 1300, as the poet is careful to specify in his narrative.

The most pervasive pilgrimage imagery in the three canticles of the *Comedy* is in *Purgatorio*. This makes sense, given that pilgrimages were

---

33 *Paradiso* XXXI.31–36, 43–45.

34 *Paradiso* XXXI.103–11.

35 Peter S. Hawkins, "Religious Culture," in *Dante in Context*, edited by Zygmunt G. Barański and Lino Pertile (Cambridge: Cambridge University Press, 2015), 333; the first quote is Hawkins's translation from the pope's proclamation.

seen as a means of atonement, which in turn is the aim of the souls on Mount Purgatory: the purification of the soul from disordered love and the harmonizing of the will with God's will. In canto II of *Purgatorio*, the souls arriving on the island of Purgatory are singing the opening of Psalm 114, *In exitu Israël de Aegypto* ("When Israel went forth from Egypt"), figuratively referring to their own imminent liberation from sin.[36] Virgil refers to them as *peregrin*,[37] and their arrival by boat recalls that of pilgrims at their holy destination. In this scene, the musician Casella informs Dante that the souls had boarded their ship "where the Tiber's water becomes salty,"[38] an allusion to the port of Ostia, at the mouth of the Tiber, which was a frequent point of departure for pilgrim ships en route to the Holy Land. In addition, this passage alludes to the fact that during the year of the Jubilee more pilgrims than usual would have been departing for the long journey to Jerusalem from the estuary of the Tiber.[39]

The ascent of Mount Purgatory becomes, writes John Demaray, a "figured pilgrimage from the Egypt of this world to the Jerusalem of the Earthly Paradise";[40] and Dante's journey in the otherworld is narrated with enough details to remind the reader of pilgrimages on earth, including ones to Jerusalem.[41] There are several correspondences between the features of Dante's climb and the medieval pilgrimage to Jerusalem. He and Virgil move, as Demeray describes,

> uphill over a desert strand, past a gate of confession and up the stone terraces and steps of Mt. Purgatory, and on to a summit Eden [*sic*] situated at the geographic center of the southern hemisphere. Then in a fulfillment of the presaging terrestrial movement of a Palmer to the temple, tomb, and cross of Redemption on the Jerusalem pilgrimage way of the cross, Dante in Eden moves to figural representations

36 *Purgatorio* II.46–48. This psalm is referred to also in *Epistle* XIII.21 to give examples for the four levels of interpretation.

37 *Purgatorio* II.63.

38 *Purgatorio* II.101.

39 John G. Demaray, *The Invention of Dante's "Commedia"* (New Haven, CT: Yale University Press, 1974), 66.

40 Ibid., 60.

41 On the pilgrimage theme in *Purgatorio*, see Honess, "City of Jerusalem," 123–29; and Demaray, *Invention of Dante's "Commedia,"* 60ff., on which much of this section draws.

of the Jerusalem temple, tomb, and cross in encountering Beatrice, a type of Christ.[42]

Indeed, the climb of Dante and Virgil up Mount Purgatory, as well as the entrance-gate to Purgatory proper, visually recalls the thirty-four hundred stone steps that led pilgrims to the stone Gate of Confession on Mount Sinai, and to the chapel of Moses beyond.[43]

The climactic scene in the Earthly Paradise on the summit of the mountain, starting in canto XXIX of *Purgatorio*, is especially rich in allusions to Jerusalem and the Book of Revelation. Beatrice appears in a stylized setting reminiscent of the Old Temple on Mount Sion. Elaborating on the imagery in this scene in the Earthly Paradise, Demaray writes:

> Dante's worldly typology in the Eden section of the *Divine Comedy*, whatever its admitted indebtedness to biblical texts and other influences, must also be [seen in terms of] the famed "ring" of stations on Mt. Sion. For on the summit of Mt. Purgatory, Dante's viewing of the heavenly procession that introduces Beatrice to Eden mirrors an earthly Christian's observation of a Palm Sunday procession into the city of Jerusalem.... [The Old and New round Temples of Jerusalem] were restored in the Middle Ages to contain nested rings of stations about which pilgrims and others circled, in imperfect but solemn imitation of divine movements like those of the angels, to the holiest points at the center: the rock of the altar of Solomon at the Old Temple and the tomb of Christ at the New Temple.[44]

During this scene, Dante turns to look toward the east at the moment of dawn, when the sun is rising.[45] In Constantine's construction of the Church of the Holy Sepulchre, there were to be three gates facing the rising sun, symbolically receiving the light of Christ. Similarly, the

42 John G. Demaray, *Dante and the Book of the Cosmos* (Philadelphia: The American Philosophical Society, 1987), 17.

43 See Demaray, *Invention of Dante's "Commedia,"* fig. 18.

44 John G. Demaray, *Cosmos and Epic Representation: Dante, Spenser, Milton and the Transformation of Renaissance Heroic Poetry* (Pittsburgh: Duquesne University Press, 1991), 63.

45 *Purgatorio* XXIX.7–12.

Temple of Solomon was believed to have been oriented to receive the first rays of the sun:

> Immediately one recalls how, in the account of St. Jerome, the pilgrim Paula stood in the Holy Land facing east and "as the sun rose, remembered the Son of righteousness"; how Constantine constructed the main basilica of the New Jerusalem with "three gates facing the rising sun" so as to receive the morning light of Christ; how the Temple of Solomon was commonly believed to have been similarly oriented to catch the sun's first rays.[46]

Next in the *Purgatorio* scene, as we saw in chapter 4, there is an allegorical procession of the twenty-four elders who represent the books of the Old Testament, as well as other figures signifying the books of the New Testament and the Church, culminating in Dante's reunion with Beatrice in a carriage drawn by a Griffin. Demaray sees in this sequence of events a mirroring of the arrival of the pilgrim in Jerusalem, who prepared to receive Christ in the Host, after watching a procession of Church dignitaries. In addition, Beatrice's arrival is heralded by angels singing *Benedictus qui venis*, Blessed you who come,[47] recalling words shouted by onlookers when Jesus entered Jerusalem on his donkey. Notably, Dante uses the masculine adjective *Benedictus* for Beatrice, suggesting that she comes not as herself but as a representative of Christ. Dante hears the first part of this biblical phrase much earlier in the pageant, when he perceives an indistinct melody of voices singing in a chorus, which he eventually realizes are uttering the word *Osanna*.[48] Beatrice is showered with flowers the way Jesus was greeted in Jerusalem with palm branches. In the arrival of Beatrice at the climax of the procession, then, Dante is like one of the onlookers in Jerusalem when Christ was entering the city. In another instance of Dante's hybridizing the imagery of Jerusalem and Rome, the angels around Beatrice are also singing words from Virgil's *Aeneid* as they toss the flowers: *Manibus ... date lilia plenis* ("Give out lilies with full hands").[49]

---

46 Demaray, *Invention of Dante's "Commedia,"* 119.
47 *Purgatorio* xxx.19.
48 *Purgatorio* xxix.51.
49 *Purgatorio* xxx.21, quoting *Aeneid* vi.883.

The allegorical pageant that Dante witnesses in the Earthly Paradise symbolically reenacts the events that pilgrims underwent in Jerusalem during Holy Week. For example, the Tree of the Knowledge of Good and Evil, at the center of the scene and obviously recalling the sin of Adam and Eve, is bare until the Griffin (usually interpreted allegorically as Christ) attaches the carriage to it, which brings about its renewal.[50] This action recalls the Crucifixion, as the shaft of the carriage represents the Cross, which traditionally was said to be made from the wood of the Tree linked to original sin. The rejoining of the shaft to the Tree, then, represents the redemption of the human soul by Christ's death. Next, the *puttana sciolta* (dissolute or immodest or half-naked harlot),[51] the *meretrix magna* of Revelation 17:1–5, who is seated on the beast and fornicates with kings, appears on the scene — a figure for the corrupt Roman Curia. As Honess observes, "Just as for John these disasters precede the Last Judgement and the coming of the Heavenly Jerusalem, so too for Dante they precede his immersion in Eunoë and his final readiness for his ascent to Heaven."[52] And lastly, an association to Jerusalem is made at the start of the final canto of *Purgatorio*, where the seven female figures around Beatrice, representing the theological and cardinal virtues, sing a fragment of Psalm 78, *Deus, venerunt gentes* ("God, the Gentiles have come"), which mourns the destruction of the Temple and its profanation. In Dante's allegory, this refers to the sacrilege of the Church by corrupt monarchs and popes.[53]

As discussed in chapters 1 and 2, the Christ- and Jerusalem-related symbolism of Beatrice had been established by Dante in the *Vita nova*, years before he composed these culminating scenes of *Purgatorio*. For example, the earth quakes in Dante's dream of Beatrice's death in the *Vita nova*, during which he hears the very words, *Osanna in excelsis*, that occur with Christ's entry into Jerusalem and his ascension into Heaven, words that Dante also quotes when Beatrice reappears in the Earthly Paradise. Dante announces Beatrice's death in the *Vita nova*, not directly, but by suddenly interjecting the passionate language of Jeremiah, mourning the destruction of Jerusalem: *Quomodo sedet sola civitas plena populo! facta est quasi vidua domina gentium!* ("How doth

---

50 *Purgatorio* XXXII.38–39, 52–60.
51 *Purgatorio* XXXII.149.
52 Honess, "City of Jerusalem," 127.
53 *Purgatorio* XXXIII.1; Psalm 78:1.

the city sit solitary that was full of people! How is she become a widow, she that was great among the nations [lit. the Lady of the nations/peoples]!").[54] The parallel could not be clearer: the death of Beatrice resembles, for Florence, the destruction of Jerusalem that Jeremiah is lamenting, which in turn is associated in Christian liturgy with the death of Christ. For example, extracts from Lamentations are used for the Matins office during the culmination of Holy Week and associated with the Passion of Christ. And other passages from Lamentations, also echoed by Dante in the *Vita nova*, have been used in liturgical verses and responses to indicate words spoken by Christ on the Cross or connected with the Crucifixion.[55] The image of Jerusalem as a widow occurs again in canto I of *Purgatorio*, when, just having emerged from Hell with Virgil, now in the Southern Hemisphere, Dante says he saw four stars that had not been seen since Adam and Eve were in the Garden. These stars represent the four cardinal virtues (fortitude, temperance, justice, and prudence), from which, Dante says, the Northern Hemisphere has been "widowed."[56] A little later in *Purgatorio*, Dante says that Italy is similarly "widowed" in its lack of an emperor who can guide and order its conflicts.[57]

The closing chapters of the *Vita nova* recall, not only Jerusalem and the Crucifixion, but the motif of pilgrimage that we have already considered in relation to the *Comedy*. Dante tells us that he had witnessed a group of pilgrims passing through Florence during Holy Week:

> At that time when many people go to see the blessed image [the Veil of Veronica] that Jesus Christ left us as an imprint of his beautiful visage, which my lady sees in glory, it happened that certain pilgrims were passing along a street that runs virtually straight through the middle of the city where that most gracious of women was born, lived, and died.[58]

---

54   *Vita nova* 19.1 (XXVIII.1); Lamentations 1:1. Dante quotes the same passage at the start of *Epistle* XI, addressed to the Italian cardinals in 1314.

55   See, e.g., the poem *O voi che per la via d'Amor passate* ("O you who pass along the road of Love"), in *Vita nova* 2.14–17 (VII.3–6); and on this topic, Ronald L. Martinez, "Dante Between Hope and Despair: The Tradition of Lamentations in the *Divine Comedy*," *Logos: A Journal of Catholic Thought and Culture* 5, no. 3 (2002): 45–76.

56   *Purgatorio* I.24–26.

57   *Purgatorio* VI.113.

58   *Vita nova* 29.1 (XL.1).

Dante says he noticed that the pilgrims seemed preoccupied, and that they apparently came from a land so far away that they had not heard of Beatrice or her death. If they had come from nearby, Dante reflects, "something in their bearing would appear disturbed as they passed through the middle of the suffering city." He decides that he will compose a sonnet in which he addresses them directly, telling them things that *farebbero piangere*, would get them to weep.[59] As discussed in chapter 1, where this sonnet is quoted in full, the poem's imagery echoes the encounter of the two disciples with Christ on the road to Emmaus, narrated in Luke.

The sonnet opens with the word *peregrini*, pilgrims. Dante's prose just before the poem glosses this term, explaining that he means *peregrino* in the broad sense of "anyone who is outside his homeland," not the narrower sense of *peregrino* used for one traveling to or from Santiago di Compostela. And he adds the following aside:

> And it is worth noting that there are three separate terms for people who travel to honor the Supreme Being: they are called *palmers* if they travel to the Holy Land, where they often carry the palm; they are called *pilgrims* if they travel to the home of Galicia, since the tomb of Saint James was farther from his homeland than that of any other apostle; they are called *romers* if they travel to Rome — the place where those I am calling *pilgrims* were headed.[60]

Palmers were those pilgrims with palm leaves wound about their walking sticks, which demonstrated they had been to the Holy Sepulchre. In *Purgatorio* Beatrice uses this word as a metaphor for Dante's prophetic writing, which will bear witness to his pilgrimage in the otherworld the way the palm bore witness to the pilgrim's journey.[61] A "romer" (*romeus*) was a pilgrim whose destination was the tomb of St. Peter and the Veronica; and we have already seen that Dante refers to the Empyrean at times as an apotheosis of Rome. Finally, as Dante

---

59   *Vita nova* 29.3–4 (XL.3–4).

60   *Vita nova* 29.7 (XL.7).

61   *Purgatorio* XXXIII.78: *che si reca il bordon di palma cinto* ("that the pilgrim's staff is carried wrapped with palm").

clearly has in mind in this scene, *peregrinus* means "stranger."[62] For Augustine, an earthly *peregrinatio* or pilgrimage is a visible image of the spiritual journey, since life itself is a state of wandering toward our spiritual home. Separated from God, we are strangers in our own lives — as the use of *patria* (homeland) for heaven was common usage in Christian hymns. As St. Paul puts it in his letter to the Ephesians, regarding the beatified spirits, "So then [as members of the mystical body of the Church] you are no longer strangers and sojourners, but you are fellow citizens with the saints and members of the household of God."[63] In *Purgatorio* XXIII, Dante refers to the souls of the gluttonous on Mount Purgatory as *peregrin pensosi*, pilgrims oblivious or lost in their thoughts, the same words he uses for the pilgrims in this early sonnet; and a few lines later in the *Purgatorio* scene he compares the emaciated bodies of the gluttonous in their state of purgation to the *gente che perdé Ierusalemme*, the people who lost Jerusalem (and were starving to death) when they were under siege by Titus. Again, losing Jerusalem is clearly a metaphor for losing the spirit's heavenly home.[64]

For Dante, the point is that home is where Beatrice has gone — Florence, without its *speculum Christi*, is not itself and certainly is not really home. In the next and penultimate chapter of the *Vita nova*, the last sonnet of the book ("Beyond the sphere that turns the widest gyre," quoted in translation in chapter 2) prophetically narrates the journey to the Empyrean around which the entire *Comedy* and its more than fourteen thousand lines are constructed — in the sonnet reduced to fourteen lines. The sigh of the lover ascends to a vision of Beatrice in glory, where his *peregrino spirito*, pilgrim-spirit, is enraptured by its contemplative gaze upon the Beloved.[65] Only in this concluding scene of the *Vita nova*, in short, does the word *peregrino* begin to assume the symbolic import that we have seen it has in the *Comedy* — where the journey to God is represented as one that begins outside the *patria* and concludes *in patria*. The very opening of *Inferno* thus begins *nel mezzo del cammin*, in the middle of our life's *journey*, or pilgrimage.

Given this sequence of events in the *Vita nova*'s final chapters, it seems likely that Dante intends a parallel between the journey of the

---

62 Isidore of Seville, *Etymologies* x.215.
63 Ephesians 2:19. See also Hebrews 11:16.
64 *Purgatorio* XXIII.16, 29.
65 *Vita nova* 30.11 (XLI.11).

pilgrims passing through Florence to see the face of Christ and the young Dante's new stage in his understanding of love and the beloved. In the chapter just before the episode of the pilgrims, Dante has a vision of Beatrice as she was the first time he saw her, when they were children. By sequencing the narrative in this manner, he implies an analogy between his vision of Beatrice and the pilgrims' anticipated viewing of the face of Christ in the Veil of Veronica. And we have already seen that Florence's grief and emptiness after Beatrice's death resemble that of Jerusalem after Christ's crucifixion. With this background, the beatified Beatrice will appear in the Earthly Paradise as the very face and guardian of the New Jerusalem.

9

The Divine Comedy *as Cosmos*

THE *DIVINE COMEDY* is a great testimony to the art of detail. The sheer quantity and vitality of particulars in the *Comedy* imitate life: we can never grasp hold of it all. Remarkably however, Dante's art harmonizes the fragments into a transcendent pattern — binding in a single volume, as he puts it in the last canto of *Paradiso* (quoted in this book's epigraph), the scattered pages of the creation. Just as his subjective experience, both pleasurable (Beatrice) and painful (exile), is eventually seen in terms of the *dolce armonia*, or sweet harmony, that suffuses and sustains existence — the vision of the One that is the culmination of the poet's journey — the *Comedy* itself is an imitation of divine order. As Dante writes in his treatise on monarchy: "As the part is to the whole, so the order of the parts is to the order of the whole. The part is to the whole as to its true end and highest good: therefore also the order of the parts is to the order of the whole as to its true end and highest good."[1] The specific context here is a discussion of the need for social unity in the figure of the emperor, but it is also evident that Dante conceived the architecture of his great poem as a microcosmic model or reconstruction of the whole of creation, or cosmos. For Dante, as Zygmunt Barański writes, "the best way to achieve an understanding of anything is to follow the example of the symbolic art of the Creator," the *Deus artifex*, and therefore the *Comedy* is a "sign in a universe of signs."[2]

It is a common notion in medieval Christian theology and in Jewish and Muslim thought as well: God left traces of Himself in all created things, which human beings can know by "reading" the Book of Creation, thereby coming to an indirect knowledge of God. The same divine language can be read in the symbolism of scripture; the *Comedy* reflects events and people from these two sourcebooks, the Book of Creation and the Book of Scripture, and Dante's reading of history (of the Roman Empire and the Church) as providential is based on this principle as

---

1 *Monarchia* I.vi.1.

2 Zygmunt G. Barański, *Dante e i segni: Saggi per una storia intellettuale di Dante Alighieri* (Naples: Liguori, 2000), 84, 108.

well. In *Paradiso* Dante refers to the Creator's *impronta* or *suggello* — the imprint or seal of the divine creative virtue — that leaves its traces in each successive level of creation. For instance, Beatrice explains how the eighth celestial sphere, that of the Fixed Stars, receives the *imago*, the archetype, from the angelic Intelligences and becomes a seal of it, an intermediary between pure spirit and manifest creation: *e 'l ciel cui tanti lumi fanno bello, / de la mente profonda che lui volve / prende l'image e fassene suggello* ("and the heaven that many lights make beautiful [i.e., the sphere of the Fixed Stars] takes the image from the deep mind [the angelic Intelligences] that makes it turn [since the angelic hierarchies are in the ninth sphere, that of the Primum Mobile or First Mover] and makes itself a seal of it [of the image]").[3] As we will see from some of the patterns that shape the narrative arc of the poem, Dante intends the *Comedy* itself to be such a *suggello*, just as the great cathedrals of the Middle Ages were built as copies of the pattern in the mind of God.

We have looked at Dante's journey in the *Comedy* as the pilgrimage of Everyman. The last chapter reviewed some specific pilgrimage imagery that patterns Dante's story, especially in *Purgatorio*. There are indications, too, that Dante intended his narrative to reflect a specific pilgrimage, the so-called Great Circle, "the oldest, longest, and most famous pilgrimage in Christendom."[4] John Demaray outlines the itinerary of the Great Circle, and other details related to it, in his synopses of medieval pilgrims' own accounts of their journeys. As he points out, Dante's focus on presenting his story as if it were *historically* true means that evoking actual pilgrimage sites for stages of the poem's journey, rather than nonspecific or fictional ones, would better fit his overall approach. As Demaray puts it, "The whole of the *Commedia* [by means of its immediacy and realism acts] as an ordered arrangement of exemplary types or figures pointing back to earth."[5] The Great Circle pilgrimage generally started with a sea voyage from Italy (Rome or Venice) to Alexandria, continued south on the Nile to the Egyptian Babylon, then went east toward the Red Sea and (led by Muslim guides) through the Sinai desert and on to Jerusalem. Most pilgrims,

---

3 *Paradiso* II.130–32.

4 John G. Demaray, *Cosmos and Epic Representation: Dante, Spenser, Milton and the Transformation of Renaissance Heroic Poetry* (Pittsburgh: Duquesne University Press, 1991), 7.

5 John G. Demaray, *The Invention of Dante's "Commedia"* (New Haven, CT: Yale University Press, 1974), 62.

passing through the desert, would stop at St. Catherine's monastery at the foot of Mount Sinai, and climb the mountain to the ring of stations near the site of Moses' vision of the burning bush. They also frequently stopped at the Dead Sea, reputed to be the mouth of Hell, where they looked upon the ancient sites of Sodom and Gomorrah. They bathed in the Jordan, the boundary separating the desert from the Holy Land, in a ritual renewal of baptism and spiritual cleansing. Then they would stop at Jericho, where each received a palm, which they wrapped around their staves as an emblem of purity before they entered Jerusalem. The pilgrim's progress in Jerusalem generally moved south through the Temple area, the southeastern part of the city, and then west and north to the Church of the Holy Sepulchre — which was the medieval Christian omphalos or center of the world. After the sojourn in Jerusalem, pilgrims would set sail for the culmination of their journey, Rome, and in particular the viewing at St. Peter's of the Veil of Veronica, which we encountered earlier, by means of which they could gaze directly on the visage of the Savior.[6]

This geographical itinerary was a profoundly symbolic and spiritual itinerary as well. Pilgrims' geography was spiritual geography; they journeyed inside the Book of Creation, not merely across the naturalistic or snapshot landscape of modern commercial tourism. The Christian pilgrims "sought above all else to 'read' spiritual truths from the iconographic Book of God's Works. They studied publications by God in the form of holy rocks, trees, rivers, mountains, hills, and caves; and these publications were elaborated into complex nests of icons by the artful markings of holy men."[7] All of these places corresponded to stations in the spirit's journey in temporal-spatial existence, and through the labyrinth of life, either away from or toward God. Egypt, in the Judeo-Christian tradition, symbolized the state of worldliness — of enslavement, as the ancient Israelites were enslaved to Pharaoh, to worldly contingencies that have lost their transparency to the Absolute and that therefore hold the spirit in captivity. Israel was the Promised Land of deliverance from bondage to the ego or the empirical self. Rome, for Dante and his European contemporaries, was the place of the martyrdom of SS. Peter and Paul, of the foundations of Christ's Church on earth. In addition, as Dante explains in *Monarchia*, Aeneas's

---

6   Ibid., 11.
7   Ibid., 19.

settling in Italy was the providential basis of the Roman Empire and its civilization, which would make possible the great diffusion of Christianity throughout the Mediterranean Basin and beyond. To relate the otherworld to this world, Dante sought keys in "the holiest 'pages' in God's Book of the World: the iconographic cities, landscapes, holy sites, and even persons on the Egypt-Jerusalem-Rome pilgrimage route."[8] The typology of the Great Circle pilgrimage was one device that Dante could use to give dramatic unity to the tremendous amount of detail in the *Comedy*, and at the same time it provided a series of symbols widely known to Dante's contemporaries that would give his story resonances, or correspondences, on many levels, including the cosmic level adumbrated by pilgrimage itself.

Dante's earliest commentators noted the centrality in the *Comedy* of the Exodus story — which the Great Circle pilgrimage emulated as well, in its itinerary from Egypt to Sinai and on to Jerusalem. Dante himself, in his letter to Cangrande della Scala, his host at Verona, explains that the *Comedy* can be better understood by reference to Psalm 114, which was quoted in the last chapter in connection with the arrival of souls in Purgatory: *In exitu Isräel de Aegypto, domus Iacob de populo barbaro, facta est Iudaea sanctificatio eius, Isräel potestas eius* ("When Israel went forth from Egypt, the house of Jacob from a people of strange language, Judah became his sanctuary, Israel his dominion").[9] Whether or not Dante himself ever made the whole pilgrimage, he certainly had at least indirect familiarity with the main features of the Great Circle. His literary sources for knowing details of the pilgrimage sites could have included Bede, Paulus Orosius, St. Jerome, or Eusebius.[10] Besides Christian texts and the possibility that he made the journey himself, Dante probably would have known or met people who had gone on the pilgrimage. In Dante's prose description of the pilgrims passing through Florence, quoted earlier, he refers to stages in the Great Circle pilgrimage, as well as to the popular pilgrimage to Santiago de Compostela. As we also have seen, the journey to Beatrice in the Earthly Paradise, and with her to the Empyrean, has its model in the progress of pilgrims on their way to Jerusalem or Rome.

---

8 Ibid., 54.

9 *Epistle* XIII.21.

10 Demaray, *Invention of Dante's "Commedia,"* 47. Both Bede and Orosius appear in the sphere of the Sun in *Paradiso* X.

The journey of Dante-Everyman in the *Comedy* progresses from Egypt-Hell, the place of total myopia, self-interest, violence, fraud, religious hypocrisy, and other manifestations of life in servitude to the narcissistic ego; to Mount Sinai–Purgatory, the place of purification in the desert; to Eden-Jerusalem, where Beatrice appears in a solemn procession in the holy precincts; and finally, after crossing the great sea of being, or the heavenly spheres, arriving in Empyrean-Rome/Jerusalem. At the very beginning of the story, Dante is in a wasteland where there is a mountain that he attempts to climb but from which he is driven back by a leopard, a lion, and a she-wolf. Commentators have noted that this episode represents a kind of failed Exodus, in that the mountain at the start of *Inferno* prefigures Mount Purgatory. But before Dante-pilgrim can start his reenactment of Exodus, he must confront the darkness of the worldly Hell; guided by Virgil, in *Inferno* he will gradually gain the insight and perspective that enable him to begin scaling Mount Sinai–Purgatory.

A further way in which Dante would have had access to Great Circle pilgrimage imagery and lore, besides the sources mentioned above, was by visiting certain sacred buildings in Italy itself. Symbolic pilgrimages were carried out in Dante's time by visiting replicas of Holy Land structures that had been built into local churches and cathedrals. The reasons for this were practical, in that not everyone could travel to Egypt and the Holy Land, as well as theological, in that the cathedrals themselves were types for the cosmos. Churches in Italy, such St. Peter's and the Lateran in Rome, St. Vitale in Ravenna, St. Stephen's in Bologna, and others were designed to reflect the round Church of the Holy Sepulchre or other churches built over the relics of saints and holy persons. For example, at St. Stephen's in Bologna there is an urn-shaped stone in front of a reconstruction of the Holy Sepulchre, replicating the stone at the world's center in Jerusalem. Pilgrims unable to go to the Holy Land could reenact a Jerusalem pilgrimage there. Similarly, at La Verna in Tuscany—the spiritual center of the Franciscans and the mountaintop where Francis of Assisi received the stigmata—the steps ascending from the grotto of Francis resemble the steps at the stone Gate of Confession at Mount Sinai, before the chapel of Moses. Mount Verna, then, was an Italian version of Holy Land pilgrimage mountains. In the biographical narrative of Francis in *Paradiso*, La Verna is referred to as the *crudo sasso*, rough stone, where Francis received the *sigillo* (seal) of Christ, the stigmata.[11] Bonaventure, who also used Temple symbolism drawn from the Book of Exodus for his contemplative writings, resided at La Verna for an extended period.

In addition, high altars in some medieval churches signified temple altars at Jerusalem. Many of these had inlaid stone labyrinths that, writes Demaray, "pointed worshippers to central rose or other medallions...[representing] the fulfilled and 'true' spiritual-geographic 'station' of Jerusalem." A number of the core medallions were scored with "small minotaur and pagan icons signifying the 'old' spiritual-geographic centers of Crete or Troy."[12] The mazes represented the entanglements of the ego-self isolated from God, the convoluted folds of delusion and sin that can be untangled only with the help of divine grace. Dante inscribes both Troy and Crete into his story—Troy as the fallen city from which came the seed of Rome, Crete as the center of the old pagan world embodied by the statue of the Old Man of Crete, whose story is told in canto XIV of *Inferno*. The Old Man is an allegory for the four ages of man: gold, silver, bronze, and iron; drawing on the Book of Daniel as well as Ovid, it is an alternative figure for the story of the Fall.[13] In *Inferno*, Virgil tells Dante that the statue, whose tears are the source of the rivers in Hell, has a head made of gold, a breast and arms made of silver, a midsection made of brass, and a lower part made of iron, except for the right foot, which is baked clay (the latter usually interpreted as a symbol for the corrupt Church).[14] Demaray discusses the symbolism of the Old Man of Crete in relation to the Great Circle pilgrimage. For example, the shoulders of the statue "indicate a traditional crusading-pilgrimage pathway, one followed even by Francis of Assisi, to or past the old pagan world center to Damietta and then to the Holy Land. The statue faces the final goal of long pilgrimage: Rome."[15]

Several commentators have noted that Dante's Hell can be viewed as a labyrinth. This seems to be especially true of Malebolge, the very large eighth circle of Hell. Malebolge is shaped like an arena, with steeply descending tiers with rock bridges that pass over the trenches or *bolgias* (literally "pouches") between them. The connecting points

---

11 *Paradiso* XI.106–7.
12 Demaray, *Cosmos and Epic*, 26.
13 See Daniel 2:31 and the beginning of Ovid's *Metamorphoses*.
14 *Inferno* XIV.94–120.
15 Demaray, *Cosmos and Epic*, 224 n. 24.

between the tiers are sometimes convoluted and tangled, or labyrinthine. Even with Virgil's expert knowledge of Hell's terrain, Dante and Virgil get lost at one point, directed off-track by the demons in the tar pits of the barraters.[16] And the labyrinth of Dante's Hell is spiritualized by its mirror-image in Dante's Heaven, the celestial Rose, whose folds are also labyrinthine. In the late cantos of *Paradiso* St. Bernard describes the vertical line of women seated in the Rose, with Mary at the highest point and several Old Testament matriarchs seated directly below her.[17] Dante's design resembles the iconographic motif of the ancestry of the Virgin, depicted for example in the great north rose window at Chartres, which illustrates the Virgin's descent from Hebrew kings in the line of David. It has been noted that below the rose on the west front at Chartres (where there are three rose windows in all) is a labyrinth set into the nave, at a distance from the west door such that if the rose were to swing down from its position above, it would fit over the labyrinth, and that such a relation reflects the connection between the labyrinth and the mandala, the latter of which, "projected onto life, [offers] . . . a means not only of finding one's way but also of differentiating between the forms of good and evil."[18] It is possible to see the same symbolism in Dante, in the relationship between the celestial Rose and the labyrinth of Hell, since blind ego consciousness and false attachments are redeemed in the folds of the Rose that germinate in the womb of the Virgin.[19]

NUMBER

Number symbolism is another means that Dante uses to resolve the episodes, personages, historical references, scientific observations, and other details of his narrative into a structure that imitates the cosmos or divine order. The most evident numerological fact of the *Comedy* is its division into three parts. The Holy Trinity leaves its trace in innumerable references to the number 3, including the tercets in which the

---

16   *Inferno* xxi–xxii.

17   *Paradiso* xxxii.7ff.

18   My thanks to the late Professor Keith Critchlow for explaining several details about the rose windows at Chartres. A lecture by Prof. Critchlow at Dartington, Devon, several years ago demonstrated that the plan and elevation of the whole cathedral were in complete harmony, the rose window "falling" on the labyrinth merely being one primary symbol. See also Painton Cowen, *Rose Window* (San Francisco: Chronicle Books, 1979), 98–99, cited in Demaray, *Cosmos and Epic*, 27.

19   *Paradiso* xxxiii.7–9.

poem is written (terza rima was invented by Dante for the occasion), each of which has 33 syllables (since the classic Italian verse line is the hendecasyllable, or eleven-syllable line).[20] The German Romantic critic August Wilhelm Schlegel, a perceptive reader of Dante, commented on the symbolic import of Dante's terza rima in lectures that Schlegel gave on art and literature in Berlin in 1802–3:

> This tripartite structure [of *terza rima*] does not ... arise ... by way of simple addition, but consists of a doubling or halving of a given unit, which then produces a mediating third entity out of itself. This process is reflected in the form of the *terza rima*: the first rhyming line represents, as it were, the Father and corresponds to the third line, while the second line both divides and unites the other two.... Each *terza rima*, by virtue of its single middle line, demands a further rhyme, just as in Nature each new creation both resolves two opposing forces within itself and at the same time already contains the seed of a new confrontation, and so on *ad infinitum*. This then is the paradigm for the interlinking of the *terza rima*, with its inherent allusion to the future and its consequent aura of the prophetic.[21]

The entire *Comedy* is a 3-and-1, since it is a single poem composed of 3 parts: it has 3 canticles, one for each of the 3 realms that Dante visits. There are 33 cantos in each canticle of the *Comedy*, canto 1 of *Inferno* acting as a proem to the narrative (the actual journey of Dante and Virgil starts in canto 11). This "extra" canto also fits into the numerological pattern, since the 3-and-1 of the Trinity is echoed by it (33 cantos in each canticle, plus the 1). Likewise, each canto ends with a lone line of verse which rhymes with the middle verse of the final tercet, thus echoing the 3-and-1 pattern. The 33-plus-1 pattern of cantos and tercets also hints at the life of Christ, since he died in his thirty-fourth

20 One could go on and on about 3's in the *Comedy*: the 3 saints (Mary, Lucia, and Beatrice) who save Dante from the dark wood (by sending Virgil), 3 heads of Cerberus, 3 traitors in 3 mouths of Lucifer, 3 steps before the gate of Purgatory, the 3 theological virtues, and so on. I am concentrating here on the number 3 as it is built into the poem's structure.

21 Schegel, from an (untitled) excerpt from his lectures, in *Dante: The Critical Heritage*, edited by Michael Caesar (London: Routledge, 1989), 423.

year at the age of 33. All 3 realms — Hell, Purgatory, Paradise — are divided into 3 main parts with a total of 10 subdivisions, which, as I will expand upon below, are also grouped into a 9-plus-1 pattern (the "antechamber" of Hell, for example, plus the 9 main circles).

What is especially significant about Dante's use of number symbolism is not his dazzling virtuosity, however impressive that is. Rather, Dante invites us, through a gradual process of realizing that little in the *Comedy* is as it first appears, to discover the intelligible order of the cosmos that models his poem. Dante was heir to a long numerological tradition, for which numerical analogy reveals relations between things that would otherwise be hidden. As the Pythagorean philosopher Philolaus put it, it is by numbers that things become known.[22] Pythagorean number theory asserts that number is behind all manifest creation. In a Christian context, Pius XI wrote that "the universe is only as resplendent with divine beauty as it is because its movements are regulated by a divine mathematical combination of numbers, for according to scripture God created everything 'with *number, weight* and *measure.*'"[23] Number — which, as every poet knows, is another word for poetic meter — therefore is essentially divine. A fragment of Orphic writing states, "Orpheus, the son of [the Muse] Calliope, having learned wisdom from his mother in the mountain Pangaeus, said that the eternal essence of Number is the most providential principle of the universe, of heaven and earth, and the intermediate nature; and further still, that it is the root of permanency of divine natures, of gods and divinities." Iamblichus infers from this that Pythagoras "learned from the Orphic writers that the essence of the gods is defined by Number."[24] The modern world uses number in a purely quantitative sense, while ancient and medieval philosophers saw it "as a *qualitative* essence, a principle of relationship or *logos.*"[25]

22   Vincent Foster Hopper, *Medieval Number Symbolism* (1938; repr., New York: Cooper Square Publishers, 1969), 34.

23   Quoted in Jean Hani, *The Symbolism of the Christian Temple*, translated by Robert Procter (San Rafael, CA: Sophia Perennis, 2007), 27. Pius XI is quoting Wisdom 11:21. Many Christian authors have cited this passage in discussing sacred number; for instance, Augustine mentions the same passage at *City of God* XI.30.

24   David Fideler, *Jesus Christ: Sun of God* (Wheaton, IL: Quest Books, 1993), 74; quoting from Kenneth Sylvan Guthrie, compositor and translator, *The Pythagorean Sourcebook and Library: An Anthology of Ancient Writings Which Relate to Pythagoras and Pythagorean Philosophy*, edited and introduced by David Fideler (Grand Rapids, MI: Phanes Press, 1987), 93–94.

25   Ibid., 60; italics in original.

The Logos can be seen as "the pattern that connects," the principle that "underlies the manifestation of harmony at its very core."[26] Such thinking is behind Augustine's view that "numbers are the thoughts of God.... The Divine Wisdom is reflected in the numbers impressed on all things.... The construction of the physical and moral world alike is based on eternal numbers."[27] Augustine is one of the main sources of Christian numerology. For him as for Dante, the contemplation of number is a way to discover traces of God in the creation. Number plays an intermediary role in the process through which physical manifestation appears to the human senses. As Plato puts it in *Timaeus*: "The various elements had different places before they were arranged so as to form the universe. At first, they were all without reason and measure. But when the world began to get into order... God fashioned [things] by form and number."[28] Through numbers, then, the transcendental world of Forms could be made intelligible — the very notion that Augustine expressed in terms of "traces." Given this tradition, Dante would have thought that the *Comedy* needed number symbolism built into its essential structure if it were to become, as John Guzzardo puts it, a "poetic microcosm which, as the Creator's macrocosm, provides clues through which man can be led back to unity with God."[29]

In Pythagorean number theory, 3 is the first number. The number 1 is represented by a point as the beginning and foundation of all other numbers; the number 2 gives extension in the form of a line between two points; and the addition of a 3rd point creates a plane figure. Thus, as Vincent Foster Hopper explains in his study of medieval number symbolism, "the triangle becomes... the basis of all objects perceptible to the senses. This is the meaning of Plato's remark that surface is composed of triangles."[30] Hopper adds that that 3 "represents all reality [as the first 'real number'], not only as the image of 'surface,' but also as having beginning, middle, and end."[31] The triad restores unity and diversity to harmony with one another, since, as Proclus writes, "the mean acting as a mediator links the other two into a single complete

---

26 Ibid., 2.
27 Quoted ibid., 25, from *De libero arbitrio* (On Free Will) II.16.
28 *Timaeus* 53b; Jowett translation.
29 John J. Guzzardo, *Dante: Numerological Studies* (New York: Peter Lang, 1987), 6.
30 Hopper, *Medieval Number Symbolism*, 35, citing *Timaeus* 55–56.
31 Ibid., 41.

order."[32] Or, as another author put it, "The triad leads to a new integration, one that does not negate the duality preceding it but rather, overcomes it, just as the child is a binding element that unites the male and female parents."[33] So, the constant references to the Trinity throughout *Paradiso* attest to the perfect fullness of Being in that realm; the first emanation of the One, described in canto xxix of *Paradiso*, is the simultaneous creation of the triad of pure spirit or angelic Intelligences (form), pure matter (*prima materia*), and spirit-matter (celestial bodies).[34] In *Inferno* the same number 3 symbolizes the mental state in which human beings have forgotten they are made in the image of God and so know only semblances and contingencies, not the real existence of things: the 3 traitors in the 3 mouths of Lucifer (a demonic parody or negation of the Trinity) are consumed by the spectral self, which has rejected the fullness of true existence in God — the very mind-forged manacles that beset all the residents of Hell.

Earlier, we saw that number 9 is Beatrice's number. The number 9 also structures the 3 realms in the *Comedy*, each of which has 9 main divisions, in addition to 1 (9 + 1 = 10) outside the main part of the realm: the antechamber in Hell; the base of Mount Purgatory, where Dante and Virgil meet Cato and the arriving souls; and the Empyrean in Paradise. In all 3 canticles of the *Comedy* the 9th canto narrates a passage to a more important level of the realm in question: Dis in Hell; the gate of Purgatory to reach Purgatory proper; the sphere of the Sun in Paradise, the first celestial sphere outside the penumbra of the earth.

JOURNEY AT THE CENTER OF TIME

Large numbers also play a role in structuring the *Comedy*. The one that is especially germane here is the number 13,000. We know that

---

32 Proclus, *Elements of Theology* 1.148, cited in ibid., 41.

33 Ludwig Paneth, cited in Annemarie Schimmel, *The Mystery of Numbers* (New York: Oxford University Press, 1993), 58.

34 *Paradiso* xxix.22–24: *Forma e materia, congiunte e purette, / usiro ad esser che non avia fallo, / come d'arco tricordo tre saette;* "Form and matter, conjoined and simple, issued from being that had no flaw, like three arrows from a three-stringed bow." *Forma* here refers to pure form, or "pure act" (the angelic intelligences), in scholastic philosophy; *materia* refers to pure matter, or "pure potential" or "prime matter," the basis of all matter; *congiunte e purette* refers to their combination, resulting in the celestial spheres. As stated in *Paradiso* vii.67–69 and 130–38, these are the three things created by God without mediation. Aristotle, in *De anima* ii.2, 414a, distinguishes between form, matter, and a compound of the two.

Dante's otherworld journey takes place in 1300, the year of the Church's first Jubilee. This year falls in the exact middle of Dante's life, since he was 35 years old at the time, half of the 70 years that biblical tradition said was the span of a human life.[35] It also turns out that, according to calculations current in Dante's time, the year 1300 was the midpoint of the duration of human life on earth, since 6,500 years had elapsed up to 1300 and the world was to last another 6,500 years. In the sphere of Venus in *Paradiso*, Dante says that the fame of the troubadour and bishop Folco of Marseille will last for 6,500 years, which some scholars have seen as an allusion to Dante's conceiving his journey as taking place at the midpoint of the 13,000-year Great Year.[36] Another instance occurs in *Paradiso*, where it is said that 6,500 (to be exact, 6,498) years have passed since God formed Adam.[37] While this Great Year number contrasts with the Great Year of the Persians and Greeks, which lasts 26,000 years (more precisely 25,920 years, the cycle of the precession of the equinoxes), Filippo Villani, a Florentine chronicler who lived just after Dante, expressly states that the *annus magnus* lasts 13,000 years.[38] As Robert Hollander comments:

> At least since Plato's time the *annus magnus* ("great year"), that cycle that brings all the stars back to their original alignment in the heavens, was thought to last 36,000 years. In *Convivio* (II.v.16) Dante accepts that traditional view. It is, however, an interesting fact that Filippo Villani, commenting on the first canto of the poem early in the fifteenth century, says that the *annus magnus* contains 13,000 years....

35 Psalm 89:10.

36 *Paradiso* IX.37–42. Most commentators have disagreed with this interpretation of the lines that give the duration of Folco's fame, preferring instead to interpret *centesimo anno ancor s'incinqua* as "this centennial year shall be multiplied by five again": in other words that five centuries will pass—most likely not exactly five hundred years, just a long time. But several Dantists have argued for the longer period, in particular Anna Maria Chiavacci Leonardi (*Paradiso*, p. 250), who points to *Aeneid* III.954 as a source; and Rodolfo Benini, *Dante tra gli splendori dei suoi enigmi risolti* (Rome: Sampaolesi, 1952), 64.

37 *Paradiso* XXVI.118–23.

38 Cited in Robert Hollander, comment to *Paradiso* IX.40, in *Paradiso*, translated by Robert and Jean Hollander (New York: Anchor Books, 2008). Hollander also writes in this comment: "There was apparently a tradition, if it is referred to derisively by St. Augustine ... that the history of humankind, from Adam until Judgment Day, would last 7,000 years. That would, according to Dante's timeline, make human history on this earth extend roughly to the year 1800, since 6498 years have passed since God formed Adam."

For Villani the number does not count the years of the great revolution of the heavens, but the years of human life on earth. His number is interesting, since it has the effect of making Dante's journey occur at nearly the precise mid-point of the cycle of the years allotted to humanity's earthly "voyage," a second sort of "great year," as it were, in the year 6499.... If we follow Villani, we can see that Dante's first verse, with something approaching terrifying precision, dates the opening of his poem to the midpoint of his own life and to that of the life of the species.[39]

René Guénon says that *half* of the years of the precession of the equinoxes was considered by the Persians and Greeks to be a Great Year, which they actually calculated as 12,000 years — according to Guénon, much less exact than Dante's 13,000 years.[40] Guénon considers this Great Year to be behind Dante's allusions to the number 6,500, described above. Whether or not Guénon's interpretation aligns with Dante's own reasons for using it — Villani, as Dante's near contemporary, is probably a more reliable source — his symbolic explanation of *why* Dante would situate his journey in the exact center of a great span of time is highly evocative:

To place oneself at the mid-point of the cycle is therefore to place oneself at the point where these two tendencies counter-balance each other.... The center of the "Wheel of Things," according to the Hindu expression, or the "Immutable Middle" of the Far-Eastern tradition; the fixed point around which the spheres rotate — the perpetual movement of the manifested world. Dante completes his journey by following the "spiritual axis" of the world; only thence, in truth, is it possible to view all things in permanent mode, because one is not oneself subject to change, and consequently has a view that is synthetic and complete.[41]

39 Robert Hollander, comment to *Inferno* I.1, in *Inferno,* translated by Robert and Jean Hollander (New York: Anchor Books, 2000). This part of the comment is not in the print edition of Hollander's commentary; it was added by Hollander to the online edition, available at the Dartmouth Dante Project, http://dante.dartmouth.edu.

40 René Guénon, *The Esoterism of Dante,* translated by C. B. Bethell (Ghent, NY: Sophia Perennis et Universalis, 1996), 57–58; Guénon's source is Benini, cited above.

41 Ibid., 62.

There is no question that Dante saw his journey in the *Comedy* as enacting such a movement toward the "spiritual axis." It would be entirely in keeping with Dante's inexhaustible creative energy and precision that he would calculate his journey to take place at the exact center of time (whether the center of the precession of equinoxes or that of human life on earth). Guénon concludes that Dante's aim as poet-prophet was symbolically to effect a "return [of all things] to [their primordial] origins ... the restoration of the 'Edenic state'"[42] The year 1300, in other words, is the midpoint of a temporal mandala.

CONVERSION AND THE NUMBER 7

The number 7 is embedded in the *Comedy* in many places. For example, there are 7 terraces in Purgatory, and the 7 sins and beatitudes associated with them; and 7 planetary spheres, which Dante looks back on at the end of canto XXVII of *Paradiso*, while ascending with Beatrice to the sphere of the Fixed Stars. Charles Singleton has argued for the central importance of the number 7 in a still more subtle sense. The gist of his hypothesis is that 7 is coded into the central cantos of the poem, and that it also "frames" the entire *Comedy*, since the first 7 cantos of *Inferno* and the last 7 of *Paradiso* are set off from the rest. Canto VIII of *Inferno* begins, *Io dico, seguitando* ("I say, to continue ..."), which Boccaccio said refers to the fact that Dante wrote the first 7 cantos at an earlier stage, when he was still in Florence. Most modern commentators doubt Boccaccio's claim, but however one interprets it, canto VIII opens with a demarcation of sorts. Similarly, at the end of *Paradiso* XXVI, Adam tells Dante how long he remained in Eden before the Fall: "from the first hour to the one that follows ... the sixth." Dante has asked Adam four questions, which Adam answers out of sequence — surely a significant detail for an artist as deliberate as Dante. As Singleton comments on this line: "By answering this question [how long Adam remained in Eden] last, the poet is able to present explicitly, as the last word, the number *six* explicitly expressed (sesta), but *the number seven* in actual meaning (the seventh hour). Since there are thirty-three cantos in *Paradiso* this last word of the present canto may be seen to mark off the remaining area of the poem, made up of seven cantos."[43]

---

42 Ibid., 66.

43 Comment to *Paradiso* XXVI.142, in *The Divine Comedy*, translated and with a commentary by Charles S. Singleton (Princeton, NJ: Princeton University Press, 1970–75).

The embedding of the number 7 in the center of the *Comedy* is even more complex and subtle. The middle canto of the entire *Comedy*, canto XVII of *Purgatorio*, is the center of a triptych of cantos on the theme of free will and love, which has been mentioned a few times in this book. In canto XVI, Marco Lombardo, a northern Italian nobleman, says that the soul at birth innocently follows its pleasures, simple at first, but that the blind pursuit of pleasure ("natural love," as Dante calls it) leads to increasingly complex objects of desire and to self-deception:

> *l'anima semplicetta che sa nulla,*
> *salvo che, mossa da lieto fattore,*
> *volontier torna a ciò che la trastulla.*
> *   Di picciol bene in pria sente sapore;*
> *quivi s'inganna, e dietro ad esso corre,*
> *se guida o fren non torce suo amore.*[44]

(the simple little soul that knows nothing, other than that, moved by its happy maker, willingly it turns to what pleases it. At first it gets a taste of a small good; then it is deceived, and runs behind it, if a guide or some restraint does not redirect its love.)

Free will, which is not under the same natural compulsion and astral influence as are the natural instincts and other "sublunar" bodies,[45] must be brought to bear on which pleasures to follow and which not. In canto XVII, after Dante and Virgil have passed from the terrace of the wrathful, the third terrace of Purgatory, onto that of the slothful, the middle of the 7 terraces, hearing as they pass the absolving angel chanting the 7th beatitude, "Blessed are the peacemakers," as night falls, Virgil teaches Dante about love as the central force of all created things — plants, animals, stones, and flames, as well as human beings. I discussed this theme earlier, but I will review it here since it is crucial to the present discussion and so central to Dante's work as a whole.

Love is of two kinds: natural or freely chosen. Natural love is *sempre sanza errore*, it never errs, but love that involves free choice can err

44 *Purgatorio* XVI.88–93.
45 *Purgatorio* XVI.75.

"through mistaking the object of love, or by excessive, or insufficient love."[46] As long as freely chosen love is directed toward the First Good, God, it cannot go astray. Christian doctrine teaches that "the purgation of the affections consists in referring them to their appointed end,"[47] and that the root of evil was where reason set itself above God, perverting its power of choice. This is because, as Thomas Aquinas writes, only God is *essentially* good.[48] The ultimate object of all love is God. The teaching that disordered love is the source of the seven capital vices and that mastering it is the way to become free of them was to be found also in the most popular penitential handbook of Dante's era, the *Summa virtutum ac vitiorum* (Summa of Virtues and Vices), by the thirteenth-century Dominican William Perault.

Finally, in canto XVIII, the last part of this triptych of cantos, Virgil explains to Dante that the tendency to love (as Marco Lombardo has already stated) is always good, since it is put into us by God, but that not every object of love is good: "its matter is always good, but not every seal [love in act] is good merely because the wax [love in potential] is good."[49] Then Dante asks the key question of the long discourse: if the object of love comes from outside of us, and if the soul cannot be moved without being moved from without, how is it possible that the soul is guilty when it chooses badly? Virgil's response to this is that free will can accept or refuse the impulse as good or not good. Love really is the desire for the good, and only human beings can choose to follow that love or to choose false idols instead. Virgil sums up the discussion in these lines: "Therefore, let us suppose that every love that burns within [human beings] arises from necessity; still, the power to harness it is also within you."[50] Singleton comments on these verses: "Each and every love may be awakened in us of necessity, but it lies within our power to check it, at the first stage of love, and before the inclination and complacency in the object which is properly

---

46 *Purgatorio* XVII.94-96. The sins on the first three terraces — pride, envy, and wrath — have to do with mistaking the object of love; the middle terrace, of the slothful, with insufficient love; and the final three terraces — avarice, gluttony, and lust, with excessive love or attachment to an object.

47 Étienne Gilson, *Mystical Theology of St. Bernard*, translated by A. H. C. Downes (Kalamazoo, MI: Cistercian Publications, 1990), 240 n. 211.

48 *Summa theologiae* I, q. 6, a. 3.

49 *Purgatorio* XVIII.37-39.

50 *Purgatorio* XVIII.70-72.

so termed becomes a desire and moves toward possession of the object, thus crossing the 'threshold of assent.'"[51]

To return to the symbolism of the number 7: Singleton points out that the cantos in which this discussion takes places "are really one, which extends out from [the] center, so to speak, out from the exact center of canto 17 into the two adjacent cantos, thus marking off three cantos at the center of the structure—a number that . . . is seldom without meaning in Dante's work."[52] He says that if we count the tercets to either side of the central canto, XVII, we find that the argument on free will and love is 50 tercets long, exactly balanced on either side of the central canto, totaling 25 tercets on either side. Applying standard numerological practice to this number we get 2 + 5 (of the number 25) = 7. In addition, the central line of canto XVII, which is the central canto of the *Comedy*, is line 70, again, as 7 + 0, a number 7.[53] The last tercet of Virgil's discourse begins, *La nobile virtù Beatrice intende* ("The noble virtue that Beatrice understands"),[54] "which couples her name with the key term *libero arbitrio* [free will] in the central verse of this 25th terzina, counting from the end of canto 17." In addition, if we count back from the beginning of canto XVII we come, in the 25th tercet, not to the beginning of Marco's discourse but to the tercets in which *libero arbitrio* is first mentioned in his disquisition, rebutting the notion that planetary motions compel all human action: *Se così fosse, in voi fora distrutto / libero arbitrio* ("If it were like this, free will would be destroyed in you").[55] Thus, both love and free will are framed in the very number of the verses. We also recall that the episode is set in the center of the terraces of Purgatory, as it is also set in the center of the poem's architecture.

And there is still more to Singleton's calculations. Composing a list of the total number of verses in each canto, arranging them in columns for each canticle, he discovers another pattern of 7. Looking

51   Comment to *Purgatorio* XVIII.70–72.

52   Charles S. Singleton, "The Poet's Number at the Center," *Modern Language Notes* 80 (1965): 1–10; 2.

53   The central line of the 14,233 lines of the *Comedy* is actually line 126 of this canto, but we can forgive Dante for not knowing at this point *exactly* how many lines were to be in the entire poem. He certainly did know when he wrote this canto, however, that the canto itself would be the center of the *Comedy*.

54   *Purgatorio* XVIII.73.

55   *Purgatorio* XVI.70–71.

at the list of numbers of lines for cantos XIV–XX for both *Purgatorio* and *Paradiso*, we see:

Canto	*Purgatorio*		*Paradiso*	
	Lines	Sum[56]	Lines	Sum
XIV	151	7	139	13
XV	145	10	148	13
XVI	145	10	154	10
XVII	139	13	142	7
XVIII	145	10	136	10
XIX	145	10	148	13
XX	151	7	148	13

Canto XVII of *Purgatorio* has 139 verses, and this canto is situated in the center of *Purgatorio*, cantos XIV–XX, which are the central 7 cantos of the canticle. The number 139, as Singleton says, is the only number that has 70 at its center. The framing numbers of the list for *Purgatorio* are both 151 (= 1 + 5 + 1 = 7). Singleton sums up how the number 7 is embedded in this numerical pattern: "Here, then, are framing canto numbers (151) whose sum is 7, here are framing *terzine* [as discussed above] (25 to either side) the sum of whose number is 7, and here finally at the exact center of the poem is a verse whose number is 70, the sum of which is 7!"

Glancing at the table above, we see that there is an exactly complementary pattern between the "Sum" columns of these cantos of *Purgatorio* and *Paradiso*. In the latter we find that the number 7 is at the center instead of framing the list. Singleton believes that this pattern of chiasmus between the total number of verses in each of these cantos of *Purgatorio* and *Paradiso* is intentional and meaningful.[57] Singleton explains that "what is thus framed [in *Purgatorio* cantos] amounts to nothing less than the central pivot of the whole poem in terms of the

56   I.e., the sum of the number of lines, in standard numerological practice—e.g., for 151, 1 + 5 + 1 = 7.

57   Richard Lansing counters that the summing of digits as Singleton does for the number of lines in cantos nearly always results in a number with symbolic significance and that the symmetrical pattern can be found elsewhere in the poem: e.g., *Purgatorio* III–IX. But that does not disprove Singleton's argument; if anything, it suggests that there is still more number symbolism to discover. Richard H. Lansing, s.v. "Numerology," in *Dante Encyclopedia*, ed. idem (New York: Garland Publishing, 2000), 653.

action, in terms, that is, of what happens to the wayfarer Dante as he 'passes through the center.'"[58] The 7 cantos in *Purgatorio* hold the

> experience of a "conversion" at the center, that begins with the words spoken by Guido del Duca at Purg. 14.86–87,[59] the question concerns the radical difference that there is between possessing earthly goods and possessing heavenly goods. This heaven-bound pilgrim is being told, over and over again through this center, that he must learn to "look up," and understand how things are up there, where lies his proper goal, that he must adjust the eyes of his mind to a polarity of difference between cupidity of material things (which means looking down at them) and the charity of Heaven, where possession of spiritual goods increases by sharing. This argument, which passes then through the matter of free will and Love, will be seen to continue to its completion, as the central, pivotal, issue of the poem, in Canto xx, where an avaricious pope lies face down for having fixed his eyes so exclusively on earthly goods.... The poet has framed [this central argument] for us as beginning in Canto xiv and ending in Canto xx. And we come thus to see that the number pattern at the center is no mere surface ornament, but that it reaches deep into the movement of the poem.[60]

The figure of the chiasmus in the numerological relations here is an image for this conversion, since chiasmus reverses the order of things. The numerical order is turned outside-in between *Purgatorio* and *Paradiso*, suggesting that the conversion has taken place in the interim.

Dante's conversion or initiation in the sense that Singleton describes above culminates in Dante-pilgrim's meeting with his great-great-grandfather Cacciaguida, who in the middle cantos of *Paradiso* guides Dante through a final recollection of his biographical, historical life until he is ready to receive Cacciaguida's blessing for his calling as poet-prophet. The transfiguration of the personal and historical

58 Singleton, "Poet's Number," 7.
59 In these lines, Guido del Duca, a Ghibelline from Ravenna who is on the terrace of the envious, rebukes humanity for coveting what cannot be shared.
60 Singleton, "Poet's Number," 7.

into the archetypal and eternal is the underlying theme in these cantos. From about the middle of canto xv through canto xvi of *Paradiso* the narrative is mostly a chronicle of Florentine life, including, as often in Dante, numerous contemporary names as well as those of forebears. Some new readers of the *Comedy* are surprised and even disappointed to find such political and social minutiae at this late stage of Dante's epic poem. *Inferno* and *Purgatorio* are full of historical details, but *Paradiso* is more focused on theological and mystical subject matter. In view of the discussion above, however, I think the reason for this reversion to history is this: the historical background of Dante's life is re-presented in its fullest form anywhere in the *Comedy* in order to give way once and for all to the metahistorical.[61] The blows of fate and the changing fortunes of Florence and of Dante are finally seen through as contingencies, a *dolce armonia*, as Cacciaguida puts it, in the mind of God: *Da indi, sì come viene ad orecchia / dolce armonia da organo, mi viene / a vista il tempo che ti s'apparecchia* ("From there [the perspective of eternity], just as the sweet harmony of an organ [or polyphonic song] comes to one's ears, the time that is being arranged for you comes into my view").[62] In Singleton's schema, shown in the table above, the number 7 that had framed the list of cantos in *Purgatorio* is now at the center, in canto xvii of *Paradiso*, where, with Cacciaguida's blessing, Dante-pilgrim's equilibrium shifts once and for all from contingency toward the Absolute.

Singleton rightly notes that such subtle application of numerology to numbers of lines in cantos would have been all the more hidden to Dante's original audience since manuscripts before printing did not have verses of cantos numbered, so that a reader would have had to count the verses. But he adds that like the intricacies of a medieval cathedral, the edifice of the *Comedy*

> was not addressed to human sight alone, indeed not primarily to human sight at all. He who sees all things and so marvelously created the world in number, weight, and measure, would see that design, no matter where its place

---

61 This impression of a summation at this point of the story is reinforced by the fact that Cacciaguida's prophecy of Dante's exile, the ninth and last in the *Comedy*, has *exactly* the same number of lines as the other eight put together (pointed out in Hollander's commentary on *Paradiso* xvii.43–99).

62 *Paradiso* xvii.43–45.

in the structure; and would surely see it as a sign that the human architect had indeed imitated that created Universe which the Divine architect had wrought for His own contemplation, first of all, and for that of angels and of men.[63]

Numerological and other structural elements, in other words, were a form of esoteric knowledge (gnosis) and a form of prayer.

If Singleton's thesis about the number 7 is correct, we may ask why Dante chose that number in particular to frame and center his poem. The number 7 is sacred in many traditions. For the Pythagoreans it was sacred because it is composed of the first even number, 4, and the first odd number, 3 (recall that 1 and 2 for the Pythagoreans were not proper numbers). Also in Pythagorean thought, 7 is "granted the distinction of absolute isolation and therefore first cousinage to the monad.... The number which Plato had distinguished in the planets as 'the movable image of eternity' is known, therefore, as Pallas, the virgin number, neither generated nor generating within the decad."[64] Christian Moevs explains the symbolism of the number 7 in terms of Macrobius's idea that "it is the number of man;... a long patristic tradition agrees, because man, the bridge between creator and creation, is made of the four corruptible elements plus will, intellect, and memory, or the love of God through heart, soul, and mind.... [As the number of man, it is] the bridge or knot... between Creator and creation, between self-subsistent and the contingent, between intellect (a three) and matter (a four)."[65] Christian tradition expresses the 4-plus-3 formula in the 4 cardinal virtues and 3 theological virtues, which Dante refers to many times in the *Comedy*, most notably in the sacred procession in the Earthly Paradise, where the 4-plus-3 maidens walk in their respective groups on either side of the carriage that bears Beatrice. And 4-plus-3, as the above quote suggests, is the combination of the body and the spirit, since 4, as the first solid figure, is associated with physical manifestation and 3 with the Trinity. In a similar vein, theologians such as Augustine wrote of the number 7 in connection

63   Singleton, "Poet's Number," 10.
64   Hopper, *Medieval Number Symbolism,* 43.
65   Christian Moevs, *The Metaphysics of Dante's "Comedy"* (Oxford: Oxford University Press, 2005), 139, 147. The patristic source is Augustine, *De doctrina christiana* (On Christian Doctrine) II.xvi.25.

with the Genesis story: associated with the day of rest, 7 signified the completion of the work of creation. In medieval tradition there were 7 tones of the Gregorian scale, 7 canonical hours in the day, 7 sciences (the trivium and quadrivium, another 4-plus-3), 7 gifts of the Holy Spirit, 7 petitions in the Lord's Prayer, and so on. Honorius of Autun measured the distance between the planets according to intervals of the musical scale, "because," he wrote, "man, being 7... has 7 voices (tones of the scale) and as microcosm, reproduces the celestial music."[66] In addition, for Augustine, 7 signified the creation, 3 the Creator, the sum of which is 10, the number that signifies the fullness of God.

Taking all of this into consideration, we might think of the 7 coded into the text in the ways that Singleton describes as signifying *humanity as such*, or *essential humanity*, as it exists in the mind of God — man "made in the image of God." This would be — to think back to the cantos of *Purgatorio* in which Singleton found the number 7 embedded — the human being restored to a right relationship to love, oriented to the Good. In short, the "conversion" that Singleton says is imaged by the chiasmus-like inverted numerical pattern between parallel *Purgatorio* and *Paradiso* cantos is one from contingent values to eternal values — a conversion to the right object of love. Such a conversion raises the human from being a 4 (the traditional number of "natural" man) to a 7.[67]

As detailed in chapter 4, this conversion of love and free will to the right object, initiated by Marco Lombardo and blessed by Dante's ancestor Cacciaguida, is completed for Dante after he has been questioned by the apostles Peter, James, and John on the three theological virtues, and is granted the vision of Adam, the primordial human being, when his sight is restored, very significantly indeed, by Beatrice's eyes. Being seen by her, Dante can see again: "So from my eyes every mote fled Beatrice with the ray of her eyes, that shone more than a thousand miles: whereupon I saw better than before; and as one stupefied I asked about a fourth light that I saw among us."[68] Immediately after

---

66   *De imagine mundi* (On the Image of the World) 1.81–83; quoted in Moevs, *Metaphysics*, 95.

67   Hopper, *Medieval Number Symbolism*, 11, writes that "4 is the number of earth"; and on p. 84 adds that "mystically, the fact that man is a tetrad is evidenced in the name, *Adam*, whose letters are the 4 winds." In Dante, there are exactly 40 inhabitants of Limbo mentioned in *Inferno*, canto IV (another 4). Limbo in Dante is where the "virtuous pagans" reside, those whose virtue in Dante's symbolic system was *only* natural.

68   *Paradiso* XXVI.76–81.

this vision Dante is finally ready to see the *riso / de l'universo*, the smile of the universe,[69] and to ascend to the sphere of the Fixed Stars, which is where history (in the form of political discourses or personal encounters) is finally left behind. Dante's conversion to 7 is completed once he has encountered Adam, the father of man and therefore of 4, the number of the natural man.

Another clue that Dante in these later cantos of *Paradiso* wants us to recall the *Purgatorio* cantos on love and free will is that there are conspicuous linguistic echoes between them. For instance, in the lines immediately following the ones just quoted, Beatrice tells Dante that "inside that light, the first soul [Adam] lovingly/desiringly contemplates [*vagheggia*] his maker—the first soul that God created."[70] The verb *vagheggiare*, used here to depict Adam's contemplation of God, was a common word in courtly love poetry; it refers to the desiring gaze of the lover. In *Purgatorio*, near the beginning of Marco Lombardo's discourse on love, the same word is used to depict God's gazing lovingly on his creature.[71] Another parallel is near the beginning of canto XXVI of *Paradiso*, where Dante tells St. John, who is questioning him on love-*caritas*, that the mind enflamed by love naturally should move toward the essence of goodness itself, of which every other good is but a stray bit of light from the main ray. Therefore, anyone who has "the good of the intellect" will necessarily love God, the source of every good.[72] Clearly, this insight echoes the discussion in the *Purgatorio* cantos on free will and love. And since Dante is now able to say these things for himself, we know that his initiation into this knowledge is complete—the weight of his life has fully shifted toward its new center of gravity, the Eternal.[73] His own life has become transparent and restored to the divine order on which the very structure of his great poem is based.

69 *Paradiso* XXVII.4–5.
70 *Paradiso* XXVI.83–84.
71 *Purgatorio* XVI.85.
72 *Paradiso* XXVI.31–36.
73 Dante images this shift of gravity in his cosmic plan as well. At the beginning of the journey, the earth is the center, while by the end the entire universe is oriented around a point of pure light. This shift began when he and Virgil climbed down Lucifer's legs to pass through the center of the earth to the other side, where, at the base of Mount Purgatory, their bodies were literally standing with their heads toward heaven. In the miasma of life on earth, in Dante's schema, our bodies stand in exactly the opposite direction, our heads pointing away from heaven.

10

Love's Scribe

WHEN DANTE AND BEATRICE reach the tenth and high-est heaven in the final cantos of *Paradiso*, Dante struggles over how to respond to the overwhelming beauty and light that greets him there. And in the same passage he tells us that, as the poet seated at his desk in Ravenna, remembering and writing about that experience, he also struggles over how to find language to express it. Recalling Beatrice's face, which has become ever more radiant during their ascent through the celestial spheres, Dante writes that the beauty he saw in the Empyrean or highest heaven exceeded not only human but also angelic capacity, such that *solo il suo fattor tutta la goda* ("only its creator may enjoy it in its entirety").[1] Earlier in *Paradiso*, the power emanating into Dante from Beatrice's face is compared to the divine virtue that entered the mythological figure Glaucus when he ate the grass that made him an immortal sea god. Glaucus had seen dead fish on the ground whose contact with that grass enabled them to leap back into the water, vibrantly alive. Likewise, the spiritual power which infuses Dante from Beatrice enables him to leap into the sea of being, alive with divine inspiration.

Dante's pilgrimage that he narrates in the *Divine Comedy* is a grad-ual initiation into sustained contemplation of the divine. As we have seen, this journey goes back to his youth in Florence, where, as he tells us in the *Vita nova*, Beatrice delivered him a jolt of beauty that woke him to a new life. Now, in the Empyrean, Dante is blinded by a sudden light which, Beatrice tells him, is a necessary prelude to a higher level of vision. Dante's intellect must grow accustomed to the realm of pure light before he can sustain attention to it or even see it. Dante then says that his *novella vista*, or new faculty of vision, which this sudden light has now awakened is so keen that no other light, no matter how bright, will be able to blind him. He adds that once the celestial light is seen, it is impossible to turn away from it, so enrap-tured is the one beholding it. However, Beatrice explains that what he now sees — celestial light in the form of a circular river — is still an

---

1 *Paradiso* XXX.19–21.

indirect vision of God's light. He will have to drink from the river of light itself to see the divine radiance directly. Dante tells us that he then drank from the river like an infant eager for his mother's breast, and that the part of his body that he drank with was his eyes — to be precise, his eye*lashes* — at which point he could see the deeper reality of what was already present. The river, he now perceives, is actually a circle formed by a ray of light that descends from the Godhead and refracts off the convex surface of the Primum Mobile or First Mover, the ninth celestial sphere just below the Empyrean. This is a symbolic way of saying that the light of God, the so-called light of glory or *lumen gloriae*, itself makes it possible to see the divine light. Dante invokes this light of glory directly:

> *O isplendor di Dio, per cu' io vidi*
> *l'alto trïunfo del regno verace,*
> *dammi virtù a dir com' ïo il vidi!*[2]

(O splendor of God, through which I saw the high triumph of the true kingdom, grant me strength to say what exactly I saw!)

Two lines before the rhyme-word *vidi* ("I saw"), used twice in the above lines, the same word is also used as a rhyme-word — the only three-time identity rhyme in the *Comedy* other than the word *Cristo*, Christ, which for Dante is too great a word to rhyme with any other. The momentous repetition of *vidi* emphasizes the *novella vista*, the novel and visionary state that Dante experiences after he has drunk with his eyes from the river in the Empyrean.

As happens repeatedly in the *Comedy*, especially in *Paradiso*, Dante's *visions* are accompanied by his desire to find a way to *tell* about them, to find *words* that rise to the occasion. The passage I just quoted, which occurs in canto XXX, is the penultimate invocation that Dante himself makes in the *Comedy*. All of Dante's invocations are pauses in the narrative during which he summons the inspirational force to continue, and alerts the reader to a newly heightened phase of vision.[3]

---

2   *Paradiso* XXX.97–99.

3   There are nine invocations spoken by Dante in the *Divine Comedy* — just as there are nine classical Muses and nine is the symbolic number of Beatrice. Both *Inferno* and

There are two invocations in the final canto of *Paradiso*. Bernard makes one of them, in his petition to the Blessed Virgin on Dante's behalf. Bernard supplicates the Virgin that Dante may be granted "such strength that with his eyes [or vision] he may rise higher toward the ultimate salvation."[4] Dante's own invocation in this concluding canto is spoken from the perspective of the poet seated at his writing table in Ravenna. Many times in the *Comedy*, Dante steps out from behind the artifice of the narrative by sharing with the reader his point of view as author in the present, writing about a visionary experience in the past. Here Dante the poet, in the midst of composing, petitions the *somma luce*, or supreme light of God, that it may concede to Dante's memory the slightest trace of Dante's ultimate vision; and that this light may grant to Dante's speech the capacity for expressing even a spark of that light's glory, so that people in the future may share in it. Just before this final invocation, he conveys the ineffability of his experience with three similes that express the dissolution of form: his experience was like waking from a dream and not remembering the details, only the *feeling* of the dream; or like snow melting and so losing its form; and it was like the leaves of the oracle of the Sibyl scattering in the wind, suggesting the loss of coherent meaning.[5]

A little later in this final canto, in preparation for transition to a still more intense stage of vision, Dante again calls our attention to himself as the exiled poet who is a guest at the court in Ravenna, trying to write about an experience which was ultimately ineffable, beyond all forms, including words and language. Not only is his speech inadequate for expressing what he recalls and has a conception of, but the conception itself, his memory of the vision, is so minuscule that it would be too much even to call it *poco*, negligible.[6]

Purgatorio contain two invocations each, and there are five in *Paradiso*: *Inferno* II.7 (the Muses generically), *Inferno* XXXII.10–12 (the Muses generically), *Purgatorio* I.7–12 (Calliope), *Purgatorio* XXIX.37–42 (Urania and the "Holy Virgins"), *Paradiso* I.13–21 (Apollo), *Paradiso* XVIII.83–87 (the *diva Pegasëa*, or "divine Pegasean," i.e., one of the Muses, associated with the winged horse Pegasus), *Paradiso* XXII.112–23 (the constellation Gemini), *Paradiso* XXX.97–99 (the splendor of God), and *Paradiso* XXXIII.67–75 (the Divine Light). St. Bernard's invocation to the Virgin in the final canto brings the number of invocations up to an even ten — probably no coincidence, since ten traditionally is the number of the Godhead and the highest heaven.

4 *Paradiso* XXXIII.25–27.
5 *Paradiso* XXXIII.58–75.
6 *Paradiso* XXXIII.121–23.

I have started this chapter on inspiration in Dante with the end of his story, because the concluding cantos of *Paradiso* encapsulate all the essentials of the subject: love, vision, imagination, memory, ineffability, surrender, and of course the great poetry itself. We might even say that a subject of the final *Paradiso* cantos *is* the spring or font of poetry. At the same time, Dante enables the reader to share in this experience in the way that Socrates in Plato's *Ion* says the inspired poet passes on his inspiration to the rhapsode or singer of poetry, whose inspired and inspiring recitations of Homer also relay a trace of the original inspiration to the audience.[7] Reading the sublime cantos of *Paradiso*, the absorbed reader wishes it were possible to linger in their warm light, just as Dante says he did not have the power to pull his eyes away from the celestial vision.

Theoretical understanding of poetic inspiration in the West in fact goes back to Plato, as well as to Aristotle and the Neoplatonists; and in Latin culture, Virgil, Cicero, Plutarch, Ovid, and others. All of these authors were in agreement that inspiration comes from the gods. As Ovid puts it: "There is a god within us; when he stirs we heat up. It is this impulse that holds the seeds of sacred mind."[8] This is related to Plato's notion of *enthousiasmos*, enthusiasm, the state of someone possessed by a god. So, as Dante writes in his letter to Cangrande della Scala, in explanation of his own invocation of Apollo in the opening canto of *Paradiso*, in order to compose visionary poetry the poet must "petition higher beings for something beyond the ordinary range of human powers, something almost in the nature of a divine gift."[9] This is related to Dante's observation in *Paradiso* that the beatified spirits are lights which move in accordance with *lor viste interne*, the quality and fervor of their vision of God.[10] Dante says that the brightness of the soul's light is proportional to its ardor, the ardor proportional to the inner vision, and the inner vision's intensity proportional to the divine grace that surpasses what the soul has merited on its own.[11] Inspiration itself, in this view, is a divine illumination of the soul.

The ecstatic poetic mania or enthusiasm of Greek thought was translated into Latin as *furor*, frenzy or fury. *Furor* could also refer to

---

7   See especially *Ion* 533e–534e, as well as *Phaedrus* 245a.

8   *Fasti* VI.5–6: *Est deus in nobis, agitante calescimus illo; / impetus hic sacrae semina mentis habet.*

9   *Epistle* XIII.47.

10   *Paradiso* VIII.21.

11   *Paradiso* XIV.40–42.

erotic and uncontrollable passion, as in Virgil's description of Dido as *subito... accensa furore*, instantly on fire with frenzy, in her love for Aeneas.[12] But *furor* above all indicated the state of being possessed by a spirit of prophecy. The close connection between prophecy and poetry, which goes back in the West at least to Pindar, is apparent in the fact that the poet in Latin is often called *vates*—a bard, seer, or prophet. *Carmina* referred not only to songs and poems, but to magic spells and incantations. The poet was the interpreter of sacred language, and sacred books were written in rhythmic, metrical language because this is the language of the gods—the language of the birds in traditional symbolism, or the language of the angels who, like the birds, are winged and feathered. Cicero wrote of the *furor divinus*, saying that the human mind is inspired in two ways: by divine frenzy and by dreams. He writes that "the human soul has an inherent power of presaging or of foreknowing infused into it from without, and made a part of it by the will of God. If that power is abnormally developed, it is called 'frenzy' or 'inspiration,' which occurs when the soul withdraws itself from the body and is violently stimulated by a divine impulse."[13] Dante makes a similar statement in canto XVII of *Purgatorio*, where he talks of imagination that steals the soul up and away so that it is oblivious to the outer world. And he says that such imagination takes form in heaven and is guided by the divine will. Dante's dream of being ravished by St. Lucy in the form of an eagle who carries him to the gate of Purgatory is clearly an image of visionary inspiration.[14] The theme of being ravished or stolen by a divine power itself relates to the Latin word *furor*, which in its verbal form means precisely to steal or to rob.

The Renaissance Neoplatonists Marsilio Ficino and Cristoforo Landino brought the concept of poetic frenzy into modern European culture.[15] For Ficino and Landino, Dante was the epitome of the inspired poet. Drawing on the Platonists and Dante himself, they defended poetry as an all-embracing form of discourse—encompassing

---

12   *Aeneid* IV.697.

13   *De divinatione* I.xxx.66; translated by William Armistead Falconer in *Cicero: On Old Age, On Friendship, On Divination*, Loeb Classical Library 154 (Cambridge, MA: Harvard University Press, 1923).

14   See *Purgatorio* XVII.13–18 and the opening of *Purgatorio* IX.

15   In Ficino's Latin epistle *De divino furore* (from December 1457), and in Landino's prologue to his *Comento* on the *Comedy*, published twenty-four years later and drawing on Ficino.

all intellectual activities in the fire of its inspiration. Most important, and certainly consistent with Dante's approach, poetry for Ficino and Landino is far more than the expression of subjective emotions and impressions; it is a form of knowledge inspired by divine grace — in other words it is gnosis, in the sense I have used in this book. Plato was wary of inspired poetic speech in which the frenzied poet has no understanding of what is spoken or sung. As discussed in chapter 3, a number of medieval Christian Neoplatonists interpreted the story of Orpheus in this light. For them, Orpheus's lover Eurydice represented the wisdom within the music which Orpheus himself, like the inspired rhapsode in Plato's *Ion*, could not comprehend. Orpheus's losing Eurydice by turning around to look at her as they were leaving Hades was interpreted as the poet-singer's remoteness from wisdom or knowledge. Dante, however, presents himself as an inspired poet who is also a knower.[16]

Probably the most famous depiction of the poetic frenzy in English — descended from the Italian Renaissance notion — is a passage in Shakespeare's *Midsummer Night's Dream*. After the wild erotic confusion and transformations that take place in the woods earlier in the play, Theseus concludes that:

> The lunatic, the lover, and the poet
> Are of imagination all compact.
> One sees more devils than vast hell can hold:
> That is the madman. The lover, all as frantic,
> Sees Helen's beauty in a brow of Egypt.
> The poet's eye, in fine frenzy rolling,
> Doth glance from heaven to Earth, from Earth to heaven.
> And as imagination bodies forth
> The forms of things unknown, the poet's pen
> Turns them to shapes and gives to airy nothing
> A local habitation and a name.
> Such tricks hath strong imagination.[17]

---

16 Cf. Blake's pronouncement in *A Vision of the Last Judgement* (p. 68): "Plato has made Socrates say that Poets & Prophets do not know or Understand what they write or Utter; this is a most Pernicious Falshood. If they do not, pray is an inferior kind to be call'd Knowing?" In *Blake: Complete Writings*, edited by Geoffrey Keynes (Oxford: Oxford University Press, 1966), 605.

17 *Midsummer Night's Dream* v.i.7–19.

Note that Dante is all three of these: lover and poet, of course, but also lunatic. The last of these is often overlooked, but even a casual reading of *Inferno* tells us that Dante sees, as Shakespeare says, "more devils than vast hell can hold." The *Comedy* opens with Dante waking up to the fact that he is lost in a *selva oscura* or dark wood. We do not know what specific life events Dante may have undergone to find himself in such a state. Commentators speculate that this image may refer to a quasi-heretical aberration in thought that led Dante astray at some point. Or it may be a reference to lustful preoccupations; or perhaps both. Some of Dante's love poetry from the period right after the *Vita nova*, in which he refers to a *donna petrosa* or stony woman who both powerfully attracts Dante and also rejects him, is quite dark and conflicted. And even some of Dante's earlier love poems explicitly about Beatrice—but which he did not include in the *Vita nova*—refer to love as a dark passion that consumes the lover and threatens to obliterate him. Likewise we recall that Lancelot, to name but one figure from medieval romance, went from being a gallant knight to a wild man running around in the woods—his own *selva oscura*—because he had been rejected by his lover, Guinevere.[18] He is eventually cured when he is shown the Holy Grail. Dante introduces the theme of ineffability, which is so prominent in *Paradiso*, into the most horrific scenes of *Inferno* as well, in the face of which our speech and intellect have *poco seno*, little receptive space to comprehend it.[19]

This, then, is another way the Muses make their presence known: the mania of passion and the dark night of the soul. As Dante, who like Lancelot was also a knight, says: Hell is where souls have lost *il ben de l'intelletto*, the good of the intellect—which he too was evidently in danger of losing at some point, so that he needed a Virgil sent by Beatrice to come to his rescue and guide him back to the *diritta via*, the straight or right path.[20] Going through the emotional upheaval of lunacy and lostness in the wilderness is apparently often a prerequisite for being or becoming an inspired lover or poet—or saint, for that matter, as we see in the case of Augustine's turbulent youth.

18 The canonical account of this episode in English is that in Sir Thomas Malory's *Morte d'Arthur* XI.viii (in Caxton's numbering). See Mallory, *Works*, edited by Eugène Vinaver, 2nd ed. (Oxford: Oxford University Press, 1971), 487. My thanks to John Carey for providing this source.

19 *Inferno* XXVIII.6.

20 *Inferno* III.18 and I.2.

Naturally we cannot discuss the notion of inspiration in Dante without recalling that the Bible is the inspired Word itself, as expressed in the term *spiritus*, or *rūaḥ* in Hebrew and *pneuma* in Greek, which all mean "spirit" or "mind" as well as "inspiration" and "wind" or "breath." In the Indian tradition also, *ātman* is both spirit and the breath of life. When the high spirits in Paradise speak in Dante's narrative, he often uses the verb *spirare* for their activity of speaking, rather than the ordinary *parlare*. And inspiration is breathed by God on human beings in the written word of scripture, as St. Paul writes in his second letter to Timothy: "All Scripture is inspired [*inspirata* in the Vulgate, literally 'breathed-in'] by God."[21] In addition, Christian theologians from Augustine to Bernard to Thomas Aquinas and Bonaventure were adamant that the touch of the Holy Spirit is the source of all wisdom, which in turn is necessary for spiritually sublime eloquence.[22] Perhaps there is no greater or more beloved image for inspiration in the Christian tradition than that of the Annunciation, where the archangel Gabriel visits the Virgin, who has been chosen as the holy vessel for the Word of God. In nearly all of Dante's work, there is no meaningful way to separate his religious faith from his poetic inspiration. Dante links the two, religion and poetry, explicitly in *Paradiso*. St. Peter's symbolic crowning of him after Dante's faith has been confirmed is associated by Dante with his hopes for being crowned as a poet back in Florence, at the very place where he was baptized, the great Baptistery which stands beside the Cathedral of Florence to this day.[23]

The spiritual roots of Dante's poetry extend into a living universe in which all things are connected in God and imbued with meaning. We have seen what great symbolic import numbers carry in Dante. The world the medieval Christian inhabited was not the quantitative and mechanistic one of our own time, but one full of corresponding and interlinked levels of being. Dante's prodigious use of numerological associations is an expression, then, not of a "belief" but of an orientation to reality. Metaphysically, participation in the nature of things results in inspired intuition and speech because the substance of reality is also our *own* substance or the essence of our own being:

21 2 Timothy 3:16. In the original Greek the adjective is *theopneustos*, literally "God-breathed." Again, my thanks to John Carey for this.

22 See, e.g., Augustine, *De doctrina christiana* (On Christian Doctrine) IV.vii.21.

23 See *Paradiso* XXV.1–12.

"Spirit." Inspiration is *knowledge* (gnosis) in which we *participate* with our whole being. In metaphysical thought the spiritual intellect is our ontological center, where, as Meister Eckhart puts it, the eye with which we see God is the same as the eye with which God sees us. Unlike other forms of knowing — that of the senses or rational knowledge, for instance, which rely on agents or mediators — the knowledge of the intellect is unmediated and direct. As Dante writes in the *Convivio*, the mind or intellect is not only the highest part of the soul but *deitade*, deity, and this, as he says in a passage quoted earlier and which is an obvious reference to inspiration, "is the place where . . . Love speaks to me about my lady," here referring to Lady Philosophy, the personification of the love of wisdom.[24] Spiritually intuitive seeing is the sort that is fundamental to poetic inspiration — the "poetic genius" or Imagination, as Blake called it, which is the human state as such, the "Divine Humanity" that Dante sees in his ultimate vision in Paradise. It is fundamental to Dante's poetry and to inspired poetry in general that the poet does not merely write *about* the subject or theme, but in some sense *is* the subject that he or she represents through the medium of language. The same can be said about all the arts. As Dante writes in a poem he composed some years before the *Comedy*, *chi pinge figura, / se non può esser lei, non la può porre* ("one who paints a figure, if he can't *be* it, also can't portray it").[25]

Much religious and metaphysical verse, however earnest or sincere, is merely didactic or mimetic. It does not evoke the *presence* of the content it is representing — and I would like to emphasize the word "presence" as an especially characteristic feature of inspired poetry, certainly Dante's. Without inspiration and the ontological presence that comes with it, all of Dante's doctrinal understanding — his theological and philosophical learning — could not transport us into its world.

The material medium for this is poetic technique, for instance the meter and rhyme scheme of the *Comedy* — Dante's great invention of terza rima, the tripartite rhyme pattern which builds a potentially infinite progression of interlinking sounds. Not only the subject matter and imagery but especially the poem's music and the atmosphere it creates are traces indicating its inspired source. When subject matter,

---

24 *Convivio* III.ii.19.

25 *Le dolci rime d'amor ch'i' solia*, lines 52–53. This poem, referred to above, in chapter 5, opens book IV of the *Convivio*.

symbolic meaning, and poetic effects seamlessly combine, we respond with recognition, though what exactly it is that we recognize, it is hard to say. The inspiration in Dante makes his great poem function as revelation; we can *feel* and experience the truth in it, because Dante's mastery and inspiration made it possible for him to use symbolism and language to convey a direct encounter with reality. As we have seen in the vast architecture of the *Comedy*, high inspiration such as Dante's bestows mathematical order, precision, and lucidity on the work of art—what Blake referred to as the minutely articulated contours of Imagination.

Recall the quote from Ovid that I mentioned earlier, in which the Roman poet says that the presence of the God heats us up, and that this impulse contains the seeds of divine mind, which appear in the imagination as archetypal-symbolic forms. This is why inspiration, far from being inimical to tradition, is actually *intrinsic* to it. As the poet-scholar Kathleen Raine wrote many times, tradition is the trace, language, and learning of inspiration—what Yeats in "Sailing to Byzantium" called the "monuments of unageing intellect." In the *Comedy*, the greatest poem of Christendom, Christianity is not presented as regurgitated doctrine or imagery—the versified theology of Thomas Aquinas, as some tone-deaf critics have claimed. Rather, Dante *renovates* Christian teaching by returning it to its source in the creative intellect.

Inspiration such as Dante's is a trace of the capacity that Adam was granted to name the things of the creation in Genesis, and poetry is an enactment of such Adamic naming. In the Islamic tradition, "Adam" is the name of the *fiṭra* or primordial self present in every human being, in which all things in the universe have their being in their essential forms. The latter is another way of saying that human beings are made in God's image—a fundamental doctrine for all the Abrahamic religions. To name things poetically, then, is to return to the primordial essence of things. As M. Ali Lakhani has elegantly put it, poetry "is...an audition of the Primordial Word...a remaking or re-membrance of the Oneness out of multiplicity, which coheres in the Heart of the poet."[26] This audition of the Primordial Word—which perfectly describes Dante's activity in the final cantos of *Paradiso*—is what poets have referred to when they describe their inspiration as a divine gift. The Welsh poet Vernon Watkins expresses this in one of his

---

26 "Metaphysics of Poetic Expression," in M. Ali Lakhani, *The Timeless Relevance of Traditional Wisdom* (Bloomington, IN: World Wisdom Books, 2010), 176–230; 200–201.

poems in the voice of the bard Taliesin. With inspiration, writes Watkins, "time's [hour] glass breaks," so that the poet reaches "the spring of vision." The illusion of the separate and unified ego falls away and the poet can touch "the pin of pivotal space," seeing as it were from within the eye socket of the creation.[27]

The muse figure par excellence for Dante's inspiration, as we have seen, is Beatrice. She is not only a beloved lady who enables the lover to rise above his own lower nature; she is the guide through beauty and love to the ineffable secrets of the creation. Beatrice's beauty changed Dante forever from the time of his youth, since his love for her awakened in him a harmony and wholeness he would spend the rest of his life trying to recapture, understand, and live by. Plotinus's observation that we possess beauty when we are true to our own being, and that our ugliness lies in going over to another order, describes the intuition that came to Dante through his unrequited love for Beatrice.

The style of lyric poetry that Dante mastered with the poems of his *Vita nova* period—the so-called *dolce stil novo* or sweet new style—was based on the notion of poetic inspiration that springs from love. As Dante famously puts it in canto XXIV of *Purgatorio*, he is *un che, quando / Amor mi spira, noto, e a quel modo / ch'e' ditta dentro vo significando* ("one who, when Love inspires me, takes note, and the way that he dictates [to me] within, I write it").[28] Note that he uses the word *spira*, inspires, which as I have mentioned also refers to breath and spirit. Another verb that Dante uses here, *significare*, which I translated as "put into words," literally means expressing through signs, using sensible forms to indicate mental states. Such was the use of this word in the Latin Bible for the speech that God via the Holy Spirit addresses to human beings.[29]

In the canzone that opens book III of the *Convivio*, *Amor che nella mente mi ragiona* ("Love, who talks to me in my mind"), composed long before the *Purgatorio* passage, Dante writes that Love is the source of his poetic speech. And Dante refers to himself in several other passages of his writing as a *scribe* of Lord Love or Amor, or a scribe of

---

27   See Watkins's poem "Taliesin and the Spring of Vision," in *Collected Poems of Vernon Watkins* (Ipswich: Golgonooza Press, 1986), 224.

28   *Purgatorio* XXIV.52–54.

29   See, e.g., Hebrews 9:8, Revelation 1:1, 1 Peter 1:11, 2 Peter 1:14.

divine speech.[30] This identification explains the connection between inspiration in the sublime cantos of *Paradiso* and that of the harsh and biting verses in *Inferno*. As we have seen in detail earlier, Virgil tells Dante in the central cantos of *Purgatorio* that all the souls and states, infernal and otherwise, are ultimately motivated or moved by love. Love as such is infallible. We human beings go wrong only in our particular desires, whether by mistaking the object of love, or by excessive or insufficient love. As Love's scribe, then, Dante is obliged to be true to all levels of experience. As he puts it near the end of *Inferno*, his inspiration in those darkest cantos must be such that his verses can "depict the very bottom of the universe," which will require language that is not fit for a "tongue that cries out for mommy or daddy." Rather, the Muses who aided the ancient poet Amphion to chant words that moved the stones in Thebes magically to form a protective circling wall around the city will have to come to Dante's aid, as he creates a magic circle of language where the rocks of Hell press down the heaviest. The art of poetry, as Dante puts it, has to do with knowing how to use language so that *dal fatto il dir non sia diverso*, the deed or situation is reflected in the manner of its telling.[31]

The genesis and composition of the praise-poem *Donne ch'avete intelletto d'amore* ("Women who understand the truth of love"; discussed in chapter 1), was Dante's early revelation of language as an instrument of supernatural inspiration. In the prose of the *Vita nova*, Dante describes this poem's conception precisely as a visitation from something beyond:

> It happened that, as I was traveling along a road beside which flowed a brook of clear water, I was seized by an impulse to compose a poem. I started to consider what manner and style I might use, and thought that it wouldn't be fitting to talk about her [Beatrice] without addressing my words to other women — and not just to any women but to those who are noble and gracious. Then, I tell you, my tongue uttered words almost as if it moved of its own accord, saying: "Women who understand the truth of love."[32]

---

30 See, e.g., *Paradiso* x.27, xv.64–69. *Divini eloquii* is from *Monarchia* III.iv.11.
31 *Inferno* XXXII.1–12.
32 *Vita nova* 10.12–13 (XIX.1–2).

Anyone who has written poetry will recognize in this vignette the moment of the first conception of a poem. Out of nowhere, it seems, an image or a cadence or a phrase enters one's mind, carrying with it a sense of heightened meaning and reality that promises more to come. The visitation may happen in the middle of a crowd or when the poet is alone, at work on something else or perhaps reading or even sleeping. It almost certainly does not come when he or she is bent over a desk, pen in hand, anxiously waiting for a poetic payoff. As the poet-critic Randall Jarrell once put it, being a poet means being in the habit of walking outdoors in storms, hoping to get struck by lightning once or twice in a lifetime.

Surely significant in Dante's account of the genesis of *Donne ch'avete intelletto d'amore* is that he is walking by a brook when it happens. Inspiration itself is a stream that waters the desiccated heart. There are many biblical passages that refer to sudden speech as a gift of the Spirit: for instance, from the Gospel of Matthew, "Out of the abundance of the heart the mouth speaks"; and from the Psalms, "As I mused, the fire burned; then I spoke with my tongue"; and "O Lord, open thou my lips, and my mouth shall show forth thy praise."[33] In *Paradiso*, as I discussed in the introduction, Dante portrays the author of the Psalms, King David, as the great poetic voice of the Holy Spirit, the poet of poets. Dante refers to David in his work more than to any other Old Testament figure, while St. Paul is the Christian who is the prototype for the divinely inspired voice of the Spirit: the *vasello / de lo Spirito Santo*, or vessel of the Holy Spirit.[34]

As we also saw earlier, Dante places David among the spirits in the sphere of Jupiter, where the beatified rulers who embodied holy justice are placed. These spirits appear to Dante collectively in the heraldic shape of an eagle seen in profile. King David is the pupil in the eye of the Eagle. When the Eagle speaks it does so with one voice, though composed of many monarchs and rulers. It is interesting to note that Dante describes the upwelling of the Eagle's words in the language of poetic inspiration, which he himself is drawing on as he writes about the sacred Eagle's speech. Like the scene in the *Vita nova* quoted above, in this scene too, which he wrote twenty-five or more years later, Dante is fascinated by the inception of poetry.

---

33 Matthew 12:34; Psalm 39:3; Psalm 51:15.
34 *Paradiso* XXI.127–28; see also *Inferno* II.28.

Below are the lines that open canto xx of *Paradiso*, which describe Dante's encounter with the Eagle of blessed political leaders. Canto xix had ended with a denunciation of leaders in Christendom who were *not* just. The phrase "left off its cry" in our passage refers to that speech at the end of canto xix. The opening simile refers to the stars appearing one by one in the heavens after sunset. In antiquity and in Dante's time, it was commonly believed that the planets and stars borrowed their splendor from the sun, the primary source of light in the cosmos. As always in Dante, the sun is also an image of God, the Light of lights. Here is my translation of these lines:

> When he who lights up all the world descends
> so low that, in our hemisphere, the white
> of day wears thin and bit by bit day ends,
>   the heavens, which only he till now made bright,
> appear all of a sudden to the eye:
> numerous sparkles of a single light.
>   I called to mind those gestures of the sky
> when the ensign of the world and heads of state
> that formed its sacred beak left off its cry,
>   because those living lights poured forth a spate
> of brilliance when they sang—fugitive sound
> my memory cannot grasp or re-create.
>   O love whose loveliness is wrapped around
> with joy, those melodies your breath inspires
> were flute-notes blown by thought that grace had found!
>   When all those incandescent, prized sapphires
> studded across the sixth celestial sphere
> had hushed their resonant angelic choirs,
>   it seemed a river's purl was drawing near,
> tripping along downhill from stone to stone—
> the bounty of its mountain source made clear;
>   the way, along a soundboard, hums the tone
> of a guitar, or from a hullabaloo
> of bagpipes breath propels a steady drone,
>   just so, without delay or more ado,
> the Eagle's purling rose up in its throat
> as if its body were an open flue.

> There it took voice, and then came out a note
> formed by its beak into the shape of words
> I waited for. My heart is where I wrote.[35]

We note in this passage the theme of memory that is not able to retain the details of ecstatic vision, which we already saw in the scene in the final cantos of *Paradiso*. In addition, Dante specifies that the Eagle's speech at the end of the previous canto was directly inspired by love, which, by means of divine grace, turns thoughts into music. Notice too that, after a brief pause, the Eagle's voice as it rises anew from deep within is compared to the bubbling up of a mountain spring, which then forms a stream — the same image we saw in the *Vita nova* scene. This imagery probably draws on the Bible, where God's voice is said to flow forth like rushing waters.[36] Dante then employs a double simile, of a lute (a guitar, in my translation) and a bagpipe, reflecting the fingering of two kinds of musical instruments in order to produce various sounds (along the neck of a lute or at the vents of a bagpipe). The sounding board of the lute and the sack of the bagpipe parallel the lower body of the Eagle, in which the various voices first murmur, then collect in the Eagle's throat, and finally emerge as words issuing from its beak. Dante ends this passage by saying that he was waiting to hear the names of the spirits in this heaven, which he will then inscribe in his heart as he writes. The passage is a time-lapse glimpse into the movements of poetic inspiration.

Of course, the classical figure for inspiration is that of the Muses. Scholars from Boccaccio to the present have struggled to explain why Dante, a Christian poet, invokes the pagan Muses. As was often the practice of medieval Christian writers confronted with such questions, Boccaccio deals with the incongruity by resorting to allegorical inter-pretation: the Muses are daughters of Zeus and Mnemosyne, or God the Father and Memory. In a passage in the *Vita nova* Dante states that the Muses are personifications of internal states, just as the god Amor-Love is for the poets of his time.[37] In addition, perhaps we can understand Dante's use of the Muses in his Christian poem in terms of how he explains the goddess Fortune in *Inferno*, whom he depicts

---

35 *Paradiso* XX.1–30.
36 E.g., Ezekiel 43:2, Revelation 1:15.
37 *Vita nova* 16.9 (xxv.9).

as a figure or minister of God's will. Likewise, the Muses can be seen as figural representations of God's grace. Dante refers to the Muses in various places in his writing as "our nurses," and "most sacred Virgins," and the "Castalian Sisters," an allusion to the Castalian spring at Delphi, which gave the gift of prophecy and of poetic inspiration.[38] The Muses, writes Dante in *Paradiso*, nourish poets with their sweet milk.[39]

Dante's attraction to the figure of the Muses is hardly surprising when we recall the high place of women and the feminine in his imagination. Certainly the kind of knowledge I described earlier as participatory knowledge has a feminine quality, intimate and deeply felt. The Muses have to do with this soulful, experiential aspect of knowledge. As the ancient Greek poet Hesiod said of them, they "pour sweet dew upon [the poet's] tongue, and from his lips flow gracious words.... Happy is he whom the Muses love: sweet flows speech from his mouth.... He forgets his heaviness and remembers not his sorrow.... The gifts of the goddesses ... turn him away from these."[40] If in our own epoch the Romantic poets and authors such as Carl Jung have revived the image of the feminine, the archetype of woman as a figure of the soul and of Sophia or holy Wisdom, Dante was a medieval forerunner of this awakening.

In my sketch of the final cantos of *Paradiso*, I alluded to the fact that the themes of inspiration and invocation in Dante are usually associated with the limits of memory and intellect, and ineffability or the limits of verbal expression. Inspiration and ineffability were related themes for Dante even during his early years in Florence. The great canzone cited earlier, *Amor che nella mente mi ragiona*, which he wrote when he was about thirty years old, is particularly concerned with this theme. This poem is explained by Dante in the *Convivio* commentary as an allegory of philosophy, which Dante understands in the etymological sense of "love of wisdom." Chapter 6 discussed how Dante personifies philosophy as a woman he is in love with. Dante considers himself a scribe of Love, which is the source of his inspiration. Yet, as this poem states, it is far from easy to understand or write down what Love dictates.

---

38   *Purgatorio* XXII.105, *Purgatorio* XXIX.37, *Eclogues* 1.54.

39   *Paradiso* XXIII.57.

40   *Theogony*, lines 80–103, translated by Hugh G. Evelyn-White in *Hesiod, the Homeric Hymns and Homerica*, Loeb Classical Library 57 (Cambridge, MA: Harvard University Press, 1914).

The poem's opening stanza says that Love's speech in Dante's mind is so pleasing that he feels powerless to say what he hears about his lady. If he wants to write down what Love says about her, he will have to omit much, not only what his intellect cannot grasp but even what he *does* have some understanding of, since he would not know how to put it into words. He closes this stanza with the disclaimer:

> So if my poetry has some defect
> as it sets out upon its praise of her,
> just blame it on the feeble intellect,
> and on our speech, whose strength is not enough
> to tell of everything that's said by Love.[41]

Later in the poem, Dante depicts celestial inspiration in connection with a noble woman, Lady Philosophy, who receives the supernal light and attracts the rapturous attention of the angelic Intelligences. Through her, the divine light descends into the lovers of wisdom on earth, namely true philosophers, who are the mortal receivers of this impulse which originates in heaven. Finally, the celestial influence issues as light in the eyes of the wise and as sighs from the chests of those whom the wise inspire. Dante in this poem describes an experience that cannot be translated into human language; it can only be talked around and indicated by symbols and by the music of verse.

As Dante will express the same idea years later in the first canto of *Paradiso*, in more compact and stately terms: *Trasumanar significar* per verba / *non si poria* ("It is impossible to put transhuman-being-ness into words").[42] My translation of *trasumanar* as "transhuman-being-ness" itself demonstrates one technique that Dante has adopted to express ineffability. He coins words as he goes—particularly in *Paradiso*, where the appearance of invented words (which are nevertheless intelligible) incites the reader's mind to reach beyond itself and its habitual categories. Dante's treatment of the theme of ecstatic vision draws on the *excessus mentis* or contemplation of the mystics. The ecstasy of liberation from mental constructs makes the mystic or inspired poet, as Bernard of Clairvaux puts it in his writings, like air flooded with

---

41   *Amor che nella mente mi ragiona*, lines 14–18.
42   *Paradiso* 1.70.

light or iron liquefied in fire.[43] This liquefaction or opening of the soul does not destroy it but, on the contrary, confirms the soul's own essential nature.

I will conclude with a passage from the metaphysician René Guénon, which is as good as anything I have seen on the intimate connection between silence and speech, poetry and the ineffable. Guénon writes:

> Just as Non-Being, or the non-manifested, comprehends or envelops Being, or the principle of manifestation, so does silence carry in itself the principle of speech; in other words, just as Unity (Being) is nothing but metaphysical Zero (Non-Being) affirmed, so speech is nothing but silence expressed.[44]

Dante's vision and poetry of Paradise, with which I began this chapter, hovers between speech and silence because this is the essential nature of poetic inspiration.

---

43   *De diligendo Deo* (On Loving God) x.28.

44   René Guénon, *The Multiple States of the Being*, translated by Henry D. Fohr (Hillsdale, NY: Sophia Perennis, 2001), 24.

ACKNOWLEDGMENTS

ALL CHAPTERS IN THIS BOOK except chapter 8 and the introduction were originally written either as lectures for the Temenos Academy in London or as essays for the Academy's journal, *Temenos Academy Review*. My thanks to the general editor of *TAR*, John Carey, for his always conscientious and generous editorial acumen. All chapters have since been revised, some substantially.

Chapter 1, originally called "Courtly Love and Sacred Love in the *Vita Nova*," and chapter 2 were published as *The Young Dante and the One Love: Two Lectures on the "Vita Nova,"* in *Temenos Academy Papers* 36 (2013). Chapters 6 and chapter 7 (the latter originally titled "The Quest for Knowledge in the *Convivio*") were published as *The Quest for Knowledge in Dante's "Convivio"* in *Temenos Academy Papers* 38 (2015). My thanks to Brian Keeble and the Golgonooza Foundation for supporting those publications.

Material from three of the chapters, 5, 6, and 7, also appeared, in earlier versions, in my introduction to the *Convivio: A Dual-Language Critical Edition* (Cambridge University Press, 2018).

In addition, I wish to thank M. Ali Lakhani for having published two of the chapters, 4 and 6, in *Sacred Web: A Journal of Tradition and Modernity* 39 and 43; and Daniela Boccassini, for publishing chapter 10 (under the title "A Divine Gift: Inspiration in Dante"), in *Oikosophia: Dall'Intelligenza del Cuore all'Ecofilosofia; From the Intelligence of the Heart to Ecophilosophy* (*Quaderni di Studi Indo-Mediterranei* 10).

I thank Zygmunt Barański, Teodolinda Barolini, Jonathan Galassi, Simon Gilson, Christian Moevs, and Rosanna Warren for sharing their insights, recommendations, and/or unpublished articles with me at various stages of my Dante work.

I dedicate this book to the Temenos Academy itself, the sustaining presence of which is invaluable to my work. I am deeply grateful to the Academy's administrators, Stephen and Genevieve Overy, and to all the Members, Fellows, and Board and Council members of the Academy, for sharing in the *temenos* of the arts of the imagination.

As always, my wife, Daphne, has been my best friend and adviser during the years I have worked on the chapters in this book.

WORKS CITED

In my translating of and writing about Dante, I am indebted to Dantists past and present more than I can say. The sources I have used for my research in this book are too numerous to name in this bibliography, so what follows is a list of sources specifically mentioned in the notes. Further bibliographic details and acknowledgments can be found in my editions of Dante's *Vita nova* and *Convivio*, cited in the front matter of this book.

Albert the Great. *Mineralium liber*. Translated by Dorothy Wykoff. Oxford: Clarendon Press, 1967.

Anderson, William. *Dante the Maker*. London: Hutchinson, 1983.

Ardizzone, Maria Luisa, ed. *Dante and Heterodoxy: The Temptations of 13th-Century Radical Thought*. With a conclusion by Teodolinda Barolini. Newcastle upon Tyne: Cambridge Scholars Publishing, 2014.

Auerbach, Erich. *Dante: Poet of the Secular World*. Translated by Ralph Manheim. Foreword by Michael Dirda. New York: New York Review of Books, 2001.

Avicenna. "A Treatise on Love by Ibn Sina." Translated by E. L. Fackenheim, *Medieval Studies* 7 (1945): 208–28.

Barański, Zygmunt G. "Dante and Doctrine (and Theology)." In *Reviewing Dante's Theology*, 2 vols., edited by Claire E. Honess and Matthew Treherne, 1: 9–64. Oxford: Peter Lang, 2013.

———. *Dante e i segni: Saggi per una storia intellettuale di Dante Alighieri*. Naples: Liguori, 2000.

———. "(Un)orthodox Dante." In *Reviewing Dante's Theology*, 2 vols., edited by Claire E. Honess and Matthew Treherne, 2: 253–330. Oxford: Peter Lang, 2013.

Barolini, Teodolinda. *Dante and the Origins of Italian Literary Culture*. New York: Fordham University Press, 2006.

———. *Dante's Lyric Poetry: Poems of Youth and of the "Vita Nuova."* With new verse translations by Richard H. Lansing, commentary translated into English by Andrew Frisardi. Toronto: University of Toronto Press, 2014.

Bemrose, Stephen. *A New Life of Dante*. Exeter: Exeter University Press, 2000.

Benini, Rodolfo. *Dante tra gli splendori dei suoi enigmi risolti*. Rome: Sampaolesi, 1952.

Biscioni, Anton Maria. *Prose di Dante Alighieri e di messer Gio. Boccacci*. Florence: Per Gio. Gaetano Tartini, e Santi Franchi, 1723.

Blake, William. *Complete Writings*. Edited by Geoffrey Keynes. Oxford: Oxford University Press, 1966.

Boynton, Susan. "The Sources and Significance of the Orpheus Myth." *Early Music History* 18 (1999): 47–74.

Burckhardt, Titus. "The Seven Liberal Arts and the West Door of Chartres Cathedral." *Studies in Comparative Religion* 16, nos. 1–2 (Winter–Spring 1984): 57–61.

Caesar, Michael, ed. *Dante: The Critical Heritage*. London: Routledge, 1989.

Capellanus, Andreas. *The Art of Courtly Love*. Introduction, translation, and notes by John Jay Parry. New York: Columbia University Press, 1990.

Cicero. *On Old Age, On Friendship, On Divination*. Translated by William Armistead Falconer. Loeb Classical Library 154. Cambridge, MA: Harvard University Press, 1923.

Collins, Cecil. "Why Does Today's Art Lack Inspiration?" In *Meditations, Poems, Pages from a Sketchbook*, edited by Brian Keeble. Ipswich: Golgonooza Press, 1997.

Corbin, Henry. *Alone with the Alone: Creative Imagination in the Sūfism of Ibn 'Arabī*. Translated by Ralph Manheim. 1969. Repr. with preface by Harold Bloom. Princeton, NJ: Princeton University Press, 1997.

Corti, Maria. "Dante and Islamic Culture." Translated by Kyle M. Hall. *Dante Studies* 125 (2007): 57–75.

Cowen, Painton. *Rose Window*. San Francisco: Chronicle Books, 1979.

Curtius, Ernst Robert. *European Literature and the Latin Middle Ages*. Translated by Willard R. Trask. Original German edition published in 1948; English trans., 1951. Repr., London: Routledge and Kegan Paul, 1979.

Dell'Oso, Lorenzo. "From Peter of Trabibus' Quodlibets to Dante's *Vita nova*." Paper read at the conference Quodlibetal Culture in Dante's Time: Europe, Italy, and Florence, University of Notre Dame, April 26–27, 2019.

Demaray, John G. *Cosmos and Epic Representation: Dante, Spenser, Milton and the Transformation of Renaissance Heroic Poetry*. Pittsburgh: Duquesne University Press, 1991.

———. *Dante and the Book of the Cosmos*. Philadelphia: The American Philosophical Society, 1987.

———. *The Invention of Dante's "Commedia."* New Haven, CT: Yale University Press, 1974.

Dronke, Peter. *Dante's Second Love: The Originality and the Contexts of the "Convivio."* Exeter: Society for Italian Studies, 1997.

———. "The Song of Songs and Medieval Love-Lyric." In *The Bible and Medieval Culture*, edited by W. Lourdaux and D. Verhelst, 236–62. Leuven: Leuven University Press, 1979.

Duncan, Robert. "The Sweetness and Greatness of Dante's *Divine Comedy*." In *The Poets' Dante: Twentieth-Century Responses*, edited by Peter S. Hawkins and Rachel Jacoff, 186–209. New York: Farrar, Straus & Giroux, 2001.

Durling, Robert M., and Ronald L. Martinez, trans. *Paradiso*, by Dante Alighieri. New York: Oxford University Press, 1996.

———. *Time and the Crystal: Studies in Dante's "Rime Petrose."* Berkeley: University of California Press, 1990.

Fideler, David. *Jesus Christ: Sun of God*. Wheaton, IL: Quest Books, 1993.

Foster, Kenelm. *The Two Dantes and Other Studies*. London: Darton, Longman & Todd, 1977.

Friedman, John Block. *Orpheus in the Middle Ages*. Syracuse, NY: Syracuse University Press, 2000.

Gardiner, Eileen. *Visions of Heaven and Hell Before Dante*. New York: Italica Press, 1989.

Gardner, Edmund G. *Dante and the Mystics: A Study of the Mystical Aspect of the "Divina Commedia" and Its Relations with Some of Its Mediaeval Sources*. 1913. Repr., Chestnut Hill, MA: Adamant Media Corporation, 2006.

Gilson, Étienne. *Mystical Theology of St. Bernard*. Translated by A.H.C. Downes. Kalamazoo, MI: Cistercian Publications, 1990.

Gilson, Simon. "Dante and Christian Aristotelianism." In *Reviewing Dante's Theology*, 2 vols., edited by Claire E. Honess and Matthew Treherne, 1: 65–110. Oxford: Peter Lang, 2013.

——. "Light Reflection, Mirror Metaphors, and Optical Framing in Dante's *Comedy*: Precedents and Transformations." *Neophilologus* 83 (1999): 241–52.

Gorni, Guglielmo. Introduction to the *Vita nova*, by Dante Alighieri. Edited by Luca Carlo Rossi. Milan: Mondadori, 1999.

——. *Lettera nome numero: L'ordine delle cose in Dante*. Bologna: Il Mulino, 1990.

Guénon, René. *The Esoterism of Dante*. Translated by C. B. Bethell. Ghent, NY: Sophia Perennis et Universalis, 1996.

——. *The Multiple States of the Being*. Translated by Henry D. Fohr. Hillsdale, NY: Sophia Perennis, 2001.

Guthrie, Kenneth Sylvan, comp. and trans. *The Pythagorean Sourcebook and Library: An Anthology of Ancient Writings Which Relate to Pythagoras and Pythagorean Philosophy*. Edited and introduced by David Fideler. Grand Rapids, MI: Phanes Press, 1987.

Guzzardo, John J. *Dante: Numerological Studies*. New York: Peter Lang, 1987.

Hani, Jean. *Divine Craftsmanship: Preliminaries to a Spirituality of Work*. Translated by Robert Procter. San Rafael, CA: Sophia Perennis, 2007.

——. *The Symbolism of the Christian Temple*. Translated by Robert Procter. San Rafael, CA: Sophia Perennis, 2007.

Hawkins, Peter S. "Religious Culture," in *Dante in Context*, edited by Zygmunt G. Barański and Lino Pertile, 319–40. Cambridge: Cambridge University Press, 2015.

Helm, R., ed., *Fabii Planciadis Fulgentii v. c. opera*. Leipzig: Teubner, 1898.

Hesiod. *The Homeric Hymns and Homerica*. Translated by Hugh G. Evelyn-White. Loeb Classical Library 57. Cambridge, MA: Harvard University Press, 1914.

Hollander, Robert, and Jean Hollander, trans. *Inferno*. New York: Anchor Books, 2000.

——, trans. *Paradiso*. New York: Anchor Books, 2008.

Honess, Claire H. "The City of Jerusalem in the *Commedia*." In *From Florence to the Heavenly City: The Poetry of Citizenship in Dante*, 107–50. Abingdon, Oxon, and New York: Routledge, 2006.

——, trans. *Dante Alighieri: Four Political Letters*. MHRA Critical Texts 6. London: Modern Humanities Research Association, 2007.

Hopper, Vincent Foster. *Medieval Number Symbolism*. 1938. Repr., New York: Cooper Square Publishers, 1969.

Lakhani, M. Ali. *The Timeless Relevance of Traditional Wisdom.* Bloomington, IN: World Wisdom Books, 2010.

Lansing, Richard H., ed. *Dante Encyclopedia.* New York: Garland Publishing, 2000.

——, trans. *Dante's "Il Convivio."* New York: Garland Publishing, 1990.

Leigh, Gertrude. *The Passing of Beatrice: A Study in the Heterodoxy of Dante.* London: Faber and Faber, 1932.

Malory, Thomas. *Works.* Edited by Eugène Vinaver. 2nd ed. Oxford: Oxford University Press, 1971.

Maritain, Jacques. *The Situation of Poetry.* New York: Philosophical Library, 1968.

Martinez, Ronald L. "Dante Between Hope and Despair: The Tradition of Lamentations in the *Divine Comedy.*" *Logos: A Journal of Catholic Thought and Culture* 5, no. 3 (2002): 45–76.

Moevs, Christian. *The Metaphysics of Dante's "Comedy."* Oxford: Oxford University Press, 2005.

Murray, Paul. "Aquinas on Poetry and Theology." *Logos: A Journal of Catholic Thought and Culture* 16, no. 2 (Spring 2013): 63–72.

Nardi, Bruno. *Dante e la cultura medievale.* Edited by Paolo Mazzatini. 2nd ed. Rome-Bari: Editori Laterza, 1990.

——. *Nel mondo di Dante.* Rome: Edizioni di Storia e Letteratura, 1944.

Nasr, Seyyed Hossein. *The Garden of Truth: The Vision and Promise of Sufism, Islam's Mystical Tradition.* New York: HarperCollins, 2007.

——. *The Heart of Islam: Enduring Values for Humanity.* San Francisco: HarperSanFrancisco 2002.

——. *Knowledge and the Sacred.* Albany: State University of New York Press, 1989.

Nasti, Paola. "Dante and Ecclesiology." In *Reviewing Dante's Theology,* 2 vols., edited by Claire E. Honess and Matthew Treherne, 2: 43–88. Oxford: Peter Lang, 2013.

——. *Favole d'amore e "saver profondo": La tradizione salomonica in Dante.* Ravenna: Longo Editore, 2007.

Ovid. *The Metamorphoses.* Translated by Horace Gregory. New York: Viking Press, 1958.

Pertile, Lino. *La puttana e il gigante: Dal "Cantico dei cantici" al Paradiso terrestre di Dante.* Ravenna: Longo, 1998.

Philokalia: The Complete Text. Translated and edited by G. E. H. Palmer, Philip Sherrard, and Kallistos Ware. Vols. 1 and 2. London: Faber & Faber, 1979, 1983.

Priest, Paul. "Dante and the Song of Songs." *Studi danteschi* 49 (1972): 79–113.

Priviero, Tommaso. "On the Service of the Soul: C. G. Jung's *Liber Novus* and Dante's *Commedia,*" *Phanes* 1 (2018): 28–57.

Prümmer, Dominicus, O.P., ed. *Fontes vitae S. Thomae Aquinatis: Notis historicis et criticis illustrati.* Toulouse: Apud ed. Privat, Bibliopolam, 1912.

Schimmel, Annemarie. *The Mystery of Numbers.* New York: Oxford University Press, 1993.

Shaw, Prue. *Reading Dante: From Here to Eternity.* New York: Liveright Publishing, 2014.

Singleton, Charles S., trans. and ed. *The Divine Comedy.* Princeton, NJ: Princeton University Press, 1970–75.

———. *An Essay on the "Vita Nuova."* 1949. 2nd ed., Baltimore: Johns Hopkins University Press, 1977.

———. *Journey to Beatrice*. Baltimore: Johns Hopkins University Press, 1977.

———. "The Poet's Number at the Center." *Modern Language Notes* 80 (1965): 1–10.

Smith, Wolfgang. *Christian Gnosis from Saint Paul to Meister Eckhart*. 2008. New ed., Kettering, Ohio: Angelico Press / Sophia Perennis, 2011.

Valency, Maurice. *In Praise of Love*. New York: Macmillan, 1961.

Valli, Luigi. *Il linguaggio segreto di Dante e dei "fedeli d'amore."* Milan: Luni Editrice, 1994.

Watkins, Vernon. *Collected Poems*. Ipswich: Golgonooza Press, 1986.

INDEX

Adam 107, 117, 126, 186, 187, 202, 204, 212, 213, 224
Aeneas 81, 91, 179, 193, 219
Aeneid 81, 89, 101, 179, 185, 202, 219
agape 59, 69
Alan of Lille 17, 168
Albert the Great 38, 87, 123, 144, 158, 164
Aldobrandeschi, Umberto 121
allegory 21, 65, 66, 67, 68, 79, 88, 91, 102, 118, 128, 131, 138, 186, 196, 230
Amphion 226
Anderson, William 86
angelic Intelligences 159, 164, 192, 201, 231
Annunciation 85, 222
Aquinas, St. Thomas 4, 40, 67, 68, 69, 87, 91, 119, 120, 123, 142, 144, 155, 156, 158, 159, 160, 164, 169, 171, 177, 206, 222, 224
  allegorical interpretation and 66
  attitude toward poetry 14, 87
  attitude toward women 20
  knowledge from senses 14
  on *claritas* 46
  on happiness 159
  on human desire for truth 155
  saying his writings looked "like straw" 4
  view of knowledge 164
  view of matter 9
  view of nobility 120
arc of life 130
Aristotelianism 18, 156, 157, 170
Aristotle 11, 102, 112, 145, 149, 155, 156, 159, 164, 168, 201, 218
  Dante echoing 160
  Dante's critique of 17, 170
  De generatione animalium 158
  influence on Dante 156–58

knowledge from senses 14
Metaphysics 11, 96, 144, 155, 164
Nicomachean Ethics 127, 142, 155, 166, 167, 170
  on intellect 163
  on self-subsistent Being 11
  on virtue 126
  potential preceding act 65
  view of matter 9
arithmetic 16, 167
art xii, 13, 15, 18, 24, 25, 26, 28, 33, 69, 96, 97, 100, 110, 111, 112, 113, 179, 191, 198, 224, 226
  as an intellectual virtue 110
  as copy of God's offspring, Nature 86
  as interior mastery 110
  as sacrament 111
  as virtue of practical intellect 94
  Beatrice as apotheosis of Dante's 100
  contemplation and 95
  divine and human 95
  Leah and 93
  no intermediary of Nature between God and his 85
  sacred 98
  work and 95
Asclepius 144
astronomy 16, 141, 167, 168
Athens 173
ātman 222
Auerbach, Erich 90, 91
Augustine, St. 72, 164, 171, 181, 199, 202, 211, 222
Averroes 158
Averroist 158, 169
Avicenna 10, 34, 35, 37, 38, 49, 164

ABOUT THE AUTHOR

ANDREW FRISARDI is author, translator, and/or editor of several books, most recently *The Harvest and the Lamp*, a collection of poetry chosen by James Matthew Wilson for the Colosseum Book series of Franciscan University Press (2020). His annotated editions of Dante's *Convivio* (Cambridge University Press, 2018) and *Vita nova* (Northwestern University Press, 2012) are internationally prominent and widely used in Dante studies and by general readers of Dante in English. His work has been awarded a Guggenheim Fellowship, a Hawthornden Literary Fellowship, and the Raiziss/de Palchi Translation Award from the Academy of American Poets. Originally from Boston, he has made his home in central Italy for a number of years. Frisardi is a fellow of and a frequent contributor to the Temenos Academy in London, which offers adult education in philosophy and the arts in the light of the sacred traditions of East and West.

www.ingramcontent.com/pod-product-compliance
Lightning Source LLC
Chambersburg PA
CBHW030639030726
47497CB00006B/1860